Awake but Dreaming

Awake but Dreaming

Maya Chendke

iUniverse, Inc.
Bloomington

Awake but Dreaming

Copyright © 2011 by Maya Chendke

All rights reserved. No part of this book may be used or reproduced by any means, graphic, electronic, or mechanical, including photocopying, recording, taping or by any information storage retrieval system without the written permission of the publisher except in the case of brief quotations embodied in critical articles and reviews.

This is a work of fiction. All of the characters, names, incidents, organizations, and dialogue in this novel are either the products of the author's imagination or are used fictitiously.

iUniverse books may be ordered through booksellers or by contacting:

iUniverse
1663 Liberty Drive
Bloomington, IN 47403
www.iuniverse.com
1-800-Authors (1-800-288-4677)

Because of the dynamic nature of the Internet, any web addresses or links contained in this book may have changed since publication and may no longer be valid. The views expressed in this work are solely those of the author and do not necessarily reflect the views of the publisher, and the publisher hereby disclaims any responsibility for them.

Any people depicted in stock imagery provided by Thinkstock are models, and such images are being used for illustrative purposes only.

Certain stock imagery © Thinkstock.

ISBN: 978-1-4620-0360-0 (sc)
ISBN: 978-1-4620-0362-4 (dj)
ISBN: 978-1-4620-0361-7 (ebk)

Printed in the United States of America

iUniverse rev. date: 03/09/2011

The storm may be turbulent. It may get scary at times.

Lighting strikes, winds push, thunder growls.

You fear it will go on forever.

But it won't.

No matter what happens in your moments of disarray, there is certainty that the clouds will lift and the chaos will settle.

Sunshine always follows the storm.
You just gotta ride it out.
There's no getting around this.

the beginning of the end.

[Paris, France—February 2013]

The phone rings. Shrill, high-pitched jangles echo off the walls of the dark hotel room.

A woman's hand fumbles to the bedside table, searching for the source of the early morning disruption. Riley wraps her black, manicured fingernails around the handset, her face still buried in the fluffy pillow.

"Hullo?" she croaks painfully, still half asleep.

"Riley! Wake up!" shrieks the woman at the other end of the line.

"What time is it? My wake-up call is for nine," slurs the drowsy sleeper.

"Shut up!" she gasps, cutting off the protest. "*Riley*! Jenna … hospital … dying!"

Riley Kohl sits up, lightning fast, having caught only some of the words coming through the line. Her long, dark brown hair is all over the place; a satin slumber mask is falling off her face.

What? she asks herself, her ears becoming fully operational.

"Riley?" whimpers the feminine, high-pitched voice on the phone. "Are you there?"

"Elle, tell me *exactly* what is going on," Riley hisses to her friend. She is now awake and grasping for control. She kicks off the ivory sheets, swinging her legs over the side of the bed. The room is still totally dark.

"Jenna … overdose … on tour in Europe. This is all his fault. He's the one who got her into the drugs. He cut us out of her life … that self-destructive psychopath … pushing her to jump off the edge." Eleanor sobs helplessly, long-distance from another continent. She's about to enter a full-blown rage or hyperventilate in distress.

The hatred is being directed at their friend's on-again, off-again, on-again boyfriend. A movie star whose idea of fun involves groping his way around dark nightclubs and making deals with gossip magazines to sell Jenna out.

"She's dead?" Riley whispers, trying to understand, to refocus the emotional conversation back on fact and reason.

"Intensive care. But I think she really did it this time. They don't know if she'll survive the night."

"Where is she?" Riley whispers, trying to quietly make her way around the hotel suite while grabbing her belongings.

She wiggles out of her men's pyjamas and grabs some clothes off the chaise at the foot of the king-size bed—a pair of dark, straight-leg jeans and a chunky turtleneck, cosy for the rain outside.

Riley flips on a dainty lamp, casting soft light onto the guy still asleep in the bed. His bare back is facing her, and a deep snore growls from his throat. The clock by the bed reads 4:30 AM Paris time.

"She collapsed after a concert in Madrid," Elle explains. "You know how much she's been partying ... it's all over the tabloids—"

"Is anyone with her?" Riley interrupts.

"No, the record label actually called Parker and me. I just got off the phone with him. He's trying to get out through JFK tomorrow morning."

Parker Ma. The tattooed pretty boy hired by Jenna's record label to give her an air of rebellion—more street cred. Born and raised in New York, but of Korean heritage, he was a young producing prodigy who drew from his interests in hip-hop and punk—the cutting edge. He was the guy who helped Jenna through recording her first album, who knew her before the cameras took notice. In his late twenties, with jet-black hair and eyes as dark as coal, Jenna swooned over him right from the start. With his carefree and artistic manner, he took her precious ideas and breathed life into them, helping to turn them into chart toppers with the right amount of hipster flair. Someone who understood her passions and unbridled mind.

As if any of that mattered at this specific moment.

"Shit. Fuck. Shit. Okay, I'll muscle my way in and set up camp first ... I'll contact the label and let them know I'll be first on scene." Riley sighs, trying to button up her jeans while cradling the phone and writing down the address of the hospital on the hotel stationery. Her left-handed chicken scratch clashes with the sophisticated letterhead reading *Le Meurice*.

"I'm heading out now—got standby on the red-eye so I'll probably get in before Parker," Elle informs.

"Elle, you know you don't have to leave your family." Riley sighs, thinking of the home Elle has so carefully built in peaceful, suburban Toronto. The anti of Jenna's very public existence: a neat house with a husband and twin baby sons, lavender in the back garden, and a station wagon in the garage.

And all fit in place before the age of 25.

Eleanor Bryans, the feminine redhead with green eyes and porcelain skin who looks like she could be torn straight from a J. Crew ad. The petite and shy girly-girl who never swears, she always found herself as the swing vote between her two brash and sassy friends. Whether in grade school or front row at Fashion Week, she always preferred peace and harmony as her way of life. Elle's dream was always to escape Jenna's skyrocket to fame, to just be a mom and live in relative anonymity.

"No! I am going!" Elle affirms. "She hasn't been herself in a long time—goodness knows I haven't spoken to her in at least a year—but she's still Jenna. She's still the girl we played monkey bars with, and she needs us both. Unfortunately, we knew this day was probably going to come, and it has. She doesn't *have* anyone else. So whether we take home a friend or a coffin, I will see you in Madrid," she shoots back defiantly, her tiny voice fighting the grim reality of Jenna's prognosis.

With that, the childhood friends hang up and scurry about, preparing to face the worst-case scenario.

Eleanor wakes her husband and leaves him an organized printout of all the information he'll need for the next few days. She slips into the bedroom of her two sons and sweetly kisses them on the forehead before the taxi whisks her away.

The car splashes through the winter slush on the highway, darting to Pearson International Airport. Elle stares out at the night sky above, slipping into nostalgic thought.

I wonder how much has actually changed, she thinks to herself, remembering the lifestyle she once lived with her two best friends. Her pale cheeks are flushed from the subzero chill outside. She hugs herself, opting to brave the freeze without a winter coat, wearing only a simple pink cardigan instead. Less bulk to travel with, a lesson much appreciated from her work as Jenna's personal assistant, suffering as the one to carry her belongings while they travelled the world. An international star was never supposed to schlep around a jacket or carry a wallet. It was totally unacceptable.

A little more than a year ago, before the current reality of car seats and wife life, Elle was one half of Jenna Ramsay's entourage (the other half being Riley). They were a small unit of friends sharing her adventure of fame and success as the rising It Girl of the music industry. The parties and nightclubs, shopping and paparazzi, all got left in the dust, along with their friendship, when change inevitably took hold of them.

Elle pulls out an orange leather journal from her purse and smiles at the picture taped inside the front cover. It's from the start of the wild ride, about three years back, a time when they could not imagine living without each other's daily contact. The image captures the sheer elation after Jenna's first big performance in London, the three girls hugging in the back of a cushy limousine. A split-second moment in the chaos of Jenna's ride to celebrity, before she grew apart from Elle and Riley.

She flips to the back of the diary and looks at a postcard sent to her from the south of France —Jenna's last communication, sent randomly a few months ago. The back is blank, a creepy sign of the emptiness of her friend's life.

Elle looks at it sadly, trying to remember the last time she actually spoke with her childhood friend. Any news about Jenna's life now has had to filter in from gossip magazines or old acquaintances. How different things had become since their school days when they'd spend hours on three-way calls, worrying about high school chemistry or learning to make out.

• • •

Back in Paris, Riley is focused on the immediate course of action she'll have to take upon arriving in Madrid. She places calls to her former employers, Jenna's record label and manager, and collects contacts for a security agency in Spain to assist in protecting the pop star. She throws a spare T-shirt in her large black Hermès bag, packing light and ready to go. She scribbles a note for her companion, opting to quietly slip out rather than wake him with news of chaos.

She stops at the door and takes one last, admiring look at him. Strong, tanned back, toned arms, matted hair … then, she reminds herself of Jenna and quietly pulls the door shut.

In the elevator, she braces herself for the hectic media circus that will surround her famous friend. The potential headlines flash in her mind's eye:

"Pop star falls off the wagon—*again*!"

"Jenna and Carter back in action!"

"The Terrible Two!"

The hypercritical press following the life of Jenna Ramsay was almost as big a wedge in their friendship as her poor choice in relationships. Everything started out great and positive with Jenna's music career. Solid support from the public, good reviews, awards, kind coverage from the media … But when her public love saga with Carter Sampson became the focus of the tabloids, she was no longer on a winning team, and bringing the couple down became sport.

The dread of feeling even a fraction of the attention constantly directed at Jenna is enough to make Riley queasy.

The way the cameras blinded them, flashes everywhere, candid photos showing up on the Internet or in magazines. Complete strangers staring and shouting, heckling with sensationalistic comments to try and provoke a response. The storm around Jenna was an instant energy zapper, forcing the three girls to forge on through the calamity and detach themselves from the outside world. It was the only way to try avoiding being hit by the fierce lightning of celebrity that struck Jenna like a golfer in a thunderstorm.

Riley twists her long brown hair into a low braid, looking at her sullen face in the elevator's elegant mirror. Her olive skin is without any trace of makeup, just freshly washed and moisturized, and looks more worn than that of a 24-year-old. A small pimple is festering in the skin at the tip of her nose. Her brown eyes are red and irritated from forcing contact lenses in so early in the morning.

"Why couldn't we stay seventeen forever?" she sighs to herself as she steps into the lobby, zipping across the green and white marble floors, and vanishing out the door.

PART I:
PREPARE FOR TAKEOFF

the beginning of the beginning.

[Toronto, Canada—June 2006]

"Now, girls, one, two, three ... smile!"

The camera flashes as the three friends proudly clutch their diplomas.

"Wait—over here! Look over here!" chimes in Eleanor's mother, holding up a camera in her dainty hands, neatly manicured in summery coral.

The girls pose for one last picture, and then begin walking, arm in arm, away from their high school history and towards the school parking lot.

"Good-bye, childhood; hello, real world!" Jenna grins, her bright blonde hair reflecting the warm sunshine, blue eyes hidden behind oversized sunglasses. She's walking in the middle of her two friends, her arms linked through theirs. The bright purple summer dress she's wearing overpowers Riley's sober black pantsuit and Elle's boring beige jumper, fading them into the background and making it seem like she's flanked by Secret Service.

"It's so strange that it's already over ... and now ... we're all going such separate ways ..." Elle sighs, teary-eyed, clutching a tissue and her patent-leather purse, gazing up at the tall blonde beside her.

"Lovee, it's not that bad! You're only a few hours away, Jenna's still in the city, and I'll be home at holidays." Riley laughs from the other side of Jenna, secretly thrilled to be the only person from their graduating class to be studying in Europe.

"I know, but I don't want things to change ... things change at times like these ... when people move and make new friends and new lives ..." she whimpers, holding Jenna's hand. Jenna leans into hug her warmly, wishing she wasn't stuck staying in Toronto—wishing she had the money to book it out of town and make it big in New York or LA, instead of having to do a four-year degree while living at home.

"Send me a postcard," Jenna says to Riley, pouting.

"Obviously." Riley rolls her eyes, the three girls having kept a tradition of sending each other postal mail during vacations and trips – or rather, Riley and Elle mostly sending them back to Jenna.

"Jenna! Can you sign my yearbook?" someone shouts from across the school's lawn. The girls turn to see a meek Chinese girl scamper up with her yearbook in hand, clutched like a prize. Her jeans are dull and, although surely the smallest size possible, still baggy on her wiry frame.

"Sure …" Jenna's raspy voice trails off. She turns to Elle, raising an eyebrow, sending the signal for her to fill in the blanks. She doesn't recognize the girl, doesn't know her name.

"Ellison," Elle says with a wink, "I love the work you did on the yearbook."

"Ellison?" Riley mouths to Jenna, scrunching her forehead comically.

Jenna shrugs, thankful for the fill-in-the-blanks, and goes back to smiling emptily at her admirer.

"Oh, thank you! It was a lot of hard work, but I hope everyone treasures it forever." Ellison beams dreamily. "I know I'm going to keep mine so I can say that I knew Jenna when she becomes famous! I've never heard anyone sing like you."

Jenna lets out a throaty laugh, her ego stroked by the adoring schoolmate she's never taken note of before. She takes the Hello Kitty pen from her and signs a generic message wishing a great summer and all the best, blah, blah, blah. Then, she smoothly scrawls her name, practised hundreds of time in the margins of her notebook in preparation for when she becomes an international star.

"I put in lots of pictures from the talent show," Ellison squeals, adjusting the frames of her colourful eyeglasses. "And your quote is the lead of the graduating class. You were voted most likely to be on a Most Beautiful People List!"

"Awesome!" Jenna cheers, her scratchy voice masking the condescending tone that only Riley picks up on. She flips through the book quickly and finds dozens of pictures of herself. As the school's lead in the choir and musical, drama club president, and person most obsessed with fashion, Jenna Ramsay was the closest thing their suburban high school had to an in-house A-lister.

"Oh, and Elle—good luck at McGill! This school will never be the same without you as student council president." Ellison sighs dramatically, waiting for Elle to autograph her yearbook as well. She pulls out a camera from her fanny pack and asks Riley to take a photo. Ellison gives a peace sign and stands geekily between her two teen idols. Riley snickers as she snaps the picture, and the high school junior skips off happily to collect more signatures.

The girls slip into Elle's red BMW two-door and lead the convoy of their family members making their way to the Bryans' monstrous home on Glen Road.

Elle moved into one of the wealthiest areas in Toronto after her father secured the top neurosurgery position at the hospital where he'd worked his entire career. She never felt at ease in the ritzy Rosedale neighbourhood, even coming from grandparents with old money. She could never get used to the cavernous feel of the Victorian mansion, the way it would groan during storms. She much preferred to stay over at her friends' while her parents were away, which was often. Medical conferences, exotic vacations, Florida weekends so her mother could shop and her father could golf. The lone Bryans child was almost a symbolic by-product of their WASPy love story, her parents more involved in their couplehood and acting like peers with her.

But Elle preferred their unique brand of noninterference parenting. Watching her mother and father so in love gave her a secret hope that not all marriages collapse under pressure, that love can conquer time just like the juiciest romance novels or epic sagas. Plus, it allowed her to fly below their radar and date an older guy all through high school.

Eleanor pulls into the semicircle driveway in front of the Bryans' mansion and coasts towards the three-car garage at the edge of the property. Jenna clicks the garage door opener from the front seat, and the sleek car rolls into its home. Elle's mother parks her white X5 SUV beside her daughter, practically having to jump down from it, both of them barely over five feet tall. A third BMW, her father's two-seater convertible, rests beside them. Perfect for romantic Sunday drives with his wife, or to sneak off for a round of golf between surgeries.

"Daddy's back!" Elle announces happily, her father missing the graduation due to an emergency procedure. Elle and her mother were long accustomed to spending time together, just the two of them, just "the girls."

The petite, neatly packaged matching family of three, the Bryans fit in with the wealthy tranquillity of their neighbourhood. Polished professionals with purebred dogs and sports cars hidden behind intercom-protected gates.

At the front of the house, Riley's father parks his blue Audi in the crescent driveway. A few minutes later, a modest, red hatchback stops behind his car, and Jenna's mother joins the group.

Three different families joined by their days at the local public school. They all head into the grandiose house and to the catered barbecue spread arranged on the back deck.

The three girls have been magnetic friends since the most awkward phases of childhood. Jenna tried to bully Elle on the playground in third grade, and Riley stepped in as the new kid in town, ready to fight the big fight. Riley got suspended, Jenna got a split lip, and they all became inseparable. Sleepovers, birthdays, first crushes, first kisses, everything was shared from that moment on.

Eleanor Bryans, the wealthy and shy doll-face with perfect eyelashes. The surgeon's daughter, the yearbook editor, the girl who wore pearls in the ninth grade when it was cool to wear fishnet stockings instead. It's fitting that the schoolyard scrap was over her—the kindest and gentlest heart anyone could ever meet. Riley loved to mock her, and Jenna wanted to be her.

Soft-spoken and innocent, she was the poster child of angelic qualities. Her deep green eyes and smooth, fair skin fit her prim sense of style. Feminine and conservative.

She was set for life: a massive trust fund, steady boyfriend, and a scholarship to study art history at McGill.

What more could anyone want?

go with the flow.

[Montreal, Canada—September 2009]

The hard wooden floor is cold beneath her face. Elle Bryans peels herself off the surface, feeling her head throb and spin uncontrollably.

She looks around and sees more people sprawled around the room, having crashed after another hard night of drinking. They are all convened at the house shared by her boyfriend and his buddies—Montreal's self-proclaimed counter-culture artists, overly dramatic and trying so hard to be wounded, dabbling in existential expressions of art and vandalism. They are the edgy outsider crowd that ridiculed the art history students at their university, turning the classroom a tense face-off between tradition and the fringe.

Elle's mouth feels like a layer of peach fuzz has grown in it, bitter to taste and rough on her tongue.

Toothbrush, is all she can think, as she slowly gets up, defying gravity in her exhausted state.

She walks to the bathroom, spotting a residue of vomit in and around the toilet. There are hairs on the counter and sink; the musk of a male household is heavy in the air. The old, dilapidated housing in this part of the city is perfect for a starving student's budget. But Elle longs for the cleanliness of her apartment across campus, in a modern building with a concierge and wood floors.

She rummages for her toothbrush, hidden safely in the medicine cabinet. The bristles scour away any traces of liquor and morning breath, already improving her grumpy mood.

The evening starts to replay in her head as she spits in the sink.

She was sitting in the basement with her boyfriend, Sebastian, as all his housemates trickled in with pizza and beer and weed. Elle watched them and their girls get into the partying zone before heading to the local dive bar, doing shots, and taking hits from their homemade bong.

For a Tuesday night, the group had done pretty well for themselves, Elle getting to the point of inebriation where she began making out with Seb in the middle of the grimy bar, ignoring a term paper due the next day and her usual modesty.

After meeting him in a photography class in her second year, the spark between Elle and Seb exploded beyond arguing about art and creativity. His brash personality made her feel like a different person, his presence dangerous and electric. Mesmerising. Their volatile fights only heightening the chemistry. They fooled around in the darkroom, and she lost her virginity to him—even though she had been planning to save it for marriage, like she'd promised her mom. The bad decisions one makes in haste, trying to play an unfamiliar role. Masquerading as a wild child.

She thinks back to their argument from the night before and feels a knot in her stomach.

Seb had been ragging on her all week for being a tense killjoy. She received a warning letter from the dean during the summer, pointing out that she was about to lose her prestigious academic standing at McGill. That she was essentially failing.

So, with the new semester, Elle vowed to pull up from her nosedive.

Except all anyone around her wanted to do was party and complain about the nature of their capitalistic society. How everyone failed miserably when trying to express themselves creatively, that art as they knew it was but a fleeting joke in the modern, commercial world.

Elle's ambitious reincarnation fell to ridicule, with Seb spearheading the nastiness, never one to miss out on knocking her down.

"I can't believe you actually want to go home and do your work ... *enfant,*" he had taunted, his French insulting her after she tried to slip out at the bar. "You don't have the stomach to be a true creative. You don't have that free spirit, the exceptional vision. This is why you're stifled."

Elle impulsively slapped him, and he grabbed her into a passionate kiss.

"What? What do I have to do?" she screamed in return, frustrated never to be doing the right thing in his eyes, having abandoned her past—the wealthy roots and family life, breaking contact with everyone she had known. Trying to reinvent herself.

A conniving smile spread across his face, as he pulled her close, the hot stink of his breath all over her.

"Why don't we share each other tonight ..." he slurred, rubbing her butt with his grimy hand, the booze thickening his heavy Quebecois accent.

Elle had to follow his gaze as it locked on one of his buddies' girlfriends, who was busy dirty dancing up on a wall, way past drunk and on a one-way train to blackout town.

"Are you insane?" she barked at him, unable to fathom watching him intimate with another person.

"What? You said you wanted to open your mind ..." he menaced, trying to bite at her neck aggressively.

"Well, why don't you get him to join, too?" she blurted out sarcastically, motioning to dancer-girl's boyfriend, making his way to peel her off the wall.

Sebastian's reaction was enough to shock everyone in the bar. Even momentarily.

He slapped her across the face so hard that Eleanor felt her teeth vibrate. The petite young woman nearly fell to the grimy floor from the force of his rage.

"Don't you ever think you can bring another man into our bed," he growled, pushing her roughly and turning to his friends, blocking her out.

At that moment, she found herself staring in horror at the company she was in. And with the most dignified of humiliation, she retreated out of the bar and made her way back to the house, shivering in the fall night's air.

Eleanor looks at her face in the bathroom mirror, the dull morning light glowing through the dirty window. A faint handprint is visible on her cheek.

If my parents saw me now ... she thinks to herself, worriedly, wishing her mother was there to brush her hair or hug her. She hasn't seen or spoken to her parents since Seb had come along. Missed holidays and birthdays. They were just paying her tuition and rent, secretly praying their daughter would navigate through this risky phase and return to her senses.

At this moment, too, she misses the innocent nature of her relationship with Benjamin Roberts, the boy she fell head over heels for in high school, who respected her wish to save her virginity until marriage. The guy she thought would be her first—and her husband.

But after starting her freshman year at McGill, she had hoped to afford herself the experience of being free to grow, and split up with him while he was away at law school. Giving up his gentle touch, his kind words, under the impression that it would be easier than loving someone thousands of miles away while he was at Stanford.

I wonder how he is ... she thinks sadly, regretting the thought that there could be bigger and better out there and that it could somehow be in the form of Sebastian.

Because, really, there was nothing wrong with Ben. She was simply romanced by the possibility of being someone she wasn't supposed to be. Of living on her own and starting out with a new persona, abandoning four years of long-distance dating.

She walks into the dirty kitchen, which contains the only computer in the house, and collects her essay from the printer. The ink is so low that her text is barely visible, but she happily staples the dozen pages together.

Glancing at the clock, she estimates she has enough time to stop at her barely used apartment to shower and change, to start the new day in a pure way. The professor would undoubtedly appreciate not seeing her tear-stained cheeks or smelling the alcohol oozing from her pores. And a little cover-up for the handprint on her face would reduce curiosity.

She tiptoes down the hallway but stops right outside of Seb's bedroom door. She peeks her head inside, taking one last look before confirming that their relationship is truly over.

And the final image she has of him makes it all the easier to want to move on. He's sprawled in his bed with two other girls, tangled in the dirty, mismatched sheets. Elle smiles to herself and heads out the door, breathing in the cold air as she walks down Sherbrooke Street.

Elle waits anxiously in the reception area outside the dean's office. She's submitted her essay on luxury and excess as influences of Victorian painting but feels the compulsion to speak to the faculty head in person.

The secretary leads her in, and Elle notices a look of surprise register on the administrator's face. He looks like a homely grandfather, with a tweed blazer and white hair. But the stiffness in his face shows he's not the type to give anyone cookies and milk.

"Miss Bryans, it's good to see you," he says a little flatly, motioning for her to take a seat in front of his desk. Elle remembers him from first year, having met all the professors at a welcome dinner for scholarship winners. Now, almost four years later, she knows he sees her in a different, less flattering light.

"Hi, sir. I'm really sorry to show up like this …"

"Nonsense," he replies. "What can I help you with? I'm assuming you've received some of our letters."

Elle nods, ashamed at his dig. She crosses her legs anxiously; the back of her jeans is too loose from the poor diet she's been consuming at Sebastian's. She's lost weight, looks like a train wreck, and needs a manicure.

"I'm here because … I'm wondering … if you have any opportunities for me to study abroad next semester," she starts. "I know it's really short notice …"

The dean peers at Elle over his glasses and slowly takes a sip from the mug on his desk.

"Eleanor. Your academic standing … would prevent you from applying for a spot," he tries to explain gently. "You've had a pretty steady decline. And abroad programs are like rewards for our most dedicated students."

Elle feels distraught. She's afraid she may faint. Her eyes dart around the room nervously.

"What's been going on, Miss Bryans?" he asks, crossing his hands neatly on the desk, interested to dig deeper into the issue at hand. Elle had been one of the department's identified prodigies, her technical potential shining when discovered by an art professor. And for a couple of years, she was all they had hoped. Until something in her broke.

She sighs loudly, and without control, collapses on the old man's desk, crying.

After a few minutes of uncontrollable sobbing, Elle gathers herself. He is beyond stunned.

"Why do you want to leave?" he asks the student frankly.

"Because if I don't go, I don't think I can make it. I need to be away—I need to be myself again. I can't work here. I need to re … re …" Elle struggles to find the word.

"Reinvent?" he offers, listening to her rambling.

She nods, taking the embroidered handkerchief that is offered to her from his jacket pocket.

"Somewhere … I lost myself. I need that back," Elle pleads. She blows her nose heartily.

The elderly dean looks at her, expressionless.

"Artists work on the influences around them, right? Well, at least that's how I work. I need new influences. I need new inspirations, and people, and a setting that can let me create," she explains, stammering.

Still silence.

Should I cry again? Elle wonders.

Finally, the white-haired man speaks. "I was curious about what happened to you, Eleanor. You were such a promising scholar, and I was sad to think you were a lost cause. I would be willing to write a recommendation—to help balance out your low grades. But there is only one more spot available this year," he starts.

I don't care if I'm in a hut in Mauritius; I need to not be here, she silently begs to the powers that be.

"It would be to study in Venice as of January."

Elle thinks she's heard wrong and doesn't react.

Venice? By Venice does he mean ... Antarctica?

"It's a significant cost. Are you in a position to be able to pay for the trip?" he asks, wondering why she hasn't responded.

She nods furiously, coming back to reality.

After thanking the dean for the thousandth time, she slips outside and sits under a tree, trying to collect herself and slow down her heartbeat. She wipes her runny nose on the back of her hand and rubs it off on the grass, not wanting to use the sleeve of her cashmere sweater.

"Thank you, thank you, thank you!" she whispers out loud, stunned that she has been serendipitously granted the opportunity of a lifetime.

Elle pulls out her cell phone, which is full of voice mails and text messages that she's ignored for so long. She places a call, crossing her fingers.

The other end picks up.

"Mom?" she asks, not having heard the cheery, high-pitched voice in a long time.

"Elle? Is that you?" she gasps. Her cute, energetic mother is sitting in the back garden of their home, drinking tea and looking at decorating swatches.

"Mom! Can I please come home this weekend? I want to see you so much!" she shrieks, tears streaming down her face. "I need to talk to you. I need you and Daddy."

Elle's mother is overjoyed to finally hear from her only child and promptly books the airline ticket. First class.

give thanks.

[Toronto, Canada—October 2009]

White.
All she sees is white.

"Jenna Ramsay—get yourself down here. I cannot put this table together myself, ya know. Rhett Kohl is one of the best interior designers in the country, and he is going to laugh at this place setting!" shouts her mother from the kitchen down the hall.

White ceiling. White walls. White door. White.

"Jen-*na* ..."

"Okay, already! I'm coming! Don't worry, it'll be fine," she assures, rolling off her twin-sized bed and checking herself in the full-length mirror behind her door. Her blue eyes sparkle among the sea of freckles dotting her cheeks.

She's wearing a fisherman knit sweater, brown cords, and wool socks, the perfect Thanksgiving outfit. With her use of accessories, no one would know the entire outfit came straight from a discount store, especially on her long and lean model-like frame. It's a fashion gift she's been blessed with, having grown up on a shoestring budget with her mother's meagre income. Champagne taste on a beer budget, as she was always scolded.

She glances at the samples of designer makeup on her small dresser but grabs the generic pharmacy brand of foundation instead. She decides to save the shiny packaging of Dior and Chanel for a special occasion—maybe to give her that extra boost of confidence the next time she performs. Knowing she's wearing the expensive stuff instead of the cheap kind seems to make her voice sound better.

She slides into slippers to complete the cosy, autumn look, craving for her mother's mashed potatoes.

I wish the Bryans were in town; those yams with marshmallows Odile makes are so good, she thinks to herself, padding down the narrow hall. The older, rent-controlled apartment feels outdated with all the new condominium properties popping up in their neighbourhood. The quiet suburb is north of the main city core, around the corner from the elementary school where her mother works. The same school where she and her friends learned to play dodgeball and Ultimate.

Jenna secretly fantasizes about their apartment building accidentally being bulldozed and having to be rebuilt with marble countertops and a Jacuzzi bathroom—out of consolation.

As she shuffles to the kitchen, she straightens a family photo on the wall. It's a small unit, so heading to the kitchen is actually all of ten steps.

All their family photos are the same. She and her mom in the department store studio at age five. She and her mom in the park when she was ten. She and her mom on the CN Tower's glass floor in middle school. She and her mom. The two of them. Together. All the time. Her dad passed away in a car accident when she was little, so they've been a one-two team ever since.

Her mother is pulling the turkey out of the oven, her lacklustre blonde hair held back with a rubber band she must've snatched from the broccoli. She's roughly the same age as Elle's mother, mid-forties, but the wear and tear is deepened with the single mother burden she's carried.

"Would you put the cranberry sauce in a dish?" she asks, breathlessly hoisting the bird onto the stovetop, splashing some grease on her blouse.

"You know, mom, even Rhett Kohl gets his cranberry sauce from a can," Jenna smirks, grabbing the can opener. Her sparkly dark blue nail polish is chipped, nails bitten down dangerously short. She reaches up high to the shelf that houses all their canned food. Her mom would need a step stool, but Jenna's long arms grab the cranberries effortlessly. She has a significant height advantage over most females. Even most males. She always stood in the back row during picture day.

"Very funny. It's only that, you girls have been friends since ... practically diapers, and he's never been here!"

Jenna dumps the maroon goo into a crystal bowl, the cranberries retaining the shape of the can, texture and all.

"Is Brian coming for dinner, too?" she asks her mother; secretly hoping Riley's cute older brother is joining in the holiday cheer. She pushes a metal spoon into the cylinder shape, breaking up the mush.

"No, he's ... somewhere. Asia? Australia? Who knows."

"That's true. Last I heard, he was thinking about moving to Haiti to help build houses or something. He's so all over the map, I don't think even Brian knows where Brian is ..." Jenna smiles enviously, taking their simple cutlery to the dining table ... approximately seven steps from the kitchen.

"Well, good for him—at least he can afford to amble around and figure it out," her mom sighs, handing over a bottle of wine, reading glasses hanging around her neck. "Are you working at the store next weekend? I wanted to get your help regrouting the shower."

Jenna cringes at the reminder of her average existence, having worked at the local hardware store all through high school and into university. Riley and Elle never had to work to pay for their prom dresses, leaving Jenna to fantasize about becoming a wealthy designer-dressed star as she watered the garden department or stacked bags of fertilizer.

"Well?" her mother probes.

"I'm off Saturday ..." she sighs, coming back to reality and wishing she could hire someone for the messy labour.

"You'll thank me when you need to scrub your own bathtub. I bet Rhett Kohl hasn't taught his kids those life skills." Her mom chuckles.

Jenna stares at the bottle of wine in her hands and heads to the table.

Brian and Riley Kohl—the gay man's children.

That's how they were known around school, at least until people learned to fear them. In a community where being gay was still a bit taboo at the time, the Kohls' move to Toronto had ignited a whirlwind of gossip in their quiet, boring suburb. Tall, European, and flawlessly handsome, Rhett irritated the women of the city for being unavailable—literally.

Brian, the eldest of his two adopted kids, did his best to enforce a no-tolerance policy of trash talking, often beating the crap out of kids who insulted them. Racking up suspensions and a bad-boy image, he was the rebel with a cause in junior high.

Riley also grew to be feared, but in different ways. She became the brain of the class—cutting kids down to size with her dry sarcasm (and the occasional black eye).

Quickly, though, the Kohls worked their way into mainstream popularity, mostly after Rhett was contracted to redecorate the Bryans' home. His creative services as an interior designer were always out of the Ramsay family's price range—he worked with celebrities and heads of government, not the school secretary. Though, if her mom had asked, he would have done their plain, white shoebox for free. But it being free would probably have been worse for Ida Ramsay's pride than spending her daughter's hard-saved college fund.

"Hey, you never told me how your midterm results were ..." her mother starts, coming at Jenna with paper napkins to fold. She leaves her daughter and darts back into the kitchen.

"Uh, well, they were okay." She shrugs, turning her back and pretending to fiddle with the fake maple leaves on the store-bought centrepiece.

"Okay as in, you passed?"

"Yeah ..." Jenna trails off, picking at her fingernails and mumbling to try mask her uncertainty.

More like barely passed! There was the one time I strolled into a morning exam still drunk from a night of singing at the jazz club ...

"Okay, well, as long as you pass and get a degree, then you can do whatever else you think you need to do," her mom trills from the kitchen, filling a bowl with box-made stuffing. "No employer is going to ask the grades of your last year in university. They want to know you stuck with it."

"You know, Mom," starts Jenna, trying to steer the topic of conversation. "I really have a good feeling about this demo I sent in. I met this intern from a record company after an open mic night at the campus pub ... I really think this could lead to something ..."

"Jenna-bean, please ..." she pleads, cooing her daughter's childhood nickname, wiping her hands on the crusty apron, and following her daughter into the dining room with a turkey baster in hand. "Why don't you think about the real world? About what's going to need to happen after you graduate. I know you have talent, you have a beautiful voice, but what about the thousands of other girls who also have beautiful voices but have nothing else to fall back on?"

"Mom ..."

"No, don't 'mom' me right now. I'm saying this because I love you and because it needs to be said. I think you have to consider ... the possibility ... that a singing career isn't going to materialize in front of you. You could always work with me at the school ... think about other options if you don't get—"

"Okay!" Jenna interrupts, aggravated. "I will. I promise. But as long as I get a degree, I can pursue this—that was our deal. So ..." She puts a finger to her lips, motioning for silence.

"Don't shush your mother!" She laughs, poking her daughter in the ribs with the turkey baster.

"Ew, Mom—that's got, like, juices ..." Jenna grimaces, throwing her arms around her mother's thin neck in a mock-headlock.

Ida wiggles free and tsk-tsk's her rambunctious child, jokingly waving a finger at her as she leaves the room. Jenna has always been a livewire, but her unquenchable pursuit of becoming a singer has definitely put a strain on her very pragmatic mother.

Jenna stares down at the plastic tablecloth and sighs. She thinks back to the jam session in her friend's basement the night before. The recognition from her peers that her raspy voice was powerful and natural, that her creativity was integral to their brainstorming of new songs. She knows that she's got something other people don't.

This is gonna happen, she affirms to herself, clutching the napkins with a crazy look in her eyes. *There is just no other option.*

reach.

[Oxford, England—November 2009]

Riley Kohl stares at the clothes hanging in her armoire, struggling to piece together an outfit. Her hair is in shambles, her glasses are on, and she's finished a long, long term paper for her literary journalism course. She's still wearing flannel pyjamas instead of changing to go out. Chinese takeout containers are scattered on her desk, drops of soy sauce dotting her notes.

She pulls out a hanger with a pair of charcoal high-waisted trousers. She inspects them, makes a weird face, and then puts them back. She considers a dark, printed dress but disinterestedly tosses it on the bed.

"I think I ... don't ... wanna go" she huffs to herself, trudging across the small apartment to warm up a cup of Darjeeling tea in the microwave. The machine hums as she feels the dread of having to attend yet another fund-raiser with her boyfriend, Matthew. His interest in networking and meeting influential people in the city has spiked since he decided to get involved with university politics. And Riley despises the thought of getting dolled up to play the role of an arm-candy girlfriend. Having grown up watching socialites fawning over her father, puppeteering their husbands' wallets, and getting googly-eyed over the most superficial of things, she harbours a disdain for trendiness.

The microwave beeps, and she pulls out the steaming mug. Her cell phone rings, and she's relieved for the disruption, even more pleased to read the caller ID.

"Why, hello, Miss Bryans." She smiles, moving to sit in her ragged armchair, curling her knees in front of her.

"Why, hello, Miss Kohl." Elle giggles across the Atlantic from Montreal.

"And what are you up to this fine... Wednesday, is it? Good grief, I don't even know." Riley smiles, setting down the mug on the windowsill, excited to catch up.

"Well, I actually just finished a pottery class, and I happen to be walking home ... thought I'd check in—" says her friend as a truck drives past, drowning her out momentarily.

"Pottery? How very ... romantic ... of you. Have you gained weight back?" Riley asks, straight to the point, thankful that her friend is back on the straight and narrow.

Elle laughs shyly. "Yes ... I've been eating nothing but smoked meat sandwiches. I'm kidding. Really, though, I'm back to normal, feeling so much better ..."

"Good, good. What about that sociopath?"

"Sebastian?" Elle laughs. "He's left me alone. Must not actually miss me. A girl kinda hopes that she's made enough of an impact that the guy realizes he can't live without you and comes running back ..."

"Don't go there. You know that's not the situation. And you know that he's a total mental case. It was never about you, Elle—it was always about him and his control issues."

Elle sighs, still secretly hoping to have made a splash with her abrupt exit.

"You're right," she mumbles, and Riley can hear her unlock a door and step inside. "I guess part of it is ... I don't know, I kind of miss the ... the ... "

"Sex?"

"No!" Elle chirps quickly. "Well, maybe a tad ... but I was trying to say, I kind of miss feeling ... so ... out there. So wild and free."

"Well, yeah, I guess it's fun to play pretend sometimes. But don't you think that it's much harder to play a character than to just be who you're supposed to be?" Riley suggests, glancing at the clothes still spread out on her bed. "To accept who you are instead of feeling the tiniest bit incomplete when parading around in slutty dress things?"

"Slutty dress things? Um ... right. Who are we talking about?" Elle jokes. "But you're seriously like a self-help book. Are you sure you don't want to study psychiatry and earn ridiculous amounts of money in private practise?"

"No way. I don't like people—let alone their stupid problems," Riley cackles bluntly.

"I was thinking, maybe you should take a class, meet some different people. Get out of that fishbowl of an apartment," Elle suggests.

"What?"

"Like, I've been taking these yoga classes, right? And aside from the fact that I'm totally improving the state of my physical and mental health, I've met some really cool people who obviously share the same interest as me."

Riley stares at the floor in horror. "Yoga?!"

"Yes."

"Yoga—like bendy freaky people who salute the sun god or whatever and eat flaxseed?"

Elle can't control her laughter. "Riley, for one of the most brilliant and secretly nice people on Earth, you are also one of the most ignorant. Yoga isn't radical tree-hugging, lovee. And besides, I'm not telling you to go and do that specific hobby. I'm saying *maybe* you could expand your horizons."

"Like an arguing team?"

"Debating?"

"Right, yeah—ob-v-i—" Riley blushes, feeling self-conscious and defensive.

"Speaking of, how's the future prime minister?" Elle coos, referring to Matthew.

Riley groans, signalling that a change in topics is necessary. She taps her fingers on the dark fabric of her chair, uncomfortable.

"Okay, okay. Well, Jenna is coming up to visit Montreal this weekend," Elle says excitedly.

"Oh, wow, how is she doing? I haven't spoken to her since Thanksgiving—only that last e-mail she sent about being totally in love with … what's his name?"

"Yeah, that's over. I think she's made a resolution to focus on her singing," Elle informs.

Riley rolls her eyes and starts to pick at a hangnail.

"I can hear that scepticism oozing through the phone," Elle trills in a singsong voice.

"What? I can't help but wonder when she's gonna get her head out of the sand with the superstar singer thing." Riley sighs. "And stop being so freakin' boy crazy! I might as well not learn names because they'll be rotated out faster than a fat kid in gym class. We should honestly call them all 'dude' as a generic label. Like, 'oh, how's Dude?' And she can talk about whoever he is without needing names."

"Well, she *is* quite good," Elle redirects, always amazed by her friend's vocal skill and, secondarily, her ability to rotate boyfriends.

"I know. But talent isn't necessarily a must, know what I mean? There are plenty of … artists, or whatever they call themselves, that don't have that talent and are doing it. Doesn't it seem like the odds are one in a million billion, that maybe there's a little element of delusion there because this sort of thing seems so luck-based."

"You're right, but she feels in her heart that it's going to happen. Haven't you ever had that? A feeling, like a ... knowing. Kind of like you know what's going to happen, or what is meant to happen." Elle says dreamily.

"Uh ... no."

"Ugh. Riley, you are so dreary sometimes."

"What? So you're telling me that you had some sort of mystical insight? As to what, exactly?"

Elle bites her lip on the other end of the line, realizing she's dug herself into a hole. "Um ..."

"Spill it, psychic hotline." Riley smirks to herself, enjoying putting the pressure on her "glass half full" friend. Taunting her beliefs of fate and magical happiness.

"Well, if you must know, I had that knowing about someone. I just chose to ignore it and acted like an overdramatic child."

"Ben," Riley hums, realizing her friend is walking down memory lane again, missing the short Jewish guy who could dish out witty sarcasm like no other. Riley always liked his razor-sharp observations, especially on Jenna's flavour of the week. Ben was a bit older than the girls, already on the path to law school, but he blended well with their little group—and adored Eleanor like crazy.

"I knew that I was meant to be with him. And somehow ... I hate to admit it, but I thought that I could be an idiot and that he'd still be there after sowing my wild oats or whatever. And that we would, regardless of said idiocy, end up together."

"And?"

Elle remains quiet.

"You think you've fucked it up and that you altered the destined path?" Riley asks, rolling her eyes.

"Jenna says that I should get in touch with him, that maybe I haven't fudged up forever."

"Are you going to?"

Elle laughs nervously, still undecided.

"I'm sure when you're ready ..." Riley suggests awkwardly, not quite sure how to comfort her friend. She's never felt that someone could be "the one." Most men fail to meet even her most basic of expectations.

Matthew himself is close to perfect on paper, but lacking a certain *je ne sais quoi*.

"How's your creative writing?" Elle asks, changing the subject again.

Riley laughs hysterically. "You're asking that as if I have something in progress!" she howls, well aware that all she's been able to write are shitty term papers about dry subjects. Only a few chapters of her creative work came into existence in the fall, and she remains stuck on them, constantly reviewing and correcting and fixating.

"Well, you have to get your bum in gear—your story isn't going to write itself." Elle laughs, impersonating Riley's dry tone.

"Hey, did you call to talk or to be a jerk?"

"Oh, please. You know as much as I do that you need to get over that little phobia of sharing things with people. You need to get yourself going, and put something out there! Take a page from Miss Ramsay—no one is out there looking for you until you show them you exist."

"It's not that easy, Elle," Riley protests.

"It is when it's finished and you can show it to people. So that they can see what you're about. But if you keep doing nothing, it's not going to write itself."

"I get that, but I don't think, even if I did finish it, that it would necessarily get published or anything," Riley admits, voicing the secret fears residing in her head. She takes a sip of her tea.

"Well, you won't get anything sitting down in your chair like an old lady with her cup o' tea." Elle teases, having an idea of what her friend is doing at that very moment.

Riley looks around the room, creeped out by how well they know each other.

"So get up and stop razzing Jenna when you're the one that needs a little shot of her … delusion."

"But don't you think there's a difference between having that … knowing, and wishful thinking?" Riley rebuts.

"Yes. But right now, no thinking is worse. Stop being mopey and wash your face!"

Riley laughs, suddenly self-conscious about the fact that she hasn't bothered to wash up after the back-to-back all-nighters she's pulled this week.

"Whatever. I'll see you next month. Tell the positive-thinking poster child I say hi." Riley smiles before hanging up.

tea time tradition.

[Toronto, Canada—December 20, 2009]

Riley grabs a hand-painted porcelain teapot from the marble island in her kitchen and heads to the living room. Jenna and Elle are already sitting cross-legged on the floor on a makeshift picnic blanket (in actuality, one of her dad's raw silk fabrics from Gujarat). Two gift boxes are in the middle of them, colourfully wrapped for Jenna's 21st birthday.

The Kohl house is situated in a ravine area known as Hoggs Hollow and was featured in *Architectural Digest* after Rhett gutted it entirely and built a "green-friendly" palace. It's about ten minutes north of the Bryans mansion and close to the public schools where they were all enrolled. As kids, Riley was able to skateboard over to Jenna's apartment every afternoon to escape the ultramodern construction work going on at home.

Futuristic layouts are accented with all-natural materials, giving the narrow three-story house a luxurious feel, complete with a state-of-the-art wine cellar and en suite steam room. Rhett Kohl has proudly filled the home with treasures from his world travels, always checking out new places for trendy materials and styles to incorporate into his designs.

Their neighbourhood is affluent but exotic, its residents seeking out an environment different than rowed mansions with three-car garages and opting for the seclusion of trees and hilly avenues surrounding their properties.

The girls are gathered for their annual holiday-time tea party, a tradition started circa grade four to celebrate Jenna's sadly timed birthday, always overlooked due to school breaks and major holidays.

Riley's father had tried to initiate Hanukkah activities with his two kids. But Riley was getting over mono and was sulky and depressed and disinterested in playing dreidel with her teenaged brother.

So, instead, Rhett invited the girls over for age-appropriate party activities. And to a full-grown gay man, this somehow meant high tea—and gifting a nine-year-old Jenna a box of Chinese tea leaves with a hand-painted pot.

Jenna and Elle had shown up at the door in puffy dresses, visibly starched and uncomfortable. Riley took them to her room and gave them sweats and T-shirts to change into instead.

And with the passing years, with the girls growing from awkward teenagers to blossoming young women, the annual tea party remained a part of their mutual history. Although they don't see each other as regularly, the year-end get-together provides a link to their past and jogs memories of jokes and scandals from their school days.

"Remember when we used to do this as kids?" Elle coos, pinching a petit four from the middle of the store-bought picnic spread. Riley can't be bothered to actually learn to cook and relies solely on catering to get through any social event.

"I *knooow*, seriously. I thought tea parties were so medieval or whatever." Jenna smiles, laughing awkwardly and rocking on her sit bones. Her black tights and bright blue long-sleeve shirt look comfortable against the stone fireplace. The all-glass walls of the house face out into the backyard, showing a light snowfall.

Jenna hasn't touched her presents, an uncharacteristic behaviour. Having two best friends from wealthy families always rendered incredible birthday and Christmas presents, things that she wouldn't normally be able to get herself, trendy clothes or doodads that the Bryans parents and Rhett Kohl loved to reward her with. She was the loyal friend of their beloved daughters; the fact that she came from a less affluent household wasn't her fault.

Hmm. There's something strange here. She is smiling way too intensely, Riley thinks to herself, carefully cradling the teapot as she sits and observes Jenna.

"So, how was the end of term for you guys?" asks the host, pouring Darjeeling into cute teacups from Sri Lanka.

"Well, now that I'm through with evil psycho boy, things are going much better!" Elle laughs, referring to her turbulent, experimental college romance. "Crazy, drug-addicted, and emo: the stuff dreams are made of!"

"That tends to happen when you date a lunatic," Riley says dryly.

"Lovee, don't even start," Elle warns, not wanting to recall the months of evidence and red flags that Seb was bad news. The evidence stared her in the face, but she didn't want to see it as she tried to live in her rebel-child phase, effectively hitting "mute" on all gut feelings.

"So, then, you'll just transfer your credits from Italy and graduate on schedule?" Riley redirects diplomatically, pulling her navy turtleneck over her jeans to cover any traces of plumber's butt.

"Yes, it's perfect! I really hope you're able to come and see me, Riles. How great would it be?" she squeals, accidentally dripping tea on her green Lacoste polo.

Jenna, however, is sitting completely still, hands clasping her knees, as if in a meditative state—except she's got a goofy grin plastered on her face. Her cup sits untouched; she is withdrawn from present company.

"Jenna?" Riley asks, shooting a "what the fuck?" look at an oblivious Elle.

I never noticed that this fabric looks maroon up close ... or would this be burgundy? Elle muses to herself cheerily, admiring the fine picnic blanket they've improvised. She gets scared by the scowl Riley gives her and forces herself to settle back into reality.

Jenna keeps smiling like a doll.

"Miss Ramsay?" Elle asks gently, now aware that there is an alien among them.

Their friend is silent and begins shaking slightly.

"Jenna, really, what the hell is going on?" Riley asks, now a bit worried, but definitely more annoyed. *Pupils are reactive, skin colour normal,* she checks off, still unsure why her friend is catatonic.

"I got picked up," Jenna whispers quickly, still staring off at nothing in particular. It sounds more like "igotpickedup."

"Huh?" Elle is now fully turned, bracing herself for something awful, her face scrunched up in anxiety.

Riley puts down her teacup in case of catastrophe.

"I. Got. Picked. Up," she repeats, breaking up her words purposefully but not making eye contact with either of her friends. Her eyes are glowing eerily, matching her shirt's deep blue intensity.

"Picked up by who?" Elle winks flirtatiously, excited at the prospect of a new dating story.

"I don't think she means by a guy," Riley clarifies, still staring hesitantly, studying her friend's body language.

"Alchemy," Jenna whispers.

"What?"

"What?!"

"Alchemy Records. Three-album deal. Jenna," she rasps, pointing at herself.

"What?" Elle asks again softly, confused.

"Shh!" Riley hisses, putting a hand out to stifle her friend. Sometimes she's a bit slow on the uptake.

Riley turns to Jenna, grabbing her face semi-violently. "Repeat that."

"I'm going to record music!" she replies, the colour starting to flood back to her cheeks.

Her two friends stare at each other in total silence. In the middle of the Kohl's living room, sitting on a piece of random silk amidst the odd decorations of tribal masks and fertility idols, a bomb has been dropped.

"Come again?" Elle repeats, still not sure she's grasped the content at hand.

"*I got signed!*" Jenna screams at the top of her lungs, jumping up into a victory dance.

"*Vhaaat?*" rumbles Rhett Kohl's deep voice from the foyer, his Dutch accent heavy and vibrating the walls around them.

He steps into the living room with his boyfriend, Kevin. They are two of the most ruggedly handsome men to exist in the modern world. They're in matching cashmere sweaters and designer jeans, heading out to a dinner party.

"*I got siiiiiigned!*" Jenna shrieks again, breaking octaves like a banshee.

Everyone freezes, observing her frantic gestures.

"Shit. Fuck. Shit," is all Riley can contribute.

"When?" Elle asks, breathless at all the possibilities.

"This morning." Jenna grins mischievously.

"This morning?" she echoes, shocked.

Rhett, Kevin, Elle, and Riley are now standing awkwardly, letting the information sink in.

"Kwame Roy called me in today. *Kwame Roy*—the head of Alchemy Records from *New York* who flew up here! And he had a contract … *aaand* … I signed!"

Silence hangs in the air, and then shrieking from the rest of the group slices it. They all rush at Jenna and envelope her in a hug.

"Holy sugar, holy sugar, holy sugar," Elle murmurs to herself, over and over again, her PG-13 version of swearing.

"Happy birthday to *you*!" Riley gasps, astounded by the great timing of the news gifted to her friend.

"I can't believe it. Kwame just … made it happen. It's surreal!" Jenna shouts.

"So, what now?" asks Kevin, brushing his fashionably shaggy hair out of his eyes.

"Well, I start recording after New Year's, hopefully to get an album out by fall if I can push everything?"

"Oh my *goodniss*. Jenna, did you get a lawyer to look at *zee* contract?" Rhett asks worriedly.

"Shh. You're such a worrier," Kevin scolds him, smacking his large bicep.

"No, really. I mean, *vhat* did *yur* mother say?" he continues.

"Nothing … yet. I'm going to tell her tonight. But okay, hi, hello—this is happening. I don't care if I sold my soul—this is happening," she replies defiantly, glazed over. "I have prayed for this like you wouldn't believe. And I don't even have a religion."

Oh, my God, she looks kinda possessed, Riley thinks to herself, watching her friend's eyes focused not on the people in front of her, but almost as if looking through them and at the road ahead.

"What about school?" Elle asks, delicately clasping her hands together.

"I'll finish as I record," Jenna says breezily. "But seriously, you think I'm going to pass up on this?" She grins, wiping her clammy palms on her leggings. She's been overheating all day, scared to admit anything out loud in case she imagined it all.

"Rhett, we need to run, or we're going to be super late," Kevin warns, looking at his watch.

"Jenna, *vee'll* finish *zis* discussion later. But ... *congratulayshons?*" Rhett grins, hugging her. He's known her since the talent shows and holiday recitals when all the girl wanted to do was get up and sing. Maybe this is what is meant to happen, and no one gave her credit for being so sure-footed on her path. Riley always thought she was delusional and would eventually give up when she had to start paying off a mortgage.

Elle always thought it was cool to have another openly artsy friend, a creative who was not afraid of putting her work out in the open and calling herself an "artiste." With Riley passing off her writing solely as schoolwork, Elle and Jenna were the ones most openly in tune with their talents, and optimistic enough to think that they could live such inspired callings, and not just in a daydream.

Maybe Jenna had cosmic insight all along, and that's why she never doubted the possible reality of becoming a singer. A certain gut knowing that her destiny in life was to reach the masses with her gifts. A sureness in the end result that bred stubborn faith that all the missing pieces would fall into place at precisely the right time.

Jenna Ramsay's inner lava has spewed, the news is out—she's going to do it.

lay it out.

[Toronto, Canada—December 24, 2009]

Jenna and her mother are sitting on their tiny living room floor with hot chocolate, looking at old photos. There's a miniature plastic Christmas tree in the corner; greeting cards addressed to Ida Ramsay from teachers and students line the room. Being the reliable secretary has always reaped rewards around the holiday season, most notably in the form of chocolate boxes and bottles of wine.

Jenna flips the heavy album page with faded photos of her mom's pregnant belly, appreciating her take on eighties fashion. There's a picture of her mom and dad at the hospital, holding their newborn baby.

It's the only time of year when they really acknowledge the history of their downsized family. The loss of her father still fascinates Jenna in the form of imaginary memories from infancy; she pretends to know a man she never really bonded with.

"You know, Bean," her mom starts, using her childhood nickname. "Your dad, he used to actually like when you screamed. My goodness, how you used to wail as a baby." She laughs, looking at an image of Jenna naked in the tub, shrieking.

"I must've been such a pain." She laughs, staring at her squidgy little face, red with emotion.

"You know what? Not really. You made a lot of noise, but you were always a happy baby. He used to say that you were only communicating. He claimed you had some sort of melody or harmony or something in your shrieks."

"Really?" she asks, amused, touching the photo.

Could it be possible to hear something in someone so young like that—a raw, untapped talent? A sign of a possible future path? Did her father know this?

"Oh, yeah. He used to say it was music to his ears. What a sunny way of looking at a baby's wailing, huh?" Her mom laughs, wrapping her colourful robe around herself like a hug. She looks exhausted and worn, a drastic contrast to the vivacious energy of Elle's mother. Even Elle's father, who is approaching retirement, looks as good as ever.

"I didn't know he thought that," Jenna whispers, playing with the tattered sleeve of her Roots sweatshirt, picking a chocolate from a box gifted by the school principal.

Her mom takes a sip from her mug, a grade school craft made for Father's Day. A gift Jenna had no one else to give to. The crooked printing says #1 Dad on one side.

"My gosh, you have no idea how he would get you to bang pots and pans and make a racket—glorious noise, he'd call it. Only a music teacher could take that sound and look at it as being artistic."

Jenna looks at her, feeling sadness creep in. Young and pretty Ida Ramsay fell in love with the awkward music teacher, the man who played the French horn but never quite made it to the symphony. It took him ages to work up the courage to even speak to the lovely blonde secretary in the school office.

The album is flipped to a photograph of father and daughter playing in the snow, Jenna in a bright purple one-piece snowsuit and probably around two years old. There's a plastic sled behind them.

"Hey, Mom … where were you when you found out he was gone? When you found out about the accident?"

Ida stares at the carpet in front of her, thrown off by the question. For so long, she's kept the nature of her husband's death at bay. Simply spoken to fact—he was gone, there was no changing that. Nothing to break down about. She *had* to move on and keep going, especially with a toddler to take care of.

Jenna looks at her mom worriedly, afraid she's offended her.

Ida's lip quivers. She stares at the album, her grey eyes misty. She's looking at a picture of Jenna in the elementary school talent show, dolled up in sequins and holding a microphone with a mile-long cord.

The silence in the room is so thick it's hard for Jenna to breathe. She blurts out her next sentence in a desperate attempt to lift the heaviness.

"So, um, I signed a record deal," she says with the same tone as if she were talking about doing the laundry.

Her mother's reaction is delayed, leaving a bit more silence lingering.

She doesn't speak but simply and slowly turns her head to look at her daughter sitting beside her on the carpet.

Jenna hugs her knees for support, regretting that she didn't set up the topic of conversation better.

"Pardon me?" her mother asks, wishing she's heard wrong. She tucks her greying blonde hair behind her ears, icy eyes zooming in on Jenna like lasers.

"Yeah. Um, haha. I, ah, signed a record deal. To make my music," Jenna says, forcing an overly eager smile to compensate.

Her mother sets down her mug calmly, but her hand quivers and gives away her restrained rage. "When did this happen?"

"A couple of days ago," Jenna replies.

"And you didn't think to talk to me? You signed a contract? A legally binding contract? What on Earth were you thinking?" she gasps angrily.

Jenna is shocked, not expecting this type of reaction for something she is so excited about.

"Are you completely insane, Jenna? You were supposed to graduate and get a job and begin to have an adult life. You know we don't have money like your friends—I can't support you while you search for your path or dawdle around 'making music,'" Ida continues.

"But—"

"What about your school?" she gasps, horrified. "I can't believe you're so cavalier about throwing your life away like this. You're in your last semester and this … sham of a career. They're going to use you because you're pretty and impressionable. Dear Lord, please tell me you haven't slept with someone." Her eyes flicker with ferocity.

"Mom!" Jenna shouts, offended.

But her mother is on a rampage. "They're going to use you up and spit you out, and when you're older … that's it. Do you want to end up like those clearance bin CDs? Because that is not an industry that promotes health and well-being and longevity, Bean!"

Jenna can't handle the doomsday ranting and shoots up from the floor like a spring. She strides straight into her room and locks the door, trapped in her own home. The walls are spinning around her, and her heart is beating so hard it feels like an anvil being thrown around in her rib cage.

She feels her lungs getting smaller. Tears begin to fill her eyes, and any ounce of light and excitement in her body has dissolved. She throws herself onto her bed, smothering her heaving sobs with a pillow. All she wants is for it stop.

dividing line.

[Oxford, England—December 31, 2009]

Riley sits down at her small desk. She's decided to spend New Year's on campus at the University of Oxford to start January off right, to buckle down and get through all her work. Finish the literature degree, maybe be inspired to do some creative writing and pen the next great North American novel. Or just pen something. Anything.

Night has already slipped into her apartment; a deep chill is in the air outside. But the streets are full of festive commotion.

She stares at the blank journal page in front of her. The dark leather of the book is worn and cracking.

She's quit straightening her long dark hair, annoyed by the motions of getting dressed up for a party. Makeup is strewn around; a purse sits, half packed, on the bed.

She finds herself at a fork in the road, needing to discreetly vent:

> *They say that how you spend New Year's Eve is how your year will go. That who you kiss at midnight, or the group you're with, or the things that you do ... this is what crosses you over the threshold of one year into the next. And this sets off some cosmic, magical energy thing. Could it be possible that this sort of thing is somehow ... maybe ... fractionally true? Millions of people readily believe in fate, that nothing is actually coincidence.*

She looks at the photos on the desk, tapping her fountain pen nervously. There's a picture of her, Elle, and Jenna taped up, the edges frayed and the colours faded. They're huddled together draining maple sap from a tree during a grade school field trip. She continues writing.

> *So this year, I am not at my dad's cocktail party. Or hiking ruins with Brian. Or with Jenna and Elle eating pizza in our pyjamas. This year, I'm going to a freakin' ball with Matthew. I am sitting in an expensive, stupid dress having to go to a flashy, dumb ball.*
>
> *I don't even want to go!*
>
> *Am I really that antisocial and weird?*

I don't think I can do this. More and more, I find Matt wanting to be the social butterfly ... vexing. Why can't he want to stay in and watch period movies?! Why does he want me to wear shoes that slice up my feet? So he can mingle with people who don't actually care about him? Like, if he got into a car accident, would they be at the top of his call list? Not so much. They're acquaintances at best, and totally wouldn't visit him in the hospital. God forbid. Shit.

I mean, when we started dating, things were great. He liked my edginess. I think? But with the year ending, and me moving home ... we're going to break up, right? Right?!

And, if I'm honest with myself, I have doubts about us actually being a great couple, anyway. We're not like how Elle and Ben were. Or even Rebecca and Marc from high school, who matched with their trendy outfits. Or Leo and Irene with their brainy ways. Heck, even Kim and Trevor, with their pet cats and cuteness. Matt's great but ... not perfect. Okay, I'm not perfect, either, but shouldn't you have some sort of secret language of intuitions with your loved one? That would be a great story ... a telepathic couple that can use their powers to solve mysteries ...

I guess this poses the question, Is it ever truly okay to be with someone just for the sake of being with someone? Out of convenience or loneliness? Am I being a totally unrealistic romantic that thinks her King Arthur is going to save the day? King Matt Roth? Not quite. He doesn't have the same innate self-confidence. To not care what others think, and especially not needing to impress or please them.

Does perfect even exist? Maybe for some people ... but not for everyone, right? In this lifetime, how is it statistically possible for everyone to find someone that deeply touches them so? What the fuck does "romantic" mean, anyway?

Maybe he hasn't even thought this deeply into it and now I look like a douche because I've gotten all worried and feminine about nothing.

Riley, what have you gotten yourself into?

Worse ... what now?

She closes the book, stares at the wall, and fluffs the layers of black satin on her party dress.

this is happening.

[Toronto, Canada—January 2010]

Jenna Ramsay gets out of the chauffeured car, staring up at the brick building in front of her with awe. There is no sign or street address to mark the studio she's about to step into. The downtown neighbourhood of Queen Street West is artsy and cutting edge, coffee shops and boutiques scattered around. But hidden within the dingy building in front of her, a state-of-the-art sound studio awaits. For the first time ever, she is going to get to work on her music—legitimately—to put together a sampler for her record label boss, a reference point for the PR and marketing people to start putting her out into the world.

"Right this way, J," says Mackenzie Madison, her now formally instated manager. He chatters on his cell phone, in the middle of brokering a deal, and walks quickly against the cold gusts of wind.

The middle-aged owner of Top Dog Management spotted her last summer when she was asked to sing background music at one of Rhett Kohl's big cocktail parties. Mack was a guest with his wife at the flapper-themed unveiling of the Kohls' backyard—and Rhett's new line of paint colours. Reporters for the society pages were there, taking photos of all the city's faces and of Jenna by the piano bar.

Riley wasn't even at the event; she was visiting her brother in the Andes. And her father also knew better than to put Riley into a social situation involving kiss-asses, not to tempt her to release her cynical furies and dry wit on potential clients.

But that evening proved to be the start of a partnership that would get Jenna the unthinkable—a gatekeeper to the mystery world of the mainstream music industry.

Mack secretly taped her singing on his cell phone and slipped the feed into Kwame Roy's hands, setting in motion the lucrative pairing of Jenna Ramsay and Alchemy Records.

A viral YouTube video also helped get all the hype rolling. Two hundred thousand views before Kwame's involvement with her was leaked last month—the hit maker had found his next prodigy.

Mack wipes his square glasses free of fog, having stepped in from the cold. He's a few inches shorter than Jenna but is confidently rocking a power suit as part of his megastar manager identity. His all-business rigidness contrasts her casual hot pink hoodie, which is flipped up to cover her head from the sprinkles of snow.

"So, don't be put off by this meeting. It might be a bit rickety when you meet a collaborator at first, but have faith in this guy. I've worked with him before, and I think that you'll mesh well. He's young, has his ear to the ground. It might be weird to put yourself out there, but try be totally transparent. Show him what you've written so far. He'll give feedback—you may not like it. Remember, he's here to take you to the next level. You're going to be a pro now," Mack advises, doing his best to pep talk her in his robotic tone. He means well, and Jenna trusts him, but he's just a bit too much of a tin man.

He keeps clicking away on his BlackBerry, leading her through a sleek lobby area. His bald head glows under the industrial lighting in the building.

Jenna tries to breathe, to slow down her racing heart. The yoga classes Elle gave her for her birthday come to mind, as she exhales steadily, trying to emulate what she learned, to meditate herself back down to Earth and take in the present moment.

"By the way, how's that new apartment we got you in?" he asks, suddenly shifting gears and looking at her eagerly for positive reinforcement. He stares at her intensely, his dark eyes looking beady. He knows the key to her heart is in providing all the luxuries the young girl has never been privy to.

"Oh, yeah, great, thank you. I've gotten a lot of writing done in the quiet space this past little while." She smiles sheepishly. She's still amazed at how quickly her materialistic ambitions were fulfilled by signing on the dotted line.

Her management and new record label were concerned about the stifling influence surrounding Jenna at her mother's tiny apartment and promptly moved her into a "creative oasis" to promote more songwriting—an oasis that happened to be completely removed from Ida Ramsay's resentful shadow and controlled by an intimidating concierge.

With fully stocked amenities, the novelty of living in a ritzy condo still hasn't worn off on her. Smack in the middle of the exclusive Yorkville district downtown, Jenna's wish to live among the rich and famous had been granted almost overnight. The luxury condo building was all she could have dreamed of and more. In the bustling city, but surrounded by the comforts of wealth and power, she was in the neighbourhood with luxury hotels and shops, where celebrities notoriously trolled with the paparazzi on their heels.

Except the impressive property didn't have any photos, no memories. The sterile walls without any of the lived-in signs of a real home, making her feel displaced. And the fact that she still couldn't figure out how to work the fancy bathtub wasn't helping her feel settled in.

No mail comes for her, either. No postcards from Riley's travels, the photographs of foreign countries that she taped to her desk like a visualization exercise.

Instead, she's replaced day-to-day life by meeting her peculiar neighbours, walking past all the high-street boutiques with confidence, and having her fridge stocked with organic food—she even has a housekeeper to clean everything up.

But it all comes down to this moment, the first meeting between Jenna and her first album's producer—the guy who was selected to help get her music up to snuff, while the marketing executives and stylists take care of the rest.

Her face feels hot when she thinks of how her mother handled her decision to move out, and she desperately tries to fill her lungs with air to stay grounded. Her mom had actually thrown things at the wall when she returned home to discover her daughter's belongings already packed up and moved out. The haunting, disowning voice mail left on her cell phone made Jenna vow never to look back.

Quiet your mind, she instructs herself, trying to focus back on the situation at hand, exhaling shakily.

Jenna watches Mack stroll in through a heavy metal door and pauses, feeling a shiver shoot up the back of her neck. She follows him and steps into a room full of mixing boards and lights and equipment, feeling a jolt of excitement course through her body. Like touching an open electrical current. Any anxiety about working with a collaborator has been erased with sheer anticipation. This is the moment she's been envisioning for years—thinking positively, practising her autograph for future fans, and rehearsing an awards acceptance speech in the shower.

She stares at the recording booth beyond a pane of glass, where a lone microphone is set up.

That's mine! she thinks, wanting to jump in and play. She shivers with the thought of picking up a mic—the feeling she gets when starting to sing, like a creeping warmth tingling her skin, the sensation that she's floating in the air, suspended by sheer excitement and joy. And the second any sound escapes her throat, it's like she's sending waves of energy rippling out, glowing.

She hears noise off to the side and turns to see Mack talking to a slim Asian guy, probably in his late twenties.

"You must be Jenna," he smiles, extending his hand out to her. His black eyes would normally entice her, but she stands, mesmerized by the sight of a recording space. She snaps back into consciousness, faltering, and shakes his hand clumsily.

"Something tells me you're raring to go." He laughs, introducing himself as Parker Ma. He's around the same height as her, about five-feet-eleven with jet-black hair, and tattoos running over his arms. His eyes shine with excitement as he talks to Mack about the project. He's come up from New York to work with Jenna, a care package courtesy of Alchemy Records to help create the next trend.

Jenna comes out of her trance as Mack excuses himself from the room.

"This is happening," she says, psyching herself up, unzipping her bright sweatshirt and tossing it on a swivel chair.

She hands him her notebooks, exploding with lyrics and ideas, feeling lightheaded with anticipation.

hearty home.

[Toronto, Canada—February 2010]

"Sugar, will you pass the peas?" asks Eleanor's father from the head of the dining room table. He sets down his reading glasses on the mahogany surface, rubbing the bridge of his nose tiredly.

Elle delicately picks up the china bowl and passes it to him.

The family is having dinner to celebrate Dr. Bryans's latest medical journal publication —and, of course, to celebrate their only child visiting from Italy for a week's break. But more, they're celebrating a new procedure dubbed the Bryans Brain Buster with a vintage Chardonnay.

The cavernous dining room elegantly overlooks their large back yard. The room looks more like a traditional gentlemen's club rather than a family mealtime spot, decorated in rich, earthy colours. It feels like a decanter with cognac should be on hand, to be poured by a butler named Rudolph.

Her mother walks in with a serving platter of salmon, which matches her winter "tan" (not actually a tan, but a pale person's attempt at a tan, complete with a flare-up of sun spots). They've just returned from a Valentine's getaway at their condo in Florida. Her strawberry-blonde hair is cut in a modern bob, highlighting her delicate bone structure. Hazel-green eyes glow excitedly on the petite mother of one, the picture of a yummy mummy with her tasteful sense of style and great skin care routine.

"So, lovee, have you had any luck on the job search? Pounding the pavement and all that?" She smiles as her French-manicured hands set down the fish, bought at the gourmet grocery market and reheated. Her childlike voice is shrill but happy, the same angelic tone passed on to her daughter. She puts a plate of brown rice in front of her husband at the head of the table. "My goodness, imagine you get a job in Italy! How delicious that would be—our little sugar, the art connoisseur!" she chirps.

"Well, no … not really," Elle starts slowly, lifting a fleshy portion of salmon.

"Really? With your qualifications, I would have thought someone would want to scoop you up straight out of university," her mom replies, shocked. She smooths her soft, feminine blouse before taking a seat across from her daughter.

"You know, I have a client who—" starts her father, dropping the networking angle.

Elle shoots him a look begging for noninterference, and he quiets down. His wife gently rests her hand over his. He is the calm and composed half of the marriage, handsome like a movie star but stoic like the brilliant surgeon that he is.

"I think that I might want to take a few months to travel a bit," Elle replies, spooning rice on her gold-rimmed plate.

The family has had a long-running tradition of dressing up to eat in the fancy dining room, celebrating honour-roll report cards, her mother's acquisition of rare Degas paintings for her art club, or even a stellar round of golf.

Her father is wearing a dinner jacket over a monogrammed sweater, and Elle is in a smart green dress. It looks a little ridiculous but gives Elle a chance to wear her grandmother's antique jewellery in the safety of their home.

Odile Bryans fidgets with her favourite diamond-drop earrings and continues her prodding. "Travel? Okay, great, that's direction. That's a plan. Do you have any specifics in mind?" She smiles, trying not to be too intrusive—but failing. She glows hyperactively in contrast to her even-keeled husband, who smiles at her tenderly.

"Actually, I do have some idea of what …" She blushes, avoiding her gaze. "Jenna got signed for a recording contract. So she's started working on her first album."

Her mother looks apprehensive, twisting her face up like a child sucking on a lemon. She's used to wine clubs and spas, not the music industry.

"And Riley and I will be done with school by the time it gets released. So, we're thinking of going to work for her, help her out as she travels around to promote it."

"Like what, an assistant?" gasps her mother.

"Odile …" Elle's dad warns.

"Sort of. Helping in whatever capacity she needs us to. It's something that the three of us want to be together for. And to look out for her."

Elle's father glances at his wife, and then back at his little girl, assessing the situation cautiously.

"Guys, this is huge! She got a major recording contract! She's actually getting that chance to start her dream—how crazy is that? She's not going to be singing at the karaoke bar anymore—she's going to be singing for people around the world! And Riley and I—we want to be there for her. Be there with her."

Her father rubs the bridge of his nose again, processing the information, his white hair coiffed impeccably. He is always stylishly put together, dressed by his wife. It's one of the privileges of having his right-hand woman at the ready, always thinking of him with love.

"How long do you think you would be gone?" he asks his daughter, careful not to get his wife worked up.

"It's still not set in stone. But I think we might leave in the fall, be back around winter? A lot depends on when the album is released ... how it's received ..."

"So, you could be gone for six months?" he asks calmly.

"Yeah, but ... think of it like me going back to Montreal for a semester. Or you guys being in Florida. Except I might be in Europe. Or Asia." She chuckles nervously, still not sure about the job description Jenna has begged her to take on.

"But what about all the drugs?" trills her mother, absolutely frightened, clutching the silk scarf around her neck, fraught with worry.

"*What* drugs?" her husband asks, almost ready to roll his eyes at her melodrama.

"You know, in that sort of industry, I hear there are drugs. Everywhere. All the bad influences ..."

"Mom, I think that's modelling. And even so, that's another reason for us to stick together. Keep each other grounded and all that," Elle assures, running her finger over the silver knife at her place setting.

"Well, at least they'd all be together," she says to her husband, as if Eleanor was not sitting right in front of them.

He nods intently, and then turns to his daughter. "So where do you think you might end up first?" He smiles, trying to be excited for her opportunity, but a little worried that his wife's best friend will be too far to keep her company anymore. The two little women in his life were often joined at the hip due to his busy schedule and absenteeism, acting more like girlfriends than mother and daughter with their constant text messaging.

A wave of relief washes over Elle as she realizes that they're letting her go. Not letting her go as in granting permission, but letting her go as in accepting her as a full-grown person that doesn't require babying.

She's winning back their trust after her university identity crisis. So now, while they're playing tennis on the weekends, they'll know that their daughter is out in the world, being an adult.

• • •

The following afternoon, Elle is sitting outside on the balcony of her bedroom, feeling the chill of a barren winter. She's staring out at the back yard, a blank piece of canvas in front of her. But inspiration is not coming, at least not from the gloomy, grey sky. Her wool socks itch in her rain boots; the heavy sweatshirt she's wearing is penetrated by the freeze. As she exhales out frustration, her breath smokes in the cold air.

She leans her head back on the pink, wooden Muskoka-style chair, listening and breathing. There are no birds, no insects—just the sound of icy stillness that happens to dull her cheeks. She closes her calm green eyes and absorbs the ambience.

As her thoughts wander, she lingers on memories of Ben. Her first love. The nerd she fell for in high school, whom she dated long-distance up until university. Whom she broke up with because she wanted to be "free."

What a damn mistake.

Elle's cheeks warm as she blushes, thinking of him. How they would hold hands while walking in the art gallery or the feeling of excitement every time she picked him up at the airport.

She is oblivious to the snow that has started to sprinkle down. When her sweatpants start to feel damp, she opens her eyes to find herself sitting out in a snowfall.

She quickly gathers her art supplies and dives back into the comforts of her majestic bedroom. She laughs to herself as she peels off her wet clothes and changes into a black fitted yoga suit. Her daily mat workouts and meditations have helped to calm, to recentre, her creative thoughts back into disciplined productivity.

I wonder what he's doing ... Elle thinks to herself, recalling a mental montage of Benjamin Roberts.

Why don't you find out? comes the response in her head.

Elle pauses, wondering if she's having a mental breakdown and is now hearing voices, but then takes the advice of her braver self and heads to her laptop.

She sits at her delicate Victorian desk and starts to compose a quick note to Ben, having saved his personal e-mail address for a moment of weakness like this.

Hi, Ben. It's Elle. I thought of you today and wanted to write and see how you are, what you're doing. I'm home for a bit (last semester abroad!) and was watching the snow fall outside. Are you still at Stanford? No, you must be done and working by now. Are you living in California or did you move, I wonder? Did you like law school? You might not even open this e-mail because I'm blocked or something. You might completely hate my guts, but I wanted to write because I miss you and think about you all the time and am a stupid idiot for thinking I needed to be away from you. Why am I such a jerk face scumbag? This sucks; I can't even do an e-mail right. Blah, blah, blah. Why am I doing this? I think I still love you. Moron dumb-dumb.

Elle looks at her words and releases an exasperated grunt. Riley is so much better at composing meaningful writing.

"I should save this, remind myself to let the past be passed. Things happen for a reason, right? We were meant to ... not ... be ..." she sighs to herself, defeated.

She scrolls up to click Save to Drafts and hits Send.

Eleanor stares at the computer screen in sheer terror, afraid she's going to pass out.

She recalls her yoga breathing and tries to dial it down.

"Nothing you can do now. If you're lucky, he'll delete it without opening it. Maybe he even changed his address," she says out loud to herself, preventing a hyperventilation attack. She forces herself to get up and walk towards the door.

But suddenly, her computer chimes, indicating that an e-mail has been received by her inbox.

Elle stops in her tracks, scared to move.

Oh, my God, he wrote back! she screams in her head, panicking and not wanting to see if the new message is his.

She slowly turns around and tiptoes back, her throat tight with anguish.

She sees the e-mail and breathes a temporary sigh of relief.

It's an auto response saying he's away for the week on vacation and to contact some underling at the Brag Green & Roberts Sports Management Agency in case of emergency.

Oh, thank goodness I leave tomorrow. She grins weakly. *I'll pretend his reply went to my junk mail ... if he even replies? Wow, well, he's working as a hockey agent, that's not a shock ... must be high up if his name is in the title. Anyway, crisis averted.*

She grabs her oil painting supplies and heads to the huge, open living room downstairs. There is a note taped to the banister.

Lovee,

Sarah Schwartz (the lady doctor, not the psychiatrist) is going to pick up the key for the Florida condo (she's going with her new husband— imagine that!). It's on the kitchen counter. We'll be back late after dinner. Think we might go for sushi ... call if you want us to bring you something back! I kind of feel like some cucumber rolls, actually. Maybe I will try a dynamite one! You know how we tried them once at that little hole-in-the-wall and they were quite yummy? But at the other place they weren't ... Let's go for lunch and pedicures tomorrow!

Love you, Mama

P.S. I don't want you to leave! :(

Elle laughs at her mother's penchant for detail and lights the wood-burning fireplace. She sets up her easel and stares at the canvas. With a subconscious decisiveness, she picks her first colour. She smiles as the paintbrush glides easily.

Inspiration has come to her.

As the sun sets, Elle finishes shading in some detail on her creation. Suddenly, the doorbell rings, echoing through the large house.

She peeks out the living room window, and there's a black sports car parked in the circular driveway.

Elle slides her way over in her warm sheepskin slippers, snatching her parents' condo keys on the way past the kitchen. She knocks over a pile of mail from the counter, a colourful postcard sticking out from Riley, but she puts everything back on the counter for later.

Her hair is a stringy, damp mess rolled up into a bun; her hands are dotted with different colours of paint. All she wants is to get back into the zone and finish her piece.

She deactivates the alarm and opens one of the halves of the enormous doorway.

Except she almost dies when she realizes it's not a gynaecologist standing on her stoop—it's Ben Roberts.

Without missing a beat, she swings the door shut and grabs the wall for support.

"Ohmygosh," she gasps to herself, trying to stop her heart from leaping out of her chest.

Elle quickly glances at herself in the mirror and realizes that the messy hair and unwashed yoga clothes are as good as it's gonna get for this reunion special.

She opens the door again, and Ben is still standing there, trying not to burst into laughter.

"You okay?" he asks, amused by her knee-jerk reaction.

She nods, mortified.

"So I got your e-mail …" he starts.

Elle nods again, still not speaking. She hasn't seen him in four years. The guy who she first made out with! Who felt her up in his parents' Land Rover and even took her to prom.

"Elle, it's February in Canada. Can I come in?" he asks, motioning to the snow around him, blinking in disbelief.

She blushes and lets him through. He steps out of his brown leather shoes, leaving them by the door. He's still wearing the same type of grey-and-white socks he's had since grade school—hopefully without iron-on labels printed with his name, like his mother did for summer camp.

They head into the living room and sit on the plush brown leather couches. She elects to sit across from him, still in total shock and unable to speak, content just to stare at him. Elle is squeezing the keys to the condo in the palm of her hand, reminding herself that she is awake with painful stabs to her skin. This isn't another dream fantasy; he's right in front of her, in the flesh.

"So, as I was saying. I got your e-mail. I've gotta say, I was pretty surprised to see you in my inbox," he says, holding up his phone. His warm brown eyes crinkle as he smiles.

Damn real-time e-mail, she grumbles to herself.

Ben looks better than she remembers. His acne's gone— the braces, too. He's still short, but he looks like he could be out of a Harry Rosen catalogue, polished and mature. His designer jeans look pressed, and he's wearing a red Stanford sweatshirt under his down vest. He'd be a total stud if he was only a few inches taller, but as is, he's still the perfect fit for petite Eleanor. There's a warm tan on his skin, and his hair is a lighter brown than usual, probably also effects from the sun. Has he returned from vacation? With his non-Elle girlfriend? Or wife? A romantic Valentine's getaway?

She stares at him, wide-eyed. Freaked out.

"I was ... surprised to hear from you. I'm going to assume you didn't proofread that message," he jokes, his dry sense of humour never rude but sometimes a little too defensive.

"It was a draft," she snarls cutely through clenched teeth.

"Right. So how are you?" he asks, looking at her across the coffee table and trying to relax his stiff posture a bit.

Elle stares at him, trying to breathe slowly and discreetly. She is not able to be social with this specific person in front of her. Her reactions can't be faked. He can see right through her.

"You're here from abroad?" he tries, blinking quickly. It's a sort of tic that indicates he's trying to focus intently. Now she knows that he's just as nervous as she is.

Elle nods, swallowing. "Yep. Doing my last semester in Venice," she says slowly, still squeezing the keys rhythmically, her palms aching and sweaty.

Ben seems impressed.

"Almost flunked out of school, so it's pretty great that they let me go," she blurts out nervously, rubbing the moisture from her hands on her thighs.

Oh ... my ... gosh ... she thinks to herself, embarrassed by her verbal diarrhea.

Ben looks at her a little funny.

"What about you? What have you been up to?" she asks, quickly turning the tables.

"Well, since the last time I spoke to you ..." he says, taking a sarcastic shot at her. "I graduated. Moved to LA. Was working for a boutique-style hockey agency there and worked my way up to opening an office here in Toronto. Turned thirty, live here, my parents retired and now spend most of the time travelling," he explains. "Well, so do I for work, but, that's not the point."

"Oh, wow, that's great. I knew you would be so good with the sports thing," Elle says, more to herself than to him.

"Yeah, I was the one who landed our biggest client at the time, actually. Signed him from a competitor! He's the new winger for the Leafs. So he lives here now, too. The guy got me promoted so fast that I'm actually a partner—the 'R' in BGR Sports Management! It goes to show that you never know. Being nice to someone at a party could land you the next big thing in pro sports!"

Elle grins proudly, feeling an imaginary halo of light glowing around him.

He's perfect, she thinks dreamily.

"You're still painting, I see." He smiles, motioning to the winter landscape drying by the window.

"Yeah …" She blushes, staring at the floor.

"Elle, let's cut the crap. Why did you e-mail me?"

She gasps, tensing up, not sure what to say, panicking.

Ben relaxes his face into a familiar smile, his dimples melting any false aggression.

She throws a couch cushion at him, surprised she fell for his classic trick—the deadpan shock question that stuns everyone. Her pale face reddens quickly.

He turns to her, and his tone is gentle this time. "Really, Elle. What's going on?"

She begins to stammer something, and he gets up slowly, moving to sit beside her.

She stares at his body and the mere centimetres it is from touching hers.

"Why did you contact me? After so long? You have to know it was pretty damn hard to get over you," he says. "I honestly don't get why, when I've moved on, you decide to appear."

Elle's skin feels hot; maybe she's come down with a fever and needs to excuse herself. Did he say that he's moved on? He's over her?

Ben sighs, realizing that she's not responding. "This isn't some joke, Elle," he says, shaking his head and standing up to leave, frustrated by her silence.

He's almost reached the foyer when he hears her little voice squeak. "I'm not over you."

He turns around slowly, and she repeats herself, a little louder this time. She's standing up, clasping her hands in front of her stomach, nervously.

"I'm, uh, not over you. I still think about you all the time. I still hate myself for being selfish and thinking I needed to be alone. I'm not over you."

Ben stands by the doorway, not moving forward or backward. His hands dangle at his sides, his face expressionless.

"And I get that you've moved on, maybe you're married or have someone else. But I had the biggest compulsion to reach out to you. My New Year's resolution was to do what I feel. And I did. So I'm sorry if this seems like a cruel joke or really, really bad timing. But ... I guess this is me saying that I'm not over you."

They stand, staring at each other in the peach-coloured living room.

"Are you saying that you want to give it another try?" Ben asks, still standing his ground and sounding more cynical than Elle can stomach.

She shakily moves a few steps forward. Tiny steps. "I don't want to try. I want to do it right," she says, her voice quivering, nervous that he might actually oblige—or shut her down at light speed. It feels like someone else is doing the talking for her.

Ben steadily walks towards her and puts his hands on her shoulders. He looks deep into her tearing eyes, his nervous blinks slowing down. "I've been waiting for this," he whispers, kissing her forehead and wrapping his arms around her.

unwrap me.

[Toronto, Canada—March 2010]

"You know, people in Toronto aren't as nice as you'd like to think." Parker Ma laughs, grabbing a spring roll from the container of takeout food in front of him. He's unzipped his bright purple hoodie and thrown it on the ground beside him, ready to devour dinner with his coworkers. They're distributing the Chinese food delivered to the studio at two in the morning.

"What are you *taaalking* about?" Jenna gasps, feigning insult and clutching her chopsticks near her heart.

"Like, people say Canadians are all dopey and friendly and—" he starts.

"*Excuuuse* me?" she shrieks, her blonde hair pulled up high into a messy bun. The cartoon T-shirt she's wearing makes her look like even more of a hyperactive kid, she's keyed up from the excitement of having just finished recording another song.

The backup musicians sitting with Jenna and Parker burst into laughter, their instruments waiting to be stored for the night.

"Well, I'd say that the city has gotten a lot more like New York in the past few years," snorts the drummer, Apollo, a thirty-something black guy with a mouth full of wonton.

"Please! New York is a city full of love and multiculturalism—" Parker starts, flashing exaggerated hippie free-love peace-signs.

"And muggings," interrupts Jenna.

"What?!" Parker jokingly snaps.

"Have you not seen ... most Hollywood movies?" she laughs.

"Whatever. I'm only saying that Toronto is not as ... saintly as it is seems. Yes, it doubles as New York in cinematography, but—"

"You really haven't had a chance to see this city, have you?" Jenna says forcefully.

"Not when I'm *heeere*," Parker whines comically, motioning to the recording booths around them.

"Okay, so you take him around Toronto," Apollo instructs Jenna. "And you take her around New York. And then we'll do a vote?" He smiles, eager to see the two of them hook up already. The flirty tension has been killing the group, as Parker and Jenna live in a bubble of denial.

"Take him to the St. Lawrence market," suggests the bass player, bits of fried rice dribbling out of his mouth.

"No interference! This has to be a strictly individualized snapshot of each perspective," Apollo demands, putting his hand up like a referee.

"Coney Island," coughs the guitar player.

"Hush!"

"I will take you to the best freakin' Korean food in the continental United States, and you won't know what to do with yourself," Parker smiles mischievously, clapping his hands together.

"Where's that, your mom's?" snickers the guitar player.

"Dude—my parents died in a shark attack. I was an orphan raised by a reclusive millionaire inventor with a glass elevator," Parker says flatly.

Everyone stares at each other awkwardly.

"I'm kidding. Yeah—my mum makes the best kimchi in Brooklyn."

"That is absolutely not funny," Jenna grimaces, picking at her neon pink nail polish and remembering the same deadpan sense of humour in Elle's ex-boyfriend, Ben.

"You're a morbid fuck." The bass player shivers.

"I'm in show business, man—you have to be fucked in the head to be in this world," Parker shrugs unapologetically, creating a gun out of two fingers and popping himself in the head.

"You know what I always wondered? Is why, say on the subway or something ... sometimes people are intentionally not nice to each other. It's almost like they go out of their way *not* to hold the door for you," Jenna asks aloud.

"So you're admitting that people are not nice here?" Parker asks, expressionless.

Jenna's eyes sizzle in happy frustration. Their flirting has been palpable over the past couple of months—actually, growing more and more each day as they bond over songwriting.

"No, but really, I know what you mean. It's, like, you're wasting more energy being a dick than in simply being a good person," he admits, scooping chicken onto his paper plate.

"Yeah, like, if people had a baseline of being nice and positive ... I mean, look at if someone is having a bad day, and even if you smile and hold the elevator door for them—you have singlehandedly exerted the opportunity to change their mood around," Jenna suggests.

"Right. Because people aren't looking around them and seeing others—they're only viewing the world from their very slanted perspective," Apollo adds.

"Yes! It's like—wanting to scream out at them and say, look at *this*! People can be nice to each other. Why waste your energy in being negative? Because all it'll do is attract more negativity!" Jenna gasps, feeling like she's having an epiphany.

"Look at this!" Parker teases, pointing to his General Tso's chicken.

"No, I'm serious! Look at this—look at this beautiful world we're in, the chance to make our experience here more enjoyable instead of always being pissed at one another," Jenna preaches.

The musicians around her secretly feel uplifted by her energetic sermon, thinking back to how they started their day. Did they tell their girlfriends they were beautiful? Hold the elevator for the overwhelmed single father? Smile for the sake of smiling at the old lady on the streetcar?

"You should turn that into a book," acknowledges the bass player. "Jenna Ramsay's spiritual rules for self-affirmation and attracting lots of money into your life."

"Better yet, turn it into a song." Parker winks, as he accidentally drips soy sauce on his crotch.

"I don't know what I'm trying to say exactly—but maybe if we're selective about the songs we put out there … maybe people will indirectly be inspired to be better, kinder …"

Parker looks at her; his eyes warm with appreciation for her nymphlike sweetness.

"You're one of those people who believes that love can withstand the test of time and distance and all that rom-com bullshit, huh?" The bass player grins.

Jenna looks at him, a little wounded.

"No—it's not a bad thing, Jenna. It's a great thing, actually. And it is my sincerest hope for you as your friend that you never lose that incredible mentality," Parker admits honestly.

She feels a strange irritation at hearing him use the term "friend."

Jenna takes a sip from her pop can, looking at him out of the corner of her eye. She takes a deep breath and smiles, not telling them that she's felt inspired to have that state of mind by the reality of living her dream. And having Parker along to bring it out in her.

His cell phone starts buzzing on the floor, and he grabs it, slipping out of the studio and into the hallway.

"Hey, Kwame," he says, lowering his voice and taking a slow walk in front of the studio door.

"Parker, I haven't seen your nightly report yet. What is going on right now?"

"We're still here. Eating something quick—we were working overtime on a track."

"What track?"

"Slow, inspirational ballad," Parker replies.

"Okay. Send me your progress report when they're all gone. Did that argument with Zeek get sorted out?"

"Yep. We rewrote the lyrics; she seems happier about it."

"Well, keep your ear to the ground—I placed you in this position for a reason. Keep gaining her trust, seeing where we can pull from to build a solid album. What about any boyfriends? Has she divulged any information that could help write something a bit more steamy?"

"No ... haven't really talked about ... that," Parker says, shifting his weight uncomfortably.

"Get on it. But remember, there's a fine line between getting to know her and becoming her actual friend. She's a young, impressionable girl—don't let her think there's more there. Or she'll get attached, and it won't end well for you," Kwame instructs.

Parker hangs up with his boss and squats down against the wall, exhaling with a heavy heart. He's gotten to know the deeper parts of Jenna, once she drops her guard and can act totally dorky. It started with purely professional motive, to gain her trust and help her with her music. Now he's started to look at her in a different way but knows that as soon as she's launched into the pop music universe, that side will be deeply repressed out of necessity.

He looks down at his cell phone, the ball and chain to Kwame Roy—the man who signs his paycheques.

I'll send the report from home ... I don't want to stay here longer, he tells himself, exhausted.

He heads back to the group, and they're cleaning up after their greasy meal.

"I'm gonna get you home, okay?" Parker tells her quietly, not drawing attention from the other guys in the group.

Jenna smiles at the thought of rolling into the huge bed back at the condo, of smelling the fresh sheets she's barely touched. The temptation of a restful sleep.

He sits at the swivel chair behind a mix deck and starts shutting down the computer systems for the night. The other musicians have packed up their gear and trickle out. Jenna awkwardly sits on a couch, waiting and watching.

It is, like, super late. Maybe he's just being responsible and making sure the talent doesn't go missing, she argues. *Nah, he's shy and trying to work his way in ... but for shit's sake, how much more time does he need? We've been alone recording for, like, eight nights straight. He must know I like him. Keep being coy ... coy works.*

She wiggles into her white winter coat, and he motions for them to take off.

They pop out onto the freezing street, Parker letting out a yelp from the cold shock.

"I know," Jenna whispers, as the two of them flip their hoods up over their heads.

"No cabs." Parker observes, glancing up and down the street.

"You know what, why don't we walk? It'll get our blood pumping and warm us up," Jenna suggests, reaching for excuses to keep him at her side.

Parker shrugs and pulls on his navy fleece gloves.

Jenna shrinks her arms into her coat, never one to wear gloves, a habit from losing them in grade school.

"You still don't have gloves?" Parker laughs, having noticed the skill of getting her hands to disappear into the recesses of her sleeves.

She makes a funny face, trying to look as cute as possible while being guilty.

"Did you check your pockets?" Parker asks.

"No. I don't even own gloves." She shrugs.

"Did you check your pockets?" he repeats.

Jenna looks at him as if he's unintelligent. "No ... I ... don't ... own ... gloves," she repeats comically. "I'm pretty sure the last gloves I owned got lost at the museum when I was seven."

"Did ... you ... check ... your ... pockets?" he repeats, mocking her tone.

Jenna cringes and pokes her hands out into the cold, snaking them to her hip pockets. Sure enough, she feels a bulge.

She furrows her brow in confusion, pulling out two chunks of fleece.

She stares at them in her hands and turns to look at Parker, who is shielded by the furry hood of his parka.

"You know, the purpose of them is to be put *over* your fingers, not be admired in the moonlight …" he prods, finally turning to look at her astounded face.

She blinks back to attention and quickly slips on the mittens, which match her scarf.

"Wow—you actually shut up." He snickers.

"Thank you," she says quickly, feeling warm from the thoughtful gesture. No one has ever given her anything so … relevant.

"I mean, you're normally … nonstop," he teases, making mouths out of his hands and chirping them at her face.

She smiles shyly, actually ungrounded by his sweetness.

His hands drop back down to his sides, and she feels the back of his glove brush against hers. Her eyes bulge under the cover of her fur-lined hood, as they keep walking on in silence.

"How far is your place?" he ponders out loud, never really having left the confines of the studio or the rental house.

"Like … twelve more blocks …" She giggles.

"Seriously? Jeez … are you trying to hint that I need to lose weight or something? Get buff and run a marathon? Cos there are other, more effective methods. Including donating me liposuction or a super hot personal trainer named Umantrude."

"Is that what you like? Umantrude the German body-builder goddesses?" she teases, stepping in some dirty snow with her sneaker.

"I guess I have a thing for blondes," he razzes, trying to pawn off his truth as a joke. And failing.

"Well, when was your last girlfriend?" Jenna probes.

"Oh … wow … right to the jugular, huh?"

"Well …"

Parker shifts inside his heavy jacket, uncomfortable. "Well … I split up with someone last year," he admits.

"When?"

"December …"

"Right. So like, right before last year became this year," Jenna clarifies.

He nods, the fur on his hood bobbing.

"Why?"

"She … I dunno … it wasn't working out. She was doing her thing, I was doing my thing—but we weren't doing anything together … know what I mean?"

"Like, you were existing in separate worlds at the same time?"

"Right."

Jenna hums sympathetically.

"What about you?"

"I haven't dated a guy—properly dated a guy—in … years? I mean, I've hung out with guys and stuff, but … I could never find someone who got what I was trying to do in life. So, they were existing and living their lives while I was off in another stratosphere, trying to do my own thing, too. If I had to pick love over music … I'd pick music without contest."

"So no one was ever like, 'Wow, I want to be there with you when you win your first Grammy?'" Parker asks, surprised.

"Nope. Not any guys. Not my mom. Especially not my mom—she always wanted me to follow in her footsteps and just … settle."

"What do you mean, settle? Like, settle down?" Parker asks, turning to look at her.

"No. I mean, settle for average. Be like her. I think she is scared of achieving greatness … like, she never even tried to be more. And the fact that I want so much more … it's not real to her."

"But don't you think that she only wanted you to do better than she did? Like with school and stuff?" he suggests.

"Maybe. But she's got a funny way of saying so. I mean, in all the years she's known me … can't she see where my aptitude is? Where my talent sorta trumps the fact that I can't perform on multiple-choice tests? And that I don't give a shit about saying I went to so-and-so university? Who am I kidding—I'm not a classical brainiac like Riley. But put me up on a stage and under lights … and I could pass that test with honours. That's what I don't get, why my mom can't see that I have a different set of smarts. That I'm meant to do bigger and better things. That's my path."

"Wow … it must've been hard to keep yourself going if you didn't have someone in your corner."

"Well, my two best friends always supported me. Well, one more than the other—but Riley is definitely trying to look out for me with a swift dose of reality. But Elle, she daydreams like me—we both think that the impossible *is* possible. That by being a good person, it comes full circle. She's in Italy right now; got the most beautiful postcard from her. And it took me a while to realize that it wasn't store-bought—she actually painted the front herself. It came like magic—the worst day ever, and I got home, and it was there waiting for me. As if it knew it had to come on that specific day. Both of them are old school like that—sending good karma mail."

"My best friend's a computer geek. He thinks that technology is the future, and he believes that he can develop telekinesis. He would never think to send me any feel-good love notes," Parker offers, shrugging comically.

"So at the very least, we've got one person in our lives who makes us feel that we can move mountains, even if it's not with tactile love notes" Jenna says.

"Two people," Parker smiles, putting his hand up and showing that he thinks she can do pretty much anything.

Jenna smiles warmly, comforted by his ever-present encouragement and guidance. He's been able to coax her into getting deeper with her lyrics, to express everything she feels with honesty.

"Can we make ourselves a promise?" he asks.

She turns to hear him out. "I promise you that no matter what, you will be my friend, and I will want nothing but the highest potential for you. We're not going to date and get caught up like how other people tend to do … with the analyzing and the worrying and the rules. But instead …we are gonna keep getting to know each other. Know who we are, which, I think, is infinitely more difficult." He laughs. "But may yield an even better end result. Because, right now, I'm a fucked-up mess. And you—you are incubating a baby."

She winces.

"Music baby," he clarifies.

Jenna thinks about his deep resolution for a moment.

"Agreed."

They reach the entry of the condo, and Parker gives her a quick and awkward hug, gently squeezing the back of her neck with his glove.

"Night." He nods.

"See you in a couple of hours!" Jenna laughs, as she slips inside.

walk it off.

[Toronto, Canada—April 2010]

Jenna stares at the pint of beer in front of her, sullen and gloomy. She glances up at Parker, who is sitting straight across from her in the dingy booth. His eyes are fixed on her like lasers peeking out from underneath his baseball hat.

"What?" she snaps.

He continues to sit and stare at her.

"What?!" she hisses again, waves of annoyance overpowering her mood. She's tempted to kick his shin.

He starts his words slowly. "I ... think that we were unrealistic to think that they would deviate from their plan."

Parker is referring to the meeting they've just left with Alchemy Records and Top Dog Management. The meeting where they played a variety of the songs that they've recorded over the past few months, like a little factory of music. A factory Jenna only emerged from to write bullshit university exams and occasionally shower. A place where they've been locked up through the end of winter, working on the first Jenna Ramsay album.

The evening's outing to their favourite dive bar was meant to be celebratory. To commemorate a finished album. A release date moved up to the start of summer. Not to mull over a failed attempt to enlighten the record label as to the "other" side of Jenna Ramsay, in the hopes that she might be able to reshape the sound of her first release. Not so much straight-ahead pop, but maybe a bit more jazzy blues thrown into the mix. More adult contemporary, less teen angst.

While recording the feel-good pop music the label signed her to do, Jenna convinced Parker to give her extra time in the recording booth to experiment. To let her bring out some personal stuff, a little darker and more soulful. Grittier and deeper than the basics of love and heartbreak, and more love and more heartbreak.

She got great support from him and the rest of the team that was assembled to put her first album together. But the seasoned veterans of the industry knew all too well what would be the outcome of the newbie's aspirations.

"Jenna, darlin', you can't change the industry. At least not overnight." Zeek, the mixer from Montana, sighs.

She looks at him and purses her lips anxiously. Jenna pulls a Dior lip gloss out of her bag—the first purchase made with her advance cheque. No more simple lip chap for her! She smoothes on the thick red gloss, carefully putting any extra drops back into the tube.

"Think of it like this. If you play by their rules, earn their trust, you'll be able to do your own thing later. Eventually ... maybe," he tries, narrowing his thick grey eyebrows comically.

"So until then, I've gotta be a puppet?" she snaps.

The team of burly men shrug.

"You've seen this before ..." She shakes her head, realizing the fool she must seem to them.

They nod uncomfortably.

"But we've never seen anyone so impassioned by it," Zeek assures, putting his bear paw of a hand over hers. His ratty sweatshirt is stained with hot sauce from his chicken wings.

"That's the key, though, Jenna. You can't let that go. You have to play along now, do what they want. But never stop writing. Because when you're too old to for the teenage kids, you're gonna kick yourself if you've got nothing else behind you," Parker says. He unzips his neon multicoloured hoodie and leans his head back, hot from the close quarters of six bodies jammed in the booth.

Jenna puts her hand on the notebooks of her writing, which sat unopened at the short meeting. The label executive from New York flew in, heard her songs, and introduced her to the stylists contracted to make her over into a sleek and sexy starlet.

"The way Kwame didn't even listen to the full tracks ... he just sat there and picked, could have essentially thrown darts," she marvels, almost disgusted by the quick judgements of the boss. Thirteen songs selected from their pool of 40.

"Well, you can look at the silver lining. The man's a master at picking winners. And for a first-timer, you can't screw up your launch. Maybe this is how it's supposed to happen, you know? You put up with the shit for a bit until you cut your teeth, kid," Zeek suggests. "He's a star-maker. And a smart guy—he's not gonna take a gamble on you unless he sees that star quality in you."

"That's why they call him the alchemist," adds one of the men sitting with them.

"And launching in Europe is not a big deal, either. Sometimes they can gauge where it'll be easier for your style to break through first.

And if you can hit Europe and Asia, you'll be infinitely better off than only Canada," Apollo the drummer explains, making a hand gesture signalling money-making power.

"No offence to your home and native land." Zeek laughs, noting the comparatively smaller market of Canada.

"Yeah, but I thought it would start closer to home first, know what I mean? But I guess it's good that they want to move up my release to summer. Ugh, but I'm going to have sing all those gooey songs over and over …"

"Right, but wouldn't you rather start somewhere fresh—reinvent yourself as that star? Come back and *own* this town?" Apollo grins supportively.

Jenna pauses and shrugs.

"And the album artwork is great. I love that red," Parker comments, motioning to the graphic designer who's come out for the celebratory drinks with them.

"Ramsay red!" Zeek shouts, crunching a nacho.

Jenna smiles, relieved that the photos from her first real shoot came out more than half decent. She's already updated her Facebook with the link to her Web site—ready to come out to the online world.

"Well, until I own a record label, I guess I'll agree to disagree. So until then, let's get shittered, guys." She laughs, asking the waitress for another round of shots.

Her coworkers clap in relief.

The drinks are placed in front of them, and Jenna is ready to throw hers back.

"Hey, hey, hey, wait a minute there. You gotta toast—otherwise you're a one-man party!" Zeek announces cheekily. "This here, I'm toasting to one of the coolest gals around. To a young woman with more soul than you can imagine. Check out her new album, out June first—the first of many!"

The men pound the table and cheer, throwing back the tequila shots. Jenna looks around uneasily and tips the glass into her mouth, not even tasting the burn, her disappointment snuffing it out.

After a few more toasts and lime chasers, Jenna and Parker find themselves alone, abandoned by the technicians who have headed back to their rental house to pack for their trips home.

"You know, you've got some Asian fever going on," Jenna slurs, poking at Parker's reddened face.

He pats his sweaty forehead, a little embarrassed.

"No, no—it's cute. I was just saying. Did I make you self-conscious? I'm sorry; I said what was in my head. That always happens with you," she says, slurping water through a straw.

"What happens?" Parker asks, not having heard, and pushing his glass away, ready to quit. He's sweating through his anime-emblazoned T-shirt.

"Huh?" Jenna asks, straining to hear him over the crappy music playing in the bar.

He shakes his head and throws down some money for the bill. Jenna grabs her wallet and adds her part.

"Let's peace out," she says, as they get up from the musty booth.

Outside, the fresh spring air jolts them in their drunken stupor.

"Frick, I'm moving to a more tropical region," Jenna curses, shivering in the damp alley they're cutting through. "Start fresh in a beach house with some umbrella drinks."

"I would believe that." Parker laughs.

She looks at him, raising an eyebrow.

"Hey, with what you're going to be earning soon, you can *own* warmer climates." He snorts.

"I don't want to own that. I only want a place of my own. Get my mom to stop working. Maybe a cool car …" she says dreamily.

"What kind of car?" Parker asks, hopping over a puddle.

"I don't know about cars, really. Maybe a Bimmer like Elle?"

"What? Man, that's so normal. Go for something gutsy, like a Maserati or a Ferrari. Or an Aston! You gotta rack up the speeding tickets," he teases.

They're walking along Bloor Street West, wandering along and looking at all the windows of the closed designer shops.

"Do you want to come over?" Jenna blurts out. She shoves her hands into the kanga pocket of her hoodie awkwardly. They've spent the past four months confined to their studio and haven't hung out like normal civilians. He's never made it past the lobby of her building.

Parker looks at her cautiously, the sweat cooling on his face.

"Okay." He shrugs awkwardly.

They head towards the Yorkville condo, left relatively uninhabited with her frequent sleeping on the studio's couch.

Jenna swipes her key card at the doors, and they head into the elevator, not speaking a word. Arjun, the nosy concierge, peeks over the desk at them.

They silently ride up in the elevator. Jenna leads him to the unit, opening the door and heading for the kitchen.

"Wow, this is pretty nice," Parker muses, walking into the two-bedroom condo and looking at all the classy finishes.

"It's the record label's. They supposedly use it for people coming to town and stuff. Or to get me away from my mom." Jenna sighs.

"Have you talked to her yet?" he asks, sitting down on the living room floor and checking out the funky glass coffee table appreciatively. He decides to put sweaty handprints on it, watching his body heat vanish and reappear with fascination.

He's become her closest confidante over the past few months, often having heart-to-hearts over pizza boxes late at night, talking of inspiration and wishes. Mutually forming a bond they would never admit to, thinking of each other as potentially being "the special one" people seem to always aspire to meet.

She emerges with two glasses of ice water.

"No … no mommy talk," she says, sitting on the floor beside him. "Haven't seen or spoken to her since … the night my stuff moved out. I couldn't look back."

He looks at her worriedly.

"I seriously don't think I can face her after how all this has gone down," she murmurs.

"But she's your mom. You gotta—it's kinda now or never, don't you think? I mean, don't you want her there if you get an award or …"

"She never got this about me. All the time I spent willing this to happen. All the choirs I joined, the shows I entered. The nights I'd try to convince myself it would happen … the entire time, she was praying for it *not* to happen. That's just plain wrong," she says. "She wanted me to be average at best. I couldn't be anything more to her than a secretary."

Parker looks at her and puts a hand on the back of her neck—a gesture that has grown to become comforting over the past few months. A little squeeze. A reminder he's there.

"I think you're exceptional," he whispers, resting his head on hers, her wispy blonde hair in disarray.

She feels herself glowing from the inside out. Someone sees it in her. Someone knows.

Jenna looks at him and feels the gaze of his eyes sink in through her. He's gotten to know her more than anyone else ever has. Known her real secrets, her likes and dislikes, the random thoughts racing through her mind. And then helped her translate them into something other people could listen into. Connect to.

Jenna places a hand gently on the side of his face, feeling her heart slow to a calm and steadfast pace.

They lean into each other softly, and she feels about to explode with excitement. They've been working in such close quarters for so long, getting to know their intimate thoughts and feelings, the sexual tension building steadily.

Their lips touch, feeling like lightning striking wildly. After a few seconds of bliss, Parker pulls away fast.

"Can't do this," he says firmly, rushing away from her.

Jenna stares at him, confused. "What?"

"We can't do this. This isn't gonna work," he says.

"Why?" she asks, surprised.

"Because I'm not allowed to do this. And you ... you ..."

"What? Why? I don't understand," Jenna pleads.

"I'm not allowed to fall for you. You're not supposed to fall for me. We were supposed to get comfortable enough for you to write, and then, I go back to New York, and you become a star. End of story," he explains anxiously, staying at the opposite end of the room and inserting a safe distance between them.

She stares at him in shock, standing up quickly.

"You're supposed to be the media darling, not the girl who falls for the behind-the-scenes guy. This isn't part of the plan," he tells her, moving briskly for the door.

"Why exactly isn't this part of the plan?" she snaps back.

"Because it's in my contract. This can't happen. You have to be free to ... no, this can't happen. I'm sorry. I can't be that for you. I can't have those feelings for you like that," he says, rushing out.

Jenna stares after him, the door closing after his exit.

It's as if her heart is bleeding out, drowning her in a pool of darkness. The sudden realizations make her feel helpless and lost.

She looks at the two glasses of water, condensation dripping down their sides, and can't bother to wipe up the rings that are forming beneath them. She doesn't know where coasters are in this alien home.

Instead, she trudges her way to the master bedroom to disappear into the warmth of the sleigh bed. To let the night close in around her and erase the hurt. Even for just a little bit. There's nothing else left for her to do. She has to shed her skin and become Jenna Ramsay 2.0—the version everyone now expects her to be.

papera.

[Rome, Italy—early May 2010]

The drool pooling at the corner of Riley's mouth startles her awake. She wipes it with the back of her hand, embarrassed to have fallen asleep in public. She's flying from London to Rome, meeting Elle for the last leg of her Italian sojourn. The end of an era—university accomplished.

"Ladies and gentlemen, we will now begin our descent into the city of Rome. Local time is one PM, temperature a lovely twenty-eight centigrade. On behalf of British Airways …"

She rolls her eyes and ignores the scripted announcement. The leather journal she intended to write in remains flat in her lap.

"Miss, please put your chair-back in upright position," growls a flight attendant crossly, body checking her seat as she passes in the aisle beside her.

"I just woke up!" Riley protests. But she realizes its best not to face off with the overeager woman and sits straight up in fear. The last thing she needs is to be blacklisted for giving attitude.

The plane begins to induce the familiar, dreaded pain in her ears as the cabin pressure changes. The splitting ache will keep her ears plugged for a few days, right in time to get back on the plane home.

Riley begins flipping through her diary, scanning some of the entries from the past year, seeing if she's made any tangible progress. Starting a fresh journal around a new year is an incredibly beautiful thing. A clear division between old and new, the dividing line, the hope of things to come and fill the pages with good stuff. A dramatic black-and-white postcard falls out, tucked in carefully, documenting Elle's arrival in Venice. Riley smiles and starts reading from page one of her journal.

January 1, 2010

I've decided to stop with Matt. But I just can't anymore. It'll be hard, I know, when you have someone with you for the length of time we've been together. Since freshman year, it's been all about me and Matt. Riley and Matt go to Prague. Riley and Matt write their finals. Riley and Matt sleepovers with chocolate chip pancakes. But I just can't.

Why didn't I stop myself back then—when I knew that we would never get to the point of seriousness in contemplating marriage? For shit's sake, he's never been to Toronto and met my family. Clearly, we're not a "till death do us part" type of couple.

Which raises the question, why do we date people if we know it's not going to go anywhere? The obvious answer here is the fools. The fools—this will severely be missed. The really good make outs will be really missed. But it's like knowing that continuing the sexy stuff is going to end up delaying an unavoidable parting. I have the inkling that he feels the same, but we've never talked about it one way or the other. But I have a knowing ... you know?

So, with the New Year, I will turn over a new leaf—as clichéd as it is to have resolutions.

No more Matt Roth.

No more sexy stuff. (Especially break-up sex.)

No more putting yourself through bullshit.

No more.

She smiles at the passage, realizing that it has officially been almost five months since the vow of celibacy she took. Except she's about to land in Italy—and is quite sure that this vow is going to be a challenge to enforce.

As she navigates through baggage claim and out the terminal, Riley spots Elle holding up a hand-drawn "Riley Kohl" sign covered in glitter.

Oh, Elle.

"Hi, lovee! I'm so happy to see you!" Elle squeals, wrapping the traveller in a hug, her flouncy, romantic sundress a perfect complement to her Italian art adventure. Her hair looks lighter, more strawberry-blonde, and falls naturally at her shoulders.

They start gabbing on the way out to the taxis and zoom to their hotel, Riley burning up in the jeans and motorcycle boots that were more suitable for London.

"So how was the University of Venice? Is that even what it's called? UV?" she snorts, feeling motion sick from the chaotic traffic and suffocating heat.

"Oh, my gosh, Riles. I can't even begin to tell you how inspiring the semester was for me! It put everything into place for me. Like, after the stupid stuff from the breakup, the last thing I wanted was to be in Montreal. Or even back home. I wanted out," she starts explaining. "And walking around, sitting on the terraces, I think it affected my painting like some sort of … magical … power!"

Riley nods intently, wishing some of this magical power on her writing. Some fairy dust? Please?

"I've been doing a lot of watercolour. Even simple sketches. It's like … my mind is finally buzzing!"

"I get that. You're either on, or you're off. And if you're off when you need to be on … well, then …" she huffs, thinking of her lonely MacBook at home on her desk. She hasn't cranked out any creative stories in months. The ones submitted for grading in class were hardly her best work.

"Right … oh! And our hotel is great. Really quiet. Has this amazing little gated entry—so dramatic! And the guy at the desk gave me ideas of where we can go for lunch—I'm sure you didn't eat on the plane …"

"No way. Airplane food is for mortals." She grins, feeling the ulcers burning in her stomach.

"Great, so let's leave your luggage, and we'll start exploring!"

After meeting Mario, the desk clerk of their hotel, the pair starts down Via Nazionale. They begin discussing life post-university, scouting for a beautiful patio to gorge on some wholesome food.

"Have you heard from Jenna lately?" asks Riley, fixing the sunglasses on her face, her hair tied back loosely. She's taller than her friend, even with the height of Elle's espadrilles.

"Hmm … no. Not since the last e-mail. I think she was wiped, working with that Parker guy and all."

"Did you get the feeling she likes him?"

Elle giggles and shrugs.

"Yeah, I thought so. But that would be the definition of uber-long-distance, not to mention dating a coworker, in way. I can't believe that they want to bump this album release up so much," Riley remarks of the June release for the tentatively named *Jenna.*

"I can't believe they wanted to rename her Jen. She hates it when people call her Jen," Elle announces.

They spot a beautiful café facing the Piazza Venezia. It's perfect. The girls stroll in and pick a table outside. Not too close, but not too far, from the throngs of people moving through the city of Rome.

"So what is the plan, anyway?" Elle asks, as they take their seats and commence some serious people-watching.

"Well, the first single is starting rotation in the UK soon, so I think we start there. I mean, it'll be a slow at first, right? No one really knows her ... other than on YouTube. So, what, a month there, and then maybe go where the song gets a response? Isn't that how it would work?"

"June first to leave Toronto still?"

Riley shrugs, as the waiter sets them up with water and fresh bread.

The menu looks absolutely, authentically Italian—rustically printed and made to look aged, and therefore somehow more credible to hungry travellers.

"They must hate tourists." Elle grins, as the waiter—who happens to be wearing a gondolier's hat—leaves with their order. "But do you really think this is gonna happen? That this is going to work?" she whispers, worried about the hope and future of their friend. If she fails, she'll be pulverized.

Riley holds her glass of sparkling water thoughtfully.

"You know I'm the first to nay-say." She laughs, looking at the street. "But I actually think that ... you know, she's gotten this far. And I didn't give her credit before, thought she was just a silly girl, because even when the obvious was staring her in the face, she never faltered. Never thought that she couldn't or wouldn't. And now it's gonna pay off. It made me think that if I ... if I put myself out there like she did, if I believed so vividly in my heart, that I—"

"That you could get published. Yeah, yeah, yeah—I know."

She stares at Elle in disbelief.

"You've always been a good storyteller, Riles. But that also means you take forever to get to your point." She laughs warmly.

Riley dips a piece of bread into some olive oil and chomps at it.

"So why don't you go for it?" Elle winks.

"Really ..." she scoffs sceptically, chewing.

"Well, yeah, why not? You're always working on something ..."

"Yeah, except not now. I'm dried up like a prune in the creative sense." She shrugs, violently biting the bread. "And the other, man-friend sense."

"You? Nothing to say? I find that doubtful, Miss Kohl. I'm sure that of all places, you'll get a bright idea here." Elle smiles, gesturing out around them.

"Or I could write porno," she says, deadpan, pointing to a couple making out right by the veranda of the patio.

"Riley, don't point! It's not the zoo!" Elle whispers, swatting her friend's hand.

"Please. You're totally jealous that you don't have an Italian sausage of your own."

Elle blushes a profound crimson that only a pale white girl can blush.

"Eleanor Bryans, what on Earth have you done?"

"Remember that guy … Ben … you know, that guy?"

"Hmm, let me remember. *That* guy that you sort of dated all through high school? The one who you were oh-so-in-love with? Mr. Perfect Magical Love and Gooey Goodness?"

Elle blinks innocently.

"The one you also happened to dump even though he was okay with the long-distance relationship? When you ran off to McGill and left him heartbroken at Stanford? Cross-continent devastation? That guy? While you tripped around with a drug-addicted, nympho prick bastard?"

"That's enough," Elle warns, never keen on reliving her mistakes so vividly. She pours herself more fizzy water.

"So, what about Benjamin Roberts. Do tell!"

"Well, I e-mailed him."

Riley stares at her, waiting for the rest of the story. Elle smiles coyly.

"Well, I e-mailed him a few weeks ago. Kind of by accident. And he showed up at my house the day before I was leaving back for Italy."

Riley waits eagerly for more details, ready to throw a piece of bread at her shy friend. She gestures dramatically, waiting in suspense.

"*Aaand* we're back. We've been e-mailing and video calling and messaging every day."

"*Wowowow*," she gasps, clapping her hands together.

"He's been back in Toronto, working as a hockey agent—"

"What a shock," Riley blurts out, rolling her eyes. "I never did understand what the big deal was with the whole hockey thing. They're big men on blades—doesn't that seem ridiculous to you?"

"Anyway! Let me finish. So, I'm going to see him again before we leave with Jenna. And then … well, we're going from there. Day by day."

Riley claps with glee. Eleanor and Benjamin—the ultimate puppy love story. He sniped her off when they snuck into a kegger in high school. The mysterious college guy who studied on the west coast. In

America: land of possibility. Toronto was by no means a small town, but to meet someone who was exceptionally placed in the US of A was quite the novelty. The short, nerdy jock who had a big enough brain to get into law school and make something big of himself.

"I think that this could very well be things coming together for you, lovee," Riley nods proudly.

"Of everything that has happened, this is the one thing that has always been in my gut. I think you're right."

"Did you have cybersex?" Riley shouts, not conscious of her loudness.

Elle is about ready to sink into her chair and disappear from embarrassment.

"But you did," her friend smiles mischievously, holding up a finger and reading the shyness.

She nods, and they collapse into laughter.

• • •

That night, Riley is unable to settle into sleep. She stares at the red light of the fire detector on the ceiling of the hotel room.

Elle is passed out beside her, and hearing her dreaming is irritating.

The foamy sleep mask over her eyes isn't working; the usual bedtime playlist of rock music is also ineffective to lull her. It's as if she's waiting for something. The clock reads the reminder that it's two in the morning.

But sleep is clearly not happening.

Riley wiggles out of the bed she's sharing with her friend and changes into black tights and a sweatshirt. She shoves her room key into her pocket, grabs her journal and pen, and slips out the door.

She walks through the dark streets, which seem hauntingly quiet compared with the daytime's hustle and bustle. The closed boutiques and restaurants. The tourists safely tucked away in their hotels.

Her Birkenstocks comfortably navigate the roads, and she soon finds herself at the Trevi fountain.

I let myself do the walking and I end up at couple central. She laughs to herself, recalling the amorous people they observed earlier in the day. And the plethora of tour groups.

Riley sits down on a concrete ledge, allowing herself a minute to unpack her mind. A second to breathe. To get into that state where she's still awake, but her mind is able to slip away.

She opens the journal and begins writing in stream of consciousness.

It's amazing to realize that the scripted part of my life has come to an end. Graduated high school, university ... now what am I supposed to do? I'm actually a little bit relieved to be taking the year to travel with Jenna. Maybe that will give me the time and space to figure out exactly how to get what I want for the future. What are those things?

1. Money. My own, not my dad's. Enough to travel anywhere, anytime. Maybe some Mont Blanc pens. A pet to provide some sort of unconditional, non-judgey love?

2. Success. I want to be known for having written a book. To be recognized for my own merits. And writing seems to be the thing that I'm actually really good at. It's my shtick. Maybe I could actually finish something that I've already started ... that would be a definite sense of accomplishment.

3. Love interest? Maybe find someone that can understand me ... somewhat. Not another creative—I don't think I could stomach that. But to somewhere, down the line, have the capacity to feel love. Like, a real kind of love. Not just saying the word "love" as if that gives people meaning. Actual love. That would be great. Someone who isn't a politician-type people-darling who thrives on other people's approval. Maybe I should date a loner.

4. Prestige. I think the basis of everything is that I don't want to be a "plain person." So how do I distinguish myself moving forward?

Riley looks down at the list and feels an epiphany in her brain.

"What I want to achieve ... I can do all of it through writing," she says, openly talking to herself in the dark like a sketchy weirdo.

She flips to a new page and starts to scribble ideas furiously. She burns through a dozen pages with her frantic writing, plotting new projects. Random thoughts that might connect to more down the line.

She underlines a heading that reads: *Things I know about ...*
Under it, she's made a mind map of factors like:

fear, being an outsider, gay parent stuff, literature, wine and cheese, adoption, being bitchy, travel, spelling/grammar, journalling, brawlin', feminism, history, Arthurian legend, bullying, breaking barriers, debating, dry wit

She snickers at some of the categories, but begins to feel a sense of calm emerge as she thinks of what she can write about. A new story to tell.

In the wee hours before night slips into morning, Riley Kohl has discovered the unmarked shortcut to take her down the next road in her life. She's started planning her route towards what she wants the most and is radiating a confidence that others might ignorantly view as lunacy. Her journal pages flip manically as her thoughts spill out of the ink from her pen.

big picture.

[Toronto, Canada—May 30, 2010]

"Girls, thank you for coming into meet," Mack Madison says, walking Riley and Elle through the lobby of Top Dog Management's office in downtown Toronto. "It's been a busy past few weeks, but everything is mushrooming nicely."

He's wearing a dark haberdashery shirt over dress pants, everything expertly tailored to his compact frame. His head is fully shaved, and he's wearing a new pair of designer eyeglasses. The small guy with superman force in the media, he walks with purpose. Riley stands the same height as him, and she can't help but laugh at the thought of Jenna towering over him like an Amazon goddess. Especially in stilettos. Jenna's had model height since the fifth grade.

They pass the reception area, with its steel fixtures and minimalist design. In the main office sits a pool of worker bees at their desks. Phones are buzzing and computers clicking as arrangements are made and information is passed instantaneously. The dozen or so people trying to make the life of their bosses so easy that they get promoted to become assistants. A chance to get closer to the fame and glory they sell. They're all dressed impeccably fashion-forward, especially compared with the simplicity of Riley and Elle's blue jeans and boring shirts.

The walls around them are lined with famous faces under Mack's care, a newly mounted picture of Jenna smiles to everyone, her blonde hair cascading like a pinup doll as her blue eyes stare you down aggressively from every angle. She already looks like a star, the bulldog ferocity in her face giving Riley the shivers.

Mack opens the door to a boardroom with a large glass table, where bottles of fancy imported water are chilled and ready for their meeting.

The girls sit beside each other. Mack is across from them, and a video conferencing console is in the middle.

"Before we speak to Kwame from Alchemy in New York and sign the contracts formally, I wanted to talk to you a bit from my side," he starts. "Jenna has an incredible opportunity here. I am extremely proud of the company that she signed with. As you know, this was a very lucrative deal …"

Riley reaches for a bottle of water, seeking something to fiddle with as Mack starts his monotone pep talk.

"But that being said, the company has extremely high expectations. They've invested a lot in her and want a return on their investment back in spades. I'm talking millions, and on an international scale here."

"Which brings you to us," Elle whispers.

"Yes. You two are going to be on the road with her the most. I'll be with you here and there, but I have a wife and kid back here that I hate to leave. Plus, I get airsick. So I'm going to depend on you to be my eyes and ears. There are going to be a lot of hangers-on, if you know what I mean. And if the record does as I expect, there will be a lot of pressure on her, not only from the label, but all people around her. In this industry, it is so rare to find true friends—people who can have someone else's interest at heart and not see them as a meal ticket."

"Do you think this is going to be that big?" Elle asks worriedly.

Mack peers over his glasses, making her feel like she's asked the stupidest question possible. "She's got a great quality about her; that star-power magnetism is what I saw in her and why I took her on. But it's a double-edged sword because people are going to want to leech off that. They feel the seduction of it and become ... zombies ... like getting high off that power. And I'm just saying, to prepare you, but you're going to have to deal with deflecting a lot of it and preserving her. She's gotta be at the top of her game every day. Calm, rested, ready to perform, happy. And as much as we want it to seem like she's a good-time party girl, this is a business."

"So we have to babysit her?" Riley clarifies, a bit dryly.

Mack hesitates at her crude definition.

"Well ... it'll be easier for you to guide her because you already have the relationship, and you can lead by example. This is why we were okay hiring you as outsiders to the industry. People are going to be trying to sway her to the dark side. So it is your professional responsibility to maintain her in a sale-able state. Everyone wants to go out and party and get fucked up and say they did a line with a superstar. But at the end of the day, it's her career that suffers."

"So, like having a curfew?" asks Elle.

"Sort of. I mean, there'll be nights when you go out. But you have to keep her under control. I've been in this business a long time, and when people start to feel their influence and control, they buck. So be prepared for the backlash of success. It's an incredible thing to see someone climb to the top, and I sincerely am excited for you to be a part of it. She's a lovely person. But I am counting on you to help me keep her grounded, because there'll be just as many people ready to throw her back down to the bottom."

Mack slides two identical black file folders across the table to the girls, and a call comes through on the speakers.

"Hello, Riley, Eleanor," booms the voice of Kwame Roy, the head of the Alchemy Records. There's a delay of his image appearing on the flat screen monitor, but when it does, he exceeds any mental pictures the girls had for a hotshot American music mogul.

His cleanly cropped hair fits with his polished attire. Crisp lavender dress shirt, perfectly moisturized black skin, stern black eyes. His tie is fastened immaculately. He is the definition of a sophisticated New York mover and shaker. In his late thirties, he has a young arrogance that's backed up by his massive success.

"I wanted to conference you before you go out on the road. I think it's great that you've decided to help your friend. But I would like to explain the expectations of the positions Top Dog has given you from the perspective of this record label. Please open your paperwork," he says, never cracking a smile.

There are dozens of pages of writing and bullet points and footnotes. Riley and Elle discreetly shoot each other nervous glances.

"This record label—my record label—has put a lot of time and money into developing Jenna Ramsay. The character that is being fed to the public, the music, the image. And I don't pick losers for my team. So it is your job to maintain the consistency of this character ... while balancing the business realities of needing her to be in top form. She is going to come into a lot of fame and money very quickly, and you two are to control her and keep her from getting out of hand."

Riley stares at the various clauses of the contract before her, stunned.

"Eleanor, you will serve as her executive assistant. Anything that she wants, she gets. If she decides to buy the latest sports car, you get the test drive to come to her. She feels like a shopping trip? Then you go with her and hold the bags. She wants to go on a date with a random guy? You sit with them at the restaurant to deflect any claims they're seriously dating—because he will absolutely try sell her to the tabloids. You will have the resources of both companies at your disposal. Funding, contacts, experience ... so that when she gets invited to a last-minute party, you can call Roberto Cavalli's assistant directly and get a dress FedExed to her. Understand?"

"So anything Jenna wants, Jenna gets," Elle replies meekly.

"Basically. Your challenge is in trying to slow the inflation of her head. The ego will, undoubtedly, balloon. But the rate at which it grows is what impacts her image, her work ethic, her adjustment. Her first introduction to the media is as a good girl who did the unthinkable. Then she'll become increasingly glamorous as her rate of return goes up, and her identity will shift when she upgrades in life from first class to private planes. The people around her have to reflect this."

"So I represent her," she says.

"Exactly. I like your attitude, Miss Bryans. So for this you get full access to the perks, and a base salary of two hundred thousand dollars plus bonuses as outlined. It sounds amazing, I'm sure, but if Jenna Ramsay wants to go to Goa to write for her second album because that's where inspiration dwells—you better have your passport ready and be vaccinated against malaria."

Elle's jaw drops, looking at the breakdown of her income, lack of vacation time, and newly issued company car.

She taps Riley's elbow and points at the figures, and then looks at Mack with an "oh, my god?" expression.

He nods, motioning for her to be patient until the end of the call.

"And as for you, Riley. You'll have a bit of a varied role. Mack and I have decided you would best be served as the acting road manager for Jenna. You have a different dynamic than Elle, a different way of interacting with others."

"You mean, I can be a bitch." Riley laughs, trying to lighten the mood.

"Yes."

She stares at the screen, not expecting the affirmation of her "dynamic."

"Oh, don't be shocked. We need someone who has that stiff personality to keep her in line and maintain the schedule. So when she wants to go to the party being thrown by someone who is not of professional interest, you put your foot down and get her to bed. A journalist starts asking an unfavourable line of questioning, you kick them the hell out. You will act as a liaison between everyone, representing not only Top Dog, but me, while interacting with international subsidiaries, media—anyone, really."

"So then, a hard-line approach would be preferable?"

"I don't want any bullshit, Riley. And people get really easily caught up in the presence of such image. People will try to take advantage of her; you need to be like a goddamn hawk. Guys will try fuck her and sell the story; people will take pictures of you all; her life is going to be under complete and total scrutiny. Don't be shocked when the media starts counting her calories—because they eventually will when it's time to sell a story because someone in her high school math class thought she might've been bulimic. Cellulite photographs earn more money than hookers on a good night."

Riley cringes, reading over her contract page.

"You're going to appreciate that I'm being up front with you ladies. This is not an easy thing. It seems like fun and games, but this is a serious business and a lot of hard work. I acknowledge that you are making the commitment to work with your friend. But don't blame me if she doesn't stay your friend. You can't freeze time—change happens whether you're on board or not."

"What is going to be my most immediate concern, Kwame?" Riley asks, reading footnotes about paparazzi and hiring private security and how to initiate a restraining order.

"The album sounds great; the music will sell itself. Already doing great in the UK. But she's a total unknown. So we have to keep the character she is playing to the media and the public consistent. She is the kind of person who will stop and talk to anyone who likes her music, sign autographs, and be the glamorous girl next door you cheer for. But you have to keep her moving—focus on the bigger picture. If she can't get into the performance because she's signing autographs out front … she's losing out on the fans who've paid to see her concert, know what I mean?"

"Bigger picture."

"Bigger picture," Mack repeats in agreement.

"Riley, you will be paid the same and receive the same perks. You might work a lot more from, say, a hotel room coordinating plans, but it is advisable not to let her too far out of your sight. And protect her from the people trying to penetrate the circle we're creating here."

"So this contract commits you to one year of field work on behalf of Top Dog Management," says Mack. "You will travel and support and facilitate and report. You are to live in Jenna Ramsay's shadow, work from the wings."

"But we're going to make her so huge, at least it'll be one damn big shadow," Kwame says proudly.

Riley and Elle are holding hands under the table, a little taken aback by the brash executive and his demands. Riley picks up a pen in her left hand, Elle picks up a pen in her right hand, and they sign their documents while still clutching each other out of sight.

Before the call is terminated, Kwame announces the first leg of Jenna's promotional tour and their travel arrangements are confirmed.

"This is going to be a very intensive year. We've decided to launch a new single every month. So you girls will be busy, and the thing you're pushing and promoting is going to be ever-changing. When we leaked "Look at This" in the UK, it was less than a week, and she debuted in the top ten. We'll be moving you through Europe, and in a month she'll launch in Asia officially. So pack light; there'll be plenty of clothes couriered to keep you fresh and current."

Mack nods in agreement. "And it will get to the point where you may find yourself on different continents within the span of one week. We have to go with how the flow takes this."

The itinerary looks dizzying. Never more than a week in one place. Definitely no time for actual recreational activities.

"What about North America?" Riley asks aloud, seeing places like Greece, Spain, Japan, Korea, Thailand ... but not cities like Philadelphia, Chicago, or Vancouver.

"Well, that ... will be played by ear. Depending on how quickly she catches overseas, we'll launch her simultaneously here. But we'll see," Mack says. "I have an associate who will be handling the North American launch exclusively. This market can be a picky entity."

He hands them two first-class tickets to London.

"For now, your focus is on getting her out and about in front of the British paparazzi, getting her name out there in a fun, nondramatic way. Pictures of you shopping, having dinner, being three girls having fun—that's great. No stumbling around stupid drunk," Kwame threatens.

Mack then hands them two sets of car keys.

"Those are for your company vehicles in Toronto. If Jenna wants to go to lunch, you drive her in them," Kwame explains. "No cabs, no civilian cars."

Riley holds the heavy key fob in her hand, feeling the embossed writing, a little nervous for the potential suicide mission she's signed up for.

The call ends, and Mack wraps up the meeting.

"The advantage that we were eager to sign you for is that you already have a friendship, a history. So this, in theory, should ease the transition. To have people around her who aren't total strangers, or total kiss-asses. Keep focus on the bigger picture, and everything will fall into place."

He leads them out the back door, as the office staff sneak glances at the new girls handling Jenna Ramsay.

Outside, two matching Range Rovers are parked side by side. They're a custom-painted red that was used on Jenna's album, dubbed "Ramsay red." The black rims give the car a stealthy sleekness.

"Fully loaded, beautiful specimens, girls. I hope you enjoy! See you on the plane." Mack says, proudly admiring the luxury SUVs he's picked. He steps back into the office, content that he's found them to take on the nitty-gritty of what they will soon learn to be an unglamorous job. He can now happily recline in his big leather office chair and read updates over e-mail, instead of flying around the world and moving a mile a minute.

Elle and Riley stand, staring at their cars in the warm spring sunshine.

"I don't know *when* we'll enjoy them ..." Riley mutters, referring to their hectic travel schedule ahead.

"Let's go pick up Jenna and go for a joyride." Elle smiles, trying to turn the situation around with some positive thinking.

"You always have to be glass half full ..." Riley sighs as they unlock their cars.

round one.

[London, England—June 2010]

The airplane begins its descent into London, and Jenna Ramsay has not slept at all. She's anxiously tapping her stiletto-booted feet, sitting fully upright like a dog at attention. The new wardrobe she's been styled into is sitting in designer suitcases within the plane's underbelly—ready to be shown off as she debuts in Europe. Her hair is freshly coloured and styled—a lighter, incandescent blonde that screams, "My hair is so high maintenance, of course I'm somebody!"

Riley scrunches her face in discomfort, her ears popping at the change in altitude. She digs her fingers into the armrest, trying to shut out anything around her, wearing her hair up in a bun, a stiff white dress shirt making her look like an equestrian riding instructor.

"I can't believe this; this is so exciting!" Jenna whispers, tightly grabbing Elle's hand beside her. "I've never been out of the country before! Let alone for my ... *European press tour* ..."

Her friend is curled up in the roomy first-class seat, smiling happily, calmly waiting for the landing. Her relaxed jeans and sweater are looser than the designer dress Jenna's enveloped in. She gazes at Jenna lovingly, feeling such joy in seeing her on cloud nine.

The three girls each have an orange leather Hermès journal in their lap—a gift from Jenna to document their upcoming year of insanity. Mid-flight, she gifted her friends the books, tearfully thanking them for joining her on the journey of her dreams, explaining that the journals would symbolically hold the memories they would soon create together. Elle clapped with glee, and Riley tried to appreciate the over-emotionality of her girlfriends. Mack looked on groggily from his seat, not displaying any particular emotion, thanks to sleeping pills.

Now he is passed out from the medication. His thick, red plastic glasses sit crooked on his face, his skull shiny with airplane sweat.

Mack will be with them for round one of promotional work to support Jenna's first single, to show them the ropes of the game. But only for a couple of days before heading to New York, then back to Toronto and to the luxury of a stable office and home. He's made it clear to the three of them that they've got to hit the ground running and be quick studies.

Riley squeezes her journal, anxiously looking out the window as the plane's landing gear engages.

After clearing customs, the group is ushered to a waiting limo, and they head straight for their hotel. Mack gives them the rundown en route as they start the day.

"All right, so we've got in-person interviews first. That'll be the next three hours. A fifteen-minute break for lunch, and then we'll have some phone interviews with other European regions. Radio stations, mostly. That'll be ten to fifteen minutes each for another two hours. Then we'll have dinner, and you can have the evening free," Mack says, not trying to sugarcoat the nature of a hectic celebrity life.

"Elle, you are to meet with a stylist this afternoon to select some wardrobe pieces for key events. She has a cocktail party tomorrow night, a brunch the day after, and a dinner with the record label's UK office that evening. Jenna, give her any specifics you want—but remember, first impressions can make or break you. Riley, you are to work from the hotel and sit in on all of Jenna's interviews. If someone gets out of line, show them out. I'll be with you for a bit to get you on your feet. But I would *love* to squeeze in a trip to my Saville Row tailor this afternoon …"

"Are we going to all the events?" Elle asks naively.

Mack peers over his glasses, staring at the innocent girl.

"That would be a yes …" she announces, blushing, never feeling quite at ease with his sharp manner. He means well and has proven to be a nice man, but his delivery is too abrupt for her sweetness.

"Jenna, it's going to get old fast—repeating the same stories over and over again," Mack says. "But each person is talking to you for the first time—so fake the enthusiasm because—"

"First impressions can make or break you?" Jenna interrupts.

Mack nods and turns back to his phone.

"How is the song doing here?" Riley asks aloud.

"'Look at This' is in the Top Five and quickly climbing. It's become the most requested song this week. But as of July first, we launch 'Walk By.' But don't leak that yet. Keep them on what's going on *now*. Get the hype up. And then, shock them with novelty so that she dominates."

"Wow—is that like … a business strategy thing?" Jenna marvels, amazed by Mack's seasoned acumen.

He lets out a nasal laugh. "J, darling—have you not realized that I'm a bit of a pro at this by now? There's a reason why Kwame sticks with my formula."

The girls acknowledge his proven track record of talent management. Two decades in the business without having to barely lift a finger, he is the ultimate "manager."

The car pulls up in front of the fancy hotel, and the group gets out. They're shown up to a grand suite with separate bedrooms joined through a shared living room. There's a spread of food on the dining table, but Mack pulls Jenna and Riley back into the elevator without letting them get any. He marches them to a meeting room, comfortably decorated with a fireplace and leather couches, and they wait as a journalist is brought in.

Introductions go around as the journalist begins asking Jenna questions about writing and recording her first album. Pretty standard stuff.

"So, Jenna—what are you most excited about right now?" she asks towards the end of the interview.

Jenna squints her eyes and exhales, thinking carefully. Processing her hopes and dreams, what she'd like most to achieve.

"Wow, that's such a nice question … I mean, I'm excited about sharing my music. Because I think it's fun and positive and that people need that good energy nowadays … I'm excited about travelling with my girlfriends so that we can meet a ton of people out there and get them into my album. To share everything I've been working on, and finally celebrate how awesome it feels to be able to pay it forward …"

The reporter from the *Telegraph* newspaper smiles with a sense of relief, refreshed by the exuberant honesty and optimism.

"I think I'll call your piece 'Pay it Forward.'" She laughs, shaking Jenna's hand and snapping a picture of her by the window to run in the paper. "It was a pleasure meeting you—you seem like such a decent young woman. I wish you incredible success."

"Thank you so much. It was nice to meet you." Jenna smiles warmly, using her ability to make everyone feel as if they're part of the in-crowd with her.

The reporter is led out of the room as they await the next one.

Mack explains their system to Riley, that the local label rep is waiting downstairs receiving the press, bringing them up for their appointments.

"But keep an eye on the time; these guys don't stop unless you cut them off," he says dryly of the reporters. "If Jenna needs a little buffer time, cut them off early—gives her an air of importance."

By the sixth reporter, Riley is amazed that Jenna is still perky and upbeat, having told the same rags-to-riches story so often in a short span of time. Mack has long slipped out, bored to death.

"So, Jen, are you single?" asks the last reporter of the day, a wannabe hipster man from a teen magazine.

"Why, got anyone good in mind?" Jenna winks, trying to charm him with wit and her raspy laugh.

"If you could go on a date with any celebrity, who would it be, Jen?" he asks, trying to reframe the question.

Jenna looks a little annoyed with this particular angle, focusing on her love life more than her music.

"Well, I don't know. Maybe a yummy actor or musician ... I've always liked guys in bands." She gives a fake laugh.

The interviewer doesn't pick up on her coldness and lists possible names, a bunch of British television hosts she's never even heard of.

"My God—fine! James Franco? Okay?! Is that good enough for you?" Jenna snaps, trying to satisfy the line of questioning. "And my name isn't Jen, it's Jenna!"

The man tries to ask more questions about her celebrity crushes, and Riley steps in.

"I think that's enough. Great, thank you. Please do send us a copy," she says, practically pushing him out the door.

The man representing the label is outside, waiting to take this last reporter back to the lobby.

"Thanks, Tom. She needs to wrap up some last-minute things," Riley lies, handing off the pest and heading back into the room.

Jenna is chugging a bottle of water, her voice getting hoarse.

"Wow—it's like you're a grade school bully again!" She laughs. "Thank God they sent me for media training before this. I would have spazzed out four interviews ago!"

"Well, at least I'm not bullying you, but for you instead." Riley laughs, waving a fist at her menacingly. "So, that part of the day is done. We'll have some food, and then phoners after, okay, lovee?"

"Yeah. I mean, it's kinda intense that all these people actually want to hear what I have to say. Like my music actually matters." Jenna smiles, feeling a bit overwhelmed by those clamouring to hear her story.

Riley motions for her to get up out of the cushy chair, and they head to the suite for room service.

They stroll into the modern penthouse and gasp.

"Hey, how'd it go?" Elle smiles excitedly. A rack of clothing is randomly in the middle of the living room, hangers of clothes draped around the minimalist furniture. Shoeboxes are littered all over the floor. It looks like an expensive fashion tornado has swept through.

"Good so far ... what the heck is going on?" Riley asks, stunned as she motions to all the clothing.

"Pulled some clothes. I figure, lovee, you can pick what you want to wear. If it was me, I'd probably show up in a cardigan." Elle laughs, mocking her tame outfit.

Jenna ogles the array of dresses, skirts, tops, and pants, and begins picking out pieces like a child ransacking a sugar shop.

"Oh, this will be for the cocktail party." She smiles, handing Elle a hanger with a bright Miu Miu dress.

"And this for the dinner ..." she says, handing her a Stella McCartney number.

"Oh, and this for the brunch, I think this is good. Not too outrageous, but still funky and British," she says, passing another hanger with Burberry's latest on it.

"And shoes, I mean, the higher the heel, the better. Oh, my freakin' ... look at these!" Jenna shrieks, raiding a box with gold Atwood heels.

"I think she's met her soul mate," Riley says dryly, opting to start inhaling a club sandwich instead of browsing.

"Please tell me that you do not love these," Jenna threatens, waving the sharp heel at her friend in a threatening way.

"No, they're nice, but ... isn't it, um, a shoe?" Riley asks.

There is no reasoning with Jenna. She begins sifting through the other merchandise hungrily.

The door swings open with a swoosh.

"Um ..." Mack trails off, walking in on Jenna's ravenous episode. He pauses and looks to the other two girls, who are helpless on the sidelines. He sets down some garment bags, staring at his blonde client, manic with excitement.

"*Ahh!*" she screeches, hugging an Yves Saint-Laurent purse.

"I was going to say that ... my contact in the bar district has offered to host you guys tonight at his latest venture. A really hip, exclusive lounge-club thing. We can tip off photographers and get a nice 'welcome to the city' type of thing going," he starts, opting to talk to Riley and Elle.

"Oh, cool, um, yeah, maybe we should go out and celebrate our first night!" Elle squeaks, forcing enthusiasm.

"Yes. And I will wear *this*!" Jenna announces, holding up a red-and-white minidress.

Riley looks about as ecstatic to go partying as she would to have a root canal without anaesthetic.

"Oh, Elle, you can wear this," Jenna says, throwing her a charcoal dress with a sweetheart neckline.

"And Riley can wear this!" She grins insanely, whipping a black dress at her with such force that it nearly knocks her down.

Riley holds it up to inspect the garment. "It's a plain black dress," she says flatly.

"No, it's a little black dress by *Givenchy*, if you must get all gloomy-like," Jenna huffs. She continues picking at the shoes. She's never seen so many incredibly expensive, beautiful, shiny things put together in the same space. And for her choosing.

"Can I wear flats?" Elle asks meekly.

"No!" Jenna growls, thrusting a shoebox at her.

"I'll wear jeans and a simple top," Riley says frankly.

Jenna looks at her with homicidal madness in her eyes.

Riley obediently takes her Givenchy LBD and tries to psych herself up for their outing. It's been a long day, and tomorrow will only get longer.

• • •

"*Loveees!* I am so happy we decided to come!" Riley screams over the loud, thumping music. She's holding a glass of champagne, the bottle on ice to her side.

"I'm glad you came, stick-in-the-mud!" Jenna shouts back, finishing the contents of her flute.

The three girls are dancing inside a chic club unknown to the average person, only accessible to the best-looking and wealthiest elite by invitation. The owner happily set them up in a booth with champagne and plenty of cute guys vying for their attention. The only payment necessary was a photo of Jenna with him to proudly display in his office along with all the other celebrity memorabilia.

Elle is dizzy with glee, holding her friends' hands in hers as they hop around. She's tempted to slip off the monstrous platform heels she's been forced into wearing. But Jenna would instantly notice the drop in her height.

Riley grabs the bottle and pours a round for each girl, her head bobbing to the house beats, unnaturally relaxed.

"Hey … so …" a guy trails off, sidling up beside the brunette.

Riley turns to look at him awkwardly.

He smiles at her, and then looks down at her bottle and holds up his empty glass.

"Really?! You want a freebie? Back off, creeper!" she shouts, disgusted by his audacity to score some bubbly.

He slinks off, defeated and empty-handed.

Jenna laughs at her friend's harsh rejection.

The song fades into a familiar backbeat, and the girls start shrieking.

"Look at This" is being mixed in by the DJ!

Jenna jumps onto the plush banquette of the booth, throwing her hands up in victory as her friends hug wildly in front of her.

"This is the first time I'm hearing my song!" she screams over the music to the girls, her eyes wild with surprise.

"Oh, my God—this is for real!" shouts Riley, looking around frantically.

"This is so for real!" Elle yells, dancing around madly.

No one else even notices their celebration; they're completely absorbed in their own dancing.

Except for one person.

Jenna puts down the bottle of Veuve Clicquot, having taken a brazen victory chug from it. Her gaze travels across to the bar, where there is a small group of guys clustered.

One of them, with wispy light brown hair and piercing blue eyes, locks his stare on her. He's wearing a crisp but extremely vibrant orange T-shirt, shining out in the dark cave of the club.

Jenna realizes that she's completely stopped moving and is standing absolutely still on the couch while the music swirls around her.

She shakes off his gaze and turns back to her friends, stepping down carefully.

"The guy across the room … don't look!" she whispers, grabbing Elle's face to stop her from baiting them out. "He's wearing an orange shirt. He totally gave me the shivers."

Elle tries to casually catch a glimpse, but still stands out with her overt coolness.

"When you said orange, I didn't realize you meant ... orange." She giggles. "He's really cute, lovee!"

"I know. He looks, like, heartthrob movie-star cute ..." she trails off dreamily.

"More beverage!" Riley screams at them, stumbling up with another bottle.

"Why don't you invite them over?" Jenna asks Riley, motioning to the guys, and hoping that her friend is inebriated enough to act boldly out of character.

"No way! I can't penetrate that!" she shouts.

Jenna stares at her, confused by the choice of words, and trying not to laugh in her face.

"What if he's gay?" Elle asks.

"What?"

"Orange man. Maybe he's gay; all the hot ones are. Or he's an attention whore. *Whooore!*" Riley screams.

"Riley, really, when is the last time you went drinking?" Jenna laughs, surprised by her friend's low tolerance.

"I haven't had sex in many months!" Riley exclaims, not having understood the question.

"All right ..." Elle grins, realizing she'll have to stay the most sober tonight. Not a problem, though. She prefers to stay in control—particularly after getting back together with Ben. Calm and in control. A real adult. No flashbacks of clinging to a toilet after a night of cheap beer.

"Oh, my God, he's coming over *heeere* ..." Jenna gasps, turning her back to the club in a panic.

"Hey," he says loudly, point blank, forcing them to turn and face him. He puts his hand out to Jenna.

"Hey," she says, shaking his hand daintily, trying to be laid back.

"What's your name?"

Jenna feels as if the rest of the room has faded into a black abyss behind her. This guy's charm has relegated everyone into nonexistence.

"My name? Jenna," she says, struggling to snap out of her trance.

"Hey, Jenna. I'm Carter," he says, keeping his perfect smile fixed on her, his voice even and charming.

"Carter ..." she mumbles to herself, liking the flow of his name on her tongue.

"So I take it that was your song that played?" he says flirtatiously. "I've never seen such excitement … it has to be yours."

Jenna blushes. Her cheeks respond enough to show his intense attention is working on her.

A hostess approaches them with a tray of dark shots.

"I thought I'd congratulate you personally. I thought it was a great song …" He winks, handing her a glass.

Jenna has never been quite so tripped up by attention or by Greek god–like looks.

Carter's about six feet tall and built like Adonis's cousin. Not quite a statue but definitely no mortal. He has an even tan that makes his eyes pop, and a funky hairstyle completes his look. His style is more New Age chic, with the bright, tight T-shirt and fitted jeans.

He waves Riley and Elle over to partake in the toast.

"To my new friend Jenna, with music as beautiful as she is," he announces. They down the shot and bang the glasses down on the table.

"That was disgusting, orange man!" Riley screams at him, stalking off towards the bathroom like a child throwing a tantrum.

Elle scurries after her, desperate to wash the taste of whiskey from her cheeks.

Carter can't help but smile at them. He and Jenna sit down on the couch, where he can still see his friends watching him from the main bar with amazement.

"So, where are you from, Jenna?" he asks, leaning into her. He's so close that his breath is hitting her neck as he whispers.

"C-c-c-Canada," she stammers, shaking off a shiver. "Toronto."

"Really? I'm from BC." He smiles. "But I was recently in Toronto." He puts a hand on her bare knee.

Fuuuckin'shiiit … she thinks to herself, staring at his hand, imagining passionate bolts of electricity zapping at her from his fingers.

"W-w-why?" she asks, trying to keep her focus on being normal. The alcohol isn't helping, though.

"Oh, I shot a movie there," he says nonchalantly.

"A movie?" she asks, taking a minute to study his face. He doesn't look particularly familiar, but he definitely would be photogenic.

"Yeah, it was pretty great. We're in post-production now. Maybe you'll watch it soon …?" He smiles.

Jenna nods furiously.

"And what brings you to London?" he asks.

Jenna snaps back into her super-powerful megastar identity, thawing from Carter's seductive grip.

"Well, actually, I'm here doing promotional work for my first album," she says, restoring her air of cool and sitting up straighter. She remembers the superstar confidence she's fantasized about all these years, the smiling and waving she's practised in her bedroom mirror.

"Really? That's great. How long are you here for?" he asks, a little surprised to see her bounce back with such a poised response.

"Um, about a week."

"Then you move on. I get it, I get it—it's the industry." He smiles sympathetically.

"And what about you—what brings you to London?" she asks, watching her friends approach from the washroom. She tries to send them psychic messages to stay away, to leave her with the hot actor in their flirtatious little bubble.

"Same thing. Start the buzz for the movie. Then I start shooting a new one in the States. Might actually squeeze in another in Toronto in the new year …" He winks. "In case you're home then."

Riley and Elle run up to their friend and playfully tackle her on the couch.

Carter looks up at his buddies and motions for them to join the group. Four guys stroll up to the booth, and Carter introduces them as models and actors.

"And this is Riley and Eleanor," Jenna adds.

Everyone shakes hands, and Jenna invites the group to their champagne.

"So what's his deal?" Elle whispers to Jenna, pulling her aside.

"Movie actor!" she squeals, grabbing her friend's arm and pretending to faint.

"Really? Cos it looks like they're kinda drinkin' out our booth …" Riley announces, throwing her arms around the girls.

"Riles …" Elle warns.

Jenna shrugs her off, not the least bit concerned.

fake it.

[Rome, Italy—July 2010]

Jenna struggles to get herself out of bed. Her body is feverish, ravaged by an intense flu that's been around way past its welcome. It's only been four weeks, and her body has already started rebelling against the constant movement and uprooting, unaccustomed to the crazy hours of her new schedule.

There's a soft knock at the door, and Elle slips into the hotel room.

"Hey, lovee, how are you feeling?" she asks tenderly.

Jenna groans and rolls on to her side to face away from her friend.

"I've been talking with Riley, and we think we should modify your schedule, so we're asking Mack," she whispers, sitting on the bed beside her pasty, sweaty friend. Her pale yellow dress makes a crinkling noise as she moves, trying to check her friend's temperature.

Still well above normal and not breaking.

There's another, louder knock at the door, and Riley strolls in without waiting for a response.

"Mack's approved our changes," she announces. "How are you doing?"

Jenna doesn't speak, her throat too sore for words. It's still sensitive from the tongue depressor used by the physician called in by the hotel.

"Dr. Argento says that you need a solid three days of bed rest. So, we're going to finish half a day today—if you can—and then move to the next location," Riley begins, pacing around in her knee-high leather boots, jeans tucked into them with a green crewneck T-shirt overtop.

Jenna nods, trying to listen, but her head is throbbing.

"So we'll arrive in Scotland a few days ahead of schedule, take some rest, and then do the promo work there. I got us a reservation at a castle out in the country so we can get some peace and quiet. We can return to Italy another time. You need to be alive to do so," Riley continues, refilling the glass by Jenna's bedside with bottled water.

"So what do we have left here? The shopping trip?" asks Elle.

Riley nods.

"Okay, so we'll do a walk down Via dei Condotti, do the Armani store for a bit, and fulfill our promise to get the pictures taken. Then head straight out?" Elle clarifies.

"Yeah. So, Jenna—can you do that?" Riley asks, worriedly looking at her friend. "We gotta get the pictures we agreed to in time for the launch of the new collection to the media. Or Kwame will flip."

She nods, clearing her throat, wiping her nose with the sleeve of her pyjamas, but still not turning to look at her friends.

"Yeah ... I need a minute. Drain the sinuses. Don't want them to photograph this—don't want them thinking I'm a whiny baby."

"Okay, so I'll get everything here packed up. You guys get ready. We'll leave in half an hour? Elle, you pick an outfit so all she has to do is change and walk. Jenna, do you want any more toast?" Riley asks, looking at the empty room service tray on the floor.

"No ..." she whimpers.

Elle looks at Riley sadly, and they leave the room quietly.

"She's working too hard," Elle warns.

"I know. But Mack says this usually happens when people start out. Their body's immunity isn't used to being a jet-set superstar," Riley says, heading to her laptop. "Imagine when she's in the U.S. and taking a jet to knock out three cities in a day! To think that's what they aspire her to do ... it's frightening how someone can have that sort of stamina."

"Do you want any help?" Elle offers, approaching the dining room table that is Riley's makeshift office.

Their breakfast lays devoured at the other end of the table, espresso cups sucked dry.

Riley sighs, looking at the week's calendar she has to go through and cancel.

"Yeah, can I give you these places to call and cancel her appearances? Let them know they can contact Alchemy about rebooking," she says, printing out a spreadsheet.

"Wow, Riles, you're really organized ..." Elle marvels, tapping her ankle-wrap espadrilles as she scans the information.

Riley shrugs. *With a multimillion dollar career in my hands ... I gotta be*, she thinks, sighing heavily.

Riley is on the phone with an Italian TV station when she sees an e-mail from Mack pop up, warning about paparazzi activity and confirming the use of security for their publicity walk.

She writes back an acknowledgement, and a knock on the door reveals three big Italian bodyguards in suits. They patiently wait in the living room, reading the current gossip newspapers with stories about Jenna, George Clooney, and a Shania Twain tribute exhibit.

Riley quickly changes into Armani trousers and puts on a fresh white dress shirt underneath a charcoal blazer. It has become her basic uniform—polished and professional in a world where sprinting from the paparazzi has become daily reality. The interest in Jenna's girl-next-door story has turned her not only into a number one singer, but a media darling—essentially overnight.

Elle takes a garment bag into Jenna's room to get her ready.

Riley grabs a bottle of water and mixes in the electrolyte crystals left by the doctor. She takes a minute to speak with the guards about the current state of the client.

"Jenna is extremely sick; she's been burning a fever for a couple of days now. So we need to keep her out of the sun as much as possible. Not waste too much time getting into the shop," she explains, shaking the water up.

"Do we drive straight there, then?" asks the head guard.

Jenna appears in the doorway, holding onto Elle's arm for support as she wobbles in her strappy sandals and summer dress. She quickly sits down on a couch, struggling to keep her eyes open.

"Hi …" she croaks to the three men who are staring.

They smile a greeting to her, feeling infinitely bad for the young woman. She looks perfectly put together, but seeing her skin up close, she can't hide how debilitated she is.

"I've been instructed to have her walk down the street for at least a block. She can look into a couple of windows, and realistically, she's going to be walking quite slowly. But … we want to minimize how weak she'll get. Elle and I will walk with her. Jenna, I've got your water," Riley explains as they get up to leave.

"The paparazzi will swarm at sighting the car," one of the men tries to explain in choppy English. "They have becoming more an more aggressive with all the vacationing movie stars."

The six people head to the elevator and down to the parking garage, where two black, tinted Mercedes executive cars await them.

The girls get into one with the head guard. The other two guards stow their luggage, and then lead the way in the other car.

The dark windows let Jenna flop into a mucousy mess in the backseat as the streets of Rome whizz by.

"We are here," announces the driver as the cars approach the Via dei Condotti area. Tourists are trickling around the shopping district steadily, taking photos of themselves standing in front of shop windows—capturing themselves with Italian design icons that they're too meek to encounter with their wallets.

"Wait—I need a minute," Jenna says, stopping anyone from opening the doors.

As predicted, a rush of people approaches the cars, cameras going off with lots of shouting and screaming through the darkened windows.

The two other guards are positioned by the girls' car, ready to run interception.

Jenna blows her nose and takes moment of pause.

"*Ooo-kay*," she says, her voice hoarse and pained, handing Elle the snotty tissue. Elle looks at it, disturbed. She's never been handed something like that before—let alone from her friend.

With that, the passenger door is opened, and the intensity of the crowd multiplies.

Riley slides out first, followed by Eleanor. Jenna comes out last, dressed head to toe in the latest Armani summer style. She links her arms through those of her two friends, and they attempt to move forward with the bodyguards around them.

"Okay, easy does it," Riley whispers, as her friend smiles and weakly waves to the cameras.

They slowly walk the block, the act of perusing the windows rather conducive to a slowed pace.

I would love to go into each and every store, Jenna thinks to herself sadly, already resolved to the jam-packed schedule that has become her life. It's been a month in Europe, and she's already a sensation, her first music video viewed at record quantities.

She creates a mental bull's-eye of the Armani storefront but feels her vision go loopy for a second.

"Stop, stop a minute," she hisses to the girls.

They pause in front of a shop, the guards flanking them and keeping the hyperactive crowd at arm's length. Tourists are screaming in different languages, whipping out cell phone cameras.

"Do you want water?" Riley asks as she tries to estimate how many more steps it will take to get her through the door and safely into the air-conditioned store.

Jenna shakes her head and starts forward again, the girls following suit.

I wish I could see those steps ... and just be a tourist, she thinks, having gazed at the Spanish Steps feverishly and imaging herself eating gelato like a regular visitor to Rome.

The photographers are frantically speaking in broken English or shouting in Italian. Loud and overwhelming.

"Hey, Jenna—what's the matter?" yells a man with a perfect American accent. "Don't you like the fame game?"

Riley looks at him suspiciously as Jenna tries to ignore the commotion. He looks familiar, probably shadowing their travel to try to get exclusive shots of the blooming starlet. Be the Jenna Ramsay pioneer.

The photographer looks at Jenna intently but keeps snapping pictures, heckling her about being hung over. Riley snaps a photo of him on her cell phone to e-mail to Top Dog, for documentation in case he gets in the way again.

They reach the store, one of the guards already ahead and securing the door. The three girls walk in, and Jenna steadies herself on a table, breathless.

A shop attendant rushes to get a chair, placing it around a corner and away from curious eyes outside.

Riley pulls the water bottle out of her blazer pocket, and Jenna thirstily drinks the entire thing.

A jovial man in his fifties appears, holding a folder and dressed in impeccable European style. He is the marketing rep for Giorgio Armani and has offered to host the highly public singer at their store.

"*Mees* Ramsay!" he calls. "Oh, *Mees* Ramsay ... you are unwell!"

Jenna smiles meekly, her hands getting the shakes.

"I'm sorry; she won't be able to stay long. She's been running a fever for a few days now," Riley apologizes.

"Yes, we will take the photos fast, then ... yes ... oh, *Mees* Ramsay ... I am so sorry. May I get you anything?"

One of the shop girls wraps the shivering singer in a luxurious mohair throw.

"No, thank you ...?" she replies weakly, not sure of his name.

"Agostino." He smiles warmly, looking at her with extreme pity. His English is strong, but with a heavy Italian accent. "I am sorry Giorgio could not be here today, but we look forward to reviewing you as a potential sponsorship."

"Better—he would regret if I got him sick." Jenna winces, feeling her eyes glaze over.

Agostino smiles, charmed by the good-natured girl but wondering how quickly her star will fizzle out if she's already showing signs of exhaustion.

"Please, let me show you the collection," Agostino offers as he gives her his arm and begins to walk her through the boutique.

"Elle, please hold the clothes while I walk," Jenna instructs, not confident in having the energy to shop—the most basic joy in her life. She hands Riley the mohair throw and braces herself for the flashbulbs coming through the window.

Agostino takes some time to tell her about the new creative inspirations, carefully observing her, evaluating her potential as a spokesmodel for their next fragrance campaign. Kwame Roy has put his hat in the ring for them to seriously consider his latest prodigy.

After a half hour of visiting, the girls excuse themselves politely.

"I hope that next time we can meet, you are your vibrant self again." Agostino smiles, remembering the bright youth he has seen on television. Her second single is already a staple at all the hip clubs.

Jenna nods appreciatively and is walked out of the upscale store by Elle and Riley, who are holding the bags of merchandise.

The guards have brought their cars right up to the entrance, and the girls dive in.

Jenna collapses into a wet, phlegmy cough.

"I just shopped—and bought stuff at *Giorgio Armani* ..." she wails, embarrassed by the condition she was paraded around the sacred ground of one of her style idols. "I dreamt of something like this for so long—and how it's come to life ... is so ... not ... ugh!" She closes her eyes, afraid she's humiliated herself completely with such a prominent business contact.

The cars zoom off to the airstrip, and the girls catch their flight.

connect.

[Outside of Edinburgh, Scotland—July 2010]

Riley is sitting out on a large, stone balcony of their rented Scottish castle, looking at the landscape below. She's high up on the third floor, getting the lay of the land, breathing in the natural surroundings and thankful to be away from the growing public interest in Jenna.

This is like a freakin' daydream, she thinks to herself, amazed that she's actually hanging out at an ancient fortress. She imagines King Arthur and the Knights of the Round Table cantering through fields much like those in front of her, the lush forest with magic in the air and Merlin whipping up some spells. *I'm totally nerding out,* she admits silently.

Her laptop is open before her and she has been diligently typing the entire morning. Sewing together the different stories she's collected over the years, trying to piece them into her first cohesive novel.

The girls have been resting for the past two days. Jenna's condition is much improved since being able to evade lurking photographers and achieve uninterrupted sleep. The constant shuttling around Europe has meant early mornings and later nights full of strangers scrutinizing her every move, every outfit, every sign of lethargy.

Riley is typing so furiously that she doesn't even notice her two friends at ground level beneath her.

Elle and Jenna are also sitting out on a terrace facing the forest, but at ground level. They've opted to leave Riley with some much-needed creative space, the massive setting of a medieval castle affording them more than enough square feet to be able to accommodate an entire township.

They've finished eating an incredible breakfast prepared by the house chef. Flipping through the gossip magazines, they spotted a speculative article from the photographs taken in Italy. That Jenna was suffering from exhaustion, wondering if she's being mistreated or being seduced by the vices of nightlife. But the piece was written with utmost concern and care for the adored singer—not any trace of disdain like other highly followed stars.

But the trashy magazines were left in the dining room, along with any conversation pertaining to the entertainment industry, as the girls made the decision to shed the drama and enjoy the sun. Now Elle and Jenna are sipping the rest of their coffee outside, talking boys and silly things instead. And appreciating how far removed they are from the already familiar spotlight around them.

Elle begins to lightly sketch her view of the woods around them with a pencil. Jenna is writing in her orange journal, trying to think of fresh song ideas now that her mind isn't racing a mile a minute and panicked about jamming in another interview, photo shoot, or autograph. She's left her cell phone—and all the text messages from Carter—back in the house, too.

"Hello? Jenna Ramsay?" calls a voice from the garden.

The two girls gasp, grabbing one another's hands as they turn fearfully to see who it may be.

A man approaches the stone railing, waving warmly.

"Oh, my God, what if he kills us?" Jenna gasps, grabbing her teaspoon for self-defence.

"Miss Ramsay, I am Ignacio Rocafuerte," calls the man as he starts to come into focus. His voice is deep and has an odd accent, kind of like a whitewashed Hispanic.

"What?" Jenna asks, turning to Elle.

She has to pause for a moment to think, and then clues in as the thirtysomething in a business suit reaches them.

"He owns the castle!" Elle whispers, remembering his name from the rental agreement.

Jenna quickly puts down her weaponry, and the two girls approach the edge of the patio, wrapping themselves in their throw blankets to shield him from cartoon pyjamas (or negligees, in Jenna's case).

"Okay, hi, hello!" calls Jenna cheerily, evaluating him from head to toe.

He's finely tailored and wearing a brown European style of suit, fitted and with a red dress shirt. The wealthy Mexican businessman owns several prestigious properties around the world—in addition to inheriting his family's importing and exporting mammoth.

Ignacio reaches the girls and happily shakes their hands.

"I am sorry to disturb you, but I came to check the moat. I hope you are enjoying your stay," he says.

Jenna's eyes widen at the sight of such a sophisticated young man.

"Yes, it's been great," Elle says, replying for her. "Mr. Rocafuerte, I'm Eleanor Bryans, her assistant."

"Please, call me Ig." The man smiles. "But I thought I had spoken with another lady …"

"Oh, Riley Kohl. Yes, she's my road manager," Jenna says breezily, feeling totally comfortable with her identity as a person others now try to impress.

Ignacio nods thoughtfully.

"Thank you again for letting us use your property on such short notice," Elle gushes, but she's self-conscious that he can see her My Little Pony sleepwear.

"Oh, it is no problem. Miss Kohl mentioned you were ill—are you still unwell? I can call the doctor …" he offers, looking at the singer nervously.

"No, no, thank you. I am actually feeling better than ever. Being here basically about cured everything." Jenna smiles, batting her eyelashes and flirting with the magnate. Elle glances at her saucy friend, and her eyes are instantly drawn to the appearance of cleavage. Elle blushes, trying to look away from the hint of lace Jenna has allowed to peek out as she chats with Ig.

"Great. May I ask a selfish favour of you, Miss Ramsay?" he whispers playfully.

"Please, call me Jenna." She smiles.

He grins back, his dark eyes taking her in.

"May I ask you for an autograph? My niece in Mexico is such a fan of your music. She would not believe I am here with you." He laughs.

"You're being played in Mexico?" Elle whispers, astounded by the catchy appeal of Jenna's songs.

"Of course, Ig. But why don't we send her something nice? Not a piece of paper," coos Jenna, hoping to extend their interaction. Carter isn't here—Ignacio is. Why not keep entertained?

"You are too kind." Ignacio winks.

"Yes, let me grab your contact information," Elle says, going back to the table to grab her BlackBerry.

She scampers back up to find Jenna playfully hitting Ig's arm and laughing her raspy sexpot laugh.

Scotland'll do ya good! Elle smiles to herself, watching them flirt like hormonal teenagers.

"Well, I must be off. But I shall see you tonight." He confirms, leaving Elle standing idle with her phone at the ready.

"And?" she asks her friend once the mysterious man is out of earshot.

"He's coming here for dinner. With friends!" Jenna screeches excitedly.

"Oh, wow! Great job!" Elle beams, impressed by her confidence. Jenna's always been more bark than bite when it came to dating and relating, but the power of her newfound success has really upped the ante in commanding attention. Elle's gaze falls, and she has to redirect her eyes away from Jenna's still-flaunted lingerie.

• • •

Later that evening, before the sun has set, Ignacio Rocafuerte's Land Rover drives over the castle's drawbridge. He emerges with two friends, and they are led into the study where the three girls are sitting and talking. They eagerly join in on their conversation.

"Ladies, these are my college mates, Bryce and Abbott," Ig says.

The three men are dressed in neatly pressed khakis and polo shirts, like matching amigos. Their female hosts show a little more individuality, Jenna standing out in a bright cocktail dress and stilettos.

"So, Jenna, how has this place been treatin' ya?" Abbot asks, his accent Scottish. He smiles, taking a seat beside her on an old leather couch. His light ash-blonde hair matches the colour of his bushy eyebrows. He looks like a rugby player, and his boisterous nature pegs him to be the life of the party.

"Quite well. Been great to recharge," she says, holding a glass of ice water in both hands.

Ignacio wanders into the kitchen, leaving the group to talking.

The basics are covered—where are you from, what do you do, what is it like travelling with an overnight celebrity …

Abbott is particularly interested in Elle's vocation.

"So, do ya consider *yerself* an artist because ya studied it in school or because of some higher calling to express blah, blah, blah?" he asks, feigning an existential query and curious to see how the quiet redhead will react to his arrogance.

"My boyfriend is a hockey agent," Elle responds, having no other way to drop the information that she is spoken for.

The guys look at her, confused by the disconnected information.

"Well," she begins softly, smoothing her beige cotton skirt, "I consider myself someone who can not only express themselves artistically, but appreciate other people's creativity."

He looks at her, stifling a laugh. Under normal circumstances, he would mock someone for such grandiose hot air, but Eleanor seems so ridiculously sweet that he can't seem to let his cynicism taint her.

"So if I was to paint a picture with my big toe, you would consider it art?" he asks.

Elle looks at Abbott softly and Riley smiles to herself, knowing her friend to be misleading them with her childlike femininity. She may be gentle, but she's not a total idiot.

"It might not be as good as mine, but by definition, yes, I would have to consider it art," she whispers slightly sarcastically.

The group bursts into laughter at the petite girl quietly insulting the intimidating, refrigerator-sized man.

"D'you know, my mum owns a fantastic little gallery in New York," Bryce mentions casually, his British accent making him seem even more prep school. He is quite impressed by Elle's innocently transparent nature and that Abbott hasn't rattled her. He runs a hand through his dark brown hair and nervously glances at Riley beside him in a chair. She's been rather quiet, yet seems like the one not to piss off.

"Hey, why don't you show him your sketches?" Jenna asks forcefully, recognizing an opportunity to promote her friend's talent.

"Oh, they're not very good. My canvases and other pieces are back home." Elle sighs sadly.

"Would you please show me?" Bryce asks gently, curious to see if she has any discernable talent—or simply the ideal of being an artist.

Elle disappears and returns a few minutes later with a pad of drawings, including some work from Venice, and her orange journal.

He studies them carefully, his lips pursing in concentration.

"I really don't have much classical knowledge about art, but I reckon that these are quite good, Eleanor," he says. "Especially works that you consider ... pastimes."

I hope he doesn't think that I'm going to go on a date with him, Elle thinks worriedly, hoping that he's actually legit, and not dangling a possible gallery connection to get some play—with any of them.

"That would be awesome, Elle, if you got to show your work," Jenna says, trying to plant a seed into Bryce's mind. She flashes him a huge smile, and her blue eyes pop with excitement, in case flirting will help their case.

"Well, my mother's always looking for up-and-comers," he acknowledges.

"Get your mum to send photos on e-mail," Riley suggests to Elle, also excited by the potential networking angle of their dinner guests. Something to come out of a night with random strangers, when she'd much rather be in bed.

"Would that be okay?" Elle shyly asks Bryce.

"Hey, it helps us, too. I think she has a week free in mid-September, or else next year. But here, take my card. I'll pass anything along to her," he explains. "My wedding in the fall is truly taking up any extra time, so the sooner the better. God-forsaken tuxedos ..."

Wedding = unbelievable! Woohoo! Elle smiles to herself, eased by his openness and lack of creepiness.

She looks at his business card, a prestigious bank listing him as a director: Bryce Hodge.

Ig emerges with a tray of margaritas—freshly blended in the state-of-the-art kitchen.

"I had to fight off the cook to make these," he jokes, handing out his very potent creations.

"Do you guys want to head into town and go to the pub later?" suggests Abbott, wishing there were more girls around—especially ones that weren't into his friend, already taken, or possessing a frigid personality.

Jenna looks excited to continue hanging out with the lively guys. But a night of boozing wouldn't quite help her recovery. She bites her lower lip, having licked off the shiny red lip gloss.

"Well, why don't we finish dinner, and then we'll go from there?" Riley offers, her stomach not prepared to down pints, especially with the intense schedules of interviews and appointments set up for Jenna the rest of the week. It will surely be a challenge to talk her out of the excursion, the excuse to get drunk with Ig being the perfect cure to distract her from daydreams of Carter. The actor who had flowers delivered to her when he heard she was sick. Who sends the "thinking of you" messages at random, always keeping himself on her radar.

Ig's not a business interest, so I gotta stand my ground. Scotland this week, Ireland next. Then Greece, Turkey, and Croatia ... back to England, but shoot the next music video somewhere in Greece, Riley reviews on her BlackBerry as the group divides into smaller conversations. She sighs, suddenly overwhelmed that she has no choice but to keep their train chugging along, that they don't have the ability to buck like a horse and just say no. There are too many resources and plans and money put into creating Jenna's identity. There is no time to meet new people and socialize, let alone form a connection; they'll always be off to another country in a matter of days, if not hours.

Jenna, however, seems to have the opportunity to share her bed that night. Ig is lapping up her star power, making Riley's stomach turn. The intensity with which he looks at her like a dessert tray has Elle and Riley's guard up.

They're called into the dining room to begin their five-course meal.

can't escape your shadow.

[Paris, France—August 2010]

Jenna tries to keep her eyes shut tight, not wanting to wake up to a new day, the warmth of a huge hotel bed quickly becoming what she longs to return to as soon as she steps out of its comfort. From the second she gets up to start her schedule, she daydreams of the moment she'll curl back up and melt away. Something about the sturdiness of a bed frame, the comfort of the sheets—it puts her at ease.

There's a firm knock at the door, and she lets out a groan.

"Jenna ..." starts Riley, walking in without looking up from her cell phone. "Are you going to get up any time soon, lovee?"

Riley was awake before dawn, subconsciously expecting to rush off to catch a flight or join a conference call with Mack and Kwame. Her Circadian rhythms are off-kilter, and she sometimes forgets where in the world she is.

But today, the girls were allowed to sleep in a little on a rare day off. Riley's still wearing her pyjamas, indulgently being kept on as late as possible, and has spent some time on her laptop writing.

Jenna rolls over onto her stomach. She feels the familiar dread of having to get up and pick an outfit or get her hair and makeup done. Her skin feels puffy from the constant retouching, and her lips are peeling from licking off lip gloss all day, every day.

"Hey—what's the matter with you?" Riley asks crossly, staring at her friend from the foot of the king-sized bed.

Jenna stays silent, trying to breathe herself into invisibility and fade away into the Egyptian cotton.

"It's our day off, and you want to lie in bed?" her friend asks, surprised.

Jenna's eyes blink open.

No interviews or rehearsals or photo shoots today!

"Elle wants to go to the Louvre—and I'm not going alone. So you better get dressed and stare at art with us," Riley teases flatly. She's cautiously staring at her friend, suspicious of her constant low-energy state.

"*Oh ... kay ...* let me shower," Jenna says softly, lifting herself up on her elbows.

Riley steps into the suite and finds Elle finishing her breakfast in the dining room. She's neatly dressed in a light green dress and sandals. A sketchpad sticks out of her bag.

"Hey ... do you notice anything with Jenna ..." Riley starts to ask softly, as her friend bites into an oversized croissant.

Elle chews thoughtfully, putting up a finger, asking for a minute, and wipes her hands on the napkin in her lap.

"Um ... what do you mean?"

Riley scrunches her face up, not exactly sure how to describe her inkling of a shift in Jenna's always-happy exterior.

"I'm sure she's exhausted. All the pressure on her with this new single—it's a bit much, in my opinion. Is she coming with us?" Elle asks, spreading some orange marmalade on her croissant.

Riley nods and heads off to change, already having eaten breakfast alone. She rummages through her suitcase and grabs a pair of wrinkled beige wide-leg linen trousers and throws on a brown T-shirt with them. Her luggage is in disarray, never staying neatly packed or organized with their constant movement.

She grabs her new sunglasses, D&G hand-me-downs from Jenna's exploding wardrobe. When she marches back into the dining room, Jenna is drooped on the table, speaking softly with Elle.

"Hey—are we ready to go?" Riley asks, still observing her listless friend.

Elle nods, covering her room service plate and standing up excitedly. She wants to do something normal, not have to watch strangers throwing themselves at Jenna's larger-than-life persona.

Jenna forces a smile and follows them to the door, marching like a conscripted soldier. Her dark blue Vince tracksuit is a little baggy on her, the hem dragging on the floor because there's been no time to get it properly altered. This morning, there isn't the usual Jenna Ramsay glow that surrounds her. She looks like she's moving along a conveyor belt passively. Drained.

"Did you have breakfast?" Riley asks her, feeling like she's entering overbearing mother territory. She's knows for herself that she needs to be fuelled and can't skip her morning meal. Not having energy has almost floored her in their daily marathons before—and she's not even the centre stage starlet who requires extra, superhuman kilojoules to perform and smile.

Jenna shrugs and grabs a pear from the table, throwing it into her designer purse, knowing she'll toss it as soon as her friends are distracted. She just doesn't feel hungry. Ever. She feels like a zombie instead.

Riley frowns to herself as they ride the elevator down to the lobby, wondering if Jenna is depressed or bulimic or something scary like that.

"I hope the lines aren't too long," Elle says worriedly, as the three friends slip into a car with tinted windows.

"I was going to call in advance ... but maybe we can try to fly below the radar?" Riley suggests, as they weave through the morning traffic of the city. "It's almost like we become more of a spectacle when there are guards around to draw attention ..."

Jenna smiles, relieved. She can be incognito for a day. Hiding beneath her massive designer sunglasses encrusted with authentic diamonds.

The car lets them out in front of the famous museum, and the three girls walk up to the entrance together. They patiently wait in line to get in, as Elle takes in the historic structure, trying to make mental photographs for her memories.

They begin to browse through various exhibits, Elle's eyes popping with intensity as she surveys all the artwork rabidly.

"This looks kinda blotchy," Jenna whispers to Riley, staring at a painting sourly.

"Yeah ... a little ..." her friend replies, tilting her head to try to look deeper into the piece. "Yeah, I don't get it ..."

They smile at each other cynically and walk on to the next frame.

Riley notices a couple whispering nearby, looking intently at the singer but keeping their distance. They're admiring her from afar, like one of the treasures on display at the museum.

Jenna wanders up to a sculpture. The white marble looks smooth, yet porous—the woman's shape poised, but at ease.

She looks so ... okay with herself, Jenna thinks, studying the relaxed lips and stately jawline. *Like she doesn't have any sort of black hole in her gut ... she simply is who she is. She must be beautiful and worshipped, but with love, not envy.*

She faintly hears some whispering off to her side and slowly turns to look.

A bright flash blinds her and throws her off balance—totally startled like a fawn in the woods.

Two teenage boys continue to take photos of her, shoving their cameras in her face, having recognized the popular new singer. Their commotion draws attention from the rest of their school tour group, and Jenna quickly finds herself surrounded.

Riley and Elle look away from the painting they're admiring as soon as the yelping and shouting starts echoing off the walls.

"Oh, no …" Riley groans and hustles into the middle of the free-for-all.

Elle motions for the guards to intervene, and three of them rush into the mix.

"*Arrêt!*" they yell to the kids, who have swooped all around, frantically taking pictures and trying to ask for autographs in German.

Jenna's eyes are wide in terror; she can't push through all of them to get free. Her heart is pounding in her ears, her cheeks burning with panic. Hands are grabbing at her, eyes staring, mouths screaming. Jenna is stuck to the floor like the statue behind her, frozen and scared.

Suddenly, a firm grip on her elbow yanks her through the crowd, as Riley drags her through the gallery. She's like a charging lion, barrelling forward without slowing down. Elle rushes behind them, and they're soon surrounded by security ushering them out the door.

Other people notice the frantic movement and try to get closer to take pictures of the teary blonde, on the brink of a panic attack. Jenna feels like she's slipping out of her body, weak from not having eaten and scared out of her wits.

"We are coming out right now! A car better be there!" Riley yells into her cell phone, clearing the path with a thundering anger as they push through an exit.

She spots a car speeding down the street; it comes to a halt right in front of the curb.

"Move, move, move!" Riley shouts at her friends, trying to get them to speed up as the tourists outside the museum start to stampede towards them.

A woman gets right in front of Riley and tries to queue up to take a photo.

"*Allez!*" Riley shouts at her, not sure how else to command the intruder away in her rusty high school French.

The woman stands her ground as the group barrels towards her. Riley tries to navigate around, but the amateur photographer accidentally hits her in the face with the camera.

"Mother F!" Riley screams in pain, without missing a step, as they dive into the backseat of the car.

The doors are slammed and locked, and the sedan speeds back to the Ritz.

"Are you okay?" Elle gasps, grabbing Riley's face in her hands and studying the damage.

"That was fucking new!" Riley grimaces, holding her cheek and cringing. There's a small cut with blood trickling on her skin.

Jenna starts sobbing hysterically and topples over on the seat, her cries sending her body into convulsions.

"We can't even go to a damn museum without me getting in the way!" she shrieks, grabbing at her hair in distress and howling as she yanks at it.

Elle tries to hold her, to calm her down. The long and lean body of her friend flops over her, like a giant smushing a fairy.

"Shh," Elle whispers to her friend, trying to pat her head.

"I'm so sorry. I know you wanted to see it," Jenna cries, choking on her tears. She removes her grip on the lock of blonde hair she's ripped out of her scalp, and it flutters to the floor of the car.

Riley stares at her in shock, glancing at Elle nervously; neither are sure what this outburst means. The sudden breakdown of emotion is a little disturbing, like a hidden part of her personality exploding.

"Lovee, it's not your fault. It's okay," Elle tries to assure her.

"You don't think I notice all the people whispering?!" Jenna yells, almost throwing Elle off the seat in her panicked rage. "I didn't think it would be like this! I can't even walk down a street anymore!" She continues shouting. "Sometimes I want to die because I hate it."

"*Hey! Enough!*" Riley screams back, silencing her. "You don't get to do this right now. We are here for you because this is what you wanted. We are here because this is your dream, so don't freak because it's real. None of us expected this. We all have to work through it together," she says bluntly.

Jenna's sobs start to subside, and she feels less alone. They're in it with her. They're in this crazy world that has formed around her. They see how insane it's starting to get.

"This means that we'll have to keep things even stricter because people recognize you, so you are not going anywhere unaccompanied. Not because you're an idiot, but because, as we have now seen, people in this world are lunatics around celebrity bullshit," Riley says firmly. "Jenna, you're now famous. Congratulations. This isn't going to fade away if we have a day off. Now we know better."

Jenna nods, wiping her runny nose on her sleeve.

"You've wanted this all your life. We now have to adjust our expectations." Elle shrugs, as they pull up to the hotel. She leads Jenna to the lobby, and Riley quickly scoops up Jenna's lock of hair from the car's floor. Avoiding the opportunity that it could be sold on the Internet. They head up to their chic Chanel-themed hotel suite in silence.

Jenna runs into her bedroom and slams the door like a child throwing a fit.

"What do we do?" Elle asks Riley, as they stand helplessly in the living room.

Riley shrugs and sits down at her laptop to send Mack a full play-by-play.

"She must feel like she's on a deserted island or something—she can't even have a day off …" Elle whispers, her eyes darting around, frightened by the thought.

"Elle, she asked for this. Worked for this. You can't take it back once the wheels are in motion. If she backs down now, she'll be the next has-been documentary. She's has gotta get out of bed each day and realize that, yes, her dream came true, but with a serious clause on her privacy filter." Riley sighs.

Elle looks around anxiously and notices the bruising on Riley's face.

"I'm gonna get you an ice pack," she tells her friend, trying to give herself something to do to feel more useful.

PART II:
CRUISING ALTITUDE

sweet lemonade.

[Near London, England—September 2010]

"Where is the Dior sheath?" screams one of the stylists on-set at Jenna's photo shoot for *Rolling Stone* magazine.

Jenna Ramsay and her entourage are inside a rundown loft outside of London. Four months and four number one singles later, Jenna has reached a new height of "scenester." Enough to get on the cover of an iconic American music magazine, cementing her record-breaking speed of success, and winning the title of "Hottest Sleeper Hit."

"Alex, the shoes don't fit her!" screams the middle-aged female stylist, after discovering the size-six Vivienne Westwood platforms were not adequate for Jenna's size-nine feet. Her English accent trills so bitchily that everyone in the loft feels their blood curdle.

"Did *you* not order the correct size?" shrieks her business partner, a British man in his fifties, as he throws his hands up in the air. "You did realize she's, like, five-ten and not a lawn gnome, *riiiight?!* Tanya, you can be such a twat …"

"Really, it's okay," Jenna says softly, trying to dial down the tension devouring such a small space, squirming in the couture getups the two goons have put her in. The PVC is uncomfortable and makes her regret having impulsively bought leather pants the week before.

Tanya has a pixie cut with bright blue streaks swiped through her blonde hair. She is sending Alex vibes of hate from across the room, accidentally jabbing a pin into Jenna's skin as she tries to fix the outfit she's dressed her in.

"Oh, sorry, love," she murmurs, still staring at the grey-haired man making stupid faces at her. Alex ridicules her from afar, his eyes narrowing behind the geek chic glasses he's wearing. They start squabbling like kids in a sandbox, but Riley is too occupied with the photographer to tell them to shut it, having become used to acting like a nanny on occasions like these.

The makeup and hair stylists swoop in and pull Jenna towards their station, trying to engage in gossip by asking her about the hot new movie star Carter Sampson. He listed Jenna Ramsay as his top celebrity wish-date. Jenna blushes at the memory of the suave guy and fantasizes about making out with him for her next music video. As if Mack would buy that ploy.

She is dabbed with goos, and clouds of fumes are sprayed around her, creating the "look" of Jenna Ramsay 3.0. The noise of the stylists' constant arguing makes her uneasy and shakes up the environment with negative energy.

There are about a dozen people crammed into the rundown studio where the shoot is happening, each hoping to get a piece of her. They all anxiously radiate an attention-seeking wanting, watching her every move for a chance to butt in and talk to her. To say that they were there with Jenna Ramsay, maybe be lucky to get invited out for lunch if they impress her enough—become a party buddy in her entourage.

"You know what, Tanya—do not start with me right now!" shouts Alex, whipping a tangerine at her from the catering table, narrowly missing her head. Tanya stares at him in disbelief and ferociously insults his argyle sweater-vest.

Jenna looks over her shoulder as she is led from the makeup chair and onto a shiny silver backdrop.

The photographer begins clicking away, instructing Jenna in seven hundred different ways—all at the same time.

Riley is standing at the computer, waiting to see the shots, entrusted by Mack and Kwame to extract something golden for her debut North American cover.

Elle is sitting by the catering table, horrified, watching the scene unfold and feeling like she needs to give Tanya and Alex a time-out. She hugs her green sweater nervously, wishing Ben were there to smooth talk the stylists into submission and protect her from their fashion-forward venom. He has a way with words—must be the lawyer thing. Or the pro-sports-agent thing.

"You fackin' *twat*!" Alex yells, throwing a hanger with an expensive dress down on the ground and stomping on it.

Tanya grabs a half melon and hurls it at him, the pair screaming about what clothes they selected and regretting having gone into business with each other, their odd couple dynamic undeniable.

The scraggly photographer docks his camera, and the shots come up, one by one disappointingly worse than the former.

"This is ridiculous. I cannot work like this!" Tanya screeches, running out, letting the door slam after her exit.

"I told you that Marni would have been a better choice!" Alex screams, violently pushing their rolling rack of clothes.

With that, he also storms off in a huff, overturning the table of tea sandwiches angrily, leaving egg salad in his wake.

Jenna is visibly distraught by the commotion, her face in all the photos tense and awkward, looking out at the fighting instead of focusing on her still-image performance. Elle sits down with her by a set of big bay windows that overlook a field.

"I don't think I can get anything out of her like this. Either these are the photos you use, or they push the cover back an issue," sighs Al, the photographer, packing up his stuff. "I don't have time in my schedule until … two weeks at the earliest."

"So that's it?" Riley asks, annoyed.

"Well, by the time those two got sorted," he starts, motioning to the rolling rack of clothes T & A Stylists brought—and demolished. "They ate into most of your time with me. I have to get back to town and shoot an Agent Provocateur campaign." He shrugs unapologetically, walking out with his assistants.

The rest of the crew pack up and follow the photographer's exit strategy, accepting that there'll be no extra time to hang out with the singer.

Riley grabs her cell phone and calls Tom Rodgers, the record label rep in the UK.

"So you're telling me that they all up and left?" he gasps after Riley informs him of the situation. "T & A are one of the best stylists in the UK! They came with such hype, styled the top models …"

"Yeah, and the photos look like shit. Mack is going to kill me—he left me in charge of getting this cover together," Riley hisses. "Hey, have you ever had to tell Kwame Roy bad news? Probably not, because you're still *alive!*"

"Well, let me see the pictures. Maybe we can digitally alter them … make lemonade out of lemons, if you know what I mean. Keep Jenna calm; she might go nutty with other people fucking with her career …"

"Rightfully so!" Riley exclaims harshly, hanging up and growling with frustration. Her knuckles are white as she grips her phone tightly.

"What's wrong?" Elle asks, as Riley walks up to the paint-chipped window her friends are perched by.

"Well …"

"They look horrible, don't they?" Jenna grimaces.

"I think the set was too much of a distraction," Riley begins to explain, shoving her hands into the pockets of her trench coat and staring away blankly.

Jenna buries her head between her knees, assuming crash-landing position.

"Why don't you change out of that ridiculous outfit?" Elle suggests, laughing at the shiny metallic colours and pleather her friend is squeezed into, like a futuristic S&M doll.

Jenna putters off and returns in a comfy waffle robe, barefoot, her hair let down in relaxed waves. She's clutching her rhinestone-encrusted cell phone and is intensely messaging with someone.

"Whatcha writin'?" Elle winks, while Riley bangs her head on the window rhythmically.

"Carter's back in London and wants to meet up. Said he wants to make the date he wished for in that magazine article a reality," she gushes excitedly, clutching the phone close to her chest.

Elle gasps happily, ever the romantic. "You really like him, don't you?" she whispers, melting at the sweetness of their flirtations.

Jenna nods shyly, actually impressed by his persistence. The regular text messages have kept him on her brain during the busy European promo tour. Definitely more than the long-winded e-mails from Ignacio, sending flowery descriptions about the icy flows of the sea paralleling how cold he feels without her glowing warmth. These distractions are almost enough to stop the burn from Parker's unwavering silence to her e-mails.

"Well, why don't we grab some lunch? Then we'll plan your date!" suggests Elle, fixing her ballet flats.

Riley is still standing by the window, deep in thought and staring out the tall grasses below. Jenna and Elle begin to tidy some of the abandoned clothing for when the stylists return from their outbursts.

Riley glances at her friends and feels the tingle of a miracle.

"Elle." She waves her friend towards her.

"Yeah? I kinda feel like falafel, if that's okay with you …"

"No, Elle … I think I have an idea. Do you have your camera with you?" Riley asks, trying to keep her excitement from surfacing, and eyeing Jenna discreetly.

"Yeah, in the car …"

"I think you need to go get it, and we need to shoot our own cover," Riley instructs calmly, but her brown eyes are shifty with intense determination.

Eleanor pauses, looks at an unassuming Jenna in her robe, and smiles intuitively.

She vanishes for a minute and returns with one of her prized possessions—her new digital camera.

"What's going on?" Jenna asks, curious of the whispering around her. She neatly folds some clothes into a pile and approaches her friends.

"I'm making lemons into lemonade," announces Riley.

"Riley, you're a genius! But tell me what you're thinking." Jenna smiles, trying to figure out the plan.

"Well, if those morons are going to potentially damage your career like that, we are going to fight back. *Rolling Stone* wants you raw, sexy, no-holds-barred, right?"

"Right."

"So let's shoot it ourselves. We know you better than those creeps. Elle—right? Elle?"

"Let's do it!" Elle screeches, throwing a fist into the air.

"Okay, well, we're not marching to the barracks, Eleanor." Jenna laughs. "What do I wear?"

"Nothing. I mean—stay in your robe. They want Jenna uncensored, without the veil. Then you need to be as bare as possible! Relax your hair a bit, let's see what we can cook up." Riley explains.

Elle instructs Riley on adjusting the lighting a bit and starts snapping photos of Jenna by the window.

"I love the texture, you know what—this might actually be great." Elle giggles excitedly. "Lovee, you've gotta let me print some of these for my art show …"

After dozens of e-mails back and forth between Elle and his mother, Hilary, Bryce the Brit helped book her into an open slot at the Hodge Gallery in New York. The photos of her work really interested Hilary Hodge, as did the potential of having Jenna Ramsay as a publicity-generating guest. So, in the late hours after tucking Jenna into bed and before waking her to get primped, Elle has been fastidiously cataloguing and preparing her repertoire. Having an extremely available mother back in Toronto facilitated the documentation of all her works, and the selections were being couriered straight to New York that day.

Not being able to physically be there to bubble wrap her art was frustrating, but willingly overlooked for a chance to host her own showing. It may not be exactly as she had pictured in her head, but something is better than nothing, and the Hodge Gallery is absolutely better than could be expected for Elle's no-name status.

Jenna looks over her shoulder at the camera. "Maybe your show will also help me take the North American market by storm."

"I'm honestly relieved the availability of that gallery worked out with the travel schedule," Riley grumbles, struggling to hold up a reflector. "I don't think I could manage without Elle here …"

"Things happen for a reason," Jenna muses.

"Stop smiling," Elle instructs sharply, taking more photos.

• • •

Late that evening, Mack organizes a conference call to broker a deal between Eleanor Bryans's photographs and the magazine.

He has swept his wife and kid away to London for a few days of shopping, using Top Dog's resources with the excuse of checking in on his priority client. The manager of Jenna's career, the man who took a total unknown to the forefront of pop music—making a mint in the process. He sits on the couch, massaging his temples and feeling annoyed. His suit jacket is carefully draped over the arm of the plush, velvety sofa.

"So, what are we thinking here?" he asks into the speakerphone, taking notes and reviewing proposals simultaneously.

The editor-in-chief of the magazine is less than impressed to hear of his freelance stylists' conduct but is absolutely mesmerized by the images of Jenna Ramsay: Uncut.

"Mack, this nudie shot is it. This is *it*. I'm putting it on the cover," the editor gushes with glee, stroking the flat-screen computer monitor in his New York office. The black-and-white image of Jenna's bare back, face turned to look over her shoulder, with a forest blurred behind her, is reminiscent of an iconic free love moment. The freckles over her body add a sensual tone, her hair waving like a surfer goddess.

"Well, that's about as bare as you're gonna get from her. She turned down *Playboy*." Mack snickers into the phone, and Jenna collapses into muted giggles beside him.

"And these shots by the window … I love it. Raw, just … no couture to hide behind … so anti-high street …" continues the voice.

"Exactly. I'm glad you appreciate the art," Mack replies, rolling his eyes. He's fiddling with his watch, antsy to move on from this call and get to his dinner reservation on time.

Jenna, Elle, and Riley are on the couch across from him in the main room of their suite at the Lanesborough Hotel. They're already changed into sweats and pyjamas, wiped out from their busy day, ready to curl up and hibernate.

He passes them a piece of paper that reads: *How much do you want?*

"Anything you can get!" Elle whispers back, her green eyes wide with amazement that this is even happening.

"The *most* you can get," Jenna corrects.

"So when can we do the interview? With this new direction … I want this exclusive, like, yesterday."

Mack pauses, and checks his phone. "Well, we've got the gig at Top of the Pops tomorrow, and then in New York … then Toronto to regroup … then …"

"No, Mack—not New York," Jenna begs, pointing to Elle—or rather, reminding him of Elle's art show there that weekend.

"So tomorrow is gonna have to work for you," he instructs flatly.

"But before her date!" Elle whispers teasingly, holding Jenna's hand. Jenna blushes, excited to be seeing Carter again.

"Well, I can have a reporter to you at, say, one?" the editor asks.

"Sounds good. To the Lanesborough. Tom from Alchemy will meet them in the lobby," Mack confirms, ending the call.

The girls squeal in delight, hugging each other like preteens.

"I leave you in charge and go to the zoo with my kid …" he jokingly scolds Riley.

"Yeah, well, I think it ended well." She grins, incredibly relieved that her improvisation paid off.

"I can't believe I actually made that much money for my photos," Elle replies, in a trance, staring down at the zeros scrawled by Mack.

"Well, imagine how your show's going to go now! And my picture better be the biggest fucking thing there." Jenna grins broadly, slurping the rest of her supplement-infused smoothie in lieu of dinner.

"You know, J … you gotta prepare yourself for some of the drama that's going to come back at us," Mack warns. "We're in this with you, but obviously we're not the ones people are looking at. Try not to think about any of the negative stuff too much. I know from experience that it is all useless and usually formulated by ignorant shits."

Jenna looks at him and laughs, comforted by his dryness.

• • •

The next morning, the girls are relaxing in tandem massages, blissfully unaware of the tabloid stories hitting UK doorsteps.

"Jenna Ramsay throws diva fit—fires stylists!" reads one headline.

"Exclusive interview: Jenna high maintenance, awful to work for!" reads another.

Mack storms into the master bedroom, where three portable massage beds are lined up neatly. He's clutching various newspapers and exhaling heavily through his nostrils like an angry bull.

"I am like a predicting wizard!" he huffs, catching his breath.

"Mack!" Elle screeches, covering her bare back shyly.

"Sorry, but here's the plan," he states flatly, not caring about anything but his strategy to deflect the backlash.

"What?!" gasps Jenna, grabbing a paper out of his hand, reading the text. Her face twists in shock, and she looks about ready to cry.

He turns to the three ladies doing the rubdowns and stares at them crossly as if they're missing the obvious.

"Uh ... may we be *excused*?" he snaps, annoyed they didn't make themselves scarce automatically.

They hurry out, afraid of the small brash man in the fancy suit. As soon as the doors are shut behind them, Mack lets out his theory.

"They're trying to paint you as becoming a crazy, money-obsessed diva ... you need to use this magazine interview to spin this garbage around," he starts, clasping his hands together in excitement as he paces the room. He's in his element doing crisis management.

"Okay?" Jenna throws the paper to the ground, visibly upset by the content.

Riley tries to reach down for it from the massage table, keeping her chest pressed to the surface, stretching an arm out—painfully close to snatching it.

"Play up your modest roots, that you travel with your two friends, that whole rags-to-riches type of thing as usual. You don't forget the little people. You carry your own luggage. No discussing shopping or anything extravagant. Don't tell them about your new car; you still carpool. No one likes a young girl with a red Maserati who can be portrayed as unappreciative," Mack continues. "Especially one who allegedly fires single parents that don't have health insurance."

"I think this is ridiculous. Clearly, the farthest thing from the truth—she didn't fire them," Elle explains, trying to hide beneath the sheet, frightened by Mack's ferocity.

"Oh, I know. And you know. But they don't get it," Mack explains, eyes fluttering with borderline paranoia. "They don't see what goes on—they *think* they know. Even the paparazzi don't know what goes on, and they're practically in the in-crowd. So we need to tell them what they need to know. New video coming out, big show tomorrow … this is great for us. Need-to-know basis."

There's a thud, and everyone turns to look at Riley's naked body, crumpled on the floor.

"Did you seriously fall off the table?" Mack grimaces.

"Yeah." She laughs, grabbing the newspaper and covering herself.

"Right," he replies, unfazed, and heading for the door. "Going to Bond Street with the fam, interview at one, J," he calls out, reminding the girls of their return to "Schedule-ville: population three."

The girls collapse in laughter, throwing on their robes.

Elle puts her arm around Jenna's waist, comforting her against the negative press, and they head into the dining room.

"I don't understand what I did that they would want to hurt me … to try damage my career," Jenna mumbles softly, as they sit down to brunch. "They were so nice to me before …"

"Well …" Elle trails off, not quite sure how to counteract the self-pity parade.

"Like, is it because they're jealous? Do they hate me?"

"I really think …" Elle continues, wringing her hands as her friend lets dark clouds settle around her.

"Is it because now I have money? A lot of new money?"

Riley looks at Elle across the table, and Elle shrugs back, helpless and unable to penetrate the monologue.

"Why does it matter?" Riley asks bluntly, picking up a muffin.

"What?" Jenna asks distractedly, stirred out of her wallowing daze.

"Why does it matter if they don't like you?"

Jenna pauses a minute. "Um, because they could ruin my career?"

"Do you really think two diva stylists have that much power over you?" Riley asks, sipping her black coffee.

"They could tell the media things—like they did. Lies—like they did. And then people will read that," Jenna rebuts, pushing the scrambled eggs around on her plate.

"Okay, but if the things that they're telling are false, then why get mad about it? You know the truth. The people around you know the truth. Them being assholes doesn't mean that you did something wrong …" Riley tries to explain.

Jenna pauses, pondering the argument.

"Have you ever had someone hate you, Riles?" she asks dryly.

Riley laughs out loud, almost choking.

"Because it's not a nice feeling!"

"Did you forget that you went to high school with me? I was not exactly the valedictorian—no offence, Elle." Riley snickers, acknowledging Eleanor's tear-jerking speech.

"None taken." Elle winks, reaching for some strawberries.

"Okay, so fine—you're dark and edgy and all judgemental-like. That doesn't mean that I'm like that. That doesn't mean that I don't care what people think or that I'm going to start wearing black," Jenna lashes back, grabbing the tabloid paper and storming to her room.

Riley looks to Elle for a weigh-in. "Is it me?"

"No," Elle replies, pouring herself a glass of milk.

"Is it her?"

"No," she sighs. "It's just ... imagine yourself wanting something so bad that it consumes your entire being. You hope and dream and pray that it comes true. And when it does ... maybe the specifics you envisioned aren't exactly dead-on accurate."

Riley nods, listening to her friend.

"You've gotta admit, Riles. The response she's had so far has been ridiculously good. Positive reviews, great press, people *like* her as a person. There's bound to be some downs with the ups."

"Yeah, I know. But I'm worried about when the real bad stuff comes. Because it will, just like you're saying. She's so hell-bent on the Jenna-Flawless-Superstar thing that she's gonna get rocked."

"You know what, she probably will. But Jenna ... she will land on her feet." Elle smiles, thinking positive.

Riley peers at her friend over the World section of the newspaper.

"You need to be gentle."

"Gentle?" Riley scoffs.

"Sometimes you're a little too good with words, lovee." Elle shrugs, heading to get dressed. They've got a major sound check, interviews scheduled all day, and Jenna's performance that evening.

Riley stares at the breakfast spread, feeling like the wind has been knocked out of her. *But that's how I've always been...* she says to herself, a bit wounded by the realization that not everyone may like that about her.

That night, Jenna lets out a shriek as she collapses into the plush leather of her limo, elated. She's in an asymmetrical designer dress, having run straight out the door of the television studio where she's charmed most of the UK with her kick-ass performance and witty banter.

"That was … incredible!" she gasps, feeling high from the rush of having performed on live television—the way the lights warmed her skin, her cheeks flushing with the crowd's excitement. The rush made her feel invincible, like she could see clearer than 20/20 and break concrete with the echo of her voice as she sang her latest song.

When she was ushered out of the studio after, an extra surge of adrenaline kicked things up a notch, with the roar of the crowd outside swelling to a constant, ear-splitting level. The rabid teenage fan base she's accumulated has proven loud, proud, and dedicated to following her every move around the world.

She hyperactively kicks off her blue high heels, carelessly tossing the shoes around. Riley and Elle jump in the car after her. They've also absorbed the insane crowd's energy, watching them cheer on the latest pop sensation—their beloved friend. The door shuts after them, muting the deafening screams of hundreds of people outside.

"The fans … I'm … in awe …" Jenna whispers, a tear coming to her eye as she thinks of the warm audience.

"I think this has been the most real definition of madness to date!" Riley laughs, looking out the tinted windows at the barricaded crowd while the car pulls away.

They are holding hands excitedly, bewildered.

Elle pulls out her cell phone from a quilted Chanel tote and snaps a photo of the three of them, squishing together on the seat.

"Long-arm photography is not my thing." She laughs, having cut off their heads in the shot.

Jenna takes the camera and snaps a neatly centred image of the girls, glowing with happiness. She's shrieking with joy, her eye makeup ultra-dramatic, done up for the television cameras. Riley looks a little annoyed while talking on her cell phone with Kwame. And Elle sits peacefully between them, simply smiling and taking in the moment.

"So what's the plan now?" Riley asks, covering the phone, anxious to get back and review the latest specs of Jenna's tour rider, now including a yoga mat, carbonated water, her favourite lip gloss, and access to massage treatment in her dressing room. They have to be sent to next week's appearances and hotels in preparation of Jenna's arrival.

People are becoming increasingly eager to impress the singer, helping to groom her taste for the finer things in life.

"I gotta change quickly. Carter is going to meet us at the hotel," Jenna squeals excitedly, having been daydreaming all afternoon of her scheduled date.

"Great!" Elle screeches, holding hands with her friend like schoolgirls confessing their first kiss.

Riley looks at the overeager love patrol and contemplates backing out of supervising the date, fearing a serious onset of nausea. They pull up to the hotel's door and sprint past the fans converged out front.

The girls breathlessly step off the elevator and burst into the hotel room, a fury of celebration and happiness. Mack is at the dining table having a quiet candlelit dinner with his gorgeous wife, their toddler already tucked into bed. Elle smiles at Lisa, the former Starbucks barista Mack fell in love with.

"Girls, I hear everything went beyond great," he says, still holding her hand across the table. She looks stunning. Their child was blessed with her aesthetic genes and escaped Mack's stumpiness.

"It was magical, the energy was so ... electric," Jenna whispers dreamily, her vision clouded by instant replays.

"She sounded really good. Fans went nuts," Riley explains, as her two friends rush off to change for the date.

"She's going for dinner with Carter Sampson?" Mack confirms quietly.

Riley nods.

"I would recommend letting her go alone," he says.

"But I thought we were supposed to chaperone," Riley replies, holding a chair back while listening to her boss.

"Yeah, but I got an e-mail from his agent today. This is going to be crafted into a well-photographed excursion. They want him to be associated with her as much as we want her to be seen with a good-looking, successful up-and-comer," Mack explains.

"So they're using her as bait?"

He makes a face indicating he doesn't like her choice of words.

"So they understand there's more here than simply a boy and a girl meeting for foie gras?" she rephrases.

"Yes. Unfortunately, it's not going to be as clean-cut for her in this department. But it's a mutually positive arrangement. So, I would prefer if you and Elle occupied yourselves out of sight this time," he instructs.

Riley nods, relieved not to have to listen to any of Carter's smooth talking or to watch Jenna lap it up.

"So, looking to this week … in New York, you'll meet Hana. She's from my LA office and will oversee breaking into the American market. Now that 'Look at This' is number one there, we're gonna have to add in a lot of time stateside to do this right."

"Wow, that came a lot faster than I thought …" Riley trails off, amazed how quickly her popularity is covering the globe. "What about Canada?"

Mack bites his lip pensively.

"Maybe a few appearances when she's home for a break—but really, our focus has to be on where she's hit a nerve. I mean, Carter's agent has proposed having Jenna as his date to the *Felons* movie premiere in New York. It would be the night before the gallery show, so I went ahead and made the arrangements."

Riley silently grimaces at having to monitor her friend on yet another red carpet, to pull her along the conveyor belt of nosy cameras and overzealous reporters. She retreats from the candlelit dinner and heads to talk to Elle.

"Mack wants us to steer clear of the happy couple," she announces, walking in on her friend half dressed.

"Holy wow—you could knock!" She laughs, stunned by the intrusion and trying to dive for cover.

"Oh, sorry. Anyway, yeah … how do you feel about taking it easy tonight?" Riley suggests.

Elle's face relaxes into a look of elation at the thought of staying in with comfort food and watching a movie in her pyjamas.

"I honestly haven't had a decent conversation with Ben in days," she sighs, the extent of their hectic schedule finally showing on her ever-cheery demeanour. "It's been four months since we … kissed … if you know what I mean."

"Well, let him know you'll be around—see if you can get some time in on Skype or something after supper. I'll go tell Jenna." Riley smiles.

She takes off her heels halfway down the hall, relieved to be "at home." The bedrooms they've been sleeping in never look familiar; she wakes up in the middle of the night and never knows where the light switch is.

She knocks on Jenna's door and enters.

"I don't know which one to wear …" her friend whines, holding up two outfit choices torn straight from their garment bags.

Riley looks at them uneasily, neither option being quite her preferred style.

"Jenna, Mack wants to let you go alone with Carter tonight," she starts, trying to avoid having to give an opinion about two certifiably ugly looks. Just because it's expensive doesn't mean it's nice.

Jenna looks at her friend, surprised.

"But look at it this way—now you'll have one-on-one time to get to know him ... and I won't be falling asleep in my soup." Riley laughs.

Jenna shrugs, secretly ecstatic to have him to herself, and to convincingly play up to the rock star persona she loves, without people who knew her before the glamour to act as lie detectors.

"And I'd go with the red tights—they'll photograph better," Riley blurts out.

Did I give my opinion based on paparazzi shots? she thinks, horrified.

Jenna ponders the point and begins to change into the red bottoms and a black dress.

"You think I'll be photographed?" she asks her friend wringing her hands together anxiously.

Riley can't help but laugh—she's fishing for compliments.

"You have yet another number one single here. Of course you're going to be photographed." She rolls her eyes.

Jenna smiles to herself as her friend shuts the bedroom door on her way out. People are taking notice. In a big way.

• • •

Carter Sampson gazes across the dinner table at his date. The glow of the dim mood lighting gives her a heaven-sent look, her long blonde hair cascading like a goddess. He reaches his hand out, softly laying it on top of hers, the sleeve of his brown cord blazer showing a thick leather cuff underneath. A man-bracelet.

"I'm really happy to see you," he says slowly but confidently as he looks steadily into her big blue eyes.

Jenna smiles and looks away shyly. She's on top of the world. The feeling of being on the arm of a hot guy, as they're dressed to the nines, has caused her to radiate a confidence that's a high unlike any other. And then to be swarmed by curious photographers and adoring fans camped outside of her hotel—that was icing on the publicity cake.

"I wish we could see each other more often, you know. Being with you … I don't feel like this with other people. They don't make me feel the way you do," he whispers, speaking so she has to lean in close to listen. To look into his expressive, light eyes.

Jenna feels connected by hearing him talk about the same excitement she's feeling. His sandy brown hair is longer and has new lowlights in it. He looks as if he's torn straight out of *GQ*—chiselled, handsome, and modernly debonair.

"I know what you mean. Since this all started … the way people look at me, it's like all they care about is the image. Not who I am underneath," she sighs, feeling that he is psychically on the same page as her—knows what the rollercoaster ride is like and can feel the image that is imposed by the public eye.

Carter nods dramatically. "Did you know that *Felons* is expected to debut number one at the box office next weekend? I can understand what you're saying—because now all people see is me detonating explosives and flashing a gun … they don't see me how you know me," he says, taking the last sip of his wine. "It's like I'm all alone on an island; I'm not free to be myself because it pales in comparison to the characters I play."

Jenna nods dreamily, twirling a strand of hair absentmindedly.

"So, tell me about yourself—what do you want from life? Your hopes and dreams. I want to know about you as a human being," he says, touching her forearm with a finger.

Jenna blinks at the contact, and part of her wonders if his line about knowing her as a "human being" is total bullshit.

"Well … I guess … this *is* my dream, really. I've wanted this since I was a kid. Prayed for it so hard that I couldn't even … I mean, I'm not super religious or anything, but it was as if all this wouldn't be happening without some sort of divine assistance, know what I mean?"

"Exactly. If I wasn't the snowboarding instructor to a casting director during his vacation, I never would have been spotted for my first modelling campaign. It's funny how things seem to flow sometimes, don't you think?"

Jenna stares at him adoringly.

"Do you wanna get out of here?" he asks, looking around mischievously, all the restaurant patrons.

Jenna nods, and their bill is brought to the table.

Carter grabs the chequebook and slides his credit card in without looking at the total.

"Really?" Jenna asks, totally surprised and more than prepared to pay for at least her share of the meal. It's become customary that she foot bills in social situations—people expect it when the news reports how many millions of dollars she's now worth. And Top Dog uses the expenses as write-offs.

"Hey, you're my date tonight. It might seem old school, but that's just how I am," he says, his masculinity flooring her schoolgirl heart.

They walk out of the trendy restaurant, and the photographers start snapping pictures furiously, bathing them in flashes of light. Carter grabs Jenna's hand, and she feels instantly protected by this suave and charming guy. She is thrilled to be led down the sidewalk by his alpha male presence. The cameras only get more aggressive at the sign of affection, and as they block their faces. The two slip into her chauffeured car to return to the hotel.

They head up to the large suite, but everyone has already gone off to bed.

"I didn't realize it was so late." Jenna laughs, looking at her new diamond-encrusted Cartier watch—a small gift to herself to celebrate her latest #1.

"Maybe I should go?" Carter asks, feigning an uncertainty about intruding into her luxurious living quarters.

"Don't be silly … do you … want … a drink?" Jenna asks, not sure what else to do to entertain him at this hour. She's had enough to be past the point of tipsy, but the last thing she wants is for his magical, magical presence to wear off.

He smiles and nods, and they crack open the minibar.

"You know what …" he starts, taking a sip of his drink and shrugging off his blazer. He's wearing a tight white T-shirt underneath that shows off his lean but gym-sculpted body.

Jenna feels her chest constrict.

"Never mind," he sighs.

"What?"

"No, nothing. It's silly," he says.

"What? Come on—you can't leave me like that." She laughs, as they sit down beside each other on the couch.

He exhales dramatically.

"I was going to ask you something, but I don't want you to get freaked out."

Jenna looks at him, so curious to know.

"I don't want you to be spooked. It's just that I like you a lot … I wanted to know if you'd be my date to the movie's premiere in New York," he whispers. "If you're not busy … obviously."

Jenna looks at him and blushes. That's the big, scary question?

"Carter—are you kidding me? Of course I would." She beams.

"I know that girls get scared of the slightest sign of the commitment thing—I don't want you to think I'm moving too fast …"

Jenna raises an eyebrow. *Girls get scared? Isn't it usually the other way around?*

"I would love to," she trills, already thinking of what outfit to wear on the red carpet. Maybe the new Alberta Ferretti gown she saw in the look book …

"Well, there'll be a lot of press, and … you'll be photographed with me …" he explains.

Jenna nods, overjoyed that he wants to be publicly labelled with her.

"I didn't know … how you see me. People love to make guys out to be womanizers and all that—party boys. How do you see me?"

Jenna looks into his eyes, as he searches for her description of who he is.

"I think … you're trying to balance it all out. People want you to be one thing to them—the guy with the money, the guy with the girls, the guy with the cool connections. I get that. And maybe you're trying to still be yourself … even though now people expect certain things from you. I have the same problem. People want me to be one thing, when maybe, that's only part of who I am."

He nods slowly, not really following her. He was expecting the simple answers that tend to be given by girls he's seducing: you're great, you're fun, you're sexy.

"I gotta pee," she whispers randomly, and sneaks off.

Carter gets up and strolls to the window. He sucks back his drink and pours himself another, stronger one. He stares out at the city below, putting his hand in the pocket of his flashy Rock & Republic jeans, trying to find a seductive way of leaning against the wall, flexing his arms slightly.

He is amazed to be in a fancy hotel with a hot (superstar) girl and already being recognized on the street as an actor. He's come a long way from being a snowboard instructor at Whistler in British Columbia, from being discovered to model in a Tom Ford campaign, and then being cast in *Felons* as the "handsome thief" character.

He hears a noise, as Jenna stumbles into a table reentering the room, the alcohol clearly showing.

He smiles to himself, excitedly sensing her guard dropping.

"Hey, there ..." he greets softly as she shuffles up.

"Shh! Don't be loud—Riley will be mad!" she hisses jokingly, actually quite loud herself. She's staring at him in his tight T-shirt, trying to force her eyes to look at the ground instead of his pecs.

Stop staring ... she tells herself forcefully.

"Oh. Okay, I gotcha." He nods, sneaking a glance at her long and lean body when she bends down to the coffee table to pick up her drink.

"If we can't talk here, where should we go?" he asks, full well knowing that he has no intention to keep talking and getting to know her softer side.

Jenna bites her lip, thinking really hard. Her blue eyes bulge when she realizes that the only place left is her bedroom—but that it also has a bed.

Hoooly crap ... if we go there, we're going to ... oh my, she thinks to herself, trying to decide whether to let him into her private space. *I've been so focused on becoming famous that ... shit, I haven't fooled around with anyone in, what, like a year? Good grief ... he's so hot.*

The full moon shines on him like a spotlight, looking even more dangerous to touch.

Jenna takes his hand and leads him towards her room quietly.

He closes the door behind him and aggressively moves to her, pushing her up against a wall. He's recalling the gritty sex scene he shot for the movie, the heat he had to muster take after take.

Jenna's head is spinning with excitement. He's fully focused his intensity on her, and it's mesmerizing. The power of his rough touch makes her feel delicate. He leans in and bites at her neck, and she fumbles to undo the button on his jeans.

responsibilities.

[New York City, USA—September 2010]

"Is this seat taken?"

Riley turns from her martini glass and locks eyes with an absolutely stunning male-model wannabe.

He motions to the empty barstool beside her.

"Oh! Oh … uh-huh …" she stammers, caught off-guard by his jet-black eyes.

"Oh." He shrugs, about to turn and walk away.

"No, I mean—the seat is free." She laughs, flustered at her delayed reaction, distracted by his sheer … beauty. Probably in his early thirties, with a chiselled jaw, black hair, evenly tanned skin. And an impeccable grey suit, unbuttoned after a long workday.

He grins and displays an immaculate, orthodontic set of whitened teeth. "Simon." He winks, putting out his hand for a firm handshake.

"Riley." She smiles warmly, as he lowers himself to the seat.

She's alone, holed up at the Thom bar in New York to decompress among the hipsters at the artistic watering hole.

After the tense moments in London, she's been keeping her distance from Jenna—wallowing a lot in front of her laptop, trying to actually finish the so-called book she claims to be writing. Today's flight from Heathrow was silent treatment enough from her blonde friend, Jenna feeling vindictive towards Riley's harsh tone for criticizing her overnight guest in the UK.

Riley and Elle had quite the surprise when Carter Sampson sleepily sauntered up to the breakfast table in his boxer shorts. Elle was left blushing and trying to ignore his bare-chested search for coffee, as Riley contemplated the ramifications of him having stayed the night with Jenna in London.

How would this affect her publicly, but also personally, in terms of having slept with him so quickly?

So this first evening in NYC, Jenna and Elle are out at the *Felons* party with Mack's U.S. rep, Hana Rin, surely venting about Riley's stifling qualities and dishing about girl stuff, while being schmoozed by Carter.

Leaving the sourpuss to stare into her martini, trying to foretell the future from the crystal clear gin. The black trousers she's wearing are sitting a little too tightly but looks polished with a sleek white dress shirt—like an upscale waitress.

"So, Riley, are you from the city?" Simon asks, ordering a single-malt for himself.

"No, actually. I'm in town for work." She smiles, turning to face him, suddenly feeling encouraged to be social. To turn over a new leaf and be friendly, instead of being suspicious of every guy's intentions when striking up a conversation.

"Oh, that's great. How long are you here?"

"A couple of days."

Awkward silence.

"So Simon, what do you do here in New York?"

He lights up with the conversation turned to him, it seems. Eyes crinkling, he swallows his drink.

"I took over the family business. Was in finance, but did a bit of a shift in careers. Needed something a little more ... I don't know ... else. Something more. I recently moved into a new place, actually. A penthouse with tons of glass, very modern styling—cost a fortune," he explains, gesturing about ceiling heights and the cost of living in the city. "But business is good. I've got eight cars in my garages, recently traded in my Jag for the new Panamera. Now I can pick a new car every day of the week."

"But there are only seven days in a week ..."

"Exactly."

Riley stares at him uncomfortably. Her father always taught her that ostentatious wealth was a sign of male overcompensation. He'd share comical dating advice with her girlfriends, teaching them how to weed out greedy men who more than likely try to distract for their small potential and poor manners. *If he drops his real estate, cars, or stock portfolio in the first minute, drop him.*

"And what about you, Riley? I'm hogging the conversation. What do you do?" He puts a hand on her arm, flashing the smile. The perfect smile.

"I'm a personal assistant." She shrugs self-deprecatingly.

Simon nods, and orders another round for them. "Nothing wrong with that. Some people are better at working under others," he starts. Riley tilts her head to the side, amused by the alternate interpretation of his comment. "I mean, they're able to take instruction better. Like, for me, I could never be an assistant to anyone. I'm better at being a dictator." He laughs emptily.

"Yeah, it's not really like that …"

"Who do you work for? The perks must be great," he offers.

"That they are. Free stuff, world travel, luxury accommodations, time to work on my writing," she says, more to herself than to him, trying to be convincing.

"Writing? What kind of writing?" he asks slyly.

"Well …"

"You know, I was a writer. Actually had quite the artsy past in my Ivy League days. Before I grew up, know what I mean? Before the responsibilities. I was actually a poet. Won some awards."

Oh, my God, we're back to him, she thinks to herself, swallowing gulps of the martini, panicking that she's engaged with an egomaniac.

It's safe to say that tonight, in New York City, Riley Kohl has not met her future husband. Only a self-absorbed guy who likes to talk about his assets.

A writer before he had any responsibilities—what the hell is that supposed to mean? she thinks, insulted.

"Really? That's funny! What did you write?" she asks, wondering if he can recall any of the "immature" dallies from his past. Maybe a term paper or some other example of his abilities.

"Oh, wow, that's so long ago. I can't even remember …" he trails off, chuckling. He hikes up his sleeve, displaying his fancy watch, but not so subtly.

Riley clears her throat anxiously and opens her mouth to start a sentence, but he jumps in.

"Four winds blowing through the sky,
You have seen poor maidens die,
Tell me then what I shall do
That my lover may be true.

That's one of my favourites." Simon grins.

She raises an eyebrow. "You wrote *that*?"

He smiles. "Good, huh?"

Riley stares at him, feigning shock at his massive capacity for creative expression.

"Yeah. I won an award for it." He winks, putting a hand on her bare knee. Riley curbs the impulse to hit him.

"Really? That's …"

"You know, Riley," he interrupts. "Writing … is actually a lot harder than you seem to think. It's not like saying you're into photography or art or something. Everyone with a digital camera is into photography these days. Writing … is … for someone who has iron balls. Not like Virginia Woolf shit. And such a beautiful, *young* woman … you're an assistant …" he says, trying to explain some sort of misogynistic theorem of vocations.

"Aw … thank you, Simon. That gives me a lot to think about." She gives a fake smile, pulling out her wallet, ready to run and lock herself in the hotel room and vomit from his pretentiousness.

"Don't worry about it, babe," he smiles, pulling out his credit card.

"Really, it's okay," she replies dryly, pulling out her black, Top Dog-issued American Express card, winning the game of "mine's bigger."

He looks down at her plastic and looks back at her, sizing up from head to toe the brunette before him.

Riley hands the card to the bartender, rolling her eyes. He snickers sympathy, having observed the entire encounter with Simon: Superior Being to All Humans. He's an obnoxious regular who never tips.

"So, do you want to come check out my new place?" he asks, finishing the rest of his drink, trying his luck with one last attempt to get laid.

"That's okay, Simon." She smiles dryly, signing the receipt.

"I could teach you a bit more about publishing, show you some of my stuff." He grins. But his chiselled jaw doesn't have the same effect anymore.

Riley snaps the receipt holder closed. "Four winds blowing through the sky …" she repeats.

Simon winks at her like a slimy pervert.

"I really should be more grateful to be in the presence of a Pulitzer winner," she says to the bartender. "I had no idea that Sara Teasdale was alive and well, what, almost one hundred years after winning her poetry award?"

Simon's eyes pop.

"Oh, don't look so shocked. I may be a pretty lady, but that doesn't mean I'm an idiot. I studied literature at Oxford, you moron. Next time you go around bootlegging famous authors, pick something a little less dated, or pick a girl who doesn't notice your receding hairline."

"Ooh shit!" gasps the bartender happily. Every night, he's watched Simon trolling the bar and distracting women with his money like a grimy magician, and treating the wait staff like subhuman servants. But tonight, this broad has stuck it to him.

Riley heads to the door, walking slowly and throwing her shoulders back.

Walk like a football player, was Jenna's advice to her when she first started learning to wear heels. And by this, she simply meant, try to look confident. Her ankles wobble a little in the black sling-backs, but she exits with superior grace.

Riley's face is burning from the audacity of such a twerp. She slides into the elevator of the Thompson hotel, pulling out her BlackBerry and furiously typing up a note.

> *So what if you're good-looking, if you have money, a fancy house, or a powerful last name? Instead of belittling others by exaggerating your accomplishments, wouldn't it be more beneficial to society if you chose to affect the people around you for better rather than bring them down to subservience? To be the bigger man, the better man, and not have to inflate yourself to surpass any pathetic insecurities you possess. Not reduce others into nothingness to feel like all you've done and worked towards is actually worth something. Because it's not—I don't give a shit.*

She saves the thought for future inspiration; maybe she could develop a character out of Simon's sociopathic tendencies.

Her inbox chimes with a message from Mack.

This was passed on by Tom in London.

Riley opens the attachment and finds pictures of Carter manhandling a woman who is clearly not Jenna.

She grimaces at the new hurdles this will bring, particularly after being Carter's date at his premiere.

Is this out already? she types back to her boss.

Not yet. I'm sure they'll be sold fast, though. This was his night out in Paris. Guys night out, if you will.

Riley groans to herself. This is going to be great news to deliver to a friend with whom she's already skating on thin ice.

debutante.

[New York City, USA—September 2010]

Elle Bryans steps out of a New York yellow cab and onto the curb, a crescent moon starting to show in the sky. Her leather satchel is overflowing with extra supplies and weighing down her petite shoulder. She distractedly hands the cab driver a 50-dollar bill, overtipping him gingerly. He screeches away right as she realizes her mistake.

"Silly money is all the same colour," she growls to herself, stuffing the Gucci wallet Jenna gave her into her bag. She hops over a puddle, not wanting to soak her TOMS and flared jeans.

Elle walks through the doors of the Hodge Gallery, ready to inspect her artwork on display that evening, to check that all her pieces were carefully transported from her parents' basement and set up appropriately.

"Miss Bryans, welcome. Here is the pamphlet you sent, copied for your guests." The overly perky curator smiles, her bright, multicoloured clothes eccentric and mismatched. She hands Elle the sample to review, examining the young artist discreetly.

"Thank you. I'd like to walk through, before everyone gets here." Elle smiles, handing her a garment bag of clothes she'll change into. Jenna tried to stock her full of designer dresses before leaving the hotel, advising her friend that meeting potential clients in a boring pantsuit was not a smart business decision.

"Of course. Right this way," says the woman, leading Elle through a set of French doors and into a large oval-shaped room. The white walls arch up into a dome-like ceiling, almost as if walking into an egg. The soft lighting gives the large space a strange glow.

Elle's paintings and photographs are neatly lining the gallery's walls in different segments. A series from her self-destructive college years starts the show—violent, dark colours painted in oil. She walks towards the "reawakening" portion of her art, where the colours tone down in ferocity and become more abstract. She continues to smaller, more colourful pieces and her experiments in pottery and glasswork, and finally to her recent photographic endeavours, most notably the images of Jenna debuting in *Rolling Stone*, which have been blown up to monstrous proportions.

"Is everything all right, Miss Bryans?" chirps the middle-aged woman, trying so hard to be youthful in arm-warmers and gunmetal nail polish. She's trailing after Elle like a creepy stalker.

"Oh, yes, perfect. I am so happy you grouped these together," Elle coos, motioning to photos of Ben placed beside photos of architecture in Toronto.

"Oh yes, they felt so ... homey, comfortable. I could imagine myself feeling the love, wanting that love from a man as tough as this guy—with his hair and the gaze," she bullshits.

"Yes," Elle replies emptily, wanting to get rid of the woman.

"And this photo of Jenna Ramsay ... stunning. I am so amazed you were contracted to shoot her cover," she starts. "For an unknown, it is truly amazing—they sure took a gamble on you!"

Elle raises an eyebrow to the backhanded compliment and the lady snaps her mouth shut, attempts to backpedal, and then gives up.

"Well, I'll confirm that the catering is perfect, and then stow your bag in the bathroom so you can freshen up before the guests arrive."

"Thank you; you are too kind." Elle smiles sweetly, relieved she's retreating.

The gallery employee heads to the exit.

"Oh, excuse me ...? Is Mrs. Hodge going to be here?" Elle calls after her, trying not to shout in the echo-y space.

"Oh, no, dear. She's in Barbados. But she sends her best," the curator says, curtseying strangely.

Elle continues her walk down the exhibit, vividly remembering some of the moments where her ideas materialized. As soon as she hears the doors close, she begins peeling off the price cards placed by her artwork.

How incredibly tacky! No one knows who I am; how can they equate my work in dollars like this? It's like saying, 'Hey, I'm the new kid—this is how much I think I'm worth,' she thinks to herself, collecting the neatly printed numbers. Her tiny canvas shoes are silent on the marble floor as she moves about the egg.

Elle walks to the centre of the room and takes a deep breath, staring at the images in front of her.

I can't believe it's actually happening ... here ... now.

She closes her eyes, thinking about Ben getting ready in her hotel room. The timing of this showing turned out to be picture perfect. His main client, the current hotshot right-winger for the Toronto Maple

Leafs, is in town playing against the New York Rangers tomorrow night. So Ben took the opportunity to fly in for some face time with his hockey star, discuss potential endorsement deals, maybe grab a hot dog—and, of course, see his globetrotting girlfriend.

Elle checks her cocktail watch—it's nearing 7:00 PM.

Gosh, I gotta hurry up. Frazzled, she hurries out. Breezing through the lobby, she grabs a glass of Chardonnay from the makeshift bar. A huge bouquet of fresh flowers is positioned by a wall, calla lilies exploding joyously and releasing their sweetness into the air. Elle stops to examine it. A card is tucked inside from her parents, who are on a vacation. She smiles to herself, happy to be there on her own, having insisted that they not disrupt their travels.

She skips downstairs to the bathroom and locks the door. She cautiously stares at herself in the mirror, reevaluating her position in life.

Great boyfriend, great jobs, good health, good friends, healthy parents ... She checks off her list, mentally. *Life is pretty good right now! And you know what, Eleanor—things are going to be even better! When you leave this Jenna insanity, you're going to get married and have a gallery, and then get some children in the mix once you and Ben are settled. Five-year plan.*

She unzips her garment bag and pulls out a stunning dark green Zac Posen dress. The muted satin shines just enough to bring out her eyes, looking even more like emeralds.

Classic black Louboutin round-toe pumps follow, and a touch of makeup seals the deal. Elle smiles at the polished Victorian doll she sees in the mirror, her light red hair neatly fastened to the side.

She lowers the toilet seat cover and sits down to recentre herself and prepare for the big debut.

Pranic breathe, relax ... om ... ommm ... she hums to herself, getting yogic.

In her silenced state, she begins to hear the commotion growing in the lobby above. Her cell phone vibrates on the sink.

Hey, where r u? Laith Bassel's here! reads Riley's text message.

Laith Bassel? One of the most influential art critics in all of North America? Arguably *the* career make-or-breaker in New York?

Hurry the F up! reads her second transmission from upstairs.

Elle gathers herself and takes a deep breath, walking to the stairs. As she turns the landing, she feels the blood in her cheeks burn with excitement, seeing people streaming into her event.

Riley is anchored to the drink table, never one to go out of her way to mix and mingle.

"Hey, nice of you to show!" She winks, handing Elle a bottle of fizzy water. "Quite a crowd you're accumulating, lovee." She motions to the 50-odd spectators already noshing on the mini-croissants.

"Bassel?" is all Elle can squeak out, wide-eyed.

"Yeah, the last I saw, he was working through your dark years." She laughs, grabbing her friend's arm and leading her towards the display room.

"Elle!" calls a man, bursting through the gallery doors.

They turn to see Ben rushing in through the crowd, holding a bouquet of pink roses.

Elle hugs him fiercely, discreetly smelling his woodsy cologne. His gentle brown eyes shine happily as he pulls away. Riley saunters to wait by the exhibit's entrance, awkward with public displays of affection.

"How is everything going?" he asks his girlfriend, kissing her quickly. She doesn't have far to go to kiss Ben, who stands roughly five-six. Compact, slim, and the poster children of luxury and poise, they suit each other perfectly. He's in a black crewneck sweater and dress pants, deviating from his standard suit and tie. Even out of the hockey arena, he finds it hard to dress down, constantly trying to look the image of a polished negotiator.

"Oh my, I was about to introduce myself to one of the biggest art critics in the States ... I am so glad you are here," she confesses, nervously clutching her flowers.

"Baby, you don't need me ... go on ahead," he encourages, nuzzling her, proud that she wants him by her side, but anxiously looking around the room for someone rather important.

There is a burst of flashbulbs out on the street, and everyone's attention is drawn to the door. In saunters a prototypical pro athlete, dressed in casual but polished designer jeans and a sport coat. His shaggy blonde hair is light in colour, his complexion milky and complementing his blue eyes. Hunter White is the masculine hockey star believed to hold the power to resurrect a losing dynasty in a hockey town. Hero. The chosen one. Toronto's hockey deity.

"Hunter! I want you to meet Elle," gushes Ben excitedly, waving him over.

The thick, six-foot-three tower of power casually struts up to them, his dress shirt untucked but crisp under a charcoal blazer. Brown suede loafers walk the walk only an It Guy can walk.

"Elle, this ... this is Hunter. Hunter, *this* is Elle." Ben beams.

"My lady, a pleasure to finally meet ya. This guy won't stop talking about Elle this, Elle that, so it's about frickin' time," he snorts, playfully punching Ben's shoulder, a slight Southern drawl on his words. You can take the boy outta the country, but you can't take the country outta the boy!

Ben winces but maintains his smile and the small talk, as his shoulder throbs from the punch.

"Shit, damn, who is that?" Hunter blurts out, cutting off his agent. He turns his attention from the happy couple to a brunette impatiently standing by the door. Riley is tapping her wrist, trying to sign to Elle that the time of Laith Bassel is imminent.

"That ... would be my date ... grab a drink, come in, help me break the ice," Elle pleads. She hurries across the foyer, shaking hands with strangers as she passes, and melts into the gallery.

"Dude, set that shit up." Hunter gestures, watching Riley blend in behind Elle. Her black dress fits like a glove; studded heels add a rebellious rocker touch to her look. "You want a beer?"

"Okay." Ben grins meekly.

"That's my boy. No bitch drink shit tonight! We gotta get you off those."

Ben shrugs helplessly, wishing the gallery had a blender for daiquiris instead.

Hunter heads up to the cash bar and grabs two bottles, the women in the gallery turning to smile at his handsome presence. Being tall and muscular never got him attention until Ben introduced him to a personal shopper and the realm of designer clothes. Elevating his image, polishing his presence—the new face of his new hockey team. But this also put him on the radar of materialistic women who could evaluate the blend of his cashmere from afar (and therefore his income). He's had so many people throw themselves at him without even asking his name, only under the pretence that he's a professional athlete. Whether an elite performer or not, all that mattered was that he played in the big leagues. He could be the most underachieving player and still be relevant, but if he was pushed down to the farm team, then the pickings got slimmer.

He hands Ben one of the beers, politely smiling back at the females eyeing him, and he and Ben stroll into the gallery briskly.

He begins examining the dark and twisted images on the wall, fascinated by one in particular. It's predominantly black-and-red paint on a glass surface—spiderwebbed and shattering. The piece is titled

Stormy Days Turn into Nights and looks like the end of a tornado he witnessed in Missouri while in rookie training camp three years ago. The spare ice rink got demolished, and the team had to drive an hour out of the way for practice.

A man in a fine striped cardigan walks up and asks Hunter what has him so enthralled in the piece. He recalls the story for the older man, with some colourfully vivid detail, as Ben listens in. He points to the corner of the piece, where the black paint seems to drown the red.

"It's like the air, the dust settling over you, making it hard to breathe," Hunter explains of the destructive debris. "Totally freak natural disaster—shook up all the guys on the team who had relocated down with their families."

"That's quite interesting that you found a connection in such a way." The man smiles thoughtfully, studying his response intently.

"Yeah, I actually think I need to buy this now," Hunter admits. "Are you the broker?"

The man smiles, pooh-poohing the athlete, and extends his hand, introducing himself as Laith Bassel.

"Mr. Bassel, it's a pleasure. Ben Roberts—I'm Hunter's agent." Ben extends his hand firmly, recognizing the name.

He returns the handshake.

"Nice to meet you … but really, do you know who can sell this to me?" Hunter laughs, not caring who the man is.

Elle and Riley casually walk up to the group of men, having spotted their mark.

"Elle, really … I need to get this thing," Hunter tells her.

"I'm glad you like it, Hunter." She smiles warmly. "Mr. Bassel, I am so happy you could come." She turns, introducing herself to the famous columnist.

"I'm glad I came! The past few shows … so inaccessible to non-industry people. You could never fathom how highbrow it's been lately. But tonight …" starts Laith, looking around at the mixed crowd drawn to the hip gallery. "Hilary Hodge must think herself a genius for drawing in so much new blood!"

"Hey, if you can get a twenty-one-year-old jock like him to want to buy art, then I think you've done well." Ben winks, patting Hunter's wide shoulder.

"Exactly. But I do have a few questions, Ms. Bryans. May we walk?" asks Laith, looking to the photographs at the end of the hall.

"Five grand," Riley says to Hunter.

"What?"

"Five thousand dollars. The piece. It's five thousand dollars. American." She smiles dryly.

"Don't I get a discount?" He winks, elbowing Ben.

"That is the discount." Riley grins.

"Even if I'm a celebrity?"

"You haven't scored a goal in forever. Your team is at the bottom of their conference. People in Toronto don't even necessarily like you. Why don't you win a trophy, and then we'll see," she snorts. "It's not like you're Dave Matthews or anything."

Hunter stares at her, astounded. Ben swallows his beer, shifty-eyed.

"What? I sometimes see the sports section of the paper …" Riley shrugs. "We spend a lot of time travelling."

Ben bursts out in laughter. "Dude, she fucking told you," he howls.

"Tomorrow," challenges Hunter, referring to his game against the New York Rangers.

"I think that's a threat," Ben observes.

"Yes, yes, it is," Hunter squints mischievously.

Riley shrugs coyly, slurping the last of her water and glancing at Elle and Laith as they make rounds around the room. She sneaks a look back at Hunter, smiling at his competitive nature.

"You know, Miss Bryans, there's been quite a lot of talk about you lately. I was curious to see what all the fuss was about." Bassel smiles, turning his head to the young artist. "When Hilary told me she would host a relative unknown, my curiosity was quite aroused."

"I'm hoping that you don't find yourself disappointed by the speculation." Elle smiles sweetly, crinkling her rosy cheeks like a child star. People are casually watching them stroll around, hoping for a chance to get to talk to the famous Laith Bassel, but too intimidated to step up and interrupt them.

"Actually, any time I go to shows, I try to hold zero expectation. You know, that way you're not perpetually disappointed when people fail to meet your standards." He grins wryly. "But I like you. I like your spunk. I think you've got a lot to offer. It only needs to be refined a little."

Elle nods, carefully listening to his criticisms.

"I've been in this game for over thirty years, Miss Bryans. My take is that I think that your photography holds the key to the next level for you. Yes, you're good at smearing paint around. But I think your dimension is in what you see of other people through the lens," he explains.

They stop at the photo of Ben.

"See this ... this is your boyfriend, the hockey agent?"

She nods, listening intently.

"To most people, they would see a prick bastard."

Elle's jaw drops. Ben has the ability to project rigidity but is anything but frightening with her.

"Well, I'm saying, they would see the surface—a typical agent. Money hungry like a damn piranha. But in this picture, the contracts, the politics, the negotiations, the bullshit ... is the furthest thing from visible. In this picture, he just is who he is. And you capture that without being cheesy."

Elle looks at her black-and-white print. Ben is on a hammock, fast asleep, a book on his chest. A very raw depiction that contrasts the slick, designer suit–wearing, sports car–driving man most people know him as.

"Next time you're in New York, we should talk about how you're moving forward. Maybe introduce you to my circle," he suggests, handing her a business card. "Almost like brainstorming, if you will. I would hate for you to lose the great momentum you've got. So many young ones do—get caught up with the first whiff of attention."

They're now standing in front of the massive print of Jenna. Bare back, head looking over her freckle-covered shoulder, pouty lips and all.

"Congratulations on the cover, by the way. My wife loves it." Laith winks.

He steps away and exits discreetly.

His wife? Paula Brown, the fashion photographer? She loves my picture? Elle shivers nervously. *Oh myyy!*

Elle stares up at the black-and-white photo, thanking her lucky stars for the connections Jenna's situation has blessed her with. It's as if the Earth has stood still for just a moment, as she stares off, frozen by the compliment.

But there's a sudden eruption of noise and commotion, and Elle turns to see Jenna breeze in through the French doors of the room like a cyclone.

Her silence is stirred.

Jenna's high-waisted leather skirt matches the bright purple crocodile clutch she's holding.

"Where's Elle?" she calls out, throwing off her black leather jacket and handing it to the blonde woman beside her.

Hana Rin is the new member of her management contingent, straight out of the offices of Top Dog in California. The high-glossed, sexed-up tigress Mack has assigned to transition Jenna into an American dream. She's half Japanese and is the definition of hot LA style with her blonde extensions, deep tan, and artificial nails. She's in her early thirties, but passes for younger by sipping from the fountain of youth.

Elle is a little uneasy about seeing Hana again so quickly, having hung with her at Carter's movie afterparty the night before. Hana would only talk to men with ostentatious accessories, regardless of whether that was their platinum wedding band or platinum credit card. Although certainly perfect for being a cutthroat celebrity manager, Elle found herself wondering how her high-maintenance dynamic would influence their daily lives going forward. She had arranged for their car service to drive them only in flashy Cadillac Escalades, and forced Jenna into a hefty push-up bra before leaving the hotel, all the while dropping hints about breast augmentation's benefits.

Jenna zeros in on her target and beelines straight for her friend, her hair glowing from a refreshed dye job with complicated lowlights. It's as if she's gliding, not even walking on the floor—a supreme being, floating like magic, captivating everyone and making jaws drop.

"Elle, how is everything going?" Jenna coos, motioning to all the people around the room. All the people who are actually staring at her, and not at the art. She feels a rush of ego and sucks her stomach in, standing up straighter.

"Fantastic! Lovee, Laith Bassel was just here—the art critic! You can't imagine how great things are going so far!" she gushes to her friend. Riley walks up to them, protectively flanking Elle.

"Riley, how are the sales?" Jenna asks authoritatively, aware of all the people watching, waiting to see what she's like in person.

"Uh ... good? I guess? That's not really the point of the night ... aren't you going to look at the exhibit?"

"I've seen it all before. Hana thought you could use a little attention. Get some paparazzi action for you." Jenna winks, playfully hip-checking the Top Dog rep beside her.

"How...thoughtful," Riley says dryly. *Guess you're not that mad about Carter being a slutty man-whore anymore.*

"Hana, should we get martinis?" Jenna asks, eyeing the crowd for cute guys to flirt with.

"I already have bevies coming." She smiles, watching two men trot up with drinks in hand.

Bevies? Riley thinks to herself. *Beverages? Frick—she seems really ... trendy ...*

"Nice. So, tell me, what's going on?" Jenna asks, staring up at the photo of herself curiously.

"Not much. Ben's in town, and I think we're going to watch a hockey game tomorrow," Elle replies.

"Fantastic. I love sports. You'll arrange the tickets?" Jenna turns to Hana.

"Yep. I'll make reservations for after the game, too," she suggests. "In case any of the players are decent talent."

"Nice," Jenna agrees.

Hana pulls out her iPhone from an overly stylish Louis Vuitton bag and starts typing away. She is impeccably put together in a hot dress, her hair glamorously waved like a pinup, cascading over her bronze spray tan. She's quite short, looking deceivingly intense with the help of massive Chloé platforms.

The two random yuppie guys approach with drinks for the pop star and her comrade. The abundance of money reeks off their floppy hair.

"So, Jenna, how do you like New York so far?" asks the handsome brown-haired man, a sweater loosely tied around his shoulders.

"I've been here before," she quips flirtatiously.

That's a lie, but who cares?

"Of course. Do you own a place here? I have a brownstone down the street." The other guy, a redhead, winks.

"Lovely. How is its decoration? Do you need any artwork?" Jenna laughs, motioning to the installations around them.

"It could use a big photo of you." He smiles back.

"Really ..." Jenna grins darkly.

"But only if you'd come and see yourself ..."

"That could be arranged." She smiles, batting her eyelashes.

"Hey, man, I'm the one who dragged you to come out here—I want to buy the portrait!" argues his brown-haired friend. He turns to Elle furiously. "How much is it?"

"Ten grand," Jenna replies, leaving Elle open-mouthed and out of the conversation.

"I'll give you fifteen," he snaps back, wanting to seal the deal.

"Fucking asshole! Twenty, make it twenty," his redhead friend insists.

Elle and Riley stare at each other, astounded by the fervent energy their friend is commanding.

Twenty thousand dollars? This is actually absurd, Elle panics to herself, fearing one of them will suffer serious buyer's remorse after the fact.

"Autograph it, give me your number, and I'll take it for thirty," replies the brunette.

"Done." Jenna grabs a permanent marker from Hana, signs a flirty message for "Malcolm" onto the print, and breezes out the door, leaving everyone in shock.

"Hey, Seamus—I fucked your girlfriend, too!" shouts Malcolm maliciously, following Jenna and Hana out of the gallery and abandoning his redheaded friend.

"What the hell was that about?" Hunter asks, approaching with Ben, having watched the commotion from the other end of the room.

"That was Hana. It's pronounced *Hah*-nah, not 'Hannah,' in case you want to avoid being bitched at," Riley mocks.

Seamus disappears, mortified.

The gallery crowd murmurs with surprise, and Elle overhears a pair of young women near them start discussing.

"If Jenna Ramsay likes this, maybe it will be part of the next must-have list—did you hear that Kwame Roy is getting her to work with Timbaland?" one whispers to her friend.

"That's gold standard. Have you heard her songs? *Pretty* fun, and she's got killer style. Maybe I should buy that small photo over there ..."

"How much do you think it costs? Maybe that venture capitalist you went out with will buy it for you."

"Nah, I don't feel like sleeping with him. I should buy it now before this artist becomes famous. Once they break this drama on TMZ—it's over. Did you see Jenna's skirt? Hot!"

"I know, I should buy those purple Zanotti shoes ... do you think her hair is a weave?"

"Uh ... so ..." Hunter clears his throat, blocking out the airhead women by standing in front of them.

"She sold my print for thirty thousand dollars," Elle gasps, staring off into space, shocked.

"Thirty thousand dollars?" Ben winces, unable to mask his disbelief. He's a little wounded at the figure attached to his girlfriend. The earning potential for a starving artist always made him think he would be a sole breadwinner—and with his income, a very successful one at that.

Elle is flushed and panting. "Thirty thousand dollars. Like, thirty thousand American dollars. Greenbacks. Not Canadian Tire money. Thirty thousand real, money dollars," Elle gasps, bordering panic attack territory.

"This deserves a celebration drink," Hunter claps, trying to turn the mood around.

"I should sit down. This is so fast," Elle sighs. "Does that include tax? Ohmygosh …"

Ben holds her steady as she regains her thoughts.

"Why don't we grab some dinner?" Riley offers, watching the crowd disperse after Jenna's dramatic exit. "I think Jenna effectively pulled the fire alarm on this event."

"That sounds like a good idea. I don't want my blood sugar to plummet," Elle agrees, fanning herself and glancing at the spectators anxiously.

"Yeah, but after that sale—you're buying!" jokes Hunter, patting Elle's tiny shoulder.

game on.

[New York City, USA—September 2010]

"This is kind of exciting! I've never been to a hockey game before." Jenna grins as the driver navigates his way towards Madison Square Gardens.

The three girls are on their way to watch Hunter face off against the New York Rangers and are accompanied by Hana Rin.

"This game is *prob-ab-lie* going to be nuts!" Riley exclaims, wide-eyed, staring out the tinted windows of the large black SUV. "I wonder what he's like …"

"Hunter? I hear he's really aggressive," Elle starts. "But Ben likes that about him—makes him easy to sell."

"Sell to who?" Jenna asks, confused.

"You know, the media, to other teams … sell him … in general," Hana tries to explain, not quite sure what she's talking about, but desperate to break into the conversation. She's wearing a bright pink shirt that's low-cut and accidentally keeps catching Elle's attention.

Eleanor tries to divert her gaze down to the modest jeans and sweater she's wearing. Focusing so hard on the light-wash denim, she accidentally glances up and catches sight of Hana's chest again. She tries to play with her braid and look out the window.

"These fans are intense … almost as crazy as Toronto fans …" Riley muses, seeing a sea of red, white, and blue overflowing on the streets. "I've never understood die-hard sports enthusiasm."

The three girls hold hands excitedly and squeal as Hana subtly rolls her eyes. She's gotta find a way to penetrate the threesome and make them cooler. Jenna's image depends on it.

Jenna's phone chimes with a message. She reaches into her oversized leather purse and struggles to type back with her new fake nails. Hana spent the morning with her at the spa and convinced her on a set of falsies to match her own. Little details go into shaping an It Girl, and Hana has it down to a cloning formula.

"Is it Carter?" Hana asks, eyes wide and giddy.

Elle and Riley stare out at the crowds entering the arena, ignoring her enthusiasm.

"He wants to know if I'll see him tonight. He wants to apologize and explain," Jenna announces, reading off her screen.

"Apologize for what, exactly? Does he even know? Does he understand that hooking up with another girl when you're a public figure is ... um ... more *visible*?" Riley huffs, wiggling into a heavy knit sweater and doing up the buttons, her long brown hair swirling around her shoulders.

"I think you should see him," Hana says.

Elle and Riley look at each other, taken aback by this newcomer infringing on their girl talk. She may be young and hip, but her pushy nature is starting to go from overachieving to full-throttle obnoxious with the two of them. Jenna is oblivious to it and seems to be looking up to Hana like a role model. The hot Asian doll that renders men stunned with a wink from her eyelash extensions.

"I think you should see him and give him another chance. Or at least listen to what he has to say," Hana starts, expertly adding a thick layer of lipstick on her mouth. "In this industry, everyone twists reality—so you have to go to the source if you want the truth."

"But what if he doesn't like me ..." Jenna sighs.

"He made out with a random bartender. So what? Shit happens. You gotta realize this is, like ... a bump in the road, like a love saga. There are always obstacles and challenges when it comes to such intense, deep love," Hana says.

"Intense love? The guy is, like, perma-waste-faced," Riley interjects, thinking of all the drunken photos of him in the gossip magazines. "Love sagas also usually end in bittersweet disappointment and/or death."

"But when it comes down to it—he wants to be in Jenna's life. He loves her; he'll try every time he screws up to mend it. He doesn't give up. That's a sign. Maybe the reason this is so intense is because it's a past-life love ..."

With all the gooey words coming from Hana, it's obvious that Jenna's heartstrings are being plucked.

"I should really put you in touch with my psychic guide. You know, she predicted pretty much everything in my life accurately. Love, career, good news, bad news ..." Hana shrugs, trying to force out a genuine gentleness, sugarcoating her intentions to hook Jenna. "She told me to dump that rapper to avoid his bad karma, and a week later he got arrested."

Jenna falls for it easily and is intrigued by the secret advisor to this high-powered entertainment industry party girl. If the fierce young woman also needs guidance, she's not as invincible or superhuman as assumed. Maybe she also feels like a Martian, a novelty object that strangers try to curiously absorb glamour from. As a celebrity, Jenna is learning not to think of herself as a person, but as a thing.

Hana's well-connected status is already keeping Jenna out until the wee hours, happily wasted, and even bigger targets for the paparazzi trolling the nightclub circuit. There's always somewhere to be or someone to be seen with.

"Elle, what do you think?" Jenna asks, turning to the quietest person in the car, commanding an opinion.

Elle's eyes dart around, panicked, as if she's been cold-called in class without having done her homework. She can't sink any further into the seat.

"Umm ... I mean, lovee, I think you need to do what you want. What you feel is the right thing for you." She shrugs, speaking softly and as impartially as possible.

Riley opens her mouth to refute but closes it, not wanting to start another fight. Her opinion is very clearly one-sided.

The Escalade slows at the side of the arena, and all unpleasant conversation draws to a close.

Jenna types back a message to Carter, exhaling heavily before preparing her smile muscles.

The car door is opened, and they hop out.

Photographers swarm the barricade around the entrance and begin snapping photos of Jenna as the girls enter the building. She turns to wave, her bohemian outfit will certainly be plastered on best-dressed lists next week.

They breeze in through a discreet metal door, and it shuts heavily, blocking out the chaotic flashbulbs outside. A short, fat man is waiting for them on the other side—the PR guy from the home team.

"Jenna, great to have you here. When we got Miss Rin's call, one of our patrons requested to host you in his private box," greets the arena representative. He leads them down a cement corridor. "He says he was a friend of yours, Hannah?"

"I have a lot of friends," she replies dryly, forcing the bald, sweating man to look away from her awkwardly with a nervous laugh. "And it's pronounced *Hah*-nah, not Hannah."

Elle and Riley glance at each other again, still shocked by the rudeness Hana constantly emits. They slow down to walk behind the star and her representative, both in butt-hugging designer jeans.

"Is this for real?" Riley whispers to her, gesturing to the two women trotting ahead of them.

Elle shrugs, making a distressed face.

"Um, Miss Bryans ... Mr. Roberts said he would meet you in the box after the start of the second period," the man says softly, slowing pace to match the two less-threatening girls.

"Oh, that's great, thank you ...?" Elle smiles warmly.

"Drew." The man smiles, holding out his hand.

"Drew. Great," Elle replies, shaking his chubby hand gently.

"So, what's tonight's game lookin' like, Drew?" Riley asks, curious to learn about how Hunter and his team are stacked against their opponents. She cracks her knuckles as if she's getting ready to draw the first face-off herself.

"Well, there's long been speculation about mutiny in the ranks with Toronto. Ever since they traded Campbell Kates for Hunter White, people have been giving him a bit of a tough time. They love him when he scores and hate him when he doesn't. No in-between. He was one of the league's highest scorers last season—almost broke sixty. One of the top in points and goals the past couple of years—even so far this season he's a plus ten ..."

Riley stares at him blankly, not sure what the statistics really mean.

"He's doing really well, so people like him right now. I think the rest of the team is starting to believe why there was so much hype around him. And his salary bracket," Drew simplifies.

"Makes sense: prove yourself, gain respect," Elle reasons.

"So he's really good then?" Riley asks, raising an eyebrow.

"One of the best. They set him up hard, to try work on a team that was being held together by the influence of Campbell Kates. Not even the rightful captain had the hold Kates did over their morale, their social side—partying and fraternity. Which is so wrong. I hear he used to throw some out-of-control get-togethers to get everyone to like him, maybe swing the captaincy in his direction. So when you take that away, the team falls apart—but has to rebuild eventually," explains Drew as they snake through the corridors.

"But more evenly, not only have one king ... but all around ... like the Arthurian round table. Be able to work together," Riley says to herself, understanding the dynamic better in her dorky way.

They get in an elevator and shoot up to the private boxes. As they walk down the next hallway, waitresses and busboys turn and stare at Jenna with curiosity.

"She's quite popular …" Drew whispers to Elle.

"Tell me about it." She laughs softly.

A little girl runs up to Jenna with a paper and marker.

"Jenna! Jenna! Please, can I get your autograph?"

She turns and smiles at the cute blonde child, no older than ten. She has pony hair clips and is wearing a child-sized Rangers jersey.

"She's busy," Hana scoffs, grabbing Jenna by the arm and nearly body-checking the child out of their way.

Jenna resists, bending down to sign the autograph. "What's your name, lovee?"

"Frances." She smiles, unable to contain the joy of meeting the beautiful star.

"Can we get a photographer over here?" Hana shouts, snapping her fingers, adjusting to her client's reaction. A man from a daily newspaper rushes up with a camera.

"What, is she going to document every single autograph she gives to cute kids?" Riley muses sarcastically, fixing the waistband on her trouser jeans.

Jenna poses for a few more pictures, and then continues to the luxury box.

The engraved plate on the door reads "Thorpe Group."

"Oh man …" Hana smiles to herself, reading the company name and trying to discreetly primp her cleavage.

"What?" Jenna smiles, curious.

"Thorpe … this is going to be an epic night."

The girls walk into the suite, and there are bottles of premium alcohol around the leather couches in the private box.

"High roller wants to get it on with Jenna …" Elle giggles to Riley, motioning to the man at centre of a group of banker-looking guys. Their loosened ties and collars relax their finely tailored suits, the men unwinding after a long day at the office. Living a pop star's life is not a Monday-to-Friday 9-to-5. Sometimes the girls forget that other people lead stable and regulated lives. No late night parties or sound-checks, morning phone interviews with people on the other side of the world, or overnight flights to crisscross the globe. Routine versus chaos.

"It is a Monday. People have day jobs." Riley starts laughing. She suddenly shuts up, all sense knocked out of her. "Shit. Fuck. Shit."

"Riles?" Elle asks, as her friend grabs her by the elbow and violently jerks her back to the doorway.

"That's Simon," she hisses at Elle.

"Simon?"

"Simon. Egomaniac troll from the bar," Riley whispers under her breath.

"Oh, my gosh, Riley. That is so awkward!"

"Thanks, Elle. That's constructive," Riley scolds.

"I'm just saying … be the bigger man." Elle shrugs.

Drew walks by the doorway and Riley lunges out at him.

"Drew … really … any chance we can watch the game from … elsewhere? Like, the seats down there? Far, far away from this box?" Riley pleads frantically.

"I'll see, but it might be hard for so many …"

"No, no. I'm sure Jenna and Hana will gladly stay here with … their hosts."

Drew smiles softly and agrees to see what he can do for the second period.

Riley drags herself back into the box as if she were walking off a plank into shark-infested water.

"There you are! Riley, come meet these guys." Hana waves her over.

Simon turns to greet the new addition to the group and shock registers on his face.

"Riley, this is my friend Simon Thorpe, of Thorpe Group … International?" Hana asks.

"No, not international. We like to keep a monopoly over America instead." He scowls, extending his hand and squeezing hers painfully.

"Hi, Simon," Riley says through gritted teeth.

"Hi, Riley." He smiles stiffly. "You must be, what, her personal assistant?" he asks, motioning to Jenna, who already has a glass of champagne in hand.

"No, actually. Riley is one of my oldest friends. She's going to be a published writer soon …" Jenna smiles proudly.

"Published writer?" he asks, sceptical.

"Yep. Her first novel. It's great stuff," Jenna smiles, shooting Riley a look communicating that she realized who this Simon character is.

He curls his upper lip in stress and abruptly turns back to the conversation at hand with his friends.

"I really think that it was stupid of you to buy that Aston, Simon. Where are you going to be able to drive it here? Really open it up?" exclaims one of his friends.

"Percy ... really, I'm going to keep it at the beach house," Simon replies in an "isn't it obvious" manner, belittling his friend.

Percy nods intently, taking a swig from his beer.

"Not everyone is as lucky to come from your grandparents' deep pockets, Thorpester," another friend of his pipes in.

"At least I have credit," he smirks, like a brat who's grown up with nothing better to do than bully people with his money.

"So? Taxes are overrated, anyway." His friend laughs.

"In the 'pharmaceutical' business, you definitely have an adequate quantity of assets you can liquidate, Will," snorts Percy, as the guys clink their drinks together.

Riley and Elle tiptoe away to watch the game from the front of the box, scared of the upper-class drug dealer. Jenna playfully hip-checks Riley as they pass the group of well-groomed Wall Street men, signalling that she's got her friend's back with Simon.

"Pleasant guy," Elle laughs, rolling her eyes as they sit by the balcony's ledge with bottles of water in hand.

"Yeah, well, did you know he used to be a poet?" Riley snickers.

"Well, I never thought I'd actually say this, but today I realize how thankful I am that Ben is a law-abiding, tax-paying, credit-holding citizen," Elle exhales nervously.

"I don't even want to know how this lifestyle works," Riley grimaces, trying to ignore the debauchery brewing in the box. "Much prefer anonymity."

The game begins, and Simon holds court on the leather couches in front of the huge TV while some of his other friends mix drinks and chat, oblivious to the event on ice level below.

"I don't get it. You own a box ... you must like sports ... but you still watch it on a screen? It's right here!" Riley observes, excited to watch her first hockey game in the flesh.

Elle shrugs, delicately holding her mineral water.

"How *you've* never been to a game before, I don't understand," Riley adds.

"Well, Ben likes to keep his personal life separate from his public life." Elle shrugs.

"Why, do you think?" Riley wonders.

"He's the first to admit he has a sharky identity in the industry. People call him ruthless."

"How weird is it that he's the same person you know him as? Like an alter ego?" Riley grimaces.

"I think we all have alter egos, in a way. Don't you? I am Eleanor the artist, Eleanor the girlfriend, now Eleanor the personal assistant ..."

"Right, but ... there's always spillover. At least there's no fear that Elle the artist is going to have some illegal masterminding should I piss her off."

"Ben's never been like that with me. I think—okay, yes, I've seen him get ... tough ... with his work life. But with me, he's different. I'm okay with that."

"I can't see him!" Riley groans, trying to squint and spot Hunter down below.

"Riles, he's right there. With the big 'four' on his back," Elle replies, gesturing out at the ice rink.

"Where?"

"Riley, right there!" Elle says, exasperated, pointing energetically. "Would you seriously get your contact prescription adjusted? He's practically wearing a target on his back! The letters are W-H-I-T-E!"

Riley scrunches up her face, still not able to read the numbers on the players' backs to identify them, barely making out their last names.

"We're never somewhere long enough to get anything done ... maybe I can get new glasses this week."

"You are so incredibly blind." Elle laughs.

"What, maybe it's hereditary!"

"Look, there—Fantastic Four, he's right there!" Elle points.

"Oh ... yeah ... there he is." Riley nods, but not completely sure if she's looking at "4" or "9."

Hana's phone rings inside the lounge.

"Okay, okay. Sounds good. I'll get her to the front, then. Give me two minutes," she shouts over the noise. "Jen, we need you by the front of the box. They're going to pan up to you and talk about you on the sports edition of the news."

Jenna is positioned right as a referee blows his whistle.

The Jumbotron lights up with her image, her song playing—now on high rotation at all the Top 40 stations.

"Give them a wave," Hana instructs.

Jenna waves her hand, and the crowd screams even louder. "Look at This" throbs through the arena, the chorus familiar even though North America is behind a few singles on her album's release. Her

Asian fans have already made YouTube tribute videos to all the tracks on her CD.

The players on the ice look up to see what all the commotion is—no goal has been made, no penalty called.

But soon enough, play is resumed. The camera tries to flash back up to Jenna when there's another break, but she's unprepared and whispering to Elle, and Hana smiles and waves instead.

The commentator on the television informs viewers that Jenna is watching the game from the box of New York's own Simon Thorpe. As if on cue, he enters the shot of the girls, handing Jenna a drink and smiling as if they're having the grandest time.

"What a little creeper," Elle whispers to Riley as the others head back inside.

"As if Carter's any better …"

"True. Even this guy doesn't seem so … sketchy …"

"Yeah, but he's a total jack-off. All he wants is to bang her in his Aston and sell the story," Riley replies.

"Yeah, well. He did that with Hana already …" Elle winks.

"What?"

"You heard me …"

"Hana? And Simon?" Riley gasps.

"Yep. Her 'old friend.' Jenna sent me a text. They go way back … in the backseat, if you know what I mean," Elle says, flushed with embarrassment as she shows Riley the message.

They look back to the cocktail party happening in the luxury box, and Jenna winks, confirming her piece of gossip.

"Shut up! Ew, thank God I didn't converse with him further."

"Exactly. But she does have a good eye …"

"For social climbing?" Riley blurts out accidentally.

Elle acknowledges the comment with a double-blink of her eyes and turns back to the game.

New York scores with six minutes left in the first period. Simon and his friends start whooping and shouting, even though their defenseman draws a penalty right after. A fight breaks out between two players, getting the guys even more worked up. They don't care about the finesse of strategy or athleticism—they just want to see a brawl.

"I can't stand being here; these people are so pretentious and insane. Why don't you text Ben and tell him to meet us elsewhere?" Riley whispers, glancing over her shoulder at the group getting drunker by the minute.

Elle snorts, pulling out her cell phone and texting her boyfriend. "I'm sure we're already committed to going out with Hunter after."

"Yeah, not so sure how I feel about that guy yet."

"Huh?" Elle gasps, shocked.

"Not that he's not trustworthy or whatever—he's kinda not that book smart ... I dunno ... I guess I don't see how this is gonna work, if at all. He's all about the socializing guy's-guy thing, and I really am not ... He's nice, I'm interested in getting to know him ... but I can't get serious. Like, I can't be that woman who goes shopping all day and is waiting at home for her man with lingerie on and a slab of meat on the grill."

"Fair enough, if you feel that way. I think you're being a little biased, but you'll get to know what he's about. Please be clear with him about that so he doesn't have any false hopes. And stop making up plotlines in your head." Elle shrugs, disappointed that her friend didn't feel love at first sight with the handsome athlete. They could be a permanent double date with her and Ben!

"So ... what do you think you're going to do ... when we're eventually phased out of this touring stuff?" Riley asks her friend, watching Hana and Jenna taking shots off the bar without them. "It feels like it's going fast, like she's pretty okay with her new BFF."

"Well, I'd like to move back to Toronto ... sell my art, have a home ..." Elle smiles softly, drifting into a daydream she's escaped to ever since she was a child. A magical place with organza and fresh flowers, an adoring husband and cute children. And monogrammed embroidered towels beside his-and-hers sinks.

"Is said home with Ben?" Riley grins, poking her friend in the ribs playfully.

"Yeah. I mean, we haven't fully talked about it. He hasn't formally asked me, or anything—not like I have a round-cut solitaire on. But ... it's like the high school sweetheart fantasy come true. Back then, I thought it was only puppy love, that he was the idealised first. Well, not literally. You know what I mean. But more and more, I feel like we fit great together. I want that life—to stay home with my kids, to make Play-Doh peanut butter with them and fold his socks. The sort of stuff I didn't really have growing up," she says thoughtfully.

"What about the religion thing?" Riley asks her WASPy friend.

"Well, he doesn't expect me to convert ... and let's face it, since moving out, he's not particularly ... observant of the Jewishness. His parents are more social in their faith, the sense of community. They got reserved to him and I being together long ago. But I definitely want to start learning about Judaism, at least understand more for myself. And to raise my kids with the same sort of values he learned. Something more solid than my WASPiness."

"What? No cocktails at the Granite Club?" Riley laughs at the exclusive country club both their families happen to be members at, the club with the years of wait listing and exorbitant dues.

Elle looks at her sternly.

"I can understand that, though. It's tough if you don't know quite where you belong," Riley sighs, referring to her upbringing. "It makes the questioning of who you are a longer process if you don't know where to start rebelling!"

"Well, you're sort of Jewish, right? What do you think?"

Riley looks at her friend sympathetically. "I think that you're the best cook I have ever known in my life and that you would outdo any other woman at any holiday involving mass amounts of food." She laughs. "And that your kids will be the luckiest boogers alive because they'll have the most loving mother in all the universe. And that, that is what counts most of all, don't you think? Someone who's in your corner and loves you regardless of what kid you knock out at school."

Elle blushes, looking down at the floor.

"Elle, I was raised by a hipster gay man. You were raised by Florida snowbirds that have matching golf clubs—no offence. Jenna was raised by a struggling single mum. And the three of us are who we are because we were loved the same way. And I think they all did pretty good."

"Riles, I think that is the smartest thing you've ever said." Elle laughs, wiping a tear away from her eye.

The buzzer blares the end of the first period, and they stand up and cheer.

"Miss Bryans, I can take you down now," Drew says softly, having slipped into the box quietly, dodging the drunken antics. He pats his forehead with a handkerchief, wiping the sweat from having to hustle around.

Elle and Riley stand up and tell Jenna they're heading into the arena.

"We're good up here. We'll discuss what to do after, yes?" Jenna smiles, waving them away, her attention fixed on another of Simon's friends.

Riley and Elle follow Drew through the arena, arm-in-arm, laughing about Hana's scandalous past.

He leads them through the crowd and towards the front edge of seats.

"Drew, are you serious?" Riley gasps, realizing how close they're moving to the ice.

He turns and smiles, putting a finger to his lips.

"The guests who own these seats didn't bother showing up. Amazing how people blow off their platinum season tickets. I will never understand. So, I hope that you enjoy watching your team." He smiles.

Ben's already sitting down, but stands when the girls approach, like a gentleman. His grey suit blazer is unbuttoned and showing a crisp blue dress shirt underneath, his tie still fastened—he's on duty.

"Hi, ladies." He smiles, kissing Elle quickly as they scoot in.

"Drew, thank you so much. This is insane!" Riley squeals. "Like, the ice … the ice is right there. Right on the other side of this pane of glass … is the ice. And the puck and the fighting!"

Drew shakes his head sweetly, rushing back into the intermission crowd.

"So, how's Hunter?" Elle smiles, holding Ben's arm gently, happy to nuzzle into him instead of settling for a Skype session.

"Good. Real good. I think we might be keeping him in Toronto, after all." He smiles, satisfied.

"So his contract is getting extended?"

Ben grins like a Cheshire cat and kisses Elle on the forehead, not one to really discuss specifics of his dealings.

"Enough said." Riley laughs to herself, sitting at the edge of her seat and waiting for the second period to start.

"Hey, did you notice we're sitting by the away bench?" Ben smiles, nodding his head to the empty bench near Riley's seat.

"What's that?"

"The bench where the players who are … from away … sit?" He rolls his eyes, letting out a snort.

"Oh, oh—yeah, I knew that. I mean … wow. This is big. Guys, this game going to be big!" she announces, feeling the chill drift up from the ice.

"So, I really want them to love each other" Elle pouts to Ben, looking at her friend, who resembles a child waiting for Santa, on the edge of her seat.

He shrugs happily. "I think he's into her."

"Yeah, she's definitely into him. Won't admit it over her dead body. But really, when would Riley Kohl, in all the years you've known her, ever care for organized sport?"

Ben laughs, as the players hustle out from the locker room.

"Well, I think he's interested in settling down some. Shed that partying-jock image that he had in Missouri," he whispers, as he fixes the cufflinks on his sleeve.

Elle nods, excited for the potential love connection. Riley deserves to be happy, to be romanced by someone good. To find her Ben. But whether she's at the point of wanting to settle down, let alone wherever he happens to be playing ... that she's not so sure of.

"Oh, my God, look, it's Hunter! He's playing!" Riley gushes hyperactively, spotting number 4 underneath his helmet.

Hunter White skates up the ice with the rest of his first-string line and takes position for the face-off.

The puck drops, and the three spectators are glued to the intense action in front of them.

"Good googlie-mooglie!" Elle shouts in fear as a Toronto player body-checks someone into the glass right in front of her. The clear pane vibrates under the force of the hefty man.

Riley and Ben stare at her, shocked at the bizarre reaction, but turn back to the game.

Hunter passes the puck to another player, and he flicks it breezily into the net. Right over the goalie's left shoulder—a clear shot taken without hesitation, like a sniper at the ready.

They jump out of their seats, screaming with excitement.

"That was brilliant! Did you know he was brilliant?" Riley screams at Ben.

"Riles, he's my client. I'm well aware."

The girls are breathless from screaming. They look up to see other Toronto fans on the Jumbotron and shriek even louder, holding hands in total excitement.

Hunter's line skates to the bench to switch out.

He turns and looks into the stands, spotting his cheering section.

"That was *reee-diculous!*" Riley shouts, giving him a fervent thumbs-up.

He smiles modestly, sweat dripping down his face.

"Goodness, he's sweating a lot," Elle whispers to Riley.

"He's got good stamina," she replies, giving a thumbs-up. Then she pauses, looking away awkwardly after realizing the potential innuendo.

The second period ends with New York nearly scoring on a power play but getting shut down.

"Do you want a hot dog? I feel like I should be eating a hot dog and drinking beer right now," Riley asks the couple, consumed by the energy of sports action.

"No, I think the fancy lunch with Proenza Schouler filled me up," Elle says, patting her belly and hinting that Riley should still be full and not gorging on junk.

"Right. I forgot about that. But I feel like, with sports, that beer and hot dogs provide a sense of camaraderie, right? That's probably marketing ... but I'm just saying. I don't even drink beer."

The teams are locked in a 1–1 war through the third period.

Hunter's line jumps out with five minutes left, hoping to out-skate their exhausted second string.

He takes possession of the puck and starts bringing it up the side, but gets slammed into the boards right in front of his friends.

"What the shit!" Riley screams. "That's illegal! That's gotta be illegal! Right, Ben?!"

She jumps up and stares down the glass onto the ice, where Hunter is caught in the commotion of two teams fishing for the puck.

"Injure them! Injure them!" Riley screams. "Slam them now!"

Hunter gets up as the whistle blows and skates back to the bench, switching with another player.

Riley and Hunter make eye contact as he sits down, and she is glowing with excitement, he with bodily pain.

"Guys, I love athletics!" she whispers.

"Athletics love you, too ..." Ben coughs jokingly so that only Elle can hear.

The game ends with New York scoring a last-minute goal and winning.

"Bullshit! That's fucking outta control!" Riley shouts angrily.

"It's okay, Riley. The game's done now," Ben says dryly, trying to calm her down.

"Right. Besides, it isn't a playoff; they'll have more chances to win." Elle smiles supportively. "Which means, now it's time for a light supper ... I'm sure poor Hunter must be starving after that game."

"Time for camaraderie—and to feed my hungry boy," Ben says, stretching his arms.

The three file out of the main arena and head back up to the private boxes while Hunter changes and does his post-game interviews.

"So, what'd you think of NYC kicking your Canadian asses?" Simon grins as the trio enters his box. He's obviously a few Scotches past his limit.

Ben makes a horrified face at Elle, and she nods in agreement. Simon's face is sweat-drenched, and he looks sloppy, his business attire wilted. He should have an enforced cut-off point.

"Where do you guys want to go now? I can get us resos ..." interrupts Percy, holding his customized phone for everyone to see.

"What about dancing?" Hana grins, grabbing another champagne flute and draping herself seductively on the couch.

"Um, Jenna ..." Elle says softly, pulling her friend away.

"Yeah, what's up?"

"Well, we were thinking maybe we could go for dinner and kind of ... take it easy ..." she suggests.

Jenna turns to look at the group of people in the suite.

"I dunno, Elle. I mean, I think I might go out with these guys. They hosted us here and everything ... kind of an obligation," Jenna starts.

Secretly, she's dreading turning into some sort of fifth wheel with Ben-Elle and Riley-Hunter. The last thing she needs is to be the spinster.

"Okay, well, are you sure?" Elle asks worriedly. "You've got a big day tomorrow ..."

Jenna looks at her oddly, and her mood snaps. "I'll be fine," she replies dryly, turning and walking back to the group, abandoning Elle rudely.

"All right, well, maybe we should leave," Elle sighs to her two companions.

"Odd ..." Riley whispers, as they step into the hallway.

Elle shrugs.

"Hunter's ready and wants steak." Ben reads off a text message.

Drew escorts them to an unmarked area.

"It was nice meeting you ladies. Have a great evening!" He smiles, leaving the girls with the hockey agent in a hallway.

"Ben, buddy, how's it going?" A man, dressed in a sleek black suit and pale green dress shirt, greets him warmly. He's just emerged from the New York locker room, cell phone in hand.

"Phil, hey, good to see you, man." Ben smiles, as the two hockey agents start talking shop about some record-setting deal.

The girls drift off to the side, giving Ben privacy, and start contemplating Jenna's new friend.

"I really hope Mack isn't stupid enough to let Hana take over completely or something …" Riley whispers.

Elle shakes her head confused. "She's too … into the lifestyle. She actually kind of scares me. Jenna likes shiny things, yes—but … she's not only about that."

They spot Hunter walking up the hallway towards Ben and Phil.

"I know that they've got their eye on him for their top pick … but your guess is as good as mine. Anyway, Phil, buddy, next time I'm in Montreal, let's do up a Habs game," Ben suggests, glancing quickly at his client's approach.

"So stereotypical. Just because I live there doesn't mean I bleed Canadiens, Roberts. That's like saying you bleed Maple Leafs blue."

"But I do bleed Leafs," Ben says, deadpan, motioning to Hunter. "And I bleed Blackhawks, and I bleed Flames …"

Phil rolls his eyes at the young, gutsy agent. "Yeah, yeah—we bleed whatever we need to bleed. You know I'd rather watch Tampa, anyway. Weather's better," he replies, the two of them laughing.

Hunter approaches, and the three men have a few seconds of short banter before saying their good-byes.

Hunter and Ben look at each other and smile intuitively, turning to join the girls.

"That was awesome!" Riley shouts at Hunter loudly, her big brown eyes wide with excitement. She offers up a dorky high-five.

He grins happily at the sudden interest from her. "Imagine what it'd be like if we won …" He laughs to Ben.

"Man, you might have gotten laid …" Ben snickers, as Elle smacks his arm playfully.

"So I take it we're double dating?" Hunter smiles, putting an arm around Riley's neck, dropping his two-hundred-pound body on her, her knees buckle a bit.

"Uh, we're not dating!" She laughs nervously, jokingly trying to push him off like a gross leech.

"Yeah, whatever, you know you want me." He winks, as they quietly get into a car and head out into the dark city.

visible.

[Toronto, Canada—October 2, 2010]

"I'm so sorry to have to drag you out here like this, Riley," Hunter sighs, frustrated. "I gotta grab my hockey bag, and then I promise we'll go eat—anywhere you want."

Riley turns to him from the passenger's seat of his Ferrari and smiles awkwardly as they crawl out of his condo's parking garage. They're waiting to pull onto a busy street near the lakefront in downtown Toronto. The real estate near the grimy water has some of the most popular properties in the city, tons of condominiums developed for the young and deep-pocketed.

He runs a hand through his shaggy, light hair, popping his sunglasses down from the top of his head.

Take me anywhere I want? What's that supposed to mean? Does he think I'm going to pick somewhere fancy and he'll pay? Like some sort of archaic Southern gentleman, soap opera shit? she thinks to herself, wondering if he likens himself to the wealthy knight-in-shining armour, his multimillion dollar paycheque being one of the most written about topics covered in the Internet research she did on him.

"Really, it's fine. It's not a big deal at all," she replies, trying to allow him benefit of the doubt. Just because he's a hyped pro athlete doesn't mean he's a jerk. She stares out at the overcast afternoon sky.

"I feel so bad. I get you to agree to go out with me … on a real date, the two of us … and there's a wrench thrown in my plans …" he sighs, fiddling with the window of his bright yellow sports car. Not the most inconspicuous of choices in automobiles.

In a sudden burst of acceleration, he whips the car onto the street.

A dark blue V-neck sweater fits snugly over him, and he happens to smell incredible.

My God, this car draws a lot of attention, Riley thinks anxiously as they slow at a red light on Lakeshore Boulevard—the main artery of the downtown core that passes right by the hockey arena where he plays. The old, rickety car stopped beside them has its occupants staring with their jaws open, recognizing the driver and ogling his ride. It is at this moment of awkward eye contact that Riley regrets leaving her comparatively modest Range Rover at his place and letting him drive. Though it was quite a nice condo … one of the perks of being the next big thing in a hockey town, probably. The equivalent of a local celebrity—hockey players worshipped more than politicians, actors, or musicians in Canada. A fact she never could quite understand.

The light turns green, and Hunter peels away, leaving the spectators in the dust. Riley's long brown hair flicks up with the speed, and she feels her stomach hiccup.

"Wait, you had plans?" she asks, suddenly aware that Hunter White—hotshot NHL player and Toronto hero—may, in fact, be trying to win her affection all by his lonesome. Maybe he isn't a stereotypical bonehead jock … maybe he's actually a sensitive, real genius who thinks money can't buy love …

"Well, I did have plans. But …" he pouts. "When your prized piece of luggage is lost and returned to the wrong address … it's like if your laptop went missing," he compares.

"Well, at least your bag got sent to the rink and not someone's eBay account." She smiles, as they pull into an unmarked garage at the arena. He stops the sports car in the empty hull, the engine still running. Hunter tucks his fancy sunglasses in their case.

"Mr. Hunter, good to see you," says a valet who approaches the car and opens the door for him.

"Hey, Farshid. I'm taking Riley in," Hunter replies, getting out of the custom-sewn seat. He hands the young Persian boy the keys to his ray of sunshine—still with Missouri plates. It's so bright and golden that it looks like it belongs in Miami.

Hunter walks around to the passenger door and opens it to let his date out.

Farshid smiles at them innocently. He looks barely old enough to have gotten his learner's permit, let alone be driving luxury vehicles. He's very thin, and his braces make him endearingly awkward.

"The team management has wrapped their meeting already—all is clear," says the boy cryptically.

"Thanks, man." Hunter nods, leading his date towards the stadium's doors.

"Oh, I could've waited in the car," Riley blurts out nervously. She's tightly clutching the grey Mulberry bag Jenna gave for the date, straight from her suitcase. It matches nicely with the sweater she's wearing, conservatively signalling there's no chance of necking on Date #1.

"You could've … but … no." He smiles as they walk through halls lined with photos of hockey heroes past.

"Wow, this is like a maze." She laughs, disoriented and out of her element.

Organized sports were never her thing. In gym class, Riley was the one who wasn't necessarily picked last, but rather preferred to watch from the sidelines, or act as the team manager—never to get into the mix and wear a "C" on her chest or anything.

He stops suddenly at the locker room door. The door leading into the secret society of men and their sticks.

"I'll be right back." He winks, disappearing inside.

In this moment of silence, Riley finds herself confused.

I mean, yes, he's cute and everything ... but is he the one? He's cool, but probably not relationship material. Are you even relationship material? she thinks, pacing in her Frye boots.

Oh, Riley, who gives a shit. There's no such thing as one ideal person—stop reading Jane Austen, you moron, her mind argues back. She's about to refute herself when Hunter emerges with a huge duffle bag. It's so big that it looks like a body could easily be transported in it, right alongside his athletic cup.

"Ready?" he asks, brushing his hair back, his pale cheeks with a touch of rosy colouring.

"Yep." She nods, following his lead, checking out his butt in the slightly metrosexual jeans he's wearing. But paired with the latest sneakers from his athletic sponsor—such a classic, masculine look.

They start walking in the opposite direction of where they came, but she doesn't correct him right away. Maybe it's a secret passageway, and she would be a total jackass for meddling.

I'm so sick of arguing. With myself, with my friends, with my writing ... all I do is argue. And for what? I know I'm not going to change, and my friends aren't going to change, especially Jenna. I really should have become a lawyer like Dad used to say ... Riley Kohl: control freak. She gets lost in her mental soliloquy, trying to get herself to relax the fibres of her body.

Trying.

"Um, Where are we going?" she blurts out sharply, caving into her neurosis, realizing they're nowhere near the garage.

"Oh, we're almost there. Right through here," Hunter responds calmly, obviously still enjoying her "charming" Type A tendencies, and not finding her to be overbearing or nitpicky like Ben has joked.

They walk through a set of double doors, and everything around them is pitch-black. Dark. And chilly.

What the ...? Riley wonders. *Oh, my God, what if he kills me?! And stuffs me in his hockey bag!*

But with a lack of self-control she would normally find embarrassing, her hand darts out to find his. She can hear him sigh with contentment; he's winning this hard girl over.

He grips it tightly, leading her forward.

"Hunt ... really ... I have horrible night vision ..." Riley pleads, envisioning herself falling down stairs or tripping over inanimate objects.

"Why don't you just ... relax ... and trust me." He laughs.

Her boots stick on what feels like a rubber surface. She shuffles uneasily behind his lead.

All of a sudden, a bright explosion of lights engulfs them. The hockey arena is illuminated from the houselights above, blinding them for a moment and causing Riley to shriek out of anxiety.

Hunter laughs as she gets her bearings, staring at the massive stadium seating around them.

"Whoa ..." she trails off, amazed at the size of the arena. "It looks different empty ..."

Duh! That's because you've only seen it on TV, she scolds herself, wanting to slap her stupid self in the face.

"Yeah. I love being here when it's empty ... almost as much as when it's a full house." He smiles, surveying his territory proudly.

They walk the Zamboni path out to the rink. He opens a gate, and the ice looks perfect. Smooth and shiny as glass. And with a blanket in the middle of it?

Riley turns to him with a raised eyebrow, confused.

"I hope you like my plans." He smiles cutely, pointing to centre ice. Right in the middle of the big blue circle where the puck drops is the makings of a picnic.

"Wow, Hunter ... this is ..." she trails off, taken aback by his attempt at romance. Albeit athletic-slanted romance.

He steps onto the ice, and she follows him out, grabbing his arm for fear of a concussion. Perfect for a first date! As Riley is getting back into the dating game, all she needs is to knock herself unconscious and be driven out in an ambulance. A definite downgrade from the Ferrari.

When they reach the flannel blanket, she does a 360-degree turn, taking in the immense scope of what it must be like playing with your team in front of so many spectators. She imagines herself as a Roman gladiator, looking up at the masses from the pit of battle, and instantly feels like a geek.

"I thought you might like to learn about my life, but I had to throw you off a bit first." He smiles, sitting on the many layers of flannel blankets that are intended to insulate their bums. He starts opening the various containers that appear from within the hockey bag.

"It's so ... huge. I can't imagine what it's like when you have thousands of people screaming—at the good and the bad," she wonders, staring at the seats. "I can't even see the nosebleeds because this place is monstrous."

Riley sits down beside him, thankful to have worn jeans and boots and not the slinky Gucci dress Jenna tried to force on her. The chill in the air is refreshing.

She smoothes the corner of the blanket, and Hunter hands her a plate full of food.

Oh, dear God, I hate potato salad, she grimaces, staring at the white goo, but obediently eating nibbles of it, feeling horribly guilty by the effort put into this gesture. And for assuming him to be dense. She grins at the paper plate and plastic cutlery, actually thrilled not to be somewhere swanky and pretentious.

"So tell me, what do you remember most, sitting out here?" she asks, crossing her legs and motioning around the rink.

He takes a sip of wine from his paper cup and pauses thoughtfully. "You know ... there's so much. I'd say my first game here." He smiles to himself. "I was scared shitless to join this team. Coming from playing in my own city, for the team I'd watched since I was a kid ... to being here alone. It was intense to be in front of another crowd."

"Oh, you mean from ... St. Louis?"

He nods, tearing another piece of baguette for himself.

"So why did you leave?" she asks bluntly.

He smiles, and she can hear him thinking about how sports-ignorant she is.

"Well ... I got traded ..." he starts, trying to stifle his laughter. "In hockey, players get traded like bargaining chips, if you will. So Ben actually helped get the deal as my agent, get me to a team where I could have great ice time and be able to take them to the next level."

Riley jokingly scrunches her face up in scepticism. "I think Ben wanted to have a little buddy nearby!"

"Or that …" He laughs, rolling his eyes. "Way to bring down my entire career!"

"No, no, I'm kidding! I really mean that it must have been a big thing to step out of your comfort zone." She smiles apologetically, putting her hand on his knee.

Eye contact is made, and she feels flirtation being exchanged between them. Her hand darts off the multimillion dollar knee in a panic, and she stares back down at her plate.

"Well, yeah. But the thing that Ben taught me is that the game has to be played the same everywhere. Whatever team you're on, whatever city you're in … it's about living in that moment and not on false loyalties. When you're on the ice, skating hard you're … just … wild and looking for the next opportunity to score," Hunter explains breathily.

Wow. That speech was actually pretty sexy. In an alpha-male, don't-leave-a-man-behind kind of way, she thinks, suddenly inspired to join a sports team.

"And is everything is settling down after that whole Campbell Kates thing?" she asks, spreading Camembert on a piece of bread.

"Yeah. It was tough at first. You get used to playing with the same people, forming friendships—sometimes almost your own language. So, it's kinda tough to check it at the door when your buddy gets moved and a new guy takes his place. But for the first time in a long time, this team's got the chance to get to the finals. And I think we all know we're in this together … we need to man up."

"Man up?" Riley asks, surprised by the odd term.

"You know—get it together, step up to the plate … just giver," Hunter says, finding her to be more and more adorable.

Riley accepts the phrase.

"Beneath that harsh exterior of dryness … I think you're actually a softie." He grins, imagining her as a gentle belle in denial. Hiding underneath the dry sarcasm and furrowing brow of a feminist with black nail polish.

"A softie?" she snorts.

"Yeah. It's your front. You scare the crap out of people so that they can't get near you. One of the defensive players on the team is a lot like you … draws out a lot of penalties from other people—but remains guarded and in check." He laughs.

Riley rolls her eyes, automatically relegating his statement to be false simply because he can't know her well enough yet. She's scary and jaded, she always has been. That's her thing.

"Did I ever mention I'm really good at penalty killing?" he asks.

He leans in close, putting a hand on Riley's cheek. She has no idea what that means, but it sounds great.

Her palms start to sweat in nervous anticipation. But she looks at him bravely, into his playful blue eyes, as he moves in for the kiss.

Oh, my God! Oh, my God! she screams inside her head, feeling fireworks of excitement and joy … and arousal?

He pulls back, and they both smile, and she knows that the libido inside her frigid little body has been stirred from its valiant strike.

"You just want to score." She laughs as he moves in again.

And she lets him.

• • •

"I wonder how Riley's date is going …" Jenna chirps, hopping around her hotel room at the Four Seasons in downtown Toronto.

"Well, I texted her, but she hasn't written back. So I'm going to assume that means—really well, or she's burying his body somewhere." Elle giggles, sitting on the bed.

"I still think she should've worn the dress …" Jenna sighs, looking at the slinky fabric still on a hanger.

"You know she's got her own sense of style," Elle warns. "Besides, now you can wear it!"

"Ugh, whatever. Is Hana ready yet?" Jenna asks, anxiously kicking her long legs around, her black tights moving with her easily. The bright turquoise tunic she's wearing makes her look unbelievably tan. Gold thread is embroidered gently on the flouncy fabric.

"Whoa, easy there, legs." Elle smiles, amazed at the intense energy her friend is emitting.

Jenna can almost be exhausting without having to even speak. She's always been hyperactive, especially when embracing her creativity and performing. The teachers in school could never understand her one-track mind of becoming a superstar singer.

"After the last e-mail from Ig, I'm about ready to tear something apart …" Jenna cackles bitterly.

"What happened?" Elle asks, amazed that the mysterious Mexican has kept a presence in her hectic life.

"Honestly, it was only e-mailing. And then when he started sending those ridiculous rants … the bullshit poetry … then I got that all he wanted was to hook up. He didn't care about me, he wants to be that guy who could tell people we had a thing, once upon a time."

Elle nods, a little nervous about why her friend is so worked up. Maybe she's trying to get her mind off Carter again, conveniently using the next available male target as a scapegoat.

"And then he says that he saw on my Web site that I'll be in Italy and he offers me the use of his villa in God knows where. And somewhere along that thread ... he mentions that he and his fiancée are going to be moving to Switzerland or something, but that he can meet me in Italy before!"

"Whoa, whoa, whoa! As in wife-to-be?" Elle asks for clarification, shocked.

Jenna nods violently, her eyes darting around.

"And what's worse is that he's totally 'oh, of course I must've told you I was engaged ... ' and I'm like, '*nooo*,' because you'd think I could remember that and, maybe, not flirt with a practically married man!"

"He tried to tell you that he told you?" Elle gasps, throwing her hands to her face in disbelief. She feels ill with sadness.

"Yeah! And then, he has the balls to ask if he can come along with us to Spain, too. And I'm like 'okay, hi, hello—did you not just bring up your fiancée?'"

Elle shakes her head. Marriage has been the most sacred of idealizations to her ever since she was old enough to dream of her fairytale wedding.

"And then he goes even worse and says that he and his fiancée chick are super open, and that they are free to be with whoever they want—that monogamy is not strict because they travel so much or something. What the shit?!"

Elle looks at her friend, her heart breaking into tiny pieces. True love is not part of this story's end.

"Then why would they even get married?" she whispers, frightened.

Jenna shrugs dramatically.

"Thank goodness nothing *ever* happened with him," Elle sighs, relieved for the emotional well-being of her friend.

"You're telling me! We almost boned in Scotland right then and there!" Jenna screeches, still pacing around the room at an anxious, flighty speed. "Thank God Riley forced them out so we could go to sleep. Ugh."

She stops suddenly in the middle of the carpet and slaps her forehead.

"Elle, I'm so sorry. I forgot to say happy birthday!" she gasps, rushing at her friend and hugging her like a powerful grizzly bear, knocking her down on the bed.

Elle blushes from the attack.

"What do you want to do for your special day?" Jenna asks, trying to think of a trendy, lavish restaurant to take her friend to make up for forgetting about her 22nd. Perhaps a popular steakhouse or oyster bar.

"Really ... not much. Maybe have a quiet dinner ... I don't know," she says softly. "I'm honestly amazed we are here, and that so are my parents! I can't wait to sleep at home ... or, well, I guess Ben's, you know what I mean."

There's a knock at the door, and Elle hops up to answer it. Hana peers at them through her sunglasses, the lenses blocking almost half her face. She is wearing flashy jeans with a bright white form-fitting leather jacket, the zipper done up just under her boobs, propping them up like a shelf.

"Ready?" Jenna asks excitedly, slipping into trendy Vivienne Westwood clogs.

"Yeah, the car's downstairs," Hana announces a little flatly as they walk to the elevators.

Wow, I'm kinda outta place, Elle thinks to herself, noticing that she's wearing a simple brown jersey dress and moccasins in stark contrast to Hana's white leather and Jenna's turquoise tunic. The two of them radiate unreal wealth and fashion, the kind of people you know would never wear the same outfit twice.

The women get into a tinted black car and are driven through the upscale Yorkville neighbourhood and straight to the doors of Holt Renfrew, only a couple of blocks away.

Holts is the quintessential Canadian high-end department store that Jenna always window-shopped, aspiring to be able to have a designer closet someday. Where she'd pretend to be disinterested in the clothes she browsed, so that the employees and other shoppers couldn't see her secret longing. She'd act as if luxury goods were something she purchased every day, and there was nothing special that caught her eye. When in reality, if she had a money tree, she would buy almost everything in sight. A temple of style and fashion beyond her wildest comprehension, it was always in her superstar plan—for the days when she could indulge her champagne tastes, but no longer on a beer budget.

Holts is also the place where Elle's mom sees a personal shopper every season. Where she selects new pieces for herself and her husband to update their wardrobes with classy simplicity. The secret role model to Jenna, Odile Bryans was a timeless, chic woman that she one day hoped to be like.

"So there'll be photographers out front; the store will remain open. Keep smiling as everyone stares with envy." Hana grins mischievously. Maximum exposure for her nouveau riche client, to brand her as someone everyone wants to be. Mack will be surprised that she's gotten such a stirring in his own backyard. Maybe show him she's not a force to be reckoned with in the PR world.

Hana has already planned a hoity-toity nightclub party for later, commanding the promoters to create an invitation-only popularity show and to pay her to bring Jenna out. She needs a good night out of drinking in this city—she finds it so boring compared with her usual pursuits in Los Angeles or New York. When she realized she'd have to spend time getting to know Jenna in Toronto, Hana felt about as thrilled to be in Canada as she would on an agricultural farm, as she assumed that's what would be in store. She's constructed a comfortable existence of staying in pricey hotels, partying with beautiful people, and indulging in the best drugs, clothes, and spa treatments available to humankind.

The car pulls up on Bloor Street West, and Jenna smiles at the memories of strolling down the same street with Parker not that long ago.

The store's doorman greets them as they step out of the car.

The paparazzi shout and scream, Jenna waving like a queen bee to her people. Cars stop on the street to see who the latest celebrity is, and some people cheer and honk when they recognize the hometown girl.

"Miss Ramsay, welcome. It's great to meet you," says a personal shopper. "I'm Ambur. I'll be accompanying you during your stay; please let me know if there's anything you'd like." The tall young black woman looks sleek in her trendy menswear outfit, chic glasses the finishing touch to a sexy secretary style.

Ambur leads them to the escalators and they head up to start shopping for shoes. Hana looks around the large store, trying to feign disappointment.

"What's wrong?" Jenna asks softly.

"It's no Barney's," she replies dryly. "Or Saks, and definitely doesn't compare to Bergdorf ..." she rants, loud enough for Ambur to hear, trying to bully her. But Ambur politely pretends to be invisible around the high-maintenance critic of her store. She isn't even the celebrity being catered to, yet has the audacity to try to pick a fight.

"Trust me ... Be open!" Jenna gasps, slightly insulted.

Elle looks apologetically to the personal shopper, resisting the urge to pull Hana away by the earlobes and send her to a time-out.

"I'm so sorry. You look absolutely familiar ..." Ambur whispers to Elle, hoping the petite redhead tagging along is less of a psycho.

"Oh ... um ... my mom shops here a lot?" Elle offers meekly.

The girl studies Elle's face carefully, recognizing something in her delicate doll-like features.

"Odile Bryans?" Elle offers.

"Oh, my gosh, yes! That's so funny. She got assigned to me recently. How great!" Ambur whispers, her modern bob hairstyle swishing as she giggles.

"Elle." She smiles, extending her hand out in introduction.

"Ambur," replies the woman, shaking it firmly with a warm grin. "Yeah, your mom had a party at the country club and picked up a beautiful Tory Burch dress. But had no date ..."

"Yeah, my dad is a surgeon—so he's kinda ... unpredictable sometimes."

As they browse the shoe department, Jenna lunges at a display, grabbing a pair of Lanvin flats and caressing them lovingly.

Elle slowly walks by the displays, still overwhelmed by the amount of fashion existing in the world. Helping stylists select clothes for Jenna has proven to be next to impossible with all the different designers and collections and seasons to keep track of. As is Jenna's ever-changing, bold sense of style that is so different than her own—getting gutsier with every hit she churns out, increasing the number of eyes watching her.

Elle glances down at a pair of Prada loafers but doesn't have the same impulse-purchasing behaviour as her friend. She admires them and moves on—well aware that she'd rather save her money for building a family nest egg, that she doesn't have the pressure to be wearing the latest and greatest like the starlet. Nor would she really care. She's invested in her luxurious basics, set to last her for a few more seasons.

Jenna waves over Ambur, observing Elle in her quiet modesty as she gracefully floats through the displays, not once picking up a heel, boot, or sandal.

"Put in an extra pair in a size six, okay? Can you gift wrap that?" she whispers to the personal shopper, having seen how Elle stared at the Lanvins with restraint. "But in baby pink. Black in size ten."

Jenna continues through the section, picking out a few key pieces. Then the group is redirected towards the denim nook, where she snaps up a couple of skinny jeans and a wide-leg trouser.

"*Us Weekly* hated you in colourful denim, Jen, so I'd stick to blues or darks. Maybe you can hype up a little bit of the new Line and Vince collections? And be sure to grab a few Armani pieces for support," Hana whispers. "I'm told Giorgio's been watching you more lately—thinking of you for their next fragrance. You don't want to lose to Rachel McAdams or something, do you?"

But she doesn't even hear the instructions. Jenna is like a kid at the zoo, lovingly gazing at all the fine wares on display. Touching and feeling the fabrics, emotional for the different designers she's had the chance to meet along her world travels. The shows she's being invited to attend—front row. The free clothes she's sent every day.

"So how did you end up working for her?" Ambur whispers to Elle, watching the singer dart around chaotically with Hana, leaving Eleanor to stand on the sidelines like a nanny watching her charges at the jungle gym.

"Childhood friend, actually." Elle smiles.

"Do you have some great Canadian designers I can get? I need something for a TV interview here," Jenna asks Ambur, modelling a Diane Von Furstenberg wrap dress she's selected for a movie premiere.

An array of wonderful surprises is brought out for her to sift through, the rolling rack full of dresses and skirts and blouses.

"Remember, you're going to need something for the awards show, and start thinking about the next music video," Hana points out, coming out of a fitting room in a Theory blouse and a black leather miniskirt, checking herself out in a full-length mirror.

Jenna smiles at a Greta Constantine dress that will definitely pop on the red carpet and selects a DSquared shirt for her interview.

"Elle, do you want anything?" Jenna asks, having tried on hundreds of pieces in whirlwind time. Other shoppers are spying on them from different areas of the store, trying to see what items may be on the next Hot List. Eager to know what the homegrown celebrity will dub as "in style."

"Oh, no, lovee, don't worry about it." Elle blushes, uncomfortable that Jenna feels the need to provide for her somehow. Yes, she's accumulated millions of dollars in a short amount of time, but couldn't that money stay saved in the bank instead? What if Jenna gets marries and decides to have babies soon?

"Really? Are you sure?" Her friend smiles, pretending to seduce her with a Marc Jacobs jacket. "It's your birthday, of course …"

Elle looks at it, gritting her teeth, but still declines the purchase, feeling uneasy about using her friend's income.

Hana emerges from the fitting room with a pile of clothes and heaves them on the counter, brushing her blonde hair out of her face, exhausted.

Ambur rings them through, and the total of their bill is enough to buy a mid-sized car. Elle stares at the floor, ready to faint, as she pulls out Jenna's credit card and hands it over. Pained.

"Okay, hi, hello! I forgot to get some cosmetics!" Jenna shouts, with the same intensity as if she were announcing an impending volcano eruption.

They head to the store's street level, and she begins grabbing various containers—lip glosses and perfumes, nail polishes and candles.

"Shit, Elle … these Dior glosses seem stupid cheap here …" Jenna whispers, stocking up on her signature colour. An item that used to be considered a total splurge, instead of a careless commodity.

The dozen bags are loaded into their waiting car, as the paparazzi capture shots of a delighted Jenna Ramsay after fulfilling her shopping desire.

"Hey—can we go to Aritzia?" Jenna pipes up, her tone borderline whining as she remembers the trendy shop a few doors down.

Hana shrugs, not having anything else to do. She's never heard of this place; hopefully it will be somewhat as exciting as her usual stores on Robertson. She beckons a security guard to walk the group down the heavy-traffic street and to the women's boutique. Photographers follow them the entire block, as people in the other stores stop and stare at the commotion.

Jenna throws open the store's heavy door, and all the shoppers and salespeople turn in silence. She smiles confidently, marching in like it's nobody's business, and everyone keys up into frantic excitement over the star's presence.

Hana raises an eyebrow as she scans the store's decoration and its incredibly diverse merchandise.

Not a dump. I'm impressed by Jen's selection. Finally something worthwhile and cool, she smirks, as she gears up for Round 2 of "let's see how much money we can spend."

This ... is a little much ... Elle thinks to herself, as she follows behind the two style powerhouses, scared by all the items they start grabbing. *I can't wait to see Ben. Just one more hour,* she tries to console herself.

Spending time with someone a little less concerned about the latest handbag is starting to sound real good at this moment. To sit on the couch and eat Chinese food, even while watching sports recaps that Elle doesn't care for, seems almost heavenly compared with dressing up in case of a paparazzi attack.

"Ooh—what about this?" Jenna coos, holding up a gorgeous silk Talula Babaton blouse to her chest.

"Jenna Ramsay doesn't wear that," Hana informs, snatching the blouse and putting it back on the metal rack and taking another piece. "Here—this is better for your image."

Elle stares at the two of them uncomfortably as all the shop girls gather to dote on their famous client.

• • •

"So I made reservations for Elle's birthday dinner at Sassafraz," Hana announces, striding into Jenna's hotel room later that afternoon. With Elle at Ben's, and Riley staying at her dad's, they trimmed down their accommodations to only two bedrooms.

Mack has just left them, stopping in for a pep talk to motivate Jenna to write new songs. The timeline to start recording another album has been tentatively set, even though she's only been promoting her debut for five months. But this is long-term planning. Bigger picture.

Jenna is sitting in a leather armchair and staring out the window with her orange journal open. She's wrapped in a soft throw blanket.

"Sassafraz? I thought she wanted to go to that small French place ..." she says, not bothering to turn and look at Hana.

"Yeah. But there are always photographers in Yorkville, and this is a great event to maximize exposure—celebrating a friend's birthday shows you are a thoughtful and grounded star. And I can't get you the same sort of private area at the other place ... we always send clients here, it's easier to photograph. We gotta set the standard high for you,

Jen. You know you should foot the bill tonight, too, right? Play up the generosity card."

Jenna looks a little uncomfortable to be usurping her friend's birthday plans but gets her henchman do all the talking instead.

"Trust me, Elle." Hana's voice travels from Jenna's bathroom. "This is a great place. You've been there? Phenomenal. You didn't like it? No? Well, unfortunately, your friend has security restrictions. So this is the ideal place for her to be able to go tonight. You wouldn't want her to get attacked by crazy people, right? Okay. Good. Thank you for being flexible."

Jenna exhales heavily, looking down at the exclusive neighbourhood below, people walking through the concrete jungle like tiny ants while she's up in her protected tower.

I wonder what Mom is doing, she thinks to herself, debating whether to invite her to the celebratory dinner that evening. She recalls a memory of her mom warning her to stay away from the high-street stores. To stay away from the Yorkville neighbourhood in general. *It'll make you want things you can't have,* she had said, with the intention that Jenna would never have the resources to shop at Gucci or Louis Vuitton or Chanel. To buy Moët instead of Molson.

Except now she can.

"Okay, so after a mild battle—we are good to go for the location I want," Hana says, rolling her eyes. "Gotta say, your friends are quite melodramatic. Totally don't get this amazing life you have."

Jenna doesn't even hear her; she's lost in thought.

"Okay, well, I better leave you alone to write," Hana says flatly, annoyed that her audience isn't paying attention.

"Huh? Oh. Right. Yeah—can you do me a favour?" Jenna asks. "Can you give my mom a call and invite her out?"

Hana stares at the singer, surprised. She crosses her arms disapprovingly, knowing the backstory of Jenna Ramsay's unsupportive mother.

"Uh … I guess? Do you really want to start a reconciliation? In public?"

"It's not that. Can you … invite her. She probably won't even come," Jenna sighs. She turns back to the window, stopping the conversation abruptly.

Hana backs out of the room with no intention to call.

maximum.

[Tokyo, Japan—end of October 2010]

The massive crowd surrounding Narita International Airport is almost reaching a thousand.

Jenna Ramsay and her two assistants have just touched down in Tokyo to start a month of promotional work, hitting Japan, Hong Kong, Indonesia, and Thailand among their targets. After a summer in Europe with a steady growth of popularity, the frenetic demand in Asia outdoes any prior success tenfold.

"*Shiiit,* this is insane," Riley gasps, on the phone with the private security firm hired to help transport Jenna around the city. The arrangement being a non-negotiable from Mack, already familiar with the fervent adoration of Japanese fans towards pop icons.

"What? What's going on?" Elle asks worriedly, as she rebraids her hair. She tries to stretch her arms out and loosen up, wearing a head-to-toe yoga outfit. She unzips her grey track jacket and puts it into her carry-on.

The group is being held in an executive lounge inside the airport, the girls tired and anxious from the lengthy plane trip. Already feeling frayed and exhausted, the strenuous travel schedule doesn't bode well for the three young women.

Riley puts up a finger, asking for silence, and listening to the coordinator on the line. She hangs up, looking at her two friends, shocked. She shoves her hands into the kanga pocket of her Quiksilver hoodie, stolen from Hunter's closet. It's many sizes too big, but comfortable. She's wearing her dark plastic-framed glasses, and is in cargo pants, not concerned about her look.

"What is it? Come on, out with it!" Jenna demands impatiently, pouting like a five-year-old.

"It seems we underestimated the viral impact of your singles here." Riley laughs nervously. "There is a *preeetty* large crowd of people out front."

"How big?" Elle bites her lip.

"Big enough that they have to send extra security *and* the police before we move," Riley explains, wiping her eyeglasses on her sleeve.

"So we can't leave yet?" Jenna asks, annoyed. She plops down in a chair, her bright green tracksuit begging to be a bull's-eye for autograph seekers and photographers. She carelessly drops her newest Louis Vuitton Speedy on the ground, its contents plopping out.

"You could leave. And then you could die. So ... no, I will not be responsible for you getting trampled. The agency doesn't think they can handle the crowd, so we will wait until there's a go-ahead," Riley advises crossly.

"But, really, how big?" Elle asks, her eyes big with surprise.

"They said a few hundred."

"Hundred? Few hundred?" Elle gasps, frightened.

Jenna stares down at the floor, an eerie smile creeping across her face. A few hundred people here to see *her*.

"Okay, upwards of a thousand," Riley admits. "But don't freak out."

Elle's face drains of colour, making her even paler than her naturally porcelain skin.

Riley gets back on the phone to update Mack on their situation, but has to answer her call waiting.

"Ugh, Hunter—I don't have time to talk right now! Mack is on the other line!" she grumbles into the phone, annoyed with his constant outpourings of attention. Her Incoming Calls log is a steady reminder of him.

A few minutes later, a small contingent of private security guards enters the lounge, their commando boots thumping on the floor heavily.

"Miss Kohl?" asks a dark-haired Japanese man, he and his men all dressed in solid black, looking like they stepped out of an action movie where they all fight as one.

Riley shakes his hand firmly as he introduces himself as Nori, the team leader.

"Miss Kohl, yes, we have so many people in front of the airport that it is overwhelming for you to walk," he starts to explain in choppy English. "There is extra men to help, and the police will open the road to drive out. We must be patient."

The girls nod obediently and wait until he gets the all-clear from the teams positioned throughout the airport and out on the street.

He hands the three of them earplugs from one of his cargo pockets.

Elle looks at him, confused.

"For the screaming. Very loud," he explains gently, his walkie-talkie spouting Japanese commands.

The girls put the squishy foam in their ears, and Nori begins to lead them through the airport. They are flanked at either side with a dozen guards. Riley leads the girls, with Jenna and Elle side-by-side behind her.

This feels so silly. This is most definitely unnecessary and overdramatized, Elle assures herself as they wind through the building, no one jumping out at them or taking pictures.

But as they approach the doors exiting onto the street, she gasps at the calamity outside.

"Good googlie-mooglie," she whispers, grabbing Jenna's hand in sheer terror.

There is a sea of people shouting and holding up signs, nothing visible but human heads. For what seems like miles and miles ahead, bodies are crammed together in anticipation of a royal arrival.

As the girls get closer, the screams dramatically increase in volume.

"Stay with me," Nori shouts, as Elle and Jenna grab onto Riley's sweatshirt, like children clutching their mother.

They walk through the automatic door, and the crowd melts into a constant, ear-splitting hum.

There are posters and banners welcoming Jenna to Japan, images of her fluttering in the breeze. The emotion on the faces of the boys and girls is beyond intense, most of them having waited for hours to catch a glimpse. They all shout and sob frantically as if they're in heat.

The three girls are about to get into the car when Jenna darts out and tries to sign some autographs by the barricade. The volume surges to apocalyptic loudness, Jenna wincing in pain at the commotion. A hand reaches through the crowd and tries to grab onto her shoulder, holding her with a death-grip only a rabid teenager can muster.

Nori swoops in and yanks Jenna away ferociously, pushing her straight into the car. He hops in after her, and they speed through the police barricade and into the city.

"Never again!" Nori scolds her, breathless.

Jenna nods, gripping the leather interior of the car with sweaty palms, her heart racing.

Riley looks at Jenna, annoyed, wondering where the impulse to be such a showoff has come from. To compromise safety for a potential headline on the evening news.

"There must've actually been a thousand people there," Elle says, her eyes bulging at never having experienced such an adrenaline rush.

"Yes, absolutely. And it will not get any better," Nori advises. "They announce on the radio stations your hotel location."

Riley picks at her nails, anxious about how she's going to manage the next few weeks in such a free-for-all. And with Hunter and Ben deciding to come for a visit in a couple of days, juggling everyone's agendas will be her worst nightmare.

Why does he have to take the few days off and frickin' fly across the world? Why does his team bench him now of all times, and let him get even more mopey and emotional? she thinks of Hunter, uncomfortably. Of his forcefulness in trying to squeeze every moment with her, his weakness in letting a hand injury sideline him—and not fighting for a faster recovery. His team was less than impressed with his depressive laziness, so they dubbed him a scratch—taken from the lineup in retaliation for his lack of productivity the past few weeks.

So Hunter decided to annoy them more by hopping on a plane with Ben, his lonely comrade, for a short jaunt to Tokyo. There was nothing Riley could do when informed of it. Elle would welcome Ben with open arms, and Hunter would impose his visit at the expense of rehabilitation, like an obsessive, hormone-ruled teenager struggling to balance his rationale and emotions.

She shakes off the funny, nervous feeling in her stomach and text messages Mack:

Thousand ppl @airport. Can't do this alone. Need backup.
This is ooc. Can u send Hana?

• • •

A couple of days into the Japan journey, the three girls are stabilized with the help of Hana Rin and Mack Madison. After Riley's SOS, the two mobilized and flew to Tokyo almost immediately, catching glimpses of the madness (including Jenna's close call at the airport) on gossip talk shows. Hana arrived first, dropping everything instantly and grabbing her already-packed travel bag always left by the door of her condo. She displays military precision in her commitment to Jenna's career, deployed like a seasoned secret agent.

Nori was definitely bang-on about things not getting any easier. At every appearance and performance, the crowds waiting to catch sight of Jenna Ramsay could barely be contained, causing ridiculous traffic delays. The screaming and pandemonium went throughout the night, the girls often sneaking peeks from the safety of the Mandarin Oriental's elevation, watching the crowds below. The street near the hotel is already flooded with vigilant fans, and there have been crazies arrested in the hotel, trying to pose as guests or housekeepers.

The group is sitting around a table in the penthouse suite, discussing scheduling and upcoming plans before bedtime. The three friends are in their pyjamas, Mack still in a suit, and Hana is dressed to hit the nightclub circuit with a new fashion contact she's met.

"All right, so are the guys still arriving here on Monday?" Hana asks, referring to Hunter and Ben. Ben has been busy trying to combat the negative media attention Hunter's been receiving for his divided focus, for his lovesick ways—but unable to sway him from travelling to Japan. The sports reporters are well aware of his private life, and his long-distance relationship, using it as an excuse for poor on-ice performance lately. One article speculated Hunter was depressed without regular sex, making Riley want to vomit from story—considering they haven't even gone down that road.

"Yeah, Hunter has a game on the west coast, and they fly out right after. Even though he'll probably be benched anyway," Riley replies bitterly, looking at the calendar on her phone and taking notes at the same time.

"I think it's sweet he's trying so hard to be with you." Jenna smiles.

"*I'd* fucking bench him for this stupidity. Whining about a hand injury, and then running off like Juliet? I have other things to worry about. I need him to man up," Riley gripes.

"Easy, Romeo ..." Jenna laughs, putting her hands up in surrender.

"Well, the media commitments are finished as of Tuesday, so you have a day to sightsee if you'd like, and then they fly back to Toronto Wednesday?" Mack confirms. "It *is* an awfully long distance for only two days of visiting."

"Yep," Elle agrees. "I've confirmed their tickets. Then we'll continue our Asia tour."

"I miss North America," Hana whines.

"So in about two weeks, we land in Toronto ... spend the weekend there resting. Maybe catch a hockey game ..." Elle giggles, sipping a mug of green tea. "I'm sure he'd be inspired to show you how much he's healed playing on home ice, Riles."

Someone kicks her under the table.

"Then we'll prep for Europe Round Two—confirm the photo shoot with *Vogue* ..." Riley continues, grinding her teeth.

"Carter is going to be there for the weekend, in Toronto, I think we're going to talk ... maybe I'll stop in and see my mom," Jenna says to no one in particular, lacking business contributions to the conversation.

"Well, Jen. I want to put you up at the Hazelton this time," Hana announces, switching the focus to the Toronto trip and making Jenna feel as if she's included in her conversation thread.

Jenna looks confused.

"I'm sure you'll be busy downtown and everything. You're a star now—it's kind of a big deal that you live the star life."

"But my mother lives—"

Hana interrupts her. "And for security ... do you really want people to follow you back to your mother's home?" she gasps.

Jenna pauses thoughtfully and agrees to the hotel stay. She hasn't heard back from her mother at all. Granted, she's only really reached out during late-night drunken phone calls when she feels her bravest.

Riley and Elle glance at each other across the table, and then look at Mack, who is preoccupied with his laptop.

She's trying to keep her away from her mom, Riley observes. *And Mack has no opinion ... or no clue.*

He tunes back into the conversation, trying to focus the girls back on to the schedule.

"All right. Then you leave Sunday and fly straight to Milan, hop on a jet and do the appearance in Monaco. Then stop in England and do the gig at Albert Hall. Fly back to Rome late after that," Mack starts.

"So, twelve hours in Italy, six in Monaco. A week in the UK again. Shoot the new video. Quick trip to France for three days. Spain for two. Then jump back to the States right before Christmas for a quick boost," he continues listing.

"Yes, I'll work on everything stateside. We'll start strong with New York, LA, and the talk shows, then a few satellite cities," Hana explains. "We should arrange jet travel so we can hit multiple cities in one day. Don't know about 'Oprah' yet. We'll secure a fresh production team for the new album in the U.S., new talent—new direction. That ties us up straight through until ..."

"Holiday time?" Jenna groans, feeling overwhelmed by the thought of so many weeks in the future already being preplanned for her.

"Yep. You'll have a week off, and then back to Toronto and smaller little projects there. Sing some holiday parties or whatever, do a little charity crap," Hana instructs.

"Okay, great. New Year's?" Jenna asks, her eyes wide with excitement.

"Still seeing where you'll book for that. But I promise you, it will be epic." Hana smiles proudly, not wanting to jinx her arrangements. She feels like partying in Vegas and will try swinging her client in that direction—to expense everything out.

Jenna nods, excited by Hana's cutthroat competitiveness for only the best.

"So between now and your holidays, you have two new singles launching, which brings us up to … seven total!" Mack exclaims, taking his glasses off and rubbing his temples.

"Seven number ones! Or at least, seven top five singles at the very worst …" Hana grins proudly. "Multiplatinum, bitches."

"That's insane!" Jenna marvels, holding her coffee cup thoughtfully.

I wonder how much money I have right now. Right at this very second, she wonders. She hasn't seen her bank account since it was overdrawn last year.

"This is beyond any expectation I could have ever had," Mack admits bluntly.

"Anyway," Hana interrupts. "I guess we get through tomorrow, and then how about I take over for Monday and Tuesday?"

Riley looks at Mack, unsure.

"What? I can handle it. Give them some breathing room. They've been on the road nonstop; I'm sure they could use the time to rest up," Hana replies matter-of-factly, motioning to Riley and Elle.

"Um … thanks, Hana," Elle says, surprised she won't have to hand her boyfriend a map and tell him to enjoy Japan.

They wrap up their meeting and spread out, waiting for their food to be delivered to the suite.

Riley slips into Elle's room and gently shuts the door behind her.

"Is it me, or was that completely bizarre?" she asks, startling Elle, who was in the process of easing into her bed.

Elle catches her breath and obliges her friend's conspiracy theory. Riley hops onto the bed beside her, crossing her legs, the two friends huddling close to whisper.

"Maybe she's trying to be nice, to give us time with our loves …" Elle suggests.

Riley scrunches up her face, not buying it.

"You're right. She's not being nice. She's up to something. But ... really, to have quality time with Ben ... I don't quite care," she whimpers.

"I know. I'm just saying, that I'm not paranoid ... she's up to something, right?"

Elle nods and lets out a heavy sigh and stares out the dark window.

"I still can't believe how these people are going insane for her," she whispers, shaking her head in disbelief.

"I know, really. It's like ... some sort of heavenly figure has descended. There's no way anyone would get this kind of reaction in North America," Riley replies. "Not even Keith Urban."

"Keith Urban?"

"What? Country music is okay," Riley huffs.

Elle has to stop herself from ridiculing her friend. Riley Kohl and country music are a pairing never imagined before.

"Where is this coming from?" Elle asks, losing it and bursting into giggles.

Riley scrunches her face and mutters a response.

"Your boyfriend? Oh yes ... he is from Missouri. I forgot about that. I'm honestly surprised; you never struck me as someone that would be ... caught dead in a cowboy hat." Elle smiles.

"I dunno. I mean, if you listen to some of the lyrics of that genre, they can be pretty angsty and moody. Which is totally what I'm about." Riley winks, hopping off the bed, nearly tripping on her plaid pyjama pants. "That reminds me, I want to download this new guy on iTunes, Anthony Daniels—totally my type of wallowing!"

Elle curls up into a ball, wishing she could sink further into the mattress. Her light green satin pyjamas need to be laundered, but she doesn't care—they're familiar.

"Hey, am I a bad person for being really excited not to do this anymore come June?" she asks Riley, lowering her voice to barely a whisper.

Riley dramatically heaves a sigh of relief.

"*Ohhh*, my God, you have no idea. Part of me is seriously counting down. Some days, I wake up and hate everything."

"It sounds stupid, but all I really want right now is to live somewhere stable. Wake up in the same bed every day, get to be around Ben more. Because between his travel and my travel, it's like an estranged relationship or something. And I can't handle that at this point in my life. I want to settle down ..."

Riley nods sympathetically, touching stuff around Elle's room, nosy. She's rolled up her grey cotton long-sleeve shirt, and she picks up a bottle of perfume, sniffs, and sprays it on her pulse points.

"Don't you ever want to lock yourself in Hunter's apartment or something and never leave—not have to get on another plane?" Elle sighs.

"Well ... kind of," Riley replies, a little uncomfortable, as she flutters one of the window drapes to peek outside.

"Kind of?" Elle asks, raising an eyebrow.

"I mean, I'd love to not have to check into my two-hundredth hotel room ... but I dunno, Elle, I'm kinda ... not sure about this whole Hunter thing."

Elle lays flat on her stomach, staring at her friend with childlike curiosity.

"Well ... he mentioned me on the news, it's a bit ... er ... I don't think he realizes I'm not cut out to be that ... athlete wifey or whatever. No offence. I still want to travel the world, not be a lapdog."

Elle nods, listening to Riley's awkwardness, as her friend stiffly crosses her arms over her chest.

"Well, it is definitely different to date a player versus an agent..." she confides in her friend. "The uncertainties of trades and their grueling game schedules ..."

"Yeah, like—if I was back home, he'd be gone most of the time travelling with the hockey club. And on game days, would be at the arena ... and some people take the sport *waaay* too seriously, don't you think? I don't want people to know me, and to know me because of him."

Elle secretly thanks Ben's short stature for preventing him a professional career and making his schedule as an agent more behind the scenes than his clients'.

"Well, speaking as your friend, I think you need to really think about what you see yourself doing. Yes, he's a great guy, and he's madly in love with you already ... but ... you need to be honest with yourself. We've changed a lot in these past ... months ... we're still evolving a lot. That's perfectly okay," Elle assures softly. "Don't let him be led on if you don't see yourself with him."

"He's great, really fun and adventurous, but ... something might be off. I feel like, how he looks at me ... he's waiting for me to be something else."

"Could you also be looking at him and hoping he'd be something else?" Elle smirks.

Riley bites her lip.

"Change happens to everyone," Elle sighs.

"Between all this, and powerhouse Jenna ..." Riley trails off.

"I know! Is it me, or is she different?" Elle interrupts.

"Totally changing. And not in a way that we seem to really have an effect on. Especially with her new right-hand man," Riley grumbles.

"I know. I can't tell if it's only part of the persona, or if she's actually believing ... all this ..." Elle sighs, pointing out the window.

"I can tell you that every night, seeing all of this, has been a huge motivator to get my ass in gear and finish my book so I can get the fuck out," Riley admits, sitting down on the bed.

"You're done?" Elle gasps excitedly.

Riley looks at the ground, a little embarrassed. "Yeah. Sorta. I mean ... almost. It's not ... perfect."

Elle looks at her long-time friend and rolls her eyes. "With you, it'll never be perfect. Why don't you send it out to someone? An agent or something? What did you end up writing about?"

Riley's eyes widen in terror. "No! People can't see it! It's a paranormal mystery set in the medieval ages."

Elle laughs hysterically, her high pitch vibrating so loudly that she has to muffle herself with a pillow. "Sorry. I love sexy medieval—that's not what was funny, I swear. But, honestly, how do you expect to be published, lovee? You know, that's how I felt about my first paintings. But seriously, Riles, you are a great writer. You need to be more confident in that. You need to admit you can actually do this."

Riley glances at her nails, the manicure long wasted away and nothing really left to pick at.

"Would you let me show it to Laith?" Elle offers.

"Laith Bassel?" Riley hisses, horrified.

"Yes, Riley. He's not as scary as I thought. Yes, he's tough—but I think if you let him look at your manuscript, maybe he can help you out—put you in touch with the right person. Or at least give you feedback from the insider's point of view," Elle suggests.

Riley exhales slowly and agrees to let her friend's mentor look at her work.

"I might take a trip down to New York next time we're back ... anywhere near that part of the world for longer than a day." Elle laughs, still surprised to find herself in Japan. "I haven't gotten to actually speak to him with all of our time differences; all our discussions have been through e-mail. He's really trying to get me to spend some time down there with his circle—and to be honest, I am kinda devastated I can't. Would I even get a few days off?"

Riley smiles sympathetically but is screaming on the inside. Showing her work to a credible art insider is as good as printing up a business card and putting "writer" as her title.

Maybe thinking affirmatively will actually help her get published. Help her manifest the career she's always dreamed of, the life path she's secretly thought was meant to be. If she believes in it, and acts like it—maybe she can be it, just like Jenna has. There's no doubt that she feels this is her calling, the path she's supposed to take. But the fear of actually starting down it is crippling. There's no one to hide behind if she fails.

"Anyway, what do we wanna do with the boys when they get here?" Riley asks, clapping her hands together and walking around the bedroom.

Elle ponders for a minute and pulls out the tourist guide binder given to her by the concierge. She's marked it up with colour-coded tabs.

Riley stares at her, horrified.

• • •

Early the next morning, while Elle and Riley sleep in, Hana plans to lay the groundwork to bond with Jenna.

Hana looks at herself in the bathroom mirror and applies another coat of black mascara over her eyelash extensions, blinking. She looks at the finished product of herself happily, appreciating the beautiful Yves Saint Laurent outfit she took from one of Jenna's suitcases.

The girl has a closet specifically for free clothes she will hopefully wear. It's not like she's going to notice me taking some. She smiles to herself, smoothing the pink silk blouse.

It's six in the morning, and she's already perfectly put together. Hair extensions curled, push-up bra in place, bronzer expertly applied. The counter is littered with makeup products.

She steps out into the suite where Jenna is sitting at a table and staring at her breakfast, unmotivated to take a bite. Hana runs through the list of appointments on tap.

"It'll be hectic going from the radio station to the TV station, but we can grab lunch and eat on the way in the car," she comments. "But then we can have a really nice dinner out, the two of us, maybe grab drinks …"

Jenna nods, not really listening and kind of wishing to be out posing in front of monuments with her friends instead. But the whole "fans flocking around adoringly" thing definitely suits her best, she concedes, so playing tourist will be forfeited to get the lifestyle she desires.

She stabs a fork at her full plate of food, her stomach burning with hunger but her mind apathetic.

"Anyway, we don't have time for breakfast—you need to get changed," Hana scolds, looking at her blue satin nightgown.

Jenna disappears to change and reemerges in a pair of trendy jeans and a flowing red top, her makeup applied in record time.

"Hmm … what about different shoes?" Hana suggests, staring at the casual canvas TOMS with disgust.

"Oh, okay." Jenna shrugs and rushes off to change into sky-high heels. "I even found a purse to match!" she squeals, holding up a cherry red clutch.

"Great. See, you have an image—the sexpot thing needs to be consistent, or people will forget about you. You were okay doing the innocent, conservative thing at first … but now, people expect more. Especially after your next magazine cover. Maybe you could show your belly in a photo spread … how are your abs?" Hana asks, studying Jenna's body.

Jenna uneasily grabs her waistline.

"Oh, come on." Hana rolls her eyes, walking up to her and lifting her shirt to inspect her client's midline.

Jenna winces uncomfortably.

"Hmmm … well, I could book you in with my personal trainer to tone that up a bit. Maybe try cut down a little bit on the … food … for a week or two. Just to help speed things along. We've got a potential shoot with *Maxim* next month—do you know how powerful it is to be able to say you weren't airbrushed? If you need a cheat, you could start smoking and snack on packs of sugar—that's how I keep off the extra five pounds!"

Jenna exhales deeply, feeling a little out of body with exhaustion. She hasn't eaten a proper meal in weeks, and insomnia is draining all energy from her brain. It's like she can't slow down her thoughts long enough to relax.

"So let's get going. Do you want me to carry your stuff?" Hana asks, opening her oversized Gucci hobo and rummaging around.

Jenna shrugs, handing over her BlackBerry and a fresh tube of lip gloss. She no longer is in the habit of carrying a wallet—she has people for that.

The two girls trot out and meet Nori by the elevator.

"I still feel we should go down the service elevator to the parking garage," he says, trying to sway Hana.

"No. We need pictures of her—getting out there, signing autographs and all that. Making nice with the Japanese. So, no, we will stick to the original plan and leave through the front door. After all, that's why I'm paying you," Hana barks, staring him down.

Nori shrugs and walkie-talkies down to his men as they descend.

The elevator stops at the lobby, pausing, and then the doors open slowly. The number of people waiting in the streets takes Jenna's breath away.

As she walks out through the main door, the screams explode, and her ears feel like they're bursting. She's left Nori's earplugs in her room on purpose, not wanting to mute any part of this experience.

A group of young schoolgirls catches her eye, as they sob hysterically at the sight of her.

Jenna walks up to sign some autographs for them, as if that would console them. But they only start shrieking even more.

"*Jana! Jana!* We missed school to see you!" one of them shrieks through gasps of excitement.

Jenna stares at them in horror. They must be in middle school, still in their uniforms, and they're already cutting class? It oddly reminds her of herself.

"No, girls—go back to school. You are so young," she says kindly, touching one of them on the arm.

They start screaming even more.

Okay, not gonna listen to a word I say, Jenna thinks to herself as she moves through the crowd, scribbling her name on posters and CD cases.

"She touched me!" the girl shrieks, throwing her head up to the sky as if thanking a supernatural power.

Jenna fails to notice Hana leaning into whisper to the schoolgirls.

"Hey, if you come back tomorrow, maybe she'll invite you to her show. She loves to see her fans. Maybe become friends."

The girls start squealing, and she puts a finger to her lips, tricking them into feeling that they're in on the biggest secret ever.

Anything to draw a crowd.

Nori leads them into the waiting car, and they pull away from the barricade to start their jam-packed day.

• • •

Jenna wraps up her last interview of the day, having seen reporters for the entire afternoon and evening in the comforts of the hotel.

The last photographer, from a Tokyo daily, has annoyingly been taking pictures nonstop during the interview led by his colleague. Jenna's certain all the shots he has are of her midsentence, with her mouth open. She turns to glare at him and commands him to wait for some posed images at the end.

The reporter snaps at the overeager photographer to back off, embarrassed.

He turns back to his interview subject and asks his last question.

"So, Jenna—what are you most excited about right now?"

"Oh, wow, great question ..." She smiles blankly, staring at the carpet absentmindedly.

"Well, Jenna acquired a lovely sports car," Hana interjects, trying to lead her exhausted client.

"Oh, really?" He grins.

Jenna's eyes blink, listening to the cue. "Yeah, I got a bright red vintage Maserati ... I haven't actually driven it yet ... I hear it's fast," she taunts.

"You like cars?" the reporter probes, surprised by her sudden bitchy side. She's been portrayed as a sweetheart up until now.

"Meh. I wanted something that reflects ... me. Fun and free. Whatever." Jenna shrugs, not wanting to continue the conversation anymore and shutting down.

The reporter studies her carefully, not sure how to take in the singer's lack of focus, the glimpse of a foul temper bubbling just beneath the surface of her perfect makeup.

"Thank you, Miss Ramsay. We will now go," he announces, finishing some notes.

The photographer pops up from his seat and fires off more pictures.

Jenna's upper lip curls in annoyance, but she tries to force a fake smile.

Mack strolls into the living room of the modern suite, where they've conducted all the interviews, and listens in.

"What was the last question?" he asks Hana.

"What is she most excited about right now." She rolls her eyes.

He clears his throat and gets the attention of the reporter.

"You know, Jenna is actually working towards building a charitable foundation in the near future. She told me last night that she is extremely excited for this future project so that she can give back. She hasn't decided exactly how … but the bigger picture is to try to make a difference in the lives of others," Mack announces, feeding a suitable answer to the writer.

Jenna looks at him blankly, wishing he were sitting in the chair instead of her.

"Was the sports car a congratulatory present for yourself, then?" the reporter asks dryly.

"No, I bought that when I had my first number one single. Now I have five. It's time to do something else with myself," Jenna bites back.

"Great. Thanks. Bye," Hana says roughly, practically dragging the reporter and photographer out the door.

Silence hovers over the hotel room.

"Why did you talk about your sports car?" Mack asks, surprised. It's in direct violation to the image they've produced—a girl next door who goes from rags to riches but never quite adjusts to the high life.

Jenna shrugs, spreading out on the couch, exhausted.

"Okay … but keep the bigger picture in mind," he warns, looking more to Hana, surprised his pit bull didn't redirect the line of questioning. "My limo's downstairs. See you back in Toronto."

And with that, he slips off to gather his luggage, having extracted himself from the rest of the trip.

"That was a solid day, Jen. Great coverage!" Hana smiles, satisfied with all the arrangements she's made to promote her.

"I hope so. The intensity is … draining," she wails, unable to get up, feeling like a rag doll.

"But your commitment to pushing further, to making your career astronomical, is great. Not all artists are this self-sacrificing—don't get that the more they put out, the more they get back."

Jenna ponders the point, thinking about the number of hours she has spent putting herself out there. Hookering. Do all the prayers said at bedtime count? Or the times she's sung along to the radio, watching herself in the mirror?

"Is there anything more that I can do?" she blurts out shyly, looking at Hana for guidance, afraid she's not as astronomical as she could be.

Hana smiles, a sinister air about her, satisfied that the celebrity is turning to her. Maybe she's finally starting to trust her, even realizing that her friends don't actually know anything about managing a media phenomenon. Not like she does.

Hana sits down on the couch beside her. "Well …" she starts, a little dramatically. "You've done great in covering most of your bases. The friends, the fashion, the music. You're like the cool girl everyone wants at their party."

"But?" Jenna asks, curling her legs under her.

"But, I think that one thing that was going great for you was your relationship with Carter."

Jenna is listening, wanting to hear more.

"People loved you together. The beautiful, successful, famous couple thing is priceless in terms of press. I think that if you would consider getting back together … it might be a smart move. Get that constant buzz of tabloid coverage. You know, your photos were selling for thousands of dollars …"

Jenna bites her lip, a little uneasy at the thought of having Carter's very public thirst for attention back in her life.

"Doesn't it distract people from my music?"

"No, no! Don't be silly. He was so proud to be dating you. Jen, he was completely in love with you and only wanted people to see you. He talks about you because he cares about you, not because he's trying to brag. I mean, when it comes down to strategic partnerships, you're the only client where I can safely say that the guy totally 'gets' the industry. And actually supports your career!" she scoffs.

"This is true," Jenna says, recalling the past couple of "dates" she's had. More like group hangs to meet new people, without giving them the opportunity to sell a first-date story to the press. Awkward dinner reservations or cocktail parties with eligible bachelors of whatever city, all slyly set up by Hana.

"People have taken a lot of interest in you lately simply because your name's in lights. But if I'm not mistaken, he noticed you before all that. It's hard to meet someone who can see through the image."

Jenna thinks back to her first night in London, the bright orange shirt that took her breath away.

"How does he make you feel?" Hana asks, trying to play her best "sensitive listener" role, trying to imitate Elle slightly.

Jenna exhales loudly, hugging one of the couch cushions like a whiny toddler.

"Because I think that love and passion ... should feel like a tornado. Crazy, blinding energy that consumes you. Like being near that person makes your lungs want to explode, and being away from them does, too. I mean, you're a creative—you're better at explaining!" She laughs, throwing her hand up playfully.

Jenna scrunches her face up. "Maybe I'll get in touch with him soon ..."

Hana lights up, having argued her case successfully.

"That's great. Because being afraid to love, it seems horrible ..." she coos. "And if your friends make fun of you ... then screw them! They're only being judgmental and jealous."

Jenna turns her head, looking at Hana curiously.

"I mean, how many people out there actually find their Bens and Hunters just like that?" she says, snapping her fingers. "You deserve a chance to try make it work. Your circumstance doesn't exactly allow you to be the damsel that can be courted."

"Well, what about you? Don't you ever get sick of all the commotion? Don't you want to settle down back in LA with that special someone?" Jenna asks dreamily.

Hana stares at her as if she's spoken in German.

Jenna shrugs, getting up off the couch and stretching her long legs. "Right, then."

"So, shall we go for dinner?" Hana asks eagerly. "I want to borrow that MJ minidress thing ... and hopefully get wasted enough to forget that I'm in fucking Japan. For fuck's sake, it's worse than LA gridlock out there."

"Yeah, okay. Let me change," Jenna sighs, feeling completely zombie-like, longing for the laid-back pizza parties she's had with her two friends since grade school. But sake bombs and sashimi will have to do tonight. At least after a few drinks, the chaotic world around her will start to dull, and she'll forget about the people staring at her.

the starting point.

[Toronto, Canada—November 2010]

Riley Kohl steps off the elevator on the fourth floor of a nondescript office building. Her chunky Sorel boots squish on the carpet, worn for a sudden burst of snow in the city. Luckily, she dug them out of the basement in her father's house—she's thankful to have the resources of a home base and not to be staying in yet another hotel room. The three girls are in Toronto for less than a weekend—enough to squeeze in some personal time and regroup before their next deployment.

I should've changed in the freakin' car, Riley thinks to herself, staring at her footwear, totally out of place with her black tights and blue dress. She stops outside of an office suite marked Light Post Literary. It's Friday evening, and Riley has a last-minute appointment with a potential agent thanks to a referral from Laith Bassel.

Okay. This is it. You are a badass, she coaches herself, pushing through a heavy glass door.

A young man sits behind a glass desk. The entire reception area is decorated in sleek, futuristic finishes of metal and glass. He glances up with a fickle expression.

"Hi," he says without a particular emotion, just blank salutation. He's extremely slim, wearing all black with piercings around his face, trying very hard to look awfully tormented and artistic. Probably right out of high school, but already putting such a hard front out to the world around him.

"Um, yeah, I'm here to see Duncan Oberman," Riley replies, feeling like she walked into the wrong office and ended up at a tattoo parlour instead. The boy has intricately colorful artwork all over his arms.

"I'll let him know. Would you like a beverage?" he asks, pushing some buttons on a console, while motioning for her to take a seat in the waiting area.

"No, thank you." Riley smiles awkwardly, sitting on the hard bench near the door.

He types at his computer, smiling to himself slyly.

I bet he's having cyber sex riiight now, Riley chuckles, watching him carefully. She rests her studded black hobo bag on her lap and peeks inside to check—for the hundredth time—that her neatly printed manuscript is still there.

"Mr. Oberman will see you now," calls the guy, standing up and leading her through a set of glass doors.

He walks her to a closed door with "D. O" inscribed on the frosted glass.

He knocks a couple of times, lightly enough to hint that he's actually petrified of "D. O," and opens it to let Riley through.

She steps into the spacious room, glancing at the shelves of books that run around the walls, but are no higher than three feet tall, leaving plenty of wall space for dozens of awards and photographs.

"Good afternoon, Riley. It's a pleasure to meet you," Duncan booms, his deep voice vibrating the fear in her body.

She steps towards him, and he stands from his office chair.

Mother F ... she marvels, realizing that he stands about six-and-a-half feet tall!

His dark black skin is a little pockmarked for a 50-year-old. He has an eccentric wardrobe—a luxurious beige manteau wrapped around his shoulders, mixing hippie influences with affluence. It certainly isn't a common throw and must have cost more than the monthly payments on a house.

He extends his hand over the glass desk, powerfully shaking hers.

"Please, have a seat. Bernie, please get us some water—sparkling or flat?" he says, turning to Riley for her opinion.

"Sparkling?" she asks nervously, resisting the impulse to curtsey or bow in his presence.

"Yes, sparkling. Good choice. I like you already," he says, as Bernie scuttles away.

"So, Riley. Do tell me how on Earth, exactly, you are acquainted with Laith Bassel." He smiles as he sits, clasping his hands together dramatically.

"He's actually a bit of a ... mentor to my friend. Eleanor Bryans?" Riley offers.

"Oh, that new girl. Yes, yes ... I remember. Laith was raving about her—supposedly as sweet as pie."

"Yep, that's her." Riley smiles.

"I hate pie," Duncan quips.

"I'm not pie," Riley assures.

"Good. So, you must be something if I have Bas himself calling me to refer you. You work for Jenna Ramsay, yes?"

"Yes. Elle and I both do. For now. Sort of. I mean …"

Duncan raises an eyebrow at her mumbling.

"I'm a writer. I've been a writer as long as I can remember. Write is what I do. Jenna is like … my day job, if you will," she replies.

"Fair enough. I wondered if you were looking to tie yourself to Jenna Ramsay. Use it as an angle for media promotion. She's quite the overnight sensation."

Riley bites her lip. "I'd … prefer … not … to. I mean, I would like to have readers learn about my book on their own. Not be known as 'the girl who wrote the book who knows Jenna Ramsay.'"

Duncan smiles, impressed by her desire to stand alone.

"May I ask … how did you come to know Laith Bassel, by the way?" Riley asks, pulling her work out of the large purse.

"Bas and I dated," Duncan shrugs, deadpan, secretly watching her out of his peripheral vision.

Riley nods, handing him the spiral-bound book she put together at Kinko's on her way to the meeting.

"You're not shocked?" He laughs, taking the offering with a smirk.

"Shocked?" Riley asks, confused.

"Shocked by the gay thing?"

Riley has to stop herself from laughing at him. "No, sir. Um, my dad's gay."

Duncan cocks his head to the side, surprised. "Like, out in the community? Really? Who is he?"

"Rhett Kohl. The interior—"

"Oh, my God! That's hilarious! Rhett did my condo!" Duncan gushes excitedly, dropping his intimidating exterior. "I should have realized by the last name … oh, this is truly hilarious. Well, you tell your dad that I say hi. I never see him out and about anymore. He must be one of those old married guys now …" he jokes.

"Yeah, sorta." Riley grins, feeling more relaxed in front of such a fabled force. They have a common thread. But she can definitely see why people fear him. His size and voice alone make an intimidating package, not taking into account the scores of awards and hype he generates for his clients.

"By the way, we never dated. I only wanted to see if I could get a rise out of you. If people get weirded out by the gay thing, then I don't represent them. Bad vibes. Bas would have a field day if he thought I was insinuating he was gay. Anyway, so let's see what we have to work with …" he says to himself, putting on reading glasses and leaning back in his chair.

Riley exhales slowly, her brittle, unpainted fingernails resting on her thighs as he scans through her proposal and asks her questions about the story arc of her first book.

• • •

After her meeting with D.O, Riley hops into her Ramsay-red Range Rover and zooms to the Air Canada Centre close by. The Leafs have a game, and Riley has made a point of trying to watch Hunter's team—even while overseas on her MacBook with live streaming feed. To demonstrate an interest in his interests.

She pulls into the secret parking area, and Farshid greets her with a big wave.

"Miss Kohl, hello, good to see you!"

"Hi, Farsh. How are you?" she asks, putting the SUV in park and changing out of her clunky boots and into a pair of Chuck Taylor high-tops—still a little too tomboyish with her dress, but an improvement nonetheless.

"Doing well, Miss Kohl. I'm glad you're here; the boys could really use any extra luck this evening. Going into the third period without a goal." He opens the car door for her, smiling innocently.

"If only luck worked for me …" Riley laughs, referring to the clumsiness in her personal life. She shudders at the thought of luck.

A sports writer created a myth claiming that Riley must be Hunter's lucky rabbit's foot. Hunter's comment of feeling lucky to have met Riley was taken so out of context that the theory ended up being believed by the city's die-hard fans—desperate for their team to win the Stanley Cup at any cost. The theory left much pressure on her to preside over games and appear the perfectly poised girlfriend. Letters pleading for her to help the boys in blue make it to the Cup began pouring into her father's mailbox, people hoping that a lucky charm could throw their team into the finals of North America's most prestigious hockey championship. But Riley couldn't feign an interest in this theory, and much to Hunter's disappointment, opted not to get caught up in the excitement and be his biggest fan.

Riley heads into the arena and is led to a seat near the Toronto bench, practically rinkside.

The Leafs are playing against the St. Louis Blues, and Hunter is pumped to battle his former team.

She takes her seat as the third period starts, both teams skating out of their locker rooms, hurtling around the ice. The Toronto goalie stretches in his crease, as the players get in their zones, and the referees gather.

The crowd is screaming and chanting, intense energy filling the large arena.

Riley perches herself at the edge of her seat, straining to find Fantastic Four. She turns to the bench and waves a quick hello to the coaching staff that she's met on a couple of occasions so far.

She flags down the boy carrying concessions.

"Miss, what beer would you like?" asks the greasy teenaged boy.

"Oh, it doesn't matter. I probably won't even drink it ... it's the camaraderie," Riley replies.

He stares at her hesitantly, and pours a random selection timidly, watching her with shifty eyes.

The third period picks up with Hunter's line sending a shot blasting past the St. Louis goalie. A fluid pass constructed by Hunter to his centre, and then back to the left-winger, who shot it right between the goalie's knees.

Hunter skates by the glass in front of Riley and waves his fist in the air.

Riley jumps and cheers, the camera suddenly panning over, the fans curious about her. The pretty girl, dating the pro star, who happens to travel with an even bigger celebrity?

She looks up at the Jumbotron and makes an awkward face, afraid of what the commentary is about her on TV, uneasy with people recognizing her in public.

A few minutes later, her BlackBerry vibrates with a message from Ben.

"Nice coverage. Elle and I are watching the game at my place. Stop being so weird—your face looks weird," Riley reads to herself softly.

She types back a message telling Ben to shut it and turns back to the players.

Her phone vibrates again.

"Can't shut it. Going to propose! Wish me luck," Riley reads, whispering.

She pauses for a second, letting the message sink in, and gasps, almost dropping her phone.

"Holy shit, he's going to propose!" she says aloud to the stranger sitting beside her.

She claps her hands excitedly, sending back a message of good luck, and turning back to stare at the ice and the next puck-drop.

Hunter's line switches off again, and Riley sees the TV camera stop on him, but he's looking away from the rink and straight at her.

The TV camera then pans over to her. This time she's prepared and gives a thumbs-up sign, and the crowd cheers. She feels awkward; the attention should be on the game, not her relationship.

The game ends with the Leafs winning, the energy in the arena at fever pitch. Riley tries to blend into the happy crowd and disappears into the back corridors of the stadium with her VIP pass.

She waits for Hunter by the locker room door.

"Hey, Riley? Hunt's inside," one of his teammates tells her, motioning for her to go ahead.

She follows him into the flurry of activity as sports reporters hold recorders up to the different players standing in front of their equipment stalls. Most of them have stripped down to their underwear already, drenched in sweat. Riley stares at the floor, avoiding the half-naked bodies.

Suddenly, a player hurtles in and practically tackles one of his teammates, smashing him in the face with a paper plate.

"Happy birthday, E, you sexy fuck," shouts the attacker, rubbing the white foam on the plate in his friend's face.

"Classic. Shaving cream pie to the face," one of the reporters snorts.

"I think it was definitely a poetic game for me, being able to win against my former team, it was a tough game, their plays are tight. But we kept it together," Hunter bellows, his performance undershirt soaked through with sweat.

"How did you feel about Casey drawing that penalty at such a crucial time?" asks a reporter. "You almost let in a goal with the two-man disadvantage."

"I think Case did what any one of us would do. When one of those guys messes with your goalie, you gotta put them in their place. I would've done the same thing. You gotta back up Eugene."

"And you don't think it has anything to do with excess aggression? I hear he broke up with his girlfriend," follows up another reporter.

"That's a personal thing. I dunno, speaking personally, sometimes—yeah, you get affected by the circumstances around you. We are human, but have to try lock it up to put our best play on the line."

"So there's no coincidence between dips in scoring and visits from *your* girlfriend?" Another reporter laughs.

The group of men chuckle together, and another player whacks a towel at Hunter.

"That's an uncomfortable question with my girlfriend standing right behind you," Hunter laughs.

The reporters turn and stick their mics in her face.

"Is Jenna Ramsay here tonight? How do you feel about being called this team's lucky charm? Do you have any plans to travel with the team? What is your opinion on meditation for psychological conditioning?"

"Uh ..." Riley stares in shock. She starts backing up nervously, overwhelmed by the playful questions.

She smacks into someone behind her, turns around nervously, and shrieks. The captain of the team has come out from the showers to give some quotes, and she's bumped into him wearing just a towel around his waist.

The entire room starts laughing at her surprise, and Riley tries to divert her eyes from his bare skin.

"Maybe let's step into the hall so we can get some quiet?" calls the team's PR guy, leading the reporters out with the captain.

Hunter rushes up to his girlfriend and swallows her into a big hug, kissing her forehead and smothering her with affection. He looks wild-eyed, high off endorphins pumping through his bloodstream. All the guys in the locker room look pleasantly stoned, exhausted, especially with the positive tone from their win.

"This was big funny," snorts Eugene the goaltender, walking by in a towel and pointing at Riley. He opens the door to the shower and change room, and Riley accidentally catches a glimpse of someone's bare ass.

"Don't you people ever wear clothes?!" she gasps, staring back down at the floor, very unsettled by the dominant frat-boy testosterone of his teammates.

"Babe, we've grown up in locker rooms like this since we were kids ... this ain't fashion parties and autograph signings," he chuckles.

Riley cringes at the smell of sweat; his wet shirt has transferred the stench to her dress.

The rest of the bare-chested guys head into the shower room, laughing.

"Anyway, I'm gonna shower. I'll meet you out in a minute, 'kay?" He smiles, kissing the top of her head again.

He strips off his shirt and whips off his shorts as the team trainer tosses him a towel.

"Ohmigod," Riley rolls her eyes, turning on her heel at the naked man in front of her and running out the door.

It's not that she hasn't seen him naked before. It's just that in public, she feels like a pervert. She walks down the cement corridor and pulls out her cell phone and messages Jenna.

W/Carter out partying, comes the response.

Carter has signed on to do a movie that begins filming in Toronto in the new year, and used the trip up to acquaint himself with the city—and try another reconciliation with Jenna.

Cool, have fun. Call if you need me, Riley types back. *P.S. I think Ben's proposing tonight!*

In Toronto, at least Jenna has an ability to orient herself, to hail a cab and get to her hotel. Maybe not the exact room number, but at least the general hotel. Not to rely on Riley or Elle to navigate her around in a shrouded bubble of protection.

But Riley is secretly annoyed that Jenna is out with him. The very rare access to downtime is hungrily devoured by sleep for Elle and Riley. But Jenna seems not to know how to shut down and incubate by herself, instead seeking out new people to hang with and escape. And the fact that the Carter Sampson virus has found its way back on Jenna's radar frightens her friends. He has no qualms about being that escape outlet. In public.

I thought she realized he was using her ... Riley thinks to herself, disappointed that there were no better-quality, eligible bachelors around as a replacement. Jenna was even piqued by Hunter's goalie teammate for a nanosecond, until Hana suggested they weren't compatible astrologically—and that his poor English skills would embarrass her. Poor Eugene, the young Russian net-minding prodigy didn't know Fendi from Ferragamo to satisfy Hana.

Riley looks up from her phone and spots Hunter walking towards her with the swagger of a winner. His navy blue pea coat has a modern cut to it, and his dress pants fit snugly over his large, muscled thighs. He looks sophisticated in his tailored Astor & Black suit, but even Riley knows he'd much prefer to be in sweats and sneakers. Wearing dress clothes was part of the hockey tradition, though, putting a higher style of professionalism to the game.

"Hey, darlin'." He smiles, wrapping her in another hug and kiss. "Hope we didn't scare ya."

Riley's eyes pop comically at the sensory overload of seeing so many near-naked men.

"It's a guy thing," Hunter quips, putting his arm around her as they head to the car park.

"You don't have any bags?"

He looks at her funny. "Uh … no? We don't really carry bags …"

"Wow, you're kinda like Jenna," she mumbles to herself.

"Hey, Riley, thanks for that—the press loved it," greets the team captain, breezing by with a dolled up model on his arm.

"New girlfriend?" Riley whispers to Hunter, staring at the leggy woman in a minidress.

"Hardly. This one is Friday. We'll see who is Saturday … and maybe if she gets extended to Sunday."

She nods, feigning sympathy, as Farshid greets them at the valet station.

A few minutes later, her SUV is pulled up, and they climb in.

Farshid waves as they take off into the city.

"What do you feel like eating?" Riley asks, pulling out of the arena and straight into intense traffic.

"Steak?" Hunter smiles.

"I should have guessed with you …" she rolls her eyes, wiping the windshield free of wet snowflakes.

"What, we've been dating a couple months now, right? You're getting to know my … quirks." Hunter laughs.

"Speaking of dating and commitments and all that … guess what your agent is doing tonight?"

"Proposing," Hunter replies, already aware of the plan.

Riley turns with her jaw dropped as she slows down at a red light.

"What? There are some things that … it's a guy thing. If your buddy tells you something, you don't tell your girlfriend!"

She furrows her brow, disappointed at the secret oath between him and Ben. Does Elle know about their super secret boys club? What other things are being kept from them under their privacy clause?

"Well, how's he doing it?" she asks, curious to see what he'll divulge.

"Oh, I don't care …" He shrugs. Noticing Riley's annoyance, he decides to add to his brush-off. "He said, 'this is what I'm doing.' We don't go into details and little giddy things, babe. I dunno, us guys don't really ... care," Hunter scoffs.

Riley keeps driving silently as he flips through radio stations. The downtown streets are busy with clubbers and partygoers, and all she wants is to head home and crawl into bed instead.

They pull up in front of Barberian's Steakhouse a few minutes later and find cameras are already waiting for their arrival. Without much going on as the city slows down for the winter, the best available tabloid fodder includes snapping pictures of the favourite new local couple. Hunter has already found himself being watched on a daily basis—heading to practice, buying groceries, going for dinner with the guys—it's become interesting to the general public because it puts them one step closer to Jenna Ramsay's grand design.

"Hunter, tell us about your girl? Riley?" asks a photographer as they step out of the SUV.

"Yeah—who are you?" shouts another. "I hear you like hanging out with the team. What's the captain like naked?"

Hunter keeps walking silently, grabbing Riley's hand and leading the way through the spectators.

They step into the cozy restaurant, and the flashbulbs stop, letting them breathe a sigh of temporary relief.

As they sit down, Riley shares details of her meeting with Duncan Oberman.

"I swear, Hunter, this guy is huge. He could play hockey! Or basketball or something. I can't believe Elle got me this hookup to get in and see him! He's a huge literary agent, totally out of my realistic hopes and dreams. But he knows my dad ... maybe that's a sign?"

"Speaking of, why don't you stay with me tonight?" he interrupts with his pouty drawl, putting his hand over hers and rubbing it gently.

With her limited visitation, she has anticipated the challenge of sharing herself between family and boyfriend.

Riley pauses, thrown off her story by his request, and feeling a little torn.

"Wait, wait, wait. So, I'm sitting there talking to this man ... and ... I hope he likes it. I mean, he said he would let me know before Christmas. He's going to read over my work while he's on vacation in—get this—Monaco! On some insanely famous person's yacht. They sounded famous, I don't even know who they are ..."

Hunter is trying his best to smile and be supportive, but it's clear that what's on his mind is spending the night with her.

"I promised my dad I would stay at the house. He's staying home tomorrow morning to have breakfast with me, and he rearranged his schedule. I haven't seen him for more than five minutes in … months," Riley explains.

"But … why don't you stay with me, and, if you have to, leave for breakfast?" Hunter asks, borderline whining. "Or promise me the night after at least?"

Riley bites her lip pensively. It's not that she doesn't want to be with him and his refreshing sense of humour. She just misses more than four hours of uninterrupted sleep. And his sex drive would be keeping them awake for most of the night.

"Well, I don't want to make you do something you don't want to do …" Hunter sighs, fully guilt-tripping her.

"It's not that; you know that. But I haven't really seen my family since I left for this job. And my brother is home, too. Which is rare. Why don't you have lunch with us tomorrow?" she suggests.

Hunter shrugs a "we'll see" type of response as they continue their meal. It's not like he has anything better to do, though. His only real friend is Ben. Most of the guys on the team are from Toronto and have families here, or are married with kids and babies. Or barely speak English like Eugene.

After they finish sharing a chocolate mousse, the two prepare themselves to exit. The attention waiting for them outside is minor compared with Jenna's bubble of fame, but the fact that Riley is the one out on display is more frightening to her than the stampedes they faced in Tokyo.

Cameras start going off as they walk the few steps to their conveniently parked car.

Riley has to shield her eyes to see where she's going. Her foot steps into a puddle of sludge, her Converse sneakers soaking through. She curses under her breath, much to the amusement of the men following them.

"Hunter, man, what's going on with Casey? Are you considering hand surgery? Have you two been on a double date with Jenna Ramsay?" probes a photographer, getting in his face.

Hunter turns and calmly smiles into the camera.

"Casey's fine. The hand's doing better. I had a nice dinner with my girlfriend, Riley. She's a writer and works for Jenna Ramsay right now," he replies transparently.

Then he grabs her, jerking her back for a very public kiss. She pulls away, shocked by his sudden move, and more than a little embarrassed. The explosion of flash and camera clicks causes her face to burn crimson as she fumbles with the car keys.

They get into the SUV, and she pulls away quickly, driving to his lakefront building.

"What was that about?" she hisses, uncomfortable with the possibility that her picture may be plastered on the Internet by sunrise. Hopefully people won't be looking up "naked hockey player gossip" with their morning coffee.

"They'll get to us sooner or later," he replies nonchalantly.

Riley looks at him, surprised by the surge of ego in his personality.

"What? Come on, Riles, be honest with yourself. You're dating a public figure. It's going to come up," he sighs. "You frickin' work for one every day; don't tell me you're not used to it—or expecting this. Besides, it's not like you're here dealing with it every day like me."

She stares at the windshield silently, watching the condensation creep up.

She's stunned.

• • •

The next night brings even more headaches.

Jenna Ramsay smiles at herself in the large bathroom mirror, having re-applied a fresh coat of red lip gloss. It's her second night home in Toronto, and Saturday night's always a better night for a party. A better night to create headlines—that's what Hana preaches. With Carter in tow, she's sure the paparazzi will have her as their prime target tonight.

"Are you done yet?" hollers Riley through the door.

Jenna checks her outfit, pleased with the scandalous dress she's chosen to wear regardless of the November freeze.

She opens the door, and her friend rushes in past her to pee. Jenna breezes into the spacious hotel suite, smiling at the beautiful guests she has assembled. Hunter is drinking a shot of tequila with Carter, surrounded by long-lost friends who began Facebooking after hearing about her success. Her well-publicized, glamorous success.

"I'd like to toast to Jenna, for having us here tonight. Abnormal Psych would never have been as fun without you!" exclaims one of the girls who studied with her at the University of Toronto.

Jenna picks up a glass and joins in the blessing.

I never took Abnormal Psychology, Minnie, she thinks to herself, but flashing a great smile as she sips the cocktail.

Hearing them talk about how talented she was in school, or how incredible she's looking ... it's well worth overlooking such small misunderstandings.

"Okay, I'm good!" Riley announces, barging into the room, adjusting the waistband on her masculine trousers.

"Right. Let's call the cars," Jenna says, grabbing the phone and calling to the desk.

"We're still going out?" her friend asks anxiously, looking at the clock.

Jenna shrugs her off, ignoring the fact that it's already one in the morning and that she would benefit from sleep instead of drinking hard for a second night in a row.

"Yes, this is Jenna Ramsay. Can you bring around my drivers? Great. No, we'll come out the main door, thank you."

The group gets themselves together, shouting and laughing all the way to the three luxury cars awaiting them downstairs.

"I'm so pumped to go back here!" squeals one of the girls in their group, linking her arm through Jenna's adoringly.

Jenna's eyes also flutter excitedly.

"Oh, one of my managers set us up real nice tonight—she's so amazing. Everyone who's anyone knows her, and wants her to rep them, or at least party together!" she cackles, channeling a bit of Hana's blinding confidence.

Their cars drive the three blocks between the hotel and their destination, a trendy lounge on Bloor Street.

I heard this place is pretentious as shit, Riley laughs to herself, staring at the line up of people hoping to get in.

Their car door is opened, and Jenna steps out with her group—a sudden wave of flash coming from photographers.

Jenna waves to them like an empress greeting her subjects, and the velvet ropes are opened at light speed for her.

Carter grabs her hand as they're rushed past the onlookers. His numerous layered necklaces and rings sparkle, making him seem even more "artistic" than usual—overly accessorized with his slim-cut jeans and tight yellow T-shirt.

The group settles into her booth, bottles of alcohol already chilled and gourmet snacks laid out. The tea lights on the table leave enough glow that Jenna knows she'll still photograph well. Mood lighting.

"Hana Rin let us know you like devilled eggs ..." introduces one of the hostesses, who is trying to suck up already. Jenna stares at the tray in front of her excitedly.

"Devilled eggs?" Hunter asks her, disgusted.

"When you're booze cruising, it is *the* best," Jenna informs happily. Her group begins to filter around, attracting attention from the other partygoers, giving her the air of royalty.

"The music here is awesome." Carter smiles, closing his eyes and bobbing his head like a fool to the dance tracks.

He's already on E, isn't he, Riley worries to herself, having grown suspicious of his drug penchant.

A photographer comes around, and Riley is about to read him the riot act, but Jenna happily poses for him instead.

She grabs a bottle of champagne and pops the cork—the centre of attention and smiling for the money shot.

"To good times!" she shouts, taking a drink straight from the frothy bottle.

Her posse cheers excitedly as the bottle gets passed around for everyone to take a sip.

It's handed to Riley, and she passes it straight along without drinking from it.

"You don't want?" Hunter asks, grabbing a piece of egg.

"Germs," she whispers, looking uneasily at the random people who are pretending to be best friends with Jenna and swapping spit on the rim of Veuve.

He gags and passes the bottle along, too.

Riley moves closer to her boyfriend, and he puts an arm around her, handing her a bottle of water. His dark long-sleeve shirt is tight on his body and worn with jeans and sneakers. The only person in the place wearing non-dress-code shoes. Only because he's an athletic darling.

"In about thirty seconds, you'll see the first round—the eager autograph seekers," she whispers to him, motioning to Jenna for amusement. "They like to get to her before the booze, hoping to impress her into becoming new BFFs. That she'll invite them in the booth with us."

As if on cue, a group of trendy young women trot up to the booth, and Jenna lets them plead their case for an autograph or photo, maybe a round of shots.

"Then, the second round will be girls who pretend not to know who she is—but are dying to catch a glimpse, and then will tell people that she's not all she's cracked up to be. Even though they'll go out and try to find her dress tomorrow morning," Riley advises.

Hunter looks at his girlfriend, surprised by the dry observations she's formed while travelling with Jenna.

"And then … you get the wave of guys who want to get with her to say they got with her. And then the ones who want to get with her to sell the story because they really don't have as much money as they pretend to and hope she doesn't realize that they're wearing H&M and not Tom Ford."

"My Lord, darlin'—you are pretty damn jaded," he gasps, surprised to watch the influx of people forming around their blonde friend like rings on a tree. The club has posted two security guards to maintain traffic flow—and keep commoners away from their high-roller guest.

"Am I right or what?" She sighs sadly, looking at a guy walk by and snap a picture of the crowd on his cell phone. "I'd hate to be this … fixture. This *thing*."

"I only get insane fans or girls who think I'm in a band." He laughs, drinking his beer and feeling overwhelmed by the presence of Jenna's highly concocted image. Over the past couple of months, he's gotten to know her a little bit—and she's definitely not as refined as the media paints her. If anything, she's more normal and flawed than he could have expected—talking about her long lost love, Parker, and not knowing how much to tip a bellboy.

Riley laughs and leans into him, neatly fitting under his arm. Hunter sneaks a glance down the buttons of her blouse and kisses the top of her head.

Her gaze slowly drifts around the long, narrow lounge and lands on a woman glaring at her from the bar. Riley wonders if she knows this demonic-looking broad, because she's trying to burn holes into her head with laser beams for eyes.

"Hey, Hunter White—nice game yesterday. But fucking take Chicago next week," yells a man from the crowd outside their booth. "Or they'll skate between your legs again!"

Hunter turns and raises his bottle in cheers, and the hockey fans hoot in excitement.

"Send that man a shot—he's a legend!" shouts another guy to the busboy attempting to pass by.

"How's that right hand feeling, man?" shouts yet another fan who emerges from the depths of the club, wondering about his recent sprain.

"Good," Hunter shouts back flatly, turning back to Riley.

"I've got you in my hockey pool, so I wanna make sure you're up to snuff ..." starts the guy.

"You Canadian people seriously love your hockey," Hunter mutters, trying to break eye contact with the die-hard fan.

Riley shrugs and kisses him quickly, as the guy backs away.

"Hunter—how much will you pay me to eat the candle wax?" yells Carter, bored and unoccupied as his famous girlfriend talks to curious spectators.

"What?" Riley asks, hoping she's heard wrong.

"Five bucks," Hunter replies, hoping he's as daring as his friends back home. The mischievous guys who play beer pong and assume fake identities when picking up girls. Or light things on fire and cross-dress for laughs.

Carter Sampson picks up a candle from the table and drips the melted wax onto his palm. He squirms from the heat but proceeds to stick the substance in his mouth.

Hunter laughs hysterically at his new goofball friend and high-fives him.

"Don't pay me money—pay me *tequilaaa*," Carter shouts, his eyes already drooping from the night's heavy drinking and secret drug use.

Riley stares at him, astounded, and watches her boyfriend sit down beside the daredevil. She's too sober to witness this.

She excuses herself from the booth and weaves through the crowd in search of the bathroom. She stops at a set of stairs and looks over her shoulder, spotting the same creepy woman that was jealously staring her down from the bar.

Riley quickly hops down the stairs in her black heels, hoping to avoid any sort of confrontation with a die-hard hockey fan. Last time something like this happened, a drunken socialite tried to slap her for dating Matthew. Except Riley hit back, and sent the coffee bean princess flying across the room of the formal gala at Oxford.

She locks herself in one of the unisex stalls, listening to the pulsating music above and wishing to be at home.

But Jenna really wanted a night out to catch some hometown attention and to show Carter a good time around her city. Elle was off-duty with Ben, enjoying engagement bliss, so Riley was stuck as the chaperone.

Riley washes her hands, splashes cold water on her face, and heads back to the rager upstairs.

Hunter and Carter have a dozen shots lined up and are ready to throw them back for a photographer.

Are you serious? Riley thinks to herself, as she watches her boyfriend act like a frat boy. And with her least favourite person as his accomplice.

The guys get attention from the crowd, the DJ giving a shout-out to the beautiful people in the bar—the singer, the actor, the pro athlete.

"*Laaadies* and gentlemen, a shout out to Toronto's newest hero—number four, Hunter *Whiiite*. And getting fucked up with him is none other than the best-looking thief out there, *Caaarter* Sampson. And the queen bee of our party tonight—our home girl, *Jenna Ramsaaay!*" booms the DJ, throwing his arms up in salute to their booth.

The boys begin their tequila campaign, grunting and shouting obscenities as each shot glass gets downed one after the other.

Riley tries not to roll her eyes, waiting by the security guards operating their booth.

"Riles!" shouts Jenna, waving her friend over.

She pushes her way forward, not meeting much resistance from the drunken trendsetters all around them.

Riley drops onto the low couch beside her friend, not amused to be the most sober person on the planet at this exact moment in time.

"*Rileeey!*" Jenna screams.

She's thrown back by the volume of the yelling in her ear.

"I'm mad that Elle isn't here!" she says forcefully, not bothering to lower her voice so that the onlookers don't hear.

"Well, you know that she doesn't get to see Ben much ..." Riley says softly, whispering in the hopes that it'll keep the conversation private. The last thing she needs is to deflect headlines that Jenna is marriage-hating.

"So?" Jenna asks, shrugging dramatically and spilling some of her drink on her lap.

"My other best friend didn't want to come tonight!" Jenna shouts at a random girl. She gets a sympathetic coo in response, even though the listener has no idea what was screamed at her.

Riley is taken aback by her friend's sudden surge of self-righteousness, watching her look out to the people around her booth with evaluating eyes. Jenna knows they're all trying to bask in her presence, hoping to sidle up to her enough to feel the influence of fame and fortune. Catch a whiff of her perfume.

"She's supposed to be here for me when I want. And instead I have these randoms," Jenna huffs, turning back to Riley. "No offence to my randoms."

"Okay, well. She'll be back tomorrow—so maybe you should try have a nice time tonight and be ready for the early flight," Riley remarks defensively.

Jenna shrugs nonchalantly and reaches for another glass of champagne, only to tip over the ice bucket, sending two bottles crashing to the ground.

"Hahaha!" she screeches, not the least bit concerned about the price tag of the wasted booze.

Someone rushes forward to clean up the mess, and Jenna turns back to the booth and heads to Carter. She straddles him, and he grabs her into a steamy kiss, planting a hand firmly on her butt—much to the delight of the cell phone cameras around them.

Okay, that's it, Riley thinks to herself uncomfortably. She gets up and marches over to her friend.

"I think we should go," she whispers, trying to nudge her from the public make-out session.

"What? No way! I love this," Jenna protests, stumbling and falling, Carter grasping her arm territorially.

"Jenna, I think it's time to go," Riley says sternly, looking at her watch and realizing that they've been out long enough, and that the early takeoff to Italy should warrant rest.

"No!" Jenna shouts, turning her back to her.

"You have a plane to catch …" she starts.

"I'll fly hungover! What the hell?" Jenna snaps, quickly irritated by her friend's managerial role. "You don't own me."

"So you're going to wake up and get yourself ready and to the airport?" Riley asks threateningly.

Jenna nods.

"I'll take care of her," Carter slurs, putting his arm around her, mocking Riley's disciplinary role.

She looks at him crossly and throws her hands up in defeat. "All right. I'll let Mack know that you're handling everything perfectly."

"Good. You can go," Jenna dismisses her, waving her hand.

Riley looks at her friend in shock and glances at Hunter, who is trying to be a wallflower through the bickering.

"I'm peacing out," Riley says to him, grabbing her purse, agitated. He reluctantly puts down his drink.

"Uh … I guess I'll come with you," he says, sadly parting ways with his new drinking buddy.

Riley stomps out the door, followed by her trudging boyfriend. Cameras start flashing, catching her in a foul mood.

Great. This is perrrfect, she grumbles to herself, hailing a cab.

"Riley, wait up!" Hunter calls, trying to catch up.

"You were awfully reluctant to leave," she hisses, opening the door to a taxi.

"Come on, where are you going?" he asks, as cameras click around them.

"Get in," Riley sighs, uneasy about the photographers, and they speed down to his condo.

"We were having fun," Hunter whines, drunker than she's ever seen him before.

She narrows her eyes at him.

"Let her have fun. He's trying to make it work …" he slurs.

Riley eyes the cab driver suspiciously through the rearview mirror.

"It's hard for him with her away. I would know …" Hunter sighs.

The driver seems to be listening in on his drunken discourse.

"We'll talk about it at home," she whispers forcefully.

Hunter throws his head back, exasperated, and groans.

Riley pays for the quick ride to his building and leads him up—after he stumbles to get in and greets his concierge like a messy, drunken sorority sister.

"Why do you have to do that?" he asks, leaning against a wall once they step into the apartment. He's struggling to get his shoes off.

"Do what?" she snaps, bending down to unlace his sneakers.

"Do that. Make me feel like a kid. Make us feel like we're stupid," he says, his voice dipping with hiccups as he steps out of his shoes.

Riley looks at him, annoyed, not wanting to have this conversation with him in such a state.

"You know, no one is going to be perfect like you think. Some of us only want to enjoy what we got ..." he wails, moving towards her and awkwardly hugging her.

She stiffens under his body weight, wishing she had decided to stay at her dad's instead of helping Hunter make new friends.

"Your hair is pretty and smells like pink ..." he whispers, touching her head.

Riley rolls her eyes so that he can't see her and leads him to the bedroom.

He flops down on the bed and passes out, fully dressed.

At least he won't be pawing at me, she thinks, relieved not to have to explain to a drunken nymphomaniac that she's too aggravated to fool around.

She walks into the kitchen and rummages in the cupboard for something to ease her finicky stomach. Hunter is a really kind person—she can see it in his eyes. But his immaturity shows, and it makes Riley feel like a schoolmarm.

She sits down at the counter and spoons yogurt into her mouth, trying to coat the burning feeling in her stomach, and contemplates her love life.

On paper, he seems like an ideal guy: handsome, successful, happy disposition. But his growing high-profile status causes her anxiety, particularly as he seems to be embracing it (and a friendship with Carter). And the last thing that attracts her is potentially being someone else's publicity shield. Yes, Ben is his agent and ultimate go-to in terms of contracts and advice. But on a day-to-day basis, she is the one who has become paranoid about safety and reducing paparazzi exposure and watching what one says in public. To do it in her personal life seems dreadful. All she looks forward to is escaping that death sentence with Jenna next year.

Riley lets out a frustrated groan, her eyes roving the kitchen. She spots his hockey bag by the closet near the front door and stares at it for a moment. She slowly gets up and walks over; a hockey stick is leaned up against the wall beside it.

"I don't understand why this is so large," she says to herself, nudging the sports bag with her big toe, remembering the secret picnic from their first date. Like a Mary Poppins bag of endless food.

She glances around cautiously before kneeling down by it. She slowly undoes the zipper and pulls back the flap of the bag. A rank, moldy odor filters up to her nostrils, the spicy smell of feet and dry sweat making her gag. Riley falls backward, knocking over the stick and hitting herself on the forehead with it.

She tries to shut the bag from afar.

"For shit's sake, that is *foul*!" she wheezes, disgusted that the man she kisses can produce such a smell. She retreats into the couch.

Riley sits down the remote; the TV is full of sports channels and recorded games.

She starts watching one of the games to see Hunter playing and tries to imagine him reviewing his moves and taking notes. The obsessive need to identify and improve plays.

Riley feels anxious at the thought of this addiction over a sport she can't seem to connect with.

It's only sports…it's not like heart surgery or something, she thinks to herself. *What science could there be in this? To see if he hits hard enough? I dunno … I can't see eye to eye with him. Maybe I'm just not cut out for this. How can he do this season after season … travel nonstop, have to live such a fixed routine? I guess a lot of it is like Jenna. A slave to staying in arenas, or living out of a suitcase, even not being able to make your own travel decisions. I would quit. I'd be like, 'You want to go to LA? Fuck that, I want to go to the Bora Bora!' It's … so … predetermined.*

So, she turns off the screen and sits in the dark, staring at the wall. It's late, but she can't turn her mind off. It feels so odd not to have the unfamiliar surroundings of a hotel room or a plane, to glance over and know Jenna and Elle are sleeping soundly.

Riley curls up on the couch, her cell phone alarm ready to ring in only a couple of hours.

alone in the crowd.

[airport tarmac, Toronto, Canada—November 2010]

Jenna is the first to arrive on-deck of the private jet commissioned by Alchemy to zip her, Riley, and Elle through Europe. It's so early that the sun is barely even peeking over the horizon, the sky glows an eerie purple. She didn't bother to sleep after the late night of partying, leaving Carter in her hotel room, passed out.

After storing her carry-on bag, she walks up and down the aisle, stretching before the flight to Italy.

Then she sits quietly. For the first time in months, she's completely and utterly by herself. No assistants. No cameras. No reporters. No fans. She is totally alone.

The feeling of silence is so long forgotten that she looks around nervously, hoping someone is nearby to break it. Glancing out a window, she is overcome with an urge to jump off the plane and make a run for it. During this stay in Toronto, she hasn't seen her mother (again) and hasn't thought farther than 30 seconds into her future, only contemplating the need to get wasted and vanish.

She closes her eyes and recalls a memory of being pushed on a swing at the playground as a child. Floating through the air, free as can be. Weightless in the breeze. Laughing and living in the moment.

Her thoughts are stirred as Riley and Elle enter the plane.

"Oh, my gosh! You are not going to believe this!" squeals Elle, rushing up to her friend, and jumping into her lap. Her sweet perfume hits Jenna's nostrils heavily.

"Okay, hi, hello!" Jenna exclaims, stirred out of her thoughts and severely hungover.

"I'm getting *marrieeed!*" Elle shrieks at the top of her lungs, causing the airplane to shake.

Jenna pauses and looks at Riley for confirmation.

Riley nods, stowing her luggage. She's obviously not feeling great, wearing a huge hoodie and her reading glasses for the trip. She looks like a slob but pulls it off with swagger simply because she doesn't care.

"I heard. Wow, that's great. Congratulations!"

Elle stops shrieking, breathless. "What? That's it?" she pants.

Jenna shrugs.

"Really?" Elle whines.

"No, no. Lovee, it's just that ... it's not really a shock, exactly. You guys were perfect from back in the day. Know what I mean? I guess I should rephrase and say that I'm so happy it's *finally* happening!" Jenna grins weakly.

"Yay!" Elle screams, hopping out of Jenna's lap and bouncing around in a bubble of joy. Her skirt flutters as she hops in the aisle.

"Let me see it," Jenna says, putting up a finger to stop her friend's prancing.

Elle gently places her hand in Jenna's for careful examination.

"Very nice," Jenna replies, carefully inspecting the modest engagement ring. Heart cut set in yellow gold, very feminine and vintage-feeling, but probably bought over the counter, she observes. Ben is more a store-bought type of guy, much easier to pick something, slap down his credit card, and pay full price at Tiffany's. Signed, sealed, delivered. Shopping for deals is not a Ben-Elle trait.

"So when do you think you want to do it?" Riley asks, taking a seat across from Jenna. The tension from the night before at the club seems to have been forgotten, and Riley is not about to instigate another crisis.

Elle gathers her hands together as if praying and gives a little sigh.

"Well! I was thinking on the summer solstice. Kind of have a nice ... cheery ... holistic feel," she starts. She digs into her large Chanel purse and pulls out a binder.

"Whoa, whoa, whoa, did you not just get engaged *two nights ago*?" Riley asks, motioning to the scrapbook already gathered and alphabetically indexed.

"So?" Elle asks, not admitting that she stayed up cutting and pasting things out of bridal magazines while Ben unknowingly slept alone.

"Anyway, I think that as clichéd as it is to be a June bride, it's gonna happen. Besides, it'll be after the Stanley Cup games, and maybe even some of Ben's other players will be able to come! I'll try accommodating the schedule for him with rookie drafts and free agent trades ... but if it doesn't work, then he'll have to manage. I already e-mailed around for venues, I think we're not going to go religious. Maybe do the bridesmaids in a light green ... the groomsmen in Gatsby white? No, never mind, that's too gaudy ..."

She continues trilling off the to-do list she's devised, and Riley watches Jenna's gaze drift out the window. She looks incredibly hollow and sad.

But with Bridezilla-to-be chirping, the heart-to-heart will have to wait at least until cruising altitude.

"… maybe your dad could help, Riles!" gasps Elle. "Or at least source me some really great linens …"

Riley's about to respond, but her friend is already onto another train of thought.

By mid-flight, Elle has worn herself out and is asleep, her Bride Book clutched in her dainty hands.

Jenna is staring out the window, not speaking—a rarity.

Riley covers her pen and shuts the draft of her book that she's been editing—compulsively fixing and nitpicking.

"What's wrong?" she asks softly, trying not to draw attention to her gloomy friend.

"Hmmm? Oh. Nothing …" Jenna replies, trying to brush off the storm clouds hovering around her mind.

"That's the lousiest case of nothing I've ever seen. What's up?"

Jenna looks at her and sighs morosely.

"Yes?" Riley insists, waiting patiently, putting her hands over the manuscript like a therapist.

"Is it bad that I'm not happy?"

Riley takes in the severity of the statement. "What is the source of this unhappiness?"

Jenna's eyes dart around; she feels sketchy. But her gaze stops at Elle, and she frowns.

"We broke up," she replies.

"You and Carter?"

Jenna nods, still watching Elle sleeping.

"But I thought that you were back together …" Riley trails off, confused by the on-off, on-off in their relationship.

"Were. But I can't help but think of something. When we left the club on Friday, there were like a zillion photographers. It's as if they knew where I was, like it got leaked."

"And you think he set it up?" Riley asks, happy to be openly suspicious of the man-whore she's come to hate.

"Well, no … not necessarily. We smoked up after getting in last night, and I had this funny paranoia … I don't know, I can't put my finger on it. I mean, now I'm gone again. And he's back in LA for a couple of weeks. Maybe I could get Hana to spy on him for me. Being alone again is like a yo-yo ..."

"And hearing about imminent weddings and love and till-death-do-us-part isn't really the best remedy ..." Riley fills in.

Jenna shrugs. "I know I should be happy. She's my friend. I should be happy for her. And I will be. They're great. They're perfect. But I wonder ... about myself."

"That you won't be happy like her?" Riley asks.

Jenna laughs softly, stopping a tear from falling down her cheek. "You know, Riley Kohl, you're so dark and dreary ..." She smiles at the ease at which her friend could identify what was weighing her down.

"What can I say?" She jokingly shrugs. "But seriously, lovee ... I think we all have those feelings. I mean, Hunter ..." she trails off uncomfortably.

Jenna looks at her, raising an eyebrow. *Hunter? Handsome athlete millionaire hot body isn't so perfect?*

"It could totally all be me. But I definitely wonder ..." Riley admits.

Jenna nods, comforted by the fact that she's not the only one trying to make it through the night alone.

"Why are you nervous?" she asks, curious about Hunter's flaws.

Riley groans, scared to admit her judgments of him.

"I dunno ... it's kinda ... like, he's liking this whole attention-fame thing a little too much for me. I'm more of the wait-in-the-wings type, know what I mean?"

"Well, yeah, you're the road manager," Jenna offers.

"Right. *You're* the public figure. I'm not. And I kind of want to remain anonymous. I don't have the confidence in that way like you or him. I saw how they tore him apart on Coach's Corner—"

"Huh?" Jenna asks, confused.

"You know, the TV program ... where they talk about hockey between periods and critique the plays and stuff?"

Jenna stares at her blankly.

"The guy with the really bright blazers?" Riley tries.

"Ooh! That guy! Yeah! I know about that. What did they say on the show?"

"That he's playing without focus, and he's a public figure above an athlete lately." Riley grimaces.

"And you ...?"

"Agree ..."

Jenna nods, absorbing her friend's opinion against her boyfriend.

"Well, if the energy's not right … I guess, you'll decide when you decide, right?" she tells her, running a hand through her blonde hair. "Do what you want to do. There are plenty of other hot guys out there. You're young."

"Pot calling the kettle black, much?" Riley laughs, pointing out her friend's inability to deviate from the train wreck of Carter Sampson.

"Whatever. But Riles—you're a strong woman. And he's a strong guy, but maybe not the right type of strong to complement each other, don't you think?"

Riley nods, not wanting to admit that deep down, she already feels they're not the right complement to each other. They have fun and goof off, but at the end of it all, she has to resist the urge to throttle his unshakeable, childish optimism.

"You should try listening to your gut more … figure out what you're trying to tell yourself, know what I mean?" Jenna suggests.

"Hey, you know what helps me …" Riley starts, rummaging in her huge purse.

She pulls out bottle after bottle, still not finding what she's looking for.

"Drugs?" Jenna asks dryly, looking at the anti-motion sickness pills, the herbal supplements, the headache medication, the sleeping pills … the resident pharmacist.

"*Nooo* …" Riley says, making a stupid face at her friend. She pulls out her orange journal proudly.

"You use it?" Jenna smiles happily.

"Of course. That's how I kept track of all my thoughts for the book," Riley explains.

"Wow." Jenna beams, searching in her bag and pulling hers out.

"I keep mine for lyrics and song ideas," she says, holding it protectively.

"Exactly. So … with any of that stuff that you're feeling. Why not channel it into something productive—like your next album?" Riley smiles, energizing the singer with incredible positivity and constructive hope. "I'm sure plenty of people can relate to how you feel, what you're going through."

"Or your next marvelous book? Pot calling kettle black …"

Jenna smiles, remembering a piece of writing she was excited about, that she hoped would develop into a future song. Something she had longed to talk to Parker about, but doubts she will get to.

"You know what? Why don't we do something special for the holidays? Go somewhere without all the ..." Riley trails off, glancing over her shoulder at the jet's service staff eagerly watching Jenna.

Jenna's eyes light up excitedly. "That's a great idea! Maybe somewhere with sun and a beach ... and fruity little drinks for Ben ..."

"And let's go off the beaten path a bit so that you don't have to worry about being the next cellulite catastrophe," Riley suggests.

"Hey! I don't have cellulite," Jenna retorts.

"Oh. Okay, well, then I guess it's just *me*!" Riley cries, jokingly clutching her thighs.

"Oh, please. Hana has a doctor that can inject the shit out of you ..." Jenna winks.

"It's okay. I'll live with it. But really, let's survive the next five weeks—and then we'll be beach bums, yes?"

Jenna nods firmly, excited at the new thing she has to look forward to.

"But ... can I ask that we not bring Hana with ..." Riley whispers.

Jenna looks at her, surprised.

"For old time's sake?"

"Okay, good—I was afraid you didn't like her or something. She's actually a genius, Riles. It's amazing how well connected she is. She's going to meet us next week." Jenna smiles proudly.

Riley cringes on the inside but forces an awkward smile.

"She's going to put me in touch with her spiritual guru, maybe learn how to channel my creativity a little better. Did you know she's actually some sort of psychic healer shaman?" Jenna whispers, her eyes swelling with hope.

"I ... don't know how that stuff really works, Jenna ..." Riley says hesitantly, scared of the credentials of this so-called guide that Hana is conveniently wielding.

"Well, we'll see. She sounds legit—predicted pretty much everything in Hana's life. Anyway, maybe she'll tell us if we'll meet any eligible bachelors at Elle's wedding." Jenna laughs.

Riley rolls her eyes comically. "It's a sweet ring, though, suits them perfectly," she acknowledges.

"It's no flawless round four-carat platinum tension set, but ..." Jenna laughs.

"Are you serious? Does Ben look like the Shah of Iran? He's a freakin' hockey agent." Riley laughs.

"Well, maybe I should do a concert in Iran …" Jenna jokes.

"Yeah, *ooo-kay*," Riley says dryly.

"But don't you think it's so strange—she's actually going to belong to him now? Like, officially …" Jenna gasps, feeling the depth of her friend signing a marriage license. But she secretly longs for the romanticism of being a part of someone else, too.

Riley looks ready to puke.

"You don't want that? The knowing that out there—you are with someone. They are with you. In a different way than simply dating. That people can't break that bond because it's something between the two of you?" Jenna asks dreamily.

"I don't think I need to sign a piece of paper or have a big party for that," Riley says flatly. "Besides, people break those bonds everyday, unfortunately."

"You didn't watch *Cinderella* as a kid, did you?" Jenna laughs.

"I did. And I would have much rather convicted and imprisoned the evil stepmother and had the land deed signed over to her so that she could own her own property."

Jenna stares at her friend in shock.

"What? Equal rights."

"You're outta control," Jenna announces.

love the one you've got.

[Sydney, Australia—mid-December 2010]

Elle burrows in the giant bed in her hotel room, relieved to be resting for the day. Two live performances, half a dozen magazine interviews, and a major autograph signing had the girls crisscrossing Australia this weekend.

She shrugs her shoulders, trying to find a sweet spot in the mattress, but still feeling strange—the sheets smell *too* clean.

Elle looks at her engagement ring and feels a warm wholeness in her chest—like a happy glow reminding her of the fiancé back home. His face is a little blurry after the weeks of being apart, but she knows he's there waiting. The heart on her hand reminds her of this.

She's alone in an alien room in a faraway land and finding it hard to want to be where she is, to keep up with the massive circus of Jenna's promotional tour, and to manifest any semblance of physical endurance for the travel and commotion.

She flops around from side to side in the bed.

"Oh, my," she sighs to herself, sitting up, unable to sleep.

She kicks back the trendy dark brown duvet in despair and gets up to grab her laptop. Maybe looking at a picture of Ben will help sharpen her memory so that she can dream of him clearly.

The screen loads. Her desktop background is the two of them at her birthday dinner a couple of months ago. The dinner that Jenna hijacked, forcing a restaurant change to a "more suitable" location. The audacity of her friend to pay the entire bill without even asking left the Bryans family taken aback by the aggressive act of generosity.

There's no use getting upset; it's all in the past. She meant well, Elle corrects her thinking, looking for a silver lining.

She studies Ben's chiseled face, his dark brown hair. The same warm feeling from before, the sense of being part of someone else, intensifies happily.

Elle opens up her e-mail to send him a quick note; they've been so go-go-go that she hasn't talked to him longer than five minutes at a time. She checks her desktop calendar to make sure she's closer to their holiday break—like a prison inmate counting down the days until freedom. She might as well have tick marks going on the wall.

> *Riley says the team is doing great! I hope that Hunter will be able to join us on vacation during his little gap over the holidays ... Things are kind of tough here—Hana is like a hovering shadow of gloom. Makes Riley and I want to run for the hills. But she must be good. Jenna is so number one here, it's insane. It's so weird to see it all—I remember her from grade four when we used to play Clue Jr. Mack is going to look into letting me off early to plan the wedding. I think with Hana around all the time, Riley and I are expendable ... I hope you'll be able to be around and give your input for our wedding, but I get that it's a busy time for you with the season wrapping up ... and that you're a guy.*

She underemphasizes the fact that she feels absolutely marooned with Jenna and Hana overpowering her and Riley. And that she's exhausted beyond description.

Elle quickly scopes out a few gossip Web sites and spots some blogging about her friend. The pictures of her and Carter in Toronto are still circulating—funny comments written about their drunken misconduct.

She reads a little rant from Perez Hilton that chastises Jenna for "getting back together with such a bottom-feeder." Regardless of how hot he is.

Wow, the press really loves to hate him, she observes, reading another site showing him leaving fancy restaurants in LA, commenting on his poor tipping and his preference for attractive female guests. They all call him out as a horny social climber trying to use Jenna's rising star, while banging the pretty young things drooling after him. Getting an ego boost wherever he can.

"I wonder if he's actually cheating on her ..." Elle whispers, trying to analyze paparazzi pictures of him and some of his upcoming female costars, having business dinners but reportedly "canoodling."

She opens up another window, writing Ben another thought:

> *Have I mentioned how absolutely happy I am? I am so blessed to have you in my life because I trust you with all my heart. You are such an honest, genuine, and incredible man, Ben. I love you so much.*

no limits.

[Tobago, West Indies—December 20, 2010]

"I'm so excited for this, you guys!" Elle squeals, as their chartered jet sets down on the island of Tobago.

After six months of nonstop promoting, the girls have been allowed a few days of respite in the sun, in the hopes that it also works on Jenna's tan. Six hit singles later, with Jenna at the top of the charts, the three friends and their loves are touching down in paradise.

"This is going to be freakin' sweet. I hope they have awesome bars." Carter smiles, putting his arm around Jenna as they step off the plane. Both are wearing flashy sunglasses, and designer jeans in spite of the humid, Caribbean air.

"I want to lie in a chair and pass out." Hunter smiles, helping Riley with her luggage. "Gotta recharge before we play the Hawks next week…"

"Hawk birds?" Jenna raises an eyebrow.

"Chicago Blackhawks," Ben translates, intensely checking his e-mail as soon as he gets cell service.

"It sucks Hana couldn't come," Carter replies. "She's so much fun to party with in LA. All the movie guys love her."

"Yeah, but … this is a great time to just rest and be calm. And celebrate Jenna's birthday!" Elle smiles happily, putting a big straw sun hat over her as they step on the airstrip. Her delicate sundress billows in the light breeze outside the jet. Ben puts his hand on the small of her back as they walk.

The balmy weather instantly creates a layer of perspiration on their skin, the sun beaming down strongly.

The group navigates through the airport and gets into a waiting limo.

"I'm amazed there aren't cameras following her around yet," Hunter whispers to Riley, motioning to Jenna and Carter, who are folded into each other amorously.

"Yeah, well, I kinda got her to mention that we were going to Hawaii…" Riley grins, feeling extremely clever for the plant to the media.

"Oh, that's awesome. Now I can walk around naked *alll* day long." He winks, fumbling for his cell phone in his cargo shorts.

"No one wants to see you naked again, Hunter," Ben says matter-of-factly, looking oddly casual in a T-shirt and khakis. He seems awkward without his suit.

After a big win last week, Hunter and some teammates were photographed celebrating wildly in Calgary. At a hip bar, the group got extra rowdy in their VIP booth, with some players jumping on the couches and stripping off their shirts victoriously.

"I would like to point out the specific detail that he was not, actually, naked," Riley laughs, still a bit embarrassed that the pictures surfaced in the newspaper. For a sport where the athletes generally try keep a low profile, Hunter is the equivalent of a rising socialite.

"Thank you, darlin'. See, I have an agent … and a lawyer." He rolls his eyes.

"I want to visit the Nylon pool—they say it has healing and restorative properties!" Elle announces, pulling out a tourism brochure. "And maybe we could take a tour of a cocoa plantation …"

Carter peers over his sunglasses and makes a snoring sound.

Ben looks at him and narrows his eyes. This guy is starting to wear his patience thin. And the fact that Hunter thinks he's the coolest guy around isn't helping.

The car pulls into the Coco Reef Hotel, and the bellboys swarm around them, helping with their bags. Or rather, helping with Jenna's multiple pieces of luggage, emblazoned with designer logo.

"What the heck did you pack? It's only three days …" Ben asks, pulling his black carry-on bag with wheels, obviously more skilled at packing with his frequent business travel.

"Oh, you know. You have to be ready for everything." Jenna smiles, heading up to her room with Carter in tow like a little puppy dog.

"Guys, let's meet by the beach in fifteen minutes!" Elle shouts after them, looking out at the turquoise ocean like a wide-eyed child.

Carter waves his hand, having heard the suggestion but not particularly caring.

"Okay, see you in fifteen." Riley smiles supportively, heading in with Hunter.

• • •

Hunter throws open the door of their hotel room, and they step into the neat and clean slice of paradise. Their balcony directly faces the roaring waves below, the horizon shining invitingly.

"This is the best hotel room I've been in yet." She gasps, walking to the balcony and staring out at the view. She shuts her eyes to listen to the tranquility, a breeze coming in off the water and fluttering her hair.

"Better than Tokyo?" he snickers, recalling the first time they spent the night together. First times, plural, actually. Breaking her vow of abstaining from messy male-female relations.

He wraps his arms around her shoulders, squeezing like a python and nuzzling her.

Riley leans back into his grasp and sighs, trying to melt into calm.

"Hey, you know … we still have a few minutes before we have to be down at the beach," he whispers to her.

"Hmmm …?"

He smacks her butt, signaling his intention to have sex, right this very moment, known to her stinging rear.

"Really? Right now? We just got here … I thought …" Riley sighs, unwillingly being pulled out of her dreamy state.

Hunter groans, releasing his grip of her.

"Besides, what, five minutes? What does that say about you …?" she asks, trying to lighten the mood with humour.

"Okay, fine. But later, you know what would be great? If we got you all liquored up like the time we screwed around in the elevator … you were so much fun, all loosey-goosey," he teases, kissing her neck.

"Oh, my God …" Riley gasps, remembering the night she drank Bacardi 151 with his teammates. She was trying to take it like a man—the burning sensation and the competitive undertone.

"Another one!" shouted the team captain, after they slammed down their shot glasses.

"No … no, no, no—this is it!" Riley slurred, grabbing the table for support.

"No! Another one! Or then you're the same as these bitches!" he shouted at her, pointing to the groupies they had lining up around their booth. "No offence, randoms!"

"I'm not a whore!" she screamed at him, grabbing another glass.

"I know you're not, but prove it! These ones get all drunk off our bottle service and try fuck us because we're athletes. I think you don't give a shit that he's a star," he snorted, pointing at Hunter. "Man up!"

"Fuck that shit, man! Fuck that shit! I'm man up!" Riley screamed back, toasting with the men and throwing back a drink.

The rest of the night was essentially a write-off. She and her new boyfriend stumbled into the lobby of his building, dragged themselves to the elevator, and barely made it through the door. Hunter claims she tried—very forcefully—to go down on him in the elevator. What would be commemorated live on the security camera for the guards at the concierge desk.

"Hey, I had the self control not to make a porno that night. Yes, I don't get to see my girlfriend for weeks at a time … but I have the self control to seduce you tonight instead." He smiles cockily. "So, right now, I won't give it to you, even if you beg."

Riley laughs stiffly, but secretly feels annoyed by his forward talk. And the mental picture of her having to beg for anything.

He whips down his shorts and turns his back to her, dramatically putting on his blue swim trunks, never shy to bare his ass.

Riley grabs her black bikini and changes quickly, not wanting her exposed flesh to egg him on.

She packs a beach bag with her journal and sunscreen and their room key, and the couple head out to the sand. They spot Ben and Elle sitting by the pool.

"Hey, where are Jenna and Carter?" Elle asks, working on a fruity drink with an umbrella in it, a colorful sarong wrapped around her. A bottle of SPF 70 sunscreen is beside her, already lathered on to protect her fair skin.

Ben is holding the exact same drink in his hand and is reading a manual about the Collective Bargaining Agreement. Whatever that means. He's wearing a polo shirt over his swim trunks—nerd alert.

"Probably having sex. Man, what did I tell you about girly drinks?" Hunter gasps, ordering a beer for himself and a vodka-soda for Riley. The four of them head to lounge chairs in the sand by the sea, stripping down to their bathing suits.

After watching the waves roll into the shore, mist spritzing up at them, the two couples begin to feel at ease with their new surroundings, tension lifting layer by layer.

A loud hoot of laughter rings out from the pool bar, and Jenna and Carter are at the centre of it, entertaining some of the guests.

The rebel couple saunter up to the beach chairs, Carter double fisting his beers and drawing attention in his neon printed board shorts.

"Oh, my God, those people are great ..." Jenna giggles, falling onto the reclined chair, spilling some of her drink. She tosses the cigarette she was inhaling on the sand.

Elle cringes at the fizzling tobacco.

"Old people with money like young people who make them feel like rock stars," Carter grins, sitting beside Jenna and resting a beer bottle on her thigh.

Ben pulls a football out of Elle's tote bag and motions to Hunter and Carter for a little pigskin on the sand.

The three guys run off to the water's edge and begin throwing the ball around, yelping and splashing, Ben leading the pack.

The girls all exhale happily.

"Lovee, you are positively ... glowing," Elle laughs, as Jenna stretches in the chaise sexily.

"Sex'll do that to you. Lots of sex with *Esquire's* new cover guy." She grins mischievously. "Happy birthday sex."

"Actually? Right now?" Elle gasps.

"What? We had time for a quickie." Jenna smiles, putting her hands behind her head, watching the guys frolic in the surf.

Riley grinds her teeth together, writing in her journal.

> *Am I really a wet blanket? Not adventurous enough? I mean, I'm not asexual or anything ... I like men, I like having fun. So why is it that past boyfriends all rag on me for not being affectionate? Maybe I'm simply not an affectionate person. Or maybe, they need to say something mean when the relationship ends. I need push myself to have fun, live in the moment ... live now. To be open to freefalling happiness and not be so rigid. Hunter is a great guy. I'm happy, I guess. We have fun. He's different ... so what if he doesn't get the writer thing? There's no such thing as a perfect fit, right?*

She sets down the pen and turns to her friends. "Anyone want another drink?"

"Yeah, I'll come," Jenna replies, shakily getting up, fixing the wedgie on her red-and-white string bikini.

"Um, I'll stay here with our stuff. But maybe can you grab me another daiquiri?" Elle giggles, holding her straw hat down against a sudden breeze.

Riley and Jenna head to the bar.

"I'm really glad we're all here together." Jenna smiles, holding her friend's arm.

"Me too, lovee," Riley sighs, leaning into her.

"Jenna! Come here! Guess what Betsy just said!" calls an elderly man, white hair and crisp salmon-coloured polo shirt shining in the sun.

"What up, Paul?" Jenna calls, strolling over to the cutest retired couple she's ever seen. A couple she'd love to be someday.

Riley orders at the bar, watching her friend genuinely admire the two American tourists.

"Hey, should I get refills for the guys?" Riley calls out, as Jenna strides back up to the bar, laughing to herself.

"Oh, yeah … maybe. I'll help you carry it all. Riles, that couple is freakin' hilarious. I seriously hope that when I'm, like, seventy, I'm still in love and having as much fun as they are …" she sighs.

The bartender hands them two daiquiris, a vodka-soda, a mojito for Jenna, and two beers.

Jenna's about to walk off, but Riley is still perched and waiting at the bar.

"Riles, what are you doing?" she asks, turning back.

"Loosening up," she sighs, as the bartender pours her a shot of whiskey.

"Hey, hey, hey—look at you! Slow down and cut a girl in on that!" She laughs, motioning for the bartender to pour her a shot as well.

Riley turns to her friend, smiling meekly, a little embarrassed.

"Nuh-uh, none of that. Here's to three measly days of paradise." Jenna smiles, setting down the drinks in her hand and picking up the shot.

The girls clink their glasses and grimace at the taste.

"Feel better?" Jenna asks.

"A little bit," Riley sighs, grabbing the beers.

"Whatever you need, Riles. Whatever you need to survive."

They set down the drinks by the cluster of beach chairs, and Riley walks towards the guys. Carter throws her a pass, and she somehow manages to catch it without missing a step.

She hurls it back at him, knocking him back a little.

Pansy ass. She laughs to herself as she jumps on Hunter, wrapping her arms and legs around him as he holds her up.

"Hey … you want to join in?" He laughs.

She shakes her head no.

Jenna and Elle join the group by the shore, and Elle struggles to throw back the football Ben has passed her. Her wrap skirt gets soaked by the approaching waves as Ben scoops her into an hug.

"Okay, guys, time to hit the showers ..." Hunter announces, walking into the ocean, still holding Riley.

The cool mist of the salty ocean puts goose bumps on her arms as he walks them in until only their heads bob above the water.

"Not even if you beg ..." he whispers to her flirtatiously, over the roar of the water.

She smiles through gritted teeth.

• • •

Jenna's big blue eyes open slowly, her head beating like a heavy drum. The dull pain of what is probably the worst hangover known to mankind is consuming every ounce of energy.

She groans, her throat dry. She reaches a hand up to her forehead, wanting to disappear.

Today, they leave the island after only two nights of vacation—and they did their worst damage drinking last night. Particularly when her friends went to bed, leaving her and Carter to scour up some weed and prescription meds from some locals, getting blitzed out of their minds. There wasn't much else for them to do but drink, chain-smoke cigarettes, lie on the beach, or have gratuitous sex.

She sluggishly rolls onto her side, trying to relieve the thump of her slow-pumping blood, but it only makes the echoing worse.

Except, as she turns, she hears something squish.

"Hmph," she moans, slowly sitting up on her elbows. "Why did I even..."

Carter is passed out in the bed beside her, naked. She's wearing one of his T-shirts, a grey one with a vintage-looking logo on it, but which was actually purchased brand-new at a designer store. The fake, high-end thrift store look.

Jenna glances down and realizes her shirt's wet.

"What the ..." she murmurs, shifting on the mattress and feeling it squish again.

She raises her palms to her nose and tries to smell herself—nothing. Only a faint scent of beer in the air.

My God, he must've sweat a lot without the air-conditioning, she thinks to herself, looking at Carter.

She drowsily gets up and leaves the room, knocking on Riley's door beside her room.

Riley answers, wrapped in a robe, her hair wet.

"Hey, what's up?" she asks, a mug of coffee already in hand. Jenna pushes in past her friend, still fuzzy in her thoughts.

"Why are you ... moistened ...?" Riley asks, sipping from the white china. The shower is on in their bathroom; Hunter must be taking his turn.

"Carter ... sweating ..." Jenna murmurs, unsure. She stands in the doorway, completely disoriented.

Riley studies her friend carefully, scrunching her nose. Suddenly, her eyes widen in shock, and she covers her open mouth with a hand.

"What? What is it?" Jenna asks.

"Jenna, I don't think that's sweat ..." Riley whispers, horrified.

"Huh?"

"Jenna, how much did he have to drink?"

Her jaw drops, and she abruptly runs out of the room, leaving Riley standing at the door.

She darts back into her bedroom and peels off the wet shirt. She wraps herself in a towel and is about to step into the shower ... until she realizes Elle has her favourite shampoo.

Jenna races out and knocks on Elle's door, on the other side of hers—the girls neatly lodged in a row, one beside the other.

Ben answers, in a pair of boxers.

Jenna pushes past him.

"I need my shampoo!" she announces, as Elle covers herself with the sheets.

"Jenna!" Elle scolds, turning bright red.

"Oh, whatever, I've seen you naked," Jenna hisses grumpily.

"You have?" Ben laughs.

"I ... need ... my shampoo ..." Jenna says, taking deep breaths as if she's about to have a meltdown.

"Jenna, what is wrong with you?" Elle gasps, wrapping herself up in the linens and walking to the dresser to get the bottle.

Jenna's lip quivers, and she starts to cry.

Ben looks at Elle worriedly. She shrugs, not sure what is bothering her friend.

"What's wrong, lovee?" Elle asks, walking over and hugging her friend. She scrunches her nose at the smell of alcohol all over her.

"Carter ..." Jenna tries to start, choking on her sobs.

"You got in a fight?" Elle asks.

"Not from what we heard last night," scoffs Ben, motioning to the wall.

"I woke up and everything—everything was wet. Water dripping off the mattress. Everything was soaked," she sobs.

Elle pats her friend's damp hair, trying to comfort her, not sure what she's stammering about.

"Carter ... Carter ... peed on me!" Jenna wails, grabbing the shampoo and running out the door.

Elle and Ben stare after her in silence.

"Did you hear what I heard?" he asks his fiancée.

Elle stares at the hand that was just stroking her friend's wet hair. She is so shocked she accidentally drops the sheet, exposing herself through their open door. Ben quickly slams it shut with his foot, and they collapse into giggles.

• • •

Jenna steps out of the longest, hottest shower ever, and Carter is still passed out on the bed. She changes into a light summer dress, grabs her purse, and heads out of the room alone, disgusted.

She finds a beach chair and opens a copy of Riley's manuscript—her selected beach read for this vacation. She's about 20 pages into the story when the two other couples approach her outside.

"Hey, lovee, are you okay?" Elle asks softly, handing her friend a mango smoothie. The four of them sit in a cluster around her.

Jenna stares out at the ocean, trying to decide if she should be mad or mortified.

"Hey, if I were you, I'd be pissed, too," Riley sighs.

Ben and Hunter stifle their laughter at her poor choice of words.

"I mean ... I would be ... disappointed ..." Riley rephrases, smacking them.

"I thought he was my Ben ..." Jenna whimpers, staring down at the sand. "The match to me. He started from nothing like me, like how the magazines write about our love story ..."

Elle coos warmly, touched that her friend looks up to her relationship with Ben.

"Trust me—he's not your Ben," Ben says under his breath.

"I dunno ... I want to belong to someone, like how you guys do ..." Jenna admits, blushing brightly.

"Belong to someone?!" Riley gasps.

"You know, like being engaged, getting married, being in an adult relationship," Jenna continues.

"Oh, dear God, Jenna—being engaged nowadays is like the new form of going steady, no offence," Riley starts, motioning to Elle and Ben. "Belonging to someone means more than having a ring or something. Look at the basic archaic nature of having an engagement ring. It marks the woman—shows that she is some man's property, while, in fact, the man wears no such engagement ring."

"Huh?" Hunter croaks, amazed by the sudden onslaught from his girl. He's dreamt of the perfect proposal since before he started dating. Much like how girls dream of their weddings, he dreamed of being the white knight swooping into claim his maiden.

"I'm just saying, that when a guy proposes to a girl—because that's usually how things are expected to go, right? He marks her. She wears the ring; he might as well pee on her. Again—no offence," she says, motioning to Jenna. "But it becomes her responsibility now. If some guy talks to her at the bar, she waves her hand at him; there is a visual cue that she is someone's property. But the guy, if some girl approaches him at the bar … he could totally be … not engaged, because there's no physical proof either way."

"But wouldn't the guy say, 'sorry, I'm engaged?'" Ben asks her.

"Yeah—*you* would. But it seems to be that sometimes, it's like … lying by omission …" Riley says. "There is the distinct opportunity of 'to lie or not to lie.'"

"Like the Mexican!" Jenna gasps.

"Exactly," Riley says, throwing her hands up in the air with victory.

Elle looks down at her engagement ring, thinking carefully.

"That is kinda true … the girl gets the ring, not the guy … or rather, not both …" she whispers.

"But that's tradition!" Hunter exclaims, wounded.

"Right, okay. Fine. But in this day and age, people are malevolently finding loopholes to tradition," Riley informs.

Hunter and Ben look about ready to shrivel up and die in the sand. Hunter, in particular, is staring at his girlfriend, totally stunned by her fierce nontraditional standpoint.

"Let's go for a walk!" Elle suggests, pulling Jenna up and linking arms with Riley.

They leave the two guys to lie out in the morning sun, to mutter back and forth about their girlfriends. Riley rolls up her jeans as the three girls hold their flip-flops in hand, squishing along the wet sand. The water quickly soaks Elle's linen pants, but the warm morning sun feels great.

"I thought that things were better. We have so much fun together—he's wild and crazy like me. He gets the whole celebrity thing. But ... he freakin' peed on me," Jenna sighs.

"And that's not how anyone deserves to be treated," Riley validates. "I didn't realize what it was at first ... but because he drank so much ... the beer must've diluted? Caused loss of control of his bladder if he blacked out ... Jenna, I honestly think ..."

Jenna sniffles sadly.

"We think," Elle starts. "*We* think that he might be a little too much. And if he's into the drug use now, that's kinda like playing with fire, especially because you're so watched in the media. Lovee, I wish you were open to meeting someone else—smarter and kinder and less ... of a waste face." Elle smiles softly, trying to comfort her friend.

"I think I need to end this thing ... for good," Jenna announces, and her two friends wrap her in a hug.

"You deserve to have someone as exceptional as you. Someone who doesn't screw up in the first place simply because he's so captivated by you ... it's unfathomable. So random cocktail waitresses can't sway him in the least," Riley says, trying to be encouraging, and hoping that her friend has the strength to part with the high-profile actor, to step away from the media power-couple identity that's been crafted for them.

All the cover stories and gossip columns full of their exploits—fact or fiction—have gotten to be too much. Photographs distorted or quotes taken out of context to propel a storyline about Jenna and Carter that's far from accurate. And Carter is in the middle of it all, ready to provide an outspoken quote or fuel the fire with his Twitter activity. Even other celebrities have started to follow his updates, simply because he's so outrageous.

• • •

Back in Toronto, Riley Kohl nervously paces around the dining room table of her father's house, the city outside covered under a blanket of snow.

She stares at the unpacked suitcase by the door—yet another thing to do before they leave for New York tomorrow. To repack it full of clean clothes, refill her toiletries, and get all their scheduling hammered out. The group of friends just arrived back from their relaxing Caribbean vacation, and she's already wound up again. A cryptic message from Duncan Oberman would do that to anyone, though. He asked her to convene her friends and family for supper so that he could talk to them all.

She thinks she knows what's going on, what he's going to tell her, but doesn't want to admit it—in case she's wrong. In case she jinxes it all. He wouldn't convene them all here to humiliate her in public, right? He couldn't possibly be that mean to need an audience.

The doorbell rings and she races off to answer. The deliveryman hands her a bunch of packages, and she signs for the food.

"Need help?" her brother, Brian, asks, lumbering down the stairs in his bright green Crocs. He grabs a bunch of the packages and follows her into the kitchen, towering over her like a basketball player—not including the height of his afro-like curly brown hair.

"Everyone should be here soon," she sighs, motioning for him to unpack the gourmet food delivered from North 44, the usual family dinner spot near their house. They go to the trendy restaurant so often, the owners know Rhett by name and their menu preferences.

She races down to the wine cellar and grabs a few bottles for the meal. She paces around in the cool basement. *Should I have changed into something nicer? What am I doing?*

The front door opens upstairs, and her father's deep voice booms through the manor.

"Riley? *Vhere* are you?" he calls.

She runs up, clutching the wine, almost slipping on the marble floor in her socks.

"*Vhat* is going on?" Rhett Kohl bellows, exasperated.

"She's not telling us until everyone is here," Brian replies, picking at the food like a scavenger, rolling up the sleeves of his alpaca sweater to dig in.

Kevin helps put the food out on the table, and the guests begin to descend at the Kohl house.

"Please, everyone, have a seat," Riley instructs, standing stiffly like a statute, wondering when Jenna will grace them with her presence.

Rhett sits at the head of the table, with Kevin and Brian to his left, and Riley at his right with Hunter beside her. Elle and Ben position themselves beside Hunter.

Everyone starts small-talking, and Jenna rushes in late, flustered, slamming the heavy front door carelessly.

"I tried to drive my Maserati, but I don't know how to use manual transmission," she tries to explain, breathless and dramatic. "So I had to take the new Range that Hana picked for me. Did you know it still had, like, paper floor mats or whatever? They delivered it to the condo, and I forgot it even existed until I realized I can't drive stick! Thank God I remedied that situation!"

Everyone hums sympathetically.

"Can we start yet?" Brian asks, clutching his starving stomach.

"No!" Riley growls, not making eye contact with any of the guests and swatting away Hunter's hand-holding attempts.

The doorbell rings, and Rhett gets up to answer, his daughter stuck to her chair like cement.

"Oh, *vell,* hullo *zer!*" he greets with some inaudible chatter. Seconds later, he leads a massive man into his dining room.

"Everyone, *zis* is Duncan Oberman," introduces Rhett.

Kevin gives him a cheery, familiar wave, clearly already acquainted with the literary agent.

"Please, *haf* a seat," Rhett motions. Everyone scoots over to accommodate Duncan near the head of the table.

"Thank you," rumbles his voice, as he pulls back the dining room chair effortlessly.

Hunter looks at Riley with wide eyes as if to confirm that "yes—he is the biggest man I have ever seen."

"So, Riley, dear, will you tell us what in holy hell is going on? I can't handle all this mystery!" Kevin asks, excitedly clapping his hands and bracing himself for the news.

She's gripping the table so tightly that her knuckles have turned white.

"Riley ..." Duncan says, smiling.

"You talk. I know nothing," she shrugs, turning to the agent.

Duncan laughs heartily. "Well, she's gathered us here so that I can tell her ... or rather ... congratulate her on what will be a newly published book." Duncan grins proudly.

The table erupts into cheers, Hunter leaping out of his chair and nearly tackling his girlfriend. He smothers her with an excessive kiss, Rhett and Kevin looking at each other awkwardly, Brian about ready to vomit.

She pulls away, a bit embarrassed, and puts her arm around him instead, holding him at a distance.

"Oh my gosh—that is amazing! What happens now?" Elle gasps, her eyes tearing with pride.

"Well, it goes to editing, and eventually to print," Duncan explains. "I was recently on the yacht of a dear friend, a top publisher, if I may say. I brought along your story to examine it, but as we toured the South of France, he got his mitts on it and could not put it down."

"It was meant to be, it was a sign," Jenna informs.

"With any luck, we can expedite this project, seeing as he has a personal interest in it now. We'll have you out doing press by summer. You are officially my newest niche-market client, Miss Kohl."

"What? No ..." Riley says, putting up a hand in terror.

"No?" Duncan asks, laughing that she's trying to argue.

"*Nooo*," Riley repeats, shaking her head.

"What she's trying to say is that there is no way she is going to be able to speak publicly," Jenna explains cutely. "Trust me, I've known her for almost twenty years. She can't handle a press junket."

"What? But how else do you expect to promote the book?" Duncan asks her.

Riley opens her mouth to speak, and no sound comes out.

"Clearly by mime ..." Brian says, giving up on the group and serving himself the food.

"Well, you could do Internet stuff—chats and e-mail interviews. Hunter did one for ESPN's Web site," suggests Ben.

"Or she could blog," Jenna adds.

Duncan sighs, taking off his velvet blazer, realizing this is one battle he won't win—at least easily.

"Well, we'll manage. Point is, the story is quirky and alternative, we all loved it. And I think it could strike a chord," he admits.

"Riley, I *ham* so proud of *yew!*" Rhett gushes, getting up to hug his daughter, practically having to pry Hunter off her.

"Marvelous! But how on Earth did you get the guts to finally submit your work to someone?" Kevin asks, playfully tapping her.

"Uh ... a little help." Riley blushes, glancing at Elle.

"I got a referral from Laith Bassel. It seems someone slipped him a copy of her writing ..." Duncan explains.

"Guilty as charged." Elle grins, getting up to finally meet the famous Duncan Oberman.

"Well, you wouldn't have met him without me in the first place," Jenna blurts out.

The group looks at her awkwardly.

"I mean, I'm so happy that karma came full circle to help out," she corrects, hopping up to hug her friend. "Lovee, I am so happy for you, but so sad for me." She laughs emptily. "I'm going to be losing both my wingmen," she sighs heavily.

"What do you mean?" Kevin asks.

"Well, with Elle planning her wedding ..." Jenna trails off, realizing that June is only a few months away. "And now this. They won't be with me twenty-four-seven once their contracts are up..."

Brian finishes a plate of food, and then takes his turn to congratulate his little sister.

"Man, it's about time! Now I can finally say all your psycho rage is because you're a writer ..." he jokes, trying to mess up her hair. Riley punches him in the gut.

Ben uncorks some wine and initiates the toast.

"To our friend and loved one, who has spent all this time supporting us. We now have no choice but to support you," he teases, holding up the vintage red.

The group clinks glasses and begins to devour the food in front of them. Jenna slips away for a moment to compose herself, ducking into the ultramodern bathroom on the main floor.

She pulls out her phone and types an impulsive text:

> *In TO. Found out Riley's getting published. Elle's getting hitched. Wanted to c what major life chgs u have 2contribute. lol buddy, where r u? -j*

She splashes some cool water on her face, and stares at herself in the mirror. Her eyes have dark circles under them, and her skin looks lackluster. She was awake all night breaking up with Carter, crying and arguing with him until he finally backed out of her hotel room at 5:00 AM. Leaving her totally and utterly alone.

Throughout the night, she checks her phone nervously, but never finds a reply from Parker.

She should've known better. The feeling of being winded quickly taints Riley's celebration in her mind as she stares on through vacant eyes.

they say.

[Toronto, Canada—December 31, 2010]

Jenna Ramsay is warming up her vocal chords in her hotel room, about to perform at her city's traditional New Year's festivities. Her friends are sitting on the couch in the living room area of the suite, waiting for her call time.

"Oy, Hana was *pissed* when Mack told her she wanted to be in Toronto and not do Vegas," Riley laughs to Hunter.

"Well, I'm sure that it was a big deal for her," Ben says, making a money hand gesture, having heard from Elle exactly how intense Hana can be.

"You know that they say how you spend the New Year is what your year is supposed to be like," Elle grins, wearing a cute set of Chanel gloves, a scarf, and toque.

"What do you mean?" Hunter asks her, wrapping a classic Burberry check scarf around his neck.

"That who you're with at midnight sets the stage for how your year goes," she explains. "The feeling and vibe."

Carter Sampson bursts into the hotel suite, already a few beers into his celebration and wrapped in a bright down jacket.

Riley looks at Elle, both of them thinking that his influence is not how they'd like to set the tone for the next year.

"Okay, let's get moving," Riley announces, checking the time and calling for their drivers.

Jenna grabs her red Marc Jacobs jacket, excited to perform.

The group heads to the elevators and to the parking lot. There, they load into an oversized SUV and depart for the outdoor venue.

Jenna is headlining the evening's free concert, even though she's only slated to perform three songs. The various acts before her are signed for more stage time, but she outweighs them in international celebrity exponentially. In the past six months, she has set new records for becoming an instant star, not only in sales and money but notoriety and media coverage.

"So, where do we want to go after?" Carter asks, excited to have talked Jenna out of another breakup and ready to celebrate. He's worked hard to re-woo her, sending notes and flowers with Hana's help. All in the hopes that it'll keep him as a tabloid fixture until he can land more movie projects.

"Well, we have booths at a few different places, so I'm good with whatever," Jenna replies, drinking from a bottle of imported water.

They pull into a barricaded area and are escorted from the car and straight towards the stage. A rock band is finishing their set, and Jenna is on right after the commercial break.

She gives her friends a quick wave and rushes up the stairs to wait her cue. They all hang around backstage in the cold; it's probably well below freezing already, but luckily no sign of snow overhead.

Riley and Elle rush to peek around the massive stage, amazed to see thousands of people crowded into Nathan Philips Square in the city's core, large office buildings surrounding them.

"You know, I've never been ice-skating here," Elle whispers, motioning to the outdoor rink. Her breath vaporizes as she speaks, her cheeks turning into candy apples.

"You know, I've never been ice-skating. Period," Riley whispers back, looking over her shoulder at her hockey player boyfriend. She shoves her hands into the pockets of her dark grey peacoat.

"*Whaaat?!*" Elle laughs.

Riley glares at her friend, embarrassed, and they turn back to look at the crowd. There is a small group of preteen girls holding up homemade signs of adoration for Jenna. One of them recognizes Riley and Elle and starts screaming for their attention.

The two friends sneak up to the barrier and greet the rabid fan.

"Holy crap! They're Jenna's best friends!" she says to the group of girls with her, clearly the ringleader.

"Oh, my *gawd*!" says another one, gazing at the two young women dreamily.

"We've been waiting here since yesterday night," another girl admits, torn between talking to Riley and Elle, or watching her favourite singer about to hit the stage.

"She's amazing …" whispers one of them, having tried to replicate Jenna's new bangs—but having failed.

"Can we have your autograph?"

"Uh …" Riley groans, shocked that the kids even know who they are—and that they care for an autograph.

"You're her best friends, and we're best friends! It's so cool that you get to travel all together," one of them gasps.

"Oh, these girls are too sweet …" Elle coos, melting at the tween fervor.

Riley and Elle excuse themselves after signing some posters and return back to their group.

Meanwhile, Jenna stands motionless, waiting to be announced on stage. She closes her eyes and tries to feel her consciousness settle into her body, like pulling her spirit back into its physical confines, trying to bring her mind down to Earth. To stop feeling spaced out and weak, as if she's not in control of her body, like she's half out of it.

She blinks her eyes open, putting her electronic ear monitors in place, custom fit for her with squishy silicone. It won't drown the crowd out completely, and she loves hearing their screams fluctuate in intensity when she eggs the audience on. She's gotten so used to her performance routine that she can predict when the crowd will roar with excitement each and every time. The songs are pretty rudimentary, but they have built a huge fan following, particularly among the young and lovesick.

She swallows slowly and flutters her eyes open, hearing her name called out. As she steps out onto the stage, the overhead lights sear her skin, even in the middle of winter. Her face feels heavy under the layers of professional makeup. The crowd is huge, and her breath gets caught in her throat, just for a second. But the familiar notes of "Look at This" register in her brain, and she remembers what she's supposed to do.

The audience stretches out as far as she can see, but as soon as she opens her mouth to sing, they fade into the background, and she loses herself in the flow of the music.

After her set, Jenna is kept on stage, talking with the host of the countdown about how great it is to come home and perform.

"It must be so nice to be surrounded by friends and family back in your city!" he says, before throwing the live-to-air program into a quick commercial.

She stiffens for a moment, and her gaze filters through some of the people in the audience, wondering if her mother has ventured out in the cold to see her. They haven't spoken since her drunk-dial phone call from Tobago, telling off her mom and defending her new success.

Jenna's cheeks colour with shame, mortified that she can barely recall the short but violent conversation. But before she can wallow in her guilt, Carter rushes up behind her, wrapping his arms around her.

The audience starts cheering and screaming, and Jenna feels herself shifted back into the identity of "Jenna Ramsay—performer."

"You look so fuckin' hot!" Carter yells in her ear, positioning himself beside the television host as the program comes back from the commercial break.

The emcee introduces the actor, and the countdown begins, the crowd getting louder with each passing second.

"Ten ... nine ... eight ... seven ... six ..."

Backstage, Riley reaches her leather-gloved hand out to Hunter. He smiles to himself.

"They say how you start your New Year sets the tone ..." he whispers, turning to face her.

Ben and Elle are already gazing at each other dreamily, her arms around his neck. She discreetly touches her diamond heart trophy through her knit gloves.

"Five ... four ... three ..."

Hunter leans in.

"I love you," he whispers as the crowd continues screaming.

"Two ... one ... Happy New Year!"

Riley is dumbfounded by his confession, her eyes bulging as he kisses her.

Shit. Fuck. Shit. What? We're at love now? Really? I didn't know he was at love ...

"I love ... uh ... you, as well?" she says, trying to compensate once they pull away, mumbling her words under the cover of cheering and party horns.

He smiles down at her, hugging her tightly, oblivious to her discomfort.

Riley closes her eyes, pretending to be caught up in the moment, but actually feeling a wave of panic run through her shoulders. After he pulls away, she rests her head on his sheepskin coat, trying to compose her thoughts.

She looks over at Ben and Elle, who are still occupied.

A photographer rushes up to take a picture of the hockey star.

The video monitors nearby show all the action on-stage, mainly Carter enveloping Jenna in a major make-out session, his bright orange jacket like a publicity beacon.

Riley cringes at the scene, hoping for someone to pry him off of her friend—except the photographers are going nuts for the juicy shots.

After the singing of "Auld Lang Syne," Jenna and Carter appear backstage, high on life.

"You were the shit, babe," he says, congratulating his girlfriend with a slap on the butt.

Her eyes are shining with the thrill of so many people watching.

"Hey, lovee. There are these really adorable girls who slept overnight in the cold to see you. Would you go sign some autographs for them?" Elle smiles sweetly, still shocked that their parents would allow them to be downtown and out in the cold.

"They came here to see *me*?" Jenna gushes. "Take me to them!"

Elle and Riley lead their friend to the barricade and the group of girls begins shrieking.

"You are my *idol*!" shouts one of them.

They keep praising and fawning over the blonde singer, as she stops to sign autographs and take pictures with them.

She begins to work her way a little further down the crowd, to the hundreds of other people that are also trying to catch her attention.

"You guys made my life!" screams the preteen ringleader to Riley and Elle. She is beyond delighted; her eyes look like the happy fireworks in the sky.

Jenna spends about 15 minutes signing autographs before politely excusing herself.

"I mean, Japan was crazy, but it's so much better when you're in your own city," she says, enthralled by the affection being shown to her. She links her arms through her friends' and drags them back towards the guys.

"Let's go party!" Carter shouts as they take off.

game face.

[Vancouver, Canada—January 2011]

Hunter White digs the tip of his skate into the ice, feeling it cut through the thick white surface, grinding out the frustration he feels.

"Hunt, where is your focus? Get your head straight," yells his coach, whacking him with the curve of a hockey stick. He's just lost the puck in a face-off drill, his reaction time dimmed by the cloudy thoughts swirling in his head.

Hunter stares down at the ice, not sure where his mind has actually been during the past hour and a half of practice. He was physically there, skating and passing and making plays, but he can't remember any of it. It's all a blur.

His team is whispering around him. They've noticed him growing distant over the past few months. Either lonely and glum, or manic and desperate to hang out. Never quite the laid-back Hunter they saw at the start of the season.

"Do you really want me to bench you against the Canucks, Hunt? Come on, now. Get yourself together—you're a *professional,* after all. Why else are we paying you?" his coach taunts. He blows his whistle and calls an end to the morning skate, frustrated by his star right-winger's dull performance. He isn't present in his game, making silly rookie mistakes.

But the coach knows where his mind is—on his distant girlfriend. The problem isn't as simple as getting his Southern jock laid; Hunter is messed up emotionally by this girl. And that poses a threat to the team's dynamic, compromising the effectiveness of a key player in the lineup.

The rest of the team make their way back to the locker room, but Hunter stays back on the ice.

"Hunter, do you want company?" Eugene, the Russian goalie, asks from his net. "I feel bad."

Hunter lets out a sigh and skates up to the crease, dangling his stick and playing with a puck on the ice.

"I don't know why it feels like a battle … like there's some resistance or something? Shouldn't love be easy?" Hunter asks.

"Maybe this is not the correct type of love," Eugene offers, holding his mask under his arm.

"It's so hard to meet someone … who gets all this … don't you think?" Hunter asks.

"This is why I will marry girl from home. Have Russian wife. When ready. Not now—want have fun now."

Hunter nods, smiling at his closest friend on the team.

"Would you enjoy to shoot pucks at me? To feel happy?" Eugene offers.

"Thanks, man. But … no. Not today." Hunter laughs, touched by the gesture of offering athletic torture for stress relief. "You're an odd goalie, Eugene. But I like that."

"Yes. We are all odd in our ways."

With that, Eugene nods and skates off to the locker room, leaving his friend to stare at the empty arena. There's a hum in the air, and the ice is eerily bright to Hunter's tired eyes.

"What the fuck is going on with you, man?" he scolds himself, as he starts to skate laps around the rink. He's trying to clear his head, trying to reacquaint himself with the Hunter White he used to be: ready to dominate, ready to win.

Beads of sweat trickle down his temple, as he whips off his helmet in frustration. It bounces and skids along the ice surface, smacking into the rink boards. He's sweating under the layers of equipment, feeling constricted and having trouble breathing.

Am I having a fucking panic attack? Why am I freaking the fuck out? He laughs, starting to skate faster. His legs burn as he pushes harder against the ice, speeding up until everything blurs around him. The slicing sound of his blades on the sleek surface soothes him. He stops suddenly, sending a spray of fresh mist up and away.

He hasn't been acting like himself lately. Ever since Riley and the girls left after New Year's, he's been feeling jittery all over. Is it that he misses her? Or because he's bored and lonely?

He grabs his stick and starts hitting pucks at the open net in a blind rage. It's not about accuracy; he's trying to release the tension inside of him.

He lets out a roar as a puck flies at the net, but it hits the goal post and pops back. Miss. It's the simple difference between win and lose in his world. The real world.

He throws his stick and slowly skates to centre ice, lost in his thoughts again.

It's strange; he's never gotten this girl-crazy before. This isn't like him—usually girls are tripping over themselves to get to him, with his cute Southern accent and alpha male stature. But Riley is different. She doesn't give a shit about the image or the prestige of having made it to the pros, his plus/minus rating, or that he's a rent-a-player this season. She doesn't even care about his salary cap or the cars he has garaged at his condo. She doesn't really care about anything, it seems. Especially that he went to Japan to try to see her, spent his holidays with her and her friends, or tries to text her all the time. He even had massive flowers delivered to her for her birthday, only to receive an underwhelmed level of gratitude.

"Maybe I imagined it all, and we're not really what I want us to be," he admits out loud to the empty arena.

Hunter estimates that the rest of the team must be gone by now and trudges to the locker room to shower and change. He wants to avoid an intervention from them at all costs. He knows he's not right—but doesn't want to hear it.

His cell phone is vibrating in his bag with a message. He's already taken off his shoulder pads and has a towel around his neck when he opens the text from Carter.

Yo, man, in van city 4audition—fuckin' nailed it. Let's chill 2nite. @a sick chalet. Bring ur boys.

Hunter smiles at the message, feeling less alone. It's not a girlfriend, but at least he has a buddy out there actively trying to contact him in return. Ben is so busy flying around the continent with his other clients that he's barely in Toronto to hang out.

He texts Carter back and sends out a message to a couple of the guys on his team. A night off in Vancouver with nothing better to do? Why not hang out with his generation's future Brad Pitt?

• • •

"Gentlemen, welcome to tonight's stabbin' cabin!" Carter howls, greeting Hunter and his friends at the door of his hotel suite. Hunter's brought along Craig the defenseman, Casey the left-winger, Eugene the goalie, and their favourite athletic trainer, Jupiter.

"Wow ... Carter Sampson ... not bad," Hunter says admiringly, looking around at the penthouse.

"Seriously, your name is Jupiter?" Carter asks the trainer, sucking on a bright red lollipop as they all check out the view.

The young Chinese man shrugs; this question is pretty standard for his odd name. "They asked me to pick a name in grade school when I first came to Canada, and I didn't really speak much English, so I picked the first thing that came to mind." He laughs. "They thought my Chinese name would be too tough for the white kids."

"So your name ... is ... Jupiter?" Carter raises an eyebrow.

"Just call him Joop. It's easier that way." Casey laughs.

"Joop it is!" Carter snickers. He's impressed by Hunter's selection of male friends—twentysomething, good-looking all-American types with fun on the brain.

"Do y'all wanna get some late night shinny goin'? I'm sure we can set that up," suggests Hunter, kind of missing being back on the ice already.

"Man—we should go boarding one day ..." Carter thinks aloud, not eager to shakily get on skates with professional hockey players. His skill set comes from doing jumps with his snowboard, and he will not show weakness to them otherwise.

"Nice," agrees Casey, still taking in the hotel room's wood decor.

"Check the best part of this place ..." The actor laughs, throwing open the balcony doors and showing off an illuminated hot tub, warm vapour rising up into the night sky.

"Holy shit, that could fit, like ... twelve." Jupiter stares.

"Exactly. So let's go find ourselves some company ..." Carter smirks.

Hunter groans to himself. The last thing he wants is to have more women around. More complications. He thought Carter genuinely wanted to hang with the guys.

"Wait, where is remote? I would like to see scores," Eugene announces. The guys settle down on the leather couch.

"That was dece," Craig admits, watching Martin St. Louis whip a puck past his opposing goalie. He observes the shot replay carefully, memorizing it.

"Poor fuck had no chance in hell," Casey adds.

"Scary." Eugene nods, pointing to another play.

"Who wants a beer?" Carter asks, disinterested.

All the guys raise a hand, not flinching from the reels of that night's games, admiring the finesse of a golden overtime goal.

Carter steps out on the balcony and removes a handful of beer bottles stashed in the snow.

"That's pretty cool." Hunter notices his resourcefulness.

"Fucking room service beer is so goddamn overpriced. Fuck. Here," Carter snorts, handing them out to the guys. "But let's get some nachos if this is gonna be a TV-watching sausage fest. Anyone want some weed? Coke? Valium?"

The athletes uncomfortably pass on the offer.

"We've got a game tomorrow; they need to stay sharp," Jupiter tells the wild actor bluntly.

"Well, don't mind if *I* do." Carter huffs.

"Hey, why don't you come watch the game tomorrow? We could go eat after," Hunter suggests.

Carter nods in agreement, ordering up some room service and messaging one of his dealers in Vancouver to fill an order. He then sends out some text messages to a few of the actresses he auditioned with that morning, inviting them up to his room to chill with his buddies. Jenna is testing his last nerve with her decision to ask for space again. It's exhausting to try to keep her interest, even if it is only to help him stay in the media spotlight. Though he relishes the time he's not technically together with her, taking down as many innocent bystanders as possible. Redefining what it means to be a fun-loving, red-blooded male.

So the more the merrier tonight.

• • •

Ben Roberts is scribbling notes in his home office, revising some endorsement contracts for a new client. A microwave dinner sits untouched on the desk. His focus is on getting the most benefit for his newly traded Swedish defenseman instead.

I should get to the gym, he realizes, already changed. He checks the time, automatically converting it in his head to where Elle is travelling.

His cell phone rings sharply.

"Roberts," he answers, closing the files and locking them in his desk.

"Ben, it's Migs," announces the Toronto hockey coach, known around the league by his random nickname.

"What's up, Migs? How was practice? Hunter doing better after that physio session?" Ben starts, referring to some time spent with the athletic therapist to loosen his tight right pinky finger—a joke of an excuse for his imprecise shooting lately, but an excuse nonetheless.

"That's why I'm calling, Ben. Practice ... was a disaster."

Ben takes off his glasses and closes his eyes, bracing himself for the middle-aged coach's rant.

"I sort of believed you when you said that the little jaunt to Japan would help, but if anything, Hunt is worse off. The guy's head is … anywhere but here. I don't know what to do with him. I really don't want to humiliate the team scratching—"

"Now, now, Migs … let's talk this through," he interrupts, jumping at the mention of a healthy scratch. "You know as much as I do that benching him isn't gonna help anyone involved," Ben continues, trying to be smooth and non-confrontational. "Take me through it."

"Well … he stunk at practice. Couldn't make any decent plays. It's like he can't see anything ahead of him. Have tried to be patient, have tried tough love … but at this point, his underperforming is hurting the rest of the team."

"Okay, so his shooting is off …"

"Ben, it's not even that. His focus is … messed up. It's like he's skating drunk or something, missing the obvious plays and totally out of it. I can't coach this fucking hockey club with one of my star guys losing his marbles over some broad. Even if I sub Scott Brandon in for him, it's not the same as when his line is doing what they're *supposed* to. The chemistry is off."

Ben groans.

"Seriously, can't you talk to your fiancée and get them to break up. Something? At least we can get him over being dumped. Or have her live here with him? I'm fucking desperate. We need to make the playoffs this year—we're so goddamn close. All hands on deck."

Ben lets out a candid laugh. Getting Riley Kohl to do anything is like trying to push an elephant through a tiny doorway. Especially when it would involve modifying her career, let alone the idea of being a supportive non-vagabond spouse.

"I'm not kidding. I'm getting fed up with this kid. He had it all together … and it's fallen apart. I feel bad, but shit, this is what he gets paid to do!"

"So what happened after the practice?" Ben asks, trying to get more information out of him.

"Well, Hunt stayed out on the ice …" Migs concedes.

"So he stayed *after* the practice and did what?"

"I saw him shooting and skating …"

Ben puts his feet up on his desk and leans back in his chair. He's confident to have found an into squashing this argument.

"So he stayed after and worked on his skills. Solo. The work ethic is there, Migs. You gotta give Hunter credit there. He stayed after the team was done and kept at it."

The coach grumbles on the other line. "Right, but word on the street is that he is out right now partying his face off ... and he's dragged a couple of the guys with him," Migs says.

"It's a free night," Ben points out.

"Ben, come on. It's a free night, my ass. You know as much as I do that when we're in season, a team has to keep their shit together. How's he going to be tomorrow after a night with Jack Daniels?"

The agent is silent on the phone, staring at his running shoes.

"Exactly. He's going to need time with the 'athletic trainer' or whatever bullshit story you create for him."

"Is he depressed?" Ben asks, feeling an inkling of worry.

"I dunno. He's not himself. And he's out with that movie actor, Sampson? He's shooting a movie or something here."

"Carter Sampson," Ben sighs.

"Right. It really doesn't send the right message of what this team is about if he's out getting fucked up the night before a big game."

"I understand, Migs. I'll talk to him."

"I hope you do. Because if he's gonna keep up this kind of thing, he's gonna get sucked in by that actor's lifestyle—the partying, the booze ... God forbid he gets into the drug scene, and then he's shit outta luck with his career."

Ben tries to keep his cool and not let on that he's starting to get concerned. "I'll cancel my trip to Boston and fly out to Vancouver tomorrow morning, spend some time with him after the game. Silver lining is that you guys are leaving, and he won't be around Carter much longer."

"Right, but that doesn't help if my leading scorer has alcohol poisoning tomorrow and can't contribute goals."

"I've got this; don't worry," Ben assures as they hang up.

He tosses his phone on the desk and kicks off his sneakers, feeling defeated. There's only so much positive role modelling he can do now that his workload has grown. With the new clients that have been added to his roster, he can't babysit Hunter night and day to get him through the mopes.

I don't think the girls actually get how much trouble this Carter guy really seems to be, he thinks, getting up and heading to the kitchen.

He grabs himself a glass of milk, deep in thought about how to guide his client back in a healthful direction.

I think I gotta play the buddy card versus the agent card, Ben decides, never keen on creating a palpable difference between him and his clients. His laid-back style and sarcastic humour has helped him gain the trust of his athletes, as they turn to him not just as an agent, but a wingman and role model.

He grabs his cell phone and heads to the living room couch to catch the night's scores. He hits his speed dial.

"Hey, honey ... how's the music video going?" Ben starts, softening his voice to Elle.

"That's great ... I can't wait to see it." He pauses. "Listen, I gotta talk to you about Hunter. I hate to bring this up ... and I need you to understand that this is strictly business."

coat-tail.

[New York City, USA—February 2011]

"Guys, why don't we find a yoga class somewhere for our afternoon off?" Elle suggests, as the three girls scarf down their breakfast at five in the morning. They're already dressed and ready to roll.

"Well, after she's done on *Good Morning America* and scores that national TV exposure, I am fine with anything you want. This has to go off without a hitch, or Hana will eat us alive. I hate live performances …" Riley grumbles to herself, texting furiously with a producer at the television studio.

"Everything will go perfect. I'll ask the concierge where to go … I really think we've neglected ourselves lately—"

"Can we go shopping at some point?" Jenna interrupts, stretching her arms above her head sleepily; her high-heeled boots are carelessly strewn beside her as she pokes at her toast. She hasn't touched her food at all, and it seems like she's been surviving only off coffee and energy drinks as of late.

"Shopping? Again?" Riley groans, popping antacid pills.

"Fine. Whatever. Hana comes in tomorrow—she'll go shopping with me," Jenna grumbles.

"What about lunch?" Riley asks her friends.

"Maybe nearby? Somewhere small and secret," Elle suggests. "That way, we can get back here and take our time getting ready before we meet Kwame for dinner?"

"Or somewhere high-profile?" Jenna weighs in as she flips through the morning's paper. She disappointedly doesn't find any photos of herself from her MTV appearance yesterday. She wore a killer minidress for the acoustic performance.

"Okay, let's step back a second. I want to ace through the show, and then we'll go from there?" Riley pleads, wanting to keep Jenna's focus steady on hamming it up with the American talk show hosts, and not unleashing the inner bitch that's come out to play lately. She had to cut off a magazine interview yesterday after Jenna nearly chomped the reporter's head off for asking about her excessive shopping.

"What jacket do you want to wear?" Elle asks, hopping up from the table and grabbing two huge garment bags for Jenna to look at.

Inside are wool-cashmere winter coats for her outdoor winter-themed performance.

"I don't know … they're so nice …" Jenna smiles, stroking the fabrics and trying to imagine herself singing in them, being stared at. "I might actually sweat in them with the lights …"

Elle bites her lip nervously, afraid she's picked the wrong outfits.

"I'll wear this one now …" Jenna says, grabbing the winter-white Dior piece. "And the other one for the interview …"

"Both? Whatever. Okay, so let's get moving," Riley announces, watching the time carefully and downing the last bit of her coffee.

"Riles, you don't want to eat anything more?" Elle asks, motioning to her friend's picked-at plate. She's shoved two bowls of yogurt in her mouth and avoided the solid food.

"Ugh, I don't feel … right …" Riley grumbles, motioning to her stomach.

"When's the last time you went?" Elle whispers, neatly folding her napkin.

"Went poo?" Jenna laughs out loud.

Riley looks uneasy at the topic of conversation.

"Seriously. When's the last time you went number two? Because that could be a sign of something more … and I know if I don't go, then I can't function …" Elle says gently.

"I don't know … in a while …? It's been a while, I guess. I haven't really thought about it," Riley admits.

"Pay attention. And tell me when you go next and how it looks," Elle instructs.

"Are you serious?" Jenna snickers.

"What? I've been learning a lot about this stuff; it's kinda cool. Maybe the yoga will help, actually … Laith says that you have to be settled in yourself …"

Riley throws her hands up in defeat and pleads with them to get into the elevator and on their way to the show.

After a charming interview and performance, the girls are permitted to relish in an afternoon without commitments. No interviews, rehearsals, recording sessions, or photo shoots.

"Why don't we walk around the city a bit? It's like we're always either in a car or a hotel or a plane …" Elle asks softly, as they eat a room service lunch and change in to comfy clothes.

"Good idea!" Jenna smiles. She hopes the paparazzi are out and about to snap some candid shots of her in New York. She mentally pieces together her next outfit.

"Fine ..." Riley groans.

Elle slips into her crusty, salt-stained Ugg boots, excited to be able to spend time at an actual yoga studio instead of doing DVDs in her room.

Riley wraps her black Mackage winter coat over her workout wear and collects all their personal belongings into an oversized Longchamp carryall. She's like the mother hen, always carrying Jenna's personal effects—and a permanent marker for autographs.

Jenna skips around excitedly, having found that a courier delivered a new McQueen coat to her while she was out, too late to get it on-air this time around, but perfect for her city walk. She wraps the patterned jacket over herself and slides into a new pair of sneakers.

"So that's ... three new coats in one morning." Riley laughs, still shocked at how many pieces of clothing her friend goes through in a day. She laces up her old running shoes lazily, watching Jenna's hyperactive prancing.

"Well, you can never wear the same thing twice," Jenna says matter-of-factly.

"Says who?" Riley snaps.

"I can't be photographed in the same outfit twice ... what does that say about me?" Jenna gasps.

"I'm quite okay wearing the same thing many times." Elle grins, pulling a heavy lululemon sweater over her multiple layers.

"Yeah, but ... I'm ..." Jenna starts, trying to find a less insulting way to express her stardom.

"You're you. We get it. Let's move," Riley commands, annoyed.

The girls have the driver drop them a few blocks from the yoga studio, Riley not compromising their safety to walk from the hotel. They wander their way over, peering into shop windows, quietly absorbing a less glamorous nook of the city.

"I wouldn't mind living here ..." Jenna says out loud, admiring the couples and joggers around them.

"Well, you gotta put roots down somewhere, right?" Elle says.

"Speaking of, where do you think you and Ben will live?" Riley asks, carefully holding a hot cup of coffee like it's something precious. "In Toronto, obviously, but at his condo? Probably not if you're gonna have babies soon ..."

"He actually found a great house not too far from my parents."

Riley coos approvingly.

"Rich people area," Jenna teases.

"Anyway ... we didn't want to move more suburban, but definitely need a house because we're planning on kids in the next couple of years. Not right away—I want to get my art off the ground. I think this one is good—central. That way, he can get to the airport or to the hockey arena faster than if we were out of the city. Be near his clients. Good schools, too."

"That's great!" Riley encourages.

"And what about you?" Jenna asks her.

Riley twists her face up, unsure. "I don't know. I mean ..."

"What? You don't want to play house with the superstar?" Jenna jokes.

"I ... am ... not ... sure," Riley confesses.

"Really? You still want to keep it cool?" Elle asks, surprised.

"Well, I mean. It's just not ... certain?" Riley blabbers.

"I thought things were going awesome ..." Jenna says, curious.

"Well, there are things that I'm kinda ... not ..."

"Sure?" Jenna fills in.

Riley nods, her eyes darting around the street.

"So he's not perfect?" Elle pouts, a little devastated that her best friend may not end up settled, happily ever after with her boyfriend's best friend.

"Not quite perfect ..."

"Is it you?" Jenna asks bluntly.

"What?!"

"Is it you? Because something tells me he thinks everything is, in fact, 'perfect,'" accuses the blonde.

"Like, is it you putting too much pressure and expecting everything to be one hundred per cent flawless? Or do you think it's legitimately not meant to be?" Elle contributes, her mittens gesturing in the frosty air.

"Because maybe it's like a self-fulfilling prophecy. If you're expecting one hundred per cent flawless ... then no one will ever be able to touch that," Jenna says. "Or maybe you don't want to settle down with anyone ... regardless of who it is. You are a Capricorn, after all, you can handle being alone like that."

"That's true. Like, maybe she knows in her higher self that Hunter isn't the one, and so that's why she's not totally into it like he is ..."

Elle says to Jenna, the two of them cutting out their friend from the conversation and starting to speak about spiritual connections and destined love.

Riley stares down at the snowy sidewalk, overwhelmed by the scrutiny on her. "Can we talk about something else?" she begs.

"I e-mailed Parker," Jenna blurts out.

Riley and Elle stop, leaving her to walk a few steps ahead.

"Why?" Riley moans, throwing her hands up in the air.

"I just ... wanted to ..."

"But, lovee, he hasn't responded to you since ... what, June? July?" starts Elle.

"He once sent me a drunk text, so technically since October," Jenna offers cheekily.

"Danger!" Elle says of her friend's hang-up on Parker Ma.

"I know ... it sounds insane. But ... I never felt so ... myself ... around someone else. Like the Carter thing, that was so ... about the image. Not me or him—but the media and the gossip and all that," Jenna sighs.

Elle looks at her friend with caution.

"Thank God. So now you can move on and find someone *new*, right?" Riley hints.

Jenna shrugs, as they stop in front of the yoga studio.

• • •

Elle whimpers in the back of the cab, tears streaming down her face. She's sandwiched between her two friends and trying to breathe herself out of a panic attack.

"It's okay, Elle, don't worry—we'll make it!" Jenna assures her forcefully, looking out the window, frantically searching the busy streets of Manhattan.

"It's near here somewhere ... don't worry, we'll get help," Riley assures, also scouring the storefronts for their target.

"Stop!" shouts Jenna, spotting their mark, as Elle's lip quivers and tears well in her eyes.

The cab screeches to a halt, and the three girls barrel out.

"You go ahead!" Riley instructs valiantly, pulling out her wallet to pay for their hectic ride from the yoga studio.

Jenna grabs Elle by the bicep and drags her inside the building, pushing people out of her way.

She stops suddenly, confused.

"Elle, where am I going?" she turns to ask, not sure where exactly she's heading.

Elle turns meekly to the security guard by the door. "Service, please?"

He looks at the two frazzled girls and points them in the right direction. They look out of place in their sportswear.

Elle and Jenna rush up to the counter.

"We have an emergency!" Jenna announces to the petite woman who stares in shock as they charge towards her.

"May I help you?" she asks, taken aback by their sense of urgency.

Jenna grabs Elle's left hand and slams it down on the countertop.

"Ow!" Elle cries, as her swollen hand hits the wood surface with a thud.

"Sorry," Jenna whispers.

The lady stares down at Elle's hand, not sure what to do.

"Help me!" Elle gasps.

"Miss, I think you should have gone to a doctor ... not come to Tiffany's ..." The conservative employee blushes, staring down at the hand swelling around Elle's engagement ring.

"Can't you saw it off or something?" Jenna snaps.

"The finger?!" gasps the employee.

"No, the ring, obviously," Elle hisses.

"Well ... I've never ..." the lady trails off, surprised by their concern over the ring instead of seeking medical attention first.

Riley rushes up to her two friends, who have started to draw attention from the rest of the store. Whispers of pop star Jenna Ramsay travelled like wildfire through the bright, shiny shop. Their frantic yelps echo through the lavish New York icon.

"What's going on?" Riley asks, trying to assess the situation, noticing the ring still on Elle's tiny but bruised hand.

"*Nothiiing,*" Elle wails, desperate.

"Hi ... may I?" interrupts a man's voice from behind them, soft but confident.

They girls turn and come face-to-face with a handsome blonde man in his mid-thirties.

"Who are you?" Riley snaps.

He can't help but laugh at her outright defensiveness. "Dr. Charles Mullen. Chucky for short." He shakes hands with Riley. "I'm an orthopedic surgeon ... I can take a look at that hand if you let me," he offers, smiling.

The three girls stare at him in disbelief.

"Oh, yeah ... okay, sure ..." Riley says, embarrassedly backing down. He leads Elle to a set of armchairs so he can check out the damage.

Before they can interrogate his certifications, he's managed to massage her hand and jiggle the ring off—intact.

"Ohmigosh!" Elle gasps, the relief and joy visible in every muscle of her face.

"It's just a really bad sprain," he says, still examining her hand closely. "What happened?"

"Ummm ..." she trails off, blushing.

He looks up at the girls. In their casual layers, they look like university students and not world-travelling hipsters.

"Downward Dog. That's what happened. She fell out of her yoga pose," Riley says, relieved to have left the class early with Elle's accident. The upside-down poses caused too much blood to rush to her skull and made her feel nauseous.

Dr. Chucky laughs at her blunt explanation, and their eyes flicker with slight flirtation for a moment.

As Riley diverts her gaze, she catches a glimpse of the wedding band on his finger and forces her attention elsewhere.

"Uh ... I'm gonna go find Jenna," she announces, suddenly realizing the blonde has vanished. She leaves Elle listening intently to her new treatment protocol and noting instructions about how to bandage herself up.

She finds Jenna engaged in a colourful conversation with a short man by the cufflinks.

"So you think this would go okay with a blue striped shirt ...?" he asks Jenna, feigning total helplessness.

"Oh, absolutely. There's nothing nicer than a man in a great suit," she flirts back, batting her new mink eyelash extensions at him.

"Wow, I'm so glad that I bumped into you ..." he coos, reaching for his phone and asking for her number.

"Mr. Andrews?" calls an employee, approaching the two of them.

He turns in terror, seeing the box being brought towards him. He tries to anxiously excuse himself, but the employee reaches the counter quickly, eagerly smiling at the two of them.

"Your engagement ring?" He grins, opening the box up in front of the man and Jenna.

Engagement ring? Jenna shouts in her head, her face feeling like burning. *The entire time you've been flirting with me, you're here getting an engagement ring!*

The employee hands it to Jenna for inspection, and she slips it onto her finger.

"Aww ... thank you, honey," she trills sweetly.

Mr. Andrews stares at the situation in front of him. He's trying to pick up a gorgeous, famous blonde while picking up his fiancée's resized ring.

"I mean, the diamond's a little small, but ... it'll do for now," she sighs, staring at her hand in the light. "Oh, well, I'll meet you at Saks." She smiles, turning quickly and zipping out the door.

Riley stares at her friend in total surprise, rather impressed by her quick thinking after having been snubbed, and grabbing this inferior man by the jewels (so to speak). She watches Jenna sail out the revolving doors with a wink, and the employee smiles at Mr. Andrews.

"She's beautiful, congratulations ..." He nods, as he walks off with his presentation tray.

Riley hears a frantic commotion outside, and camera flashes filter in through the door. She darts out, but Jenna has already sped off in a cab to escape the paparazzi.

"I hope she remembers what hotel we're at ..." Riley whispers to herself, anxious that her friend has no money or cell phone on her person.

Elle joins her downstairs, and they slip out onto the street under the cover of their sweatshirt hoods.

"They're gonna think her and Carter are engaged now," Riley whispers to her friend, explaining the drama as they hail a cab and race back to the W hotel.

Elle looks on worriedly, toting her ring in a little bag. "Well, I guess this isn't really the best venue to meet single men." She shrugs.

"I wish all these gross, negative circumstances would stop happening to her—it feels like some sort of hex or something. Don't you think? Why is it so hard for her to meet a psychologically stable, non-lying person?" Riley whispers, as the cab pulls up in front of their hotel.

"Why don't we have a pizza pyjama party tonight? I'm sure she's going to be on the couch wallowing when we get upstairs. She just needs to be reminded of the good people out there. We could paint our nails ..." Elle smiles as they ride up in the elevator.

"You mean, *we* can paint our nails, and we'll have to call in a manicurist for *her*," Riley sighs. "Sorry—low blow."

They step into the hotel suite, but the place is empty.

"Jenna?" Riley calls out, as the two girls start fanning out and checking the rooms. But she's nowhere to be found.

"Where on Earth is she? Do you think she didn't come back?" Elle gasps. Her eyes dart around in panic.

What if she's been mobbed in the street by autograph seekers? Or if some sort of insane stalker abducted her?

"I have her cell phone, so that's no use. Okay, if you were her, where would you be?" Riley asks aloud.

"The spa," Elle answers, lightning fast.

Riley's head spins around quickly, her hair whipping as she sprints out the door.

She marches straight from the elevator to the hotel restaurant. Like a lemming on a mission, she zeros in on Jenna and prepares to extract her from the bar. She's surrounded by a group of businessmen, and the bartender is clearing their last round of drinks while mixing up a new batch.

"Oh *heeey, Rileyyy,*" Jenna screams out, spotting her friend storming at her.

"Let's go," Riley tells her firmly.

"*Whyyy?*" Jenna whines, reaching for a glass.

Riley leans in and whispers to her, and Jenna obediently gets up and walks out with her.

"Bye *boysss,*" Jenna giggles and waves, as Riley leads her upstairs.

"You gotta get yourself together. We have a big event with Kwame and his investors, okay? You need to be good to perform for them if needed," Riley tells her, as she places her friend in bed to sleep off the afternoon binge drink. She sticks out her hand, and Jenna grumpily hands back the hijacked engagement ring.

Riley trudges back out to where Elle is nervously curled up on the couch.

"It's not like her to be wasted like this—out of commission at four in the afternoon? Frick, how am I gonna get her to Kwame's dinner tonight if she feels like crap?" Riley asks her, annoyed.

"I don't know what's going on with her ... she's not eating, she's drowning herself in Grey Goose ... I'm scared, Riley," Elle admits.

"I don't know what to do, either, Elle. They won't give her time off—she's so high priority, she won't be able to stop unless she crashes or something."

"She's not herself these days. And it's like, when Hana hands her back to us, she's even more of a zombie. Doped up or something. It reminds me of when I dabbled in … narcotics … once upon a time," Elle admits, ashamed.

"Never touched 'em, but I get what you mean. I guess we gotta try keep her in line … maybe Mack or Kwame will step in soon enough."

"This could be dangerous if *we* don't keep an eye on her," Elle frowns.

"What? Because people might get greedy trying to make as much money possible off her, even if she's starting to dangle in the balance? Mack cares about her well-being, at least … Kwame probably sees her as an asset that needs to be maintained. And Hana … well, I think we both know where that psycho's at."

"She is definitely not helping, keeping her out to party and stuff. Not good," Elle agrees.

"And now Jenna's looking at us like loser boring people because I hate shopping and you won't give her sleeping pills," Riley snips.

"I seriously don't know how she's coping with all this. To go from nothing to … everything … so quickly. Like, how people look at her in the street and stuff. I'd hate to have that on me, or my family."

"It's like the evil eye, I think," Riley explains. "Point is, no one can feel that level of intrusion and be okay."

devil worship.

[Los Angeles, USA—March 2011]

"So, Hana ... tell me ... how do you think you could help my career *if* I took you on as my manager ..." Carter Sampson asks, staring across the dinner table at the Ivy. Smug confidence oozes from him; a tight lime-green muscle tee makes him look even more like a California playboy with his flip-flops and jeans.

Hana smiles, taking a sip from her glass of wine. "So you're actually interested in having a real manager? Paying commission instead of doing it yourself ..." she says dryly. She fixes her tight American Apparel dress under the table, her bare legs brushing him nonchalantly.

"Because I know that your voice mail ... the person who only responds to queries via e-mail, claiming to be your manager ... is, in fact, you," she cackles.

"What?" he gasps, pretending to be shocked.

"I know you're too cheap to pay for real representation, Carter. So you do it yourself—take the scripts in, read them, respond on behalf of the actor that's way too busy ... what a clever little front." She grins menacingly. "Don't worry, I'm not gonna tell anyone ... yet."

"Well, I had to be self-sufficient early on, Miss Rin. Didn't trust anyone to look out for my interests but me ..." he says, drinking his rye and ginger. His offbeat hippie style, with the layers of necklaces, bracelets, and rings, was just voted the must-have men's look for the spring season.

"I'm sure that happens when you don't possess actual talent and have to coast with your looks," she taunts, tapping her acrylic nails on the glass stem.

"Well, at least I have looks, then. A marketable asset." He grins flirtatiously.

Hana jokingly glares at him as they wait for their cheque. It's been a long drinks date, consisting of them slinging flirty insults back and forth. It's time to shift gears.

"I think ... that ... with the movies I've signed on to do, I need to consider more ... formal ... representation," he says. "And I've seen how you've grown Jenna. I want you to double that with me."

She looks at him suspiciously but is quite interested in his proposition. Her short-term plans include leaving Top Dog and taking Jenna with her. She's already got a few clients that will sign with her, but Carter would be an extra jewel in her crown.

"You know as much as I do that a man's sex appeal can keep a female audience. Look who buys all those magazines. They want to know about Jenna because they want to know about me. If I'm with her, how amazing I am, how much of a wounded bird I am … blah, blah, blah. That's what sells," he says matter-of-factly.

"Your point being?"

Carter finishes his drink and leans in closer to her.

"Use me. Use me to aggressively build the next freakin' … whatever … Jenter … Carna … you know how the tabloids mash together two names for power couples. I want us to be earning the most money out of this … situation …"

Hana smiles mischievously, surprised by the actor's forthcoming greed. "So you don't actually … love … her?" she asks slyly.

Carter glances around the ritzy celebrity haunt, spotting a director he wants to work with at a table nearby. He contemplates sending a drink over to get on his radar.

"Honestly? I knew from the second I saw her that she'd be a good networking angle. But she's so fucking … ugh … I don't know. Squeaky clean? I can honestly say that I've had other things catch my eye," he says, glancing at her collarbone.

Hana looks at him coyly, watching him eye her up and down. "I eat little boys like you for breakfast," she warns.

"I like your employee perks." He smiles.

"I think I like your challenge." She returns the smile, subtly arching her back. If her dress hasn't caught his eyes, her sky-high Gucci platform heels have. She's refined her image to channel "upscale sex thrill" with lots of leg.

"Shall we talk about our strategy elsewhere?" he suggests.

The waiter brings the cheque, and Carter reaches for it.

Hana is about to move for her purse, but he motions for her to stop.

"Hey, you're my date tonight. It might seem old school, but that's just how I am." He winks, using his trusty line.

She smiles at his attempted chivalry. Maybe this Canadian boy isn't *totally* corrupted by the scent of celebrity.

"You know, I would advise that you keep the friendship with the hockey player," she starts.

"Really?" Carter laughs. "He's so whipped," he says disgustedly.

"Yeah. Because let's face it—they're not going to last. And you can refine your badass thing with him and his teammates. Go out partying with them. Make them feel like rock stars, and you'll become an instant legend. Maybe help cook up some scandals if you're bored, sell the stories if you want extra cash."

Carter ponders the strategic partnership and realizes that he could easily pawn off their partying and have the pro athletes foot the bills. It means little to no start-up capital for him to get exposure and branding with them. Plus, it would kill downtime while filming *Erroneous Affair* in Toronto.

"So is that what you do? Sell tips?" Carter asks. "Sell Jenna's stories?"

She looks down at the table, smiling to herself. He gets it.

"Well, to stay relevant, you have to stay in the spotlight ... and people need to know where to look ..." she says, slowly running a finger down her neck, signaling she's ready to leave.

"So let's get out of here and plan the next headline," Carter whispers softly.

"Where do you want to go to ...?" she starts, clicking around on her iPhone, trying to think how to prolong their evening, and what nightclub would be worth a visit.

"I was thinking somewhere ... private," he says.

Hana cocks her head to the side, surprised by his directness. They get up from their table and head out to the valet. Her silver Porsche convertible is pulled up.

"Is that a Boxster?" he asks as the car rumbles to a stop, checking out the custom-painted pink calipers.

Hana raises an eyebrow, disgusted. "Those are for posers. You really do need me."

Carter can't help but check out her butt as she sashays to the driver's door. The two slide in and speed off to Hana's loft.

• • •

"Hey, do you guys wanna go see the LA Kings play?" Elle shouts through their hotel suite at the Mondrian as she reclines on the couch in the living room. Her legs are propped up by one of the plush, white cushions, laptop open with a chat between her and Ben in full swing.

"No, I don't want *tuberose*," she snaps at the screen, typing back to him about their wedding's flower arrangements. "How does he know what tuberose even is? Good Lordy."

"What'd you say?" Riley asks, strolling in with a toothbrush in her mouth. Her hair is wet—she's stepped right out of the shower and is already changed into her pyjamas.

"Hockey game tonight?" Elle asks.

Riley scrunches her face up, not keen on attending another game—especially if she doesn't have to watch Hunter's team.

"He wants tuberose!" Elle gasps at her friend, typing back furiously to her fiancé.

"What's tuberose?" Riley asks through a mouth full of toothpaste foam.

"Exactly. Why does he care so much?" Elle replies, still chatting.

Riley shrugs and heads back to the bathroom to spit and rinse.

"What do you think of this?" Jenna bellows, as she turns the corner into the living room, modelling a long Valentino gown.

"Magnificent—for what?" Elle asks, barely looking up. Her friend has been modelling outfits all evening and trying to find something suitable for her appearance on the "Ellen" show.

"Hockey awards in June. I figure I might as well go. Maybe check out the talent." Jenna shrugs. She's single in the city again, not having made out in way too long.

Elle feels distressed by the thought of her friend prowling around in Ben's professional circle (and using Hana's slang).

"Well, if I'm even there. Hana thinks I might have to fly in for your wedding if I'm doing 'Oprah' around that time." Jenna smiles excitedly.

Elle stares back at the screen and signs off with Ben, throwing her hands up in the air with annoyance.

"Anyway, whatever. Hana's coming over now," Jenna announces.

"Oh, okay," Elle shrugs, trying to hide her disappointment.

"She's bringing someone for me to meet. Her spiritual guide," Jenna informs, spinning around in the long silky dress.

"What the fuck's a spiritual guide?" Riley barks from the bathroom.

"You guys should meet her, too. Maybe she can read for you," Jenna says—louder so that Riley can hear.

"Read what?" Elle asks.

Jenna looks at her like she's dumb. "Uh … your future, obviously."

"Like a psychic?" Riley scoffs, joining the girls in the living room. She sits beside Elle on the couch.

"You might even learn something …" Jenna taunts, spinning on her tiptoes and heading back to her room to change.

Riley and Elle look at each other in surprise.

As if on cue, Hana storms in, her loud, obnoxious laughter echoing off the walls.

"Oh you are *tooo* much!" she cackles, as she steps into the living room with another woman, both of them roughly the same age.

The outsider is a good-looking, typical LA fashionista. She's wearing trendy jeans and a simple but expensive-looking tunic, and her wavy dark blonde hair is clipped back messily. She's average height and build, but gives off the vibe of a pro—totally confident and comfortable stepping into a stranger's five star hotel room.

"Oh, hi, guys, this is Olivia," Hana says, staring at the casually dressed girls. She carelessly drops her designer purse on the ground and sits down on the arm of couch. Her tight jeans flow over high heels, and she's wearing a fitted black tank top.

"Hi … Olivia … are you the spiritual guide psychic?" Riley asks flatly, as Elle tries to stifle her giggles.

"Psychic guide, yes," Olivia corrects, smiling in the face of opposition.

Riley and Elle keep themselves in line, as Jenna storms in.

"Olivia!" she shrieks, charging at the guest and wrapping her in a huge hug with two cheek kisses.

"It's so nice to finally meet you in person!" Olivia chirps, holding Jenna's hand lovingly.

"You guys know each other?" Riley asks dryly.

"From over the phone … once or twice …" Jenna says, trying to underemphasize her growing fixation on having a psychic advisor. She was so bang-on about Carter last week, hopefully the information that comes out today will be even more useful.

When does she have time to talk on the phone? When she's asleep? Riley thinks, her guard up around this Olivia character.

"Anyway, do you want to do your reading before dinner?" Olivia asks Jenna. "You can invite your friends, too, if you want."

Jenna looks at Riley and Elle on the couch, unsure if they'll suspend their disbelief, perhaps insult her new confidante.

"Yeah, come on, guys; it'll be fun," Hana coaxes them, having planned on getting the three of them under Olivia's spell, of planting some idea seeds in their insecurities.

"How does it work?" Elle asks, curling her knees up to her chest.

Olivia smiles at the impressionable girl and leads them to gather around the rectangular dining table.

"I'll start with Jenna—that way you can see what you think, and decide if you want a reading," says the "psychic" as she pulls out a tie-dyed cloth with a crystal ball. The bright colours of the fabric fit the mental picture Jenna had of this cool hippie chick, of how she imagined Olivia over the phone.

Jenna and Hana at either side of Olivia, who is at the head of the table. Riley and Elle sit beside Jenna, watching.

"Okay, make a wish," she instructs Jenna, while staring at the crystal intensely.

"Jenna's energy please come forward and channel through me all that she must learn. I am the vessel for knowledge to pass to her. I say this prayer for magic and love, in this circle of friends."

Jenna takes a deep breath and braces herself.

"*Ohhh* wow … your past, this is incredible …" Olivia starts. "I see a bad relationship with your parents. Your mom is domineering, if you will. I don't really see your dad's presence, though …"

"He died when I was little."

"Ah, he's passed. I see now. It was tough on you growing up with your mom. She wasn't supportive of your singing; she knew you were good, but she had jealousy …"

Jenna nods her head, absorbing the commentary with wide eyes.

"I am sorry for all the psychic pain you suffered growing up," Olivia says dramatically, reaching out and holding Jenna's hand tenderly. "But it will be okay now; things have fully transitioned into a new life for you. The pain is gone. No one here is going to hurt you. I am sending you my special psychic magic."

Jenna nods, a tear coming to her eye.

"Who is this Chinese man?" Olivia asks, tapping the crystal. "He keeps coming up in your readings. I've seen him before but never paid much attention to him."

"Chinese?"

"Yeah. Young man, Asian guy, you feel attached to him?"

"Parker? Parker's Korean …" Jenna suggests.

"You grew a bond with him, it shows here. But you entered it with an innocent heart, and he did not. Betrayal. You were meant to learn from this—he was a test. To prepare you for the next relationship ... Carter was next, right? His Aries energy is ... whoa ... you guys are sexually explosive! He's a great match to your Sagittarius fire."

Jenna nods, as Riley and Elle look on quietly.

"See, this is the same thing coming up from previous readings. Carter is definitely a past-life love; that's why the bond is so magical between you. From ancient Egypt, where you were a noble woman, and he was your lover, actually. What did you learn from Parker?"

Jenna thinks back. "I dunno—I guess he showed me that there was the ability to feel a deep connection ..."

Olivia studies her subject carefully. "You're really stuck on him, aren't you?" she observes.

Jenna blushes, thankful that the group can't read the journal entries she's written, agonizing about why the timing with Parker was definitely not right. Idealizing him into her ultimate soul mate figure.

"I think we need to cleanse you of him, you're not opening your heart because this person serves as a distraction. And from what I can tell—he's not thinking about you as much as you're thinking of him. And, honey, that is not good enough. You deserve so much more ..."

Riley and Elle give a silent "amen, sister."

After a half hour of general commentary, she switches her focus to Riley.

"You know, this guy ... he's so different than you, I think it freaks you out. He has a good heart, but you just don't care for it. And that's not nice," Olivia states sharply.

Riley stares at her defensively.

"I think you feel guilty because deep down you know he likes you more than you like him. And let's be honest—that spot's between a rock and a hard place," Olivia explains.

Riley shifts her weight uncomfortably, and Olivia knows she's nailed it—she's got the stiff brunette figured out.

She continues giving Riley more nonspecific insight, as procured by Hana, throwing in general wisdom quotes she's memorized from her Karma-a-Day desk calendar.

"You need to address your own issues. Thinking someone is less than you because they didn't go to school or come from the elites doesn't mean anything these days. Look at Jenna—she's self-made, and her wealth and status trump your stuffy bookishness," Olivia digs.

Riley stares at her, mortified, but can't drum up a response.

Maybe she thought I wasn't good enough when we were kids ... Jenna wonders to herself, looking at Riley critically. *Not like I was part of the elite, I was the damn outcast with her and Elle.*

"Um, I don't think that's it ... exactly. Hunter and I are just very different people," Riley says, more to herself than to anyone else.

"Whatever. No one likes a harsh audience. You should ask your brother. Elle, let's look at you." Olivia smiles. She has to keep herself from laughing at the eagerness and naïveté of Eleanor.

Riley grits her teeth, discrediting the reading, but making a mental note to e-mail her brother, just in case. To shake the negative feeling Olivia is trying to implant in her.

"Oh wow ... this is the most honest-to-goodness true love I've ever seen," Olivia convincingly coos, wishing she could vomit instead. "Truly honest, pure, transparent. You guys have nothing between you two, and I will say a special blessing for your union—though, you hardly need any extra magic from me."

Elle's gaze melts into reassured happiness as she imagines herself being married with angels and celestial beings presiding auspiciously. Glowing little cherubs rejoicing in their magical, magical love.

"You're a Libra who feels the serious need to be balanced, to be the middle ground and try to smooth things into peace and harmony. But you feel a big void in your inner soul—you long to let your repressed wild side emerge. To express the hedonistic energy in an almost violent way ..."

Elle blushes, frightened by the racy innuendo.

"But he—your love—he's not like that. He won't understand that about you. This is the one thing that you have to keep for yourself. A silent sin."

Elle feels mortified and wants to stop the reading immediately.

Sensing her discomfort, Olivia drives the stake in a little further by trying to assure her that everyone goes through a period of experimentation and humiliation.

"Wait, wait! Do you think you have enough energy to read me?" Hana jumps in as Olivia finishes.

Olivia smiles and prepares herself for the ultimate con.

"Oh ... my ... Hana, I'm so sorry, but we need to handle this right away. There is really bad, negative energy coming your way. Someone is trying to stifle you *big time*. What's going on there?"

She stares at the crystal and hums to herself, continuing. "Yeah, this is bad. We need to do a major cleanse on you. This is like—a hex. Someone is wishing very negative things on you, and we need to protect your energy. It looks like a man ... older ...?"

Hana looks away dramatically.

"Do you know who this could be?" Olivia asks, frightened.

Hana nods, still staring off.

"Hana—this is serious ..."

Elle and Jenna stare at each other, scared.

"This is stupid," Riley says, rolling her eyes, feeling like Hana is gunning for an acting prize.

Hana looks up and stares at her, dead straight. "It's my dad."

"Your dad?" Elle gasps.

Hana heaves a painful sigh and shifts nervously in her seat.

"I can't believe what he did ..." Olivia says, shaking her head in disbelief.

"My dad ... tried to rape me. And I testified against him, so he's in jail. And he vowed that I would never get away."

The group stares at her with bulging eyes. It's so silent in the room that they're all scared exhaling will break the sound barrier.

"I had no idea ..." Jenna whispers, touching her gently.

Hana dramatically recoils from the touch. "I'm sorry—it's not you. It's just that ... I never talk about this."

"We'll work on this. Come—we need to start immediately ... where's the bathroom? I need water for the ritual." Olivia announces.

Elle points to the hall, and Olivia leads Hana out by the hand.

The two walk silently and enter the master bedroom. They head straight for the en suite bathroom and shut the door. But once they catch a glimpse of themselves in the mirror, they break into laughter.

"Shh!" Hana hisses, trying to compose herself, clamping a hand over Olivia's mouth.

"Your dad raped you or whatever? Ridiculously evil—even by your standards," Olivia replies, prying her friend's hand off her mouth.

"I know—but it had to be bad enough that they won't ask questions. Now they'll write me off as being sad and broken, blah, blah, blah." Hana rolls her eyes. "I saw it on 'Criminal Minds.' That shit is damn creepy."

"Fuck, you were right about the three of them—total sucks." Her friend laughs, fixing her hair in the mirror.

"I know—at least now I've got them more worried about their own agendas. Divide and conquer, my girl," Hana explains.

"Oh, shit—the ritual," Olivia laughs, turning on the faucet as they start gossiping about the girls outside.

"Keep feeding Jenna the lines we agreed on … I've invested too much in her already, I need to be sure she'll leave Mack," Hana instructs before they head back out. "We need her to get into this saga with Carter for real, she can't fake it like he can."

"Are you kidding? I'm earning enough from her to redecorate my freaking apartment. The rituals I promise her—worth at least five hundred dollars! For what? Clear her psychic creativity receptor? I don't even know what that means!" she snickers.

"How did you ever get so good at this?" Hana muses.

"Same as you—hustling at boarding school. Fuck—you're my hero. Doesn't your dad live in freaking Japan or whatever?"

"Yeah? So? Not like that part of my history is ever going to make it to LA for a visit. My mum's too busy being the amazing American school teacher and dad's a workaholic." Hana stares at her through the mirror, stone-faced.

The two of them crack up again.

"Did you see the look on Riley's face when you mentioned her dad being gay?" Hana grins proudly.

"Ya, but she's the most sceptical, though. I don't think that she's fully buying it … won't she try discourage Jen?"

"Liv, in a few months, I'm gonna have Jenna all to myself. They're so not cut out for this life; they'll run for the hills and leave her with a more seasoned caretaker. All I need is to separate her from is Mack, and then I'll be collecting all the management fees."

"I am so happy your dad shipped you over here. I would've been a miserable child without you," Olivia coos.

"This shit's gonna get sick and twisted."

"I wanna make that redhead cry. My god, what a little priss." Olivia rolls her eyes.

Hana shuts off the faucet. "Get the cash from Riley. Let's go eat."

"Chateau Marmont?"

"Whatever. As long as we get some drinks in Jenna. She's no fun otherwise." Hana shrugs.

clean up aisle four.

[Toronto, Canada—April 2011]

Ben Roberts's phone rings by his bedside. The distinctive banjo tone indicates that it is Hunter calling so early in the morning.

He grabs his glasses as he answers. The clock reads 6:00 AM.

"Hunter White, please tell me that you killed someone to be calling me this early," Ben groans.

There's silence on the other end.

"Hunt?" Ben asks, growing a bit uneasy.

"I screwed up," he says, his voice muffled.

"What happened?" Ben asks, getting up and stretching. Maybe he'll go to the gym—there's no way he'll fall back asleep.

"I screwed up big," Hunter replies.

"Bud, you gotta tell me what's going on if you need help," Ben sighs, walking to the kitchen of his condo.

"I was out with Carter last night. And a few of the guys from the team. And we kinda hit the bottle a bit too hard. And there is some chick in my bed."

Ben stops in the doorway, rubbing his bare feet on the wood floor anxiously.

"She's naked," Hunter whispers.

"Didn't need to know that. Okay, so what happened? You guys were out drinking and you took home a random girl?"

"I think she's a big puck bunny. Looks like a nasty slut. I've seen her around …" Hunter admits, sitting down on his couch away from the mess in his bedroom, trying to avoid going near her. He's hanging his head, having quietly slipped out in just his boxers.

Ben bites his lip nervously. What if it's not an innocent mistake but also a potential point for extortion? It's happened before to athletes in his firm, usually with a paternity suit—these days, groupies are ruthless.

He starts his coffeemaker and sets the blend to extra strong.

Hunter exhales heavily, looking at the trail of clothes through the living room and heading to the master bedroom.

"So, she's not going to go quietly," Ben states matter-of-factly, painting the worst-case scenario.

"What do I do about Riley?" Hunter hisses.

"Bud, I'm not really worried about her right now. I'm more concerned about trying to pay off the chick to keep your image intact. We've worked so hard at getting everything smoothed out for a long-term Toronto contract."

Hunter shakes his head. It's not only about his relationship with Riley. It's the image of his relationship—and cheating is not something a franchise forward is keen to be known for.

"What if she sells me out to the tabloids?" Hunter panics, realizing that the bleached blonde with smeared makeup is the one who has all the control right now.

"Do you think she'll be reasonable?" Ben asks, heading back to the bedroom with a coffee cup. "Did you use a condom, at least?"

"I don't know anything about her! I don't even know her name! Just that she was an easy lay," Hunter hisses. "You think I want frickin' mini-mes running around here?! Fuck, at least I used a condom …"

"What happened to Carter and the other guys?"

"He left with a bunch of chicks. The guys … who knows."

"So it's safe to say he also cheated …" Ben sighs, having heard of Carter getting back together with Jenna yet again.

"I didn't mean to cheat! You can't tell the girls, Ben. You can't tell Elle. You're my agent lawyer thing. You're my boy. You can't tell them," Hunter says forcefully. "It's client privilege or whatever."

"I know. I'll be over soon; we'll sort this out," Ben says, shaking his head but trying to reassure his friend and star.

He hangs up and tosses the phone on the bed.

The empty bed makes it easier to understand why Hunter would stray. Sleeping without Eleanor beside him all these months has been numbing. It was almost harder to win her back, only to lose her to Jenna Ramsay's career.

He sits down at the foot of the bed, realizing that the mistakes Hunter and Carter have made are against the best friends of his fiancée, and that if she ever finds out, he's fucked.

Is it considered lying if I omit information? he argues with himself, exhaling deeply and taking off his glasses. *Make it part of a professional oath of confidence …*

After drafting up a contract and changing into a pair of khakis and neat blue sweater, Ben slips into his black sports car and heads to Hunter White's condo.

He doesn't even have to knock at the door; Hunter has been spying through the peephole, waiting for his friend—and professional representative.

"Is she up?" Ben asks.

Hunter shakes his head no and gratefully drinks the cappuccino Ben has brought over for him. He's still in his underwear, but they head into the kitchen to hash things out.

"Okay. Well, how much are you willing to cough up?" Ben asks him bluntly.

Hunter waves his arms in desperation, reeking alcohol from every pore on his body.

"I need you to fix this. Things were starting to get better with Riley. I was starting to get through to her. But I got so … lonely," Hunter gasps, pacing around, tapping the appliances nervously.

"Are you going to tell her?"

"No! This will do her in for sure. The girl has major trust issues—this is not going to help!"

Ben shrugs.

"You think I should tell her," Hunter observes.

"It's your prerogative, man."

"Dude, I think this random is the one who ran Campbell Kates out of town …" Hunter whispers, leaning on the granite countertop. He's recognized the trashy woman involved in the hockey player's adultery scandal. The fortysomething cougar, who, with beer goggles, grows more and more seductive and inviting to a lonely man. To a lonely athlete making a minimum of four million a season.

Ben bites his lip, remembering the scandal involving the married hockey player and the local gold digger, shuddering.

"But Campbell wasn't my client. We can handle this," Ben says, confidently holding a folder, ready for crisis management.

"Okay, so … how do we do this?" Hunter asks, opening a drawer that contains knives and rummaging around.

Ben raises an eyebrow, confused.

"I've never done this … I need you to tell me what to do," Hunter continues, trailing off nervously, like a virgin schoolboy.

"Dude, when I said we'd deal with this, I didn't mean killing the damn slut." Ben laughs morbidly.

"Oh. Right. Okay, yeah, I just … in case that's what you meant. I've never killed someone before and thought that a gun would be too loud … whatever—forget it!" Hunter slams the drawer shut.

"If that's how you guys deal with gold diggers down South …?" Ben starts, still laughing at his friend's desperate response.

Hunter brushes him off and continues to pace around.

"I think you should go for a walk, maybe let me handle this," Ben suggests to the obviously on-edge athlete.

Hunter nods, the guilt making him nauseous.

"But let's get you some clothes first," Ben suggests, pointing to Hunter's boxer shorts with cartoon tractors on them.

Ben slips into the bedroom and grabs some clothes, giving a quick look to the girl nearly falling off the bed.

She's tangled in the black satin sheets of Hunter's massive bed. Her blonde hair is showing a good set of dark roots; her long acrylic nails are painted bright red with rhinestones glued on them.

Ben shudders at the sight of her and darts back out. He is instantly grateful to have a polished lady as his future wife and not have to scum local bars, trying to get play by flashing his business card or dropping names like others.

He hands Hunter the pile of clothes and marches him into the guest room to shower.

As Ben cleans up the place a bit, Hunter lets the scalding hot water wash over him, desperate to remove any residue of the tacky, imitation girl who got so close to him. The overly sweet scent of her cheap perfume makes him gag.

"What was I thinking?" he mutters, leaning on the tiles, thinking of the obstacles he's patiently conquered with Riley. The scepticism, the long distances, her reluctance. Only recently has she been completely comfortable sitting around naked with him. And now—for one night of not sleeping alone, he basically has thrown it all away.

He feels droplets on his face, tasting salt on his lips. Realizing he's crying, he sticks his head under the water.

He thinks of Carter and curses himself for not listening to Riley about staying away from him. It was the actor's idea to turn a night of guys watching sports into a messy bar crawl. It was clear from the start that he was looking to troll for easy targets and get laid. And befriending a team of pro athletes definitely helped his pickup game.

Now Hunter was in the same category as him.

He walks out of the bathroom, cleansed and changed, and Ben ushers him out the door efficiently.

Heading down in the elevator, he catches a glimpse of his face. Hungover and dreary, he's hiding underneath the hood of his baggy sweatshirt, covering his sandy hair. His black fleecy track pants flop down to his new running shoes, and he fights the impulse to kick the wall. He can barely recognize himself, gloom surrounding his body.

Hunter White steps outside and walks down by the lakefront. The same path he likes to run alone early in the morning. Except today, he's dragging his feet, staring at the murky, polluted water.

So much has happened since his arrival in Toronto. His team is actually positioned to make it to the playoffs. His game is better and faster than it's ever been when he feels inspired. He has the girl who could be his wife. Except Riley is not much of a stay-at-home-mom type of person. Which is okay. There are nannies for that. But it's undeniable that she's exceptional. Working for Jenna, but also getting a book published. He wants so badly to settle down with someone.

Hunter always figured their kids would get the IQ from her side, maybe athletic prowess from him. Her moody attitude, his love of fun. Their competitive nature. But after this debacle, if Ben can't keep the woman upstairs quiet, the possibility of bouncing back is negligible. One thing Riley can't ever seem to do is forget. Sometimes he gets nervous that he'll fail to exceed her expectations. She may not say it, but Riley definitely wants superhuman perfection from everyone.

• • •

After about an hour of morose wandering and contemplating, Hunter heads back, chilled by the cool spring air. Ben is at the kitchen counter, eating a bagel with lox and cream cheese when he slinks in.

"How'd it go?" Hunter sighs, taking a seat on a barstool.

He shrugs.

Hunter stares at his friend, wanting to reach across and shake him for answers.

"She signed a contract. Thought she'd try squeezing you for more money, actually. But you'll find your Swiss account less five grand."

"Five? I thought it would be, like, fifty after what happened with Campbell," he says, relieved. "I heard he got fucked in the divorce."

Ben nods, chewing thoughtfully. "It must be lucrative enough that she's getting modest. Your relationship is pretty much public knowledge, too … At least you used a rubber, dude."

Hunter lets out a moan of relief. At least he had that presence of mind. He cuts himself a bagel and chews it violently.

"Hunt, imagine if she was—probably is—crawling with diseases. You could have really jeopardized your career … we need to get you tested by the team doctor, keep things quiet. To be sure," Ben advises.

"I can't even … Let's talk about something else; I can't handle this. Hey, whatcha doin' today?" he asks.

"My boy, I was gonna go to the gym until you hit me with all this. I lead a simple existence. You're a young buck—let's go dead lift the shit out of your bad luck."

Hunter grunts, chugging some juice. "Let me pack for the Ottawa game. Sometimes I wonder how the girls don't go nuts, stuck away in foreign countries without a chance to abandon ship and run home."

Ben nods. "Yeah, I mean, I know it's tough on Elle, for sure. She's not really a wanderer. That's the thing—I'm bouncing all over North America, but it's only a couple of days at a time. None of this … stuck in a hotel in Jakarta because fans mob you like—"

"Like, deadly mob," Hunter interrupts.

Ben makes a face, thankful for his comparatively tame job.

"I thought Riley would want to chill after a crazy year …"

"Man, she is going to be wandering the globe until she's ninety-eight," Ben blurts out.

Hunter shrugs, knowing this to be most true.

"That's why I kept my focus on Elle. I knew she was a good fit for me, but she had to go through her whole wild-child thing. I had to be in it for the long haul. Patience."

"Did you know she'd come back?" Hunter asks.

"Yep."

"Actually?"

"She's got the advantage of being pretty, charming, intelligent—"

"And, like, eight years younger than you."

Ben narrows his eyes. "Anyway. I think we just fit together, and I always thought she couldn't find the same thing. So I waited and built my career. When reality kicks in, girls want impressive, stable, safe."

Hunter opens his mouth to speak.

"Except Riley Kohl," Ben throws in quickly.

"That's awful helpful," Hunter groans.

"You know as much as I do. Nice girl, but is she the *right* one?"

"Anyway, whatever, gimme a minute. Did you bring your shit, or are we stopping at your place?" Hunter asks.

"My bag's in the car. I don't do anything without a plan," Ben brags.

free range.

[Miami, USA—May 2011]

Jenna steps out of a recording booth, drained.
"What's going on with your voice?" asks the sound engineer working the board at the music studio.

"What?" she rasps, still feeling woozy from the night before. The South Beach party is all a blur to her now. Her voice is even scratchier than usual, thanks to the screaming (and chain-smoking).

Hana had pushed her to attend the birthday party of some foreign billionaire on his huge yacht. Sailing left Riley motion sick, and Elle was distracted making calls for her wedding—the two of them holing up in one of the ship's bedrooms. So Jenna was left hanging out with Hana the whole night. And that meant booze cruising.

"Jenna, you need to get more sleep. Your voice is sounding shitty. I'm not even going to keep what we did today—we gotta redo it all," says the tech, shaking his head.

He sounds exactly like Riley. Before she left with Elle for Toronto that morning, Ms. Mom took an opportunity to scold her about taking it easy. With the end of their contracts quickly approaching, it felt like her two friends were *too* eager to escape and get off the carnival ride. The fact that they happily went back to look at centerpieces and taste cakes was mildly annoying.

"If we're going to finish recording this new album in time, you need to get it together …" rumbles the producer's voice through the speakers.

Jenna grabs the stacks of notebooks she's brought along and heads for the door, not wanting to hear how crappy she sounds. She can feel it in her throat. Something is off. Wearing down. She can't hit her notes the same way anymore. She misses the feeling of Parker being there to brainstorm, talking through ideas for lyrics and piecing things together.

She angrily pushes open the door with her hip, and finds Hana in the hallway, talking on her cell phone.

"Hey, yeah … I'm gonna have to call you back …" she says into the phone, leaning against the wall in her tight jeans and asymmetrical top, propped up on heels like a parakeet.

"Hey, Jen. Here, thought you could use this ..." she says, handing her a gigantic cup of iced sugary coffee and a pack of cigarettes.

Jenna drinks it, but doesn't feel her thirst quenched.

"You taking a break?" Hana probes, following in stride as the singer picks up the pace.

"No, I wanna go," Jenna says, heading for the door. "Mack's going to be pissed at me, though."

"Oh, who cares? You're Jenna Ramsay—you're the one who practically signs his fucking cheques." Hana rolls her eyes. She's been dropping hints about Mack being replaceable all month, trying to wedge herself into Jenna's confidence more than her boss. Trying to steal the cash cow for herself alone. No junior execs, business managers, or assistants to take away from her cut.

Jenna ignores her, desperate to escape from the feeling of chasing her own tail—of not being fully grounded in herself and her music. She feels a spell of the shakes coming on but walks faster, her jeans dragging under her flip flops. She's starting to look sloppy, too tired to take good enough care of herself.

She throws open the heavy metal backdoor of the studio, and the heat of the parking lot makes her brain feel even slower. She marches straight for their tinted luxury rental car.

Hana grabs the keys out of her purse and hits the unlock button, hopping into the SUV.

Jenna struggles to get the passenger door open, hands full of her lyric notebooks. They haven't been filled with anything new in a while, though, her inspiration essentially flat lining months ago. The new songs for the album are being written for her, instead of by her.

"Hey! She's out!" someone yells.

Jenna looks up and spots a dozen photographers starting to come around the corner of the building, having been lying in wait for the celebrity.

"Jenna! Jenna! What's going on? How's the new album?" they start screaming, their sound like hoofbeats in a stampede.

Jenna feels the blood in her body heat up, not expecting to have to see anyone. All she wants is to crawl into bed and disintegrate.

"Jenna!" they keep shouting, hurrying towards the car.

Jenna struggles again with the door and turns to the car parked beside her, frustrated. She blindly sets her coffee down on the sports car's roof and is about to turn back to her door handle when she realizes that the sunroof is actually wide open.

Camera shutters go off in a flurry, documenting her coffee sailing through the sunroof and onto the interior of the car. The photographers laugh hysterically.

Fuuuck! she screams in her head, letting the cigarette fall out of her mouth.

"She dropped it in the car!" one guy wheezes, having to slow down and catch his breath from laughing so hard.

She stares at the group rushing in like a deer in headlights.

Hana reaches across and opens the door for her, and Jenna dives in, humiliated.

Hana starts to drive, but Jenna begs her to stop. Their car is swarmed, the photographers jeering through the window, trying to get her to lower it and react to the faux pas.

"What?" Hana barks.

"Please drop your business card in there. I have to at least pay for that," Jenna says, shrinking into a ball in the front seat of the SUV. She's trying to shield her face from the cameras pointed through the windshield and ends up jumping in the backseat for protection.

Hana looks at her in disbelief.

"I'm serious," Jenna says.

Hana puts the car in park, grumbling to herself. She's annoyed that she forgot to put on bronzer that morning, and that she won't look perfect in the tabloid pictures.

She fishes for a business card and gets out. She quickly rushes to the black sports car, drops the card down into the messy interior, and darts back to their idling SUV.

Her brain pulsating, Jenna puts her head between her knees, trying to survive.

end of the era.

[Toronto, Canada—early June 2011]

Toronto is in the final game of the Stanley Cup playoffs. Game seven has them still pitted against their archrivals from Montreal.

"They have to win this one—they're on home ice," Riley exclaims to no one in particular.

She's sitting rink-side with Eleanor, Ben, and Jenna. Mack and his wife and son are up in a luxury box with the Kohl, Bryans, and White family members.

Darling, this is so suspenseful! Rhett Kohl text messages his daughter after a Montreal player gets a roughing penalty. The teams are locked in a 3–3 tie as the third period draws to a close.

"What now?" Jenna asks, wringing her hands nervously.

"Sudden death," Ben replies flatly, typing on his phone with colleagues. He's wearing a jersey to show his support for his star client, but it's a few sizes too big, and looks like he's playing dress-up.

"I need another drink," Jenna grumbles, hungover from the night before's club outing. "Where can I smoke?"

Elle scrunches up her face in disgust, unhappy to see her friend's new habit of inhaling cigarettes already becoming a crutch.

"Hurry back!" Riley snaps, swatting at her as she walks past.

Jenna trudges off, seeking out a vodka-water. She stops to sign a few autographs on her way to the executive lounge, standing out in the sports crowd with her bright Michael Kors dress, as sunglasses shield her exhausted raccoon eyes.

"What happens if they don't win?" Elle whispers to Ben, wearing a Maple Leafs baby tee with a pair of jeans and ballet flats.

He looks at her uncomfortably.

"You can't think that way—don't give it negative attention. Think that they're going to win—it's more productive," Riley hisses superstitiously, her sweaty palms flat on her thighs, the moisture being absorbed by the jeans she's wearing. Her blazer is thrown over the back of her seat as she sweats anxiously.

Elle nods, still unsure how the power of positive thinking is going to help when they're playing such a hyped rival. She opts to secretly cross her fingers behind her back instead.

Riley and Elle have officially been discharged from their tour of service with Top Dog. Hana Rin has taken over as Jenna's direct handler, under Mack's distant supervision. She has elected to stay at the hotel today, hung over and disinterested in the sports milestone before them.

So now, the two friends are free to do as they please. And rather relieved to shed the responsibility of what has become Jenna Ramsay's massive shadow. The change they see in her since having attained the much sought-after fame is a little frightening.

Now they have a chance to slip away from the reach of her limelight—to paint, write, get married, explore. To lead exponentially quieter existences than the glamour and grit of following a pop star around the world, of catering to her every wish.

But on this particular day, they are watching Hunter play the biggest game of his life so far. All of the friends united to cheer him on for his race to the spotlight.

Riley stops talking as soon as the teams skate out from the locker room, on the edge of her seat to the point of almost falling.

Jenna rushes back before the overtime period starts, people snapping pictures of her, her new haircut sure to be the next must-have summer look.

"Riles?" Jenna begins, about to ask if there are plans to go for dinner after the game.

Riley puts up a hand to silence her friend, and no one dares communicate until a team is crowned victorious.

The television camera pans over to her intense devotion, the commentators dropping a mention about her being Hunter's girlfriend. The camera then zooms in on Jenna's face.

As the puck drops, Riley holds her breath.

Please let them win, please let them win, please let them win, she chants to herself silently, watching as Hunter zips past them, checking someone into the boards.

Montreal pulls their goalie for an extra player on the ice. As a shot rebounds off the Toronto goalie, Hunter swipes it with his stick and breaks for the empty net.

The crowd leaps to its feet, the screaming intensifying as he powers across the rink. Montreal's players scramble and begin a pursuit, but Hunter dodges their reach and hammers a long shot straight through the empty net.

The red goal light goes off, and the crowd reaches a deafening volume, a jumbled mess of shouts and cheers and pure unadulterated excitement.

Riley jumps up from her seat, still holding her friends' hands, and they all start hopping up and down, screaming frantically.

The Toronto bench swarms the ice as a sea of white-and-blue streamers explodes over the entire arena.

The joy on the faces of the players is almost as intense as the defeat felt by their competitors. The team's coach slides his way to his players on the ice and is enveloped in the jerseys.

The sold-out crowd doesn't settle down, particularly as a red carpet is unrolled. The hockey team is bombarded with cheers and pelted with gifts.

Photographers hustle out to take photos of the scene as it unfolds, front-page news. The team hasn't had this success in over three decades; this is a moment of pride and glory.

A man in a suit announces the winner of the playoff MVP award as one of the team's alternate captains, Hunter White. He skates over to pick up the trophy and holds it proudly, smiling for the newspaper photographers, but eagerly awaiting the bigger prize.

The silvery cup is presented to the captain of the team, who does a lap around the rink with it as the crowd continues their standing ovation.

He hands it to the first alternate captain, who then hands it to Hunter. He does a lap, hands it off, and stops to talk to a few reporters.

One of the team's athletic trainers pulls Riley from her seat and leads her around to the inside of the bench. Her eyes dart back to her friends, confused.

Jenna and Elle shrug, not sure what is going on. Ben's eyes narrow, scared of what his client has failed to share with him.

As the rest of the team finishes their victory laps, Hunter effortlessly skates towards the bench.

Riley carefully steps over the equipment in her motorcycle boots and is taken to an opening that leads to the ice. Hunter is standing, waiting for her, sweating from the strenuous game. The trainer discreetly passes something into his hand and nudges Riley right up to the ice's edge.

The crowd hushes to a murmur, straining to catch a glimpse of Hunter White in action.

"What's going on?" Riley asks nervously, trying to catch his eye, begging for this to end.

But Hunter's gaze is wild and erratic; he's stoked by the rush of having just achieved his ultimate mission in life. He has won the unthinkable prize, dreamt of by essentially every North American boy at some point in his life.

Someone creeps up towards them with a microphone, and the entire crowd soon hears along with Riley, "Riley Kohl, you've been as big a part of this season as I could ever imagine." Hunter is still breathless. He slides down on one knee, a little wobbly on skates, and takes her two hands in his.

The crowd starts cheering even more madly than before.

Riley's face registers fear and shock, as she turns a deathly shade of pale.

"Oh, shit!" Jenna exclaims, looking at Elle and knowing exactly the anxiety that is going through their friend's mind.

"The only thing that can make this day even more unreal is ... if you'd please do me the honour of being my number one fan forever," Hunter continues, trying to remember the rough script he came up with during his workout that morning.

Riley's hands begin to tremble in his, and she feels like she's going to faint. Or throw up.

"Riley, will you marry me, darlin'?" he asks, sending out every last ounce of wind in her. Like being punched in the stomach. Really, really hard. And in front of a full-capacity audience.

She stares at him, stunned.

"Good googlie-mooglie ..." Elle whispers, grabbing Ben's knee nervously, her nails digging into his flesh through the light wool trousers.

The crowd is deafening, the cameras flashing and videotaping the entire play-by-play. All the players and coaches on the ice are turned to stare at the couple, and they start tapping their sticks on the ice with excitement.

Riley is still frozen in panic.

Hunter looks into her eyes, searching for any sign of life. "Riles?" he asks, tapping her hand.

Her big brown eyes lock on to his, and she looks at him in disbelief. "I know," she replies.

"What?" he asks, trying to urge her to stop leaving him hanging and just say "yes"—even if she doesn't mean it. He was not expecting this much hesitation.

She leans down to his ear, covering her mouth with her hand so that her lips can't be read.

"I know. About her. I know. And I can't believe you're doing this—like this. Right now. This has nothing to do with me, it's all you," she whispers, careful so that the microphone can't hear.

Hunter stares at her, his eyes wide with surprise.

"I was waiting until you were done; I get that this is big and you needed a united front. But this ... this fake thing ... I can't do that."

She takes a step back, away from him. His hands dangle at his sides limply, and the crowd gasps in collective shock.

Riley turns her back and bolts through the player entrance and into the maze of the arena, running wild and jumping over equipment and obstacles. She's got tunnel vision, and is hell-bent on reaching the car park, her only chance of getting out unscathed.

"Farshid, quick!" she shouts, barreling down the corridor.

He rushes off and returns seconds later with her SUV, screeching it into park and leaving the keys in the ignition.

She can hear people coming down the hall after her, but jumps in and speeds out into the night without looking back.

Hunter White is still on one knee on the ice, staring at the empty bench in front of him.

The crowd is murmuring in shock, and he can't bear to look up at the sea of faces that have witnessed his humiliation. He can feel the cameras waiting, watching, off to his side.

One of his teammates skates out to him, helping Hunter stand, and leading him back into the crowd of champions.

They trickle into the locker room, Hunter hiding in the middle of the group, rocked to the core.

For once in his life, he is completely speechless.

• • •

Riley Kohl listens to the hum of the country music station as she drives north through the city. The streetlights shine gently in the dark as people pour out of bars, having watched the game. She weaves past the lakefront and Hunter's condo, past Jenna's hotel of the week, past Elle's neighbourhood. She roars further north on Yonge Street in the direction of her dad's house.

She abandons the red Range Rover on a side street close to her house and begins walking through the forested area near it. Desperate to move around, she follows the stars above, the nervous tension in her body vibrating uncontrollably. She charges through the trees, the leaves on the ground crunching under her black boots, now covered in mud.

She finds herself at a big rock in the middle of a ravine and stares at it like a drone. It's the same spot she used to go to when she wanted to run away from the world as a kid, the spot where she began journaling and writing all her thoughts. The safest spot where only the trees and wind were witness to her breaking down to cry. She automatically climbs onto the rock.

Except this time, she stares out at the darkness around her and tries to breathe.

In ... out ... in ... out ...

She's startled out of her thoughts by chatter and light illuminating the old trees around her.

"Riley?" calls Jenna's familiar, raspy voice.

She turns to look over her shoulder and sees two spots of flashlights.

A wave of relief washes over her. Two lights. Not three. Not four or five.

Two.

Her tearstained face is illuminated as Elle and Jenna rush forward to the plateau.

"Riley, oh my gosh, are you okay?" Elle asks worriedly, fluttering up to her in her tiny ballet flats and smothering her with a hug.

Riley sniffles a bit and nods her head.

"That was such a shock!" Elle exclaims. "What happened?"

"He tried to propose," Jenna replies sarcastically as she tries to sit on the awkward rock. Her expensive dress is not well suited to being in nature.

"But why'd you say no?" Elle asks, playfully slapping Jenna.

Riley pulls out her BlackBerry and opens some pictures.

Jenna and Eleanor's jaws drop in shock.

"What the shit?" Jenna gasps.

They're racy pictures of Hunter with a trashy blonde caught on a cell phone camera.

"Holy ... wow, Riley, I'm so sorry," Elle sighs sadly.

"That's not all of it …" Riley says flatly. She scrolls down and shows them pictures of Carter with a couple of girls.

Jenna has to hold herself still on the cool stone. "Where did you get this?" she demands.

Riley looks at her friend, their eye contact recognizing the hurt and sadness of being betrayed.

"Duncan has a connection at *Hello!*—the magazine where these pictures will be printed tomorrow. The magazine that got an exclusive with these girls," Riley explains.

The three friends sit in silence. Jenna's flashlight loses power and blinks off.

"There are also quotes from the ringleader, that she signed some bullshit contract with Hunter's agent …" Riley whispers.

Neither of the girls flinches. They stare out at the forest in silence.

"This is exactly what Olivia told me," Jenna says flatly, shaking her head in disbelief. She rummages in her bag and pulls out a cigarette, trying to light up with shaky hands. This is too much for her.

"Okay. We need to get out of here!" Elle exclaims, taking charge of the situation and choosing to ignore Ben's implication for the immediate moment.

She pulls Riley and Jenna up and marches her two friends towards the park entrance.

"Where do we go?" Riley asks aloud. "What if Hunter is back at my dad's?"

"Or he'll be at Ben's," Elle responds.

"We could go to my mom's," Jenna blurts out, not knowing what else to say.

The girls get into Elle's car and drive off in the light sprinkle of rain that has started.

• • •

Rhett and Brian Kohl are sitting around their living room, discussing the events of the evening.

"I totally can't believe she ran out like that …" Brian trails off, shocked. His curly fro peeks out beneath a toque with the hockey team's logo on it. It's his attempt at supporting his sister.

"*Vhat* could it *haf* been?" Rhett wonders aloud.

Kevin walks in with three mugs of chai and hands them out.

"Well, if it's one thing I know about your girl, it's that it had to be bad if she was going to publicly humiliate her boyfriend," Kevin responds. "Or would this now be her ex-boyfriend?"

"I thought they were totally happily-ever-after," Brian says.

"I know, but there *vas* always some hesitation from *hur*. I could hear it in *hur* voice *vhen vee'd* speak. Read it in *hur* e-mails. Something *vas* off …" Rhett explains.

There's a loud banging at the front door, and the three men look at each other with wide eyes.

Kevin gets up and opens the door, and Hunter rushes into the living room in a frazzled state.

"Where is she? Is she here?" he gasps, his eyes frantic.

"Nah, man." Brian sighs.

Hunter runs a hand through his shaggy hair, exasperated. His beard, grown for the playoffs, makes him look even more desperate and wild.

"What happened?" Kevin asks bluntly, taking a seat on the white leather couch. He glances at Rhett across the coffee table, and then back to Hunter.

Hunter's eyes dart around between the three men in the room. He hangs his head in shame, not being able to wiggle out of the truth.

"What happened?" Kevin repeats.

"I cheated on her," Hunter says flatly.

Silence falls over the room for a couple of minutes.

"You *vhat*?" Rhett booms, realizing what her daughter's attempted fiancé has said. He stands up from his chair, matching the height of the professional athlete.

Brian and Kevin dart in front of him and have to hold back the angry European man from inflicting injuries.

"Calm down, it's okay, calm down," Kevin tries to soothe, blocking his path to Hunter.

"Yeah, dad, it'll be okay," Brian assures him. There is a pause as Hunter is about to start a sentence. But Brian turns to face the distressed hockey player and punches him square in the jaw.

Hunter collapses to the floor, stunned.

"Get out of my house," Brian commands, pointing to the door.

Hunter gets himself to his feet and slips out, not bothering to explain himself or wipe the smear of blood that splattered on the floor.

"Good *vun*, son," Rhett says, for once in his life condoning violence.

Awake but Dreaming

• • •

Jenna Ramsay has to buzz up to her mother's apartment, her key long lost in the shuffle of becoming a global voyager.

"Hello?" croaks Ida Ramsay's voice on the intercom.

Jenna stares at the device, shocked to actually be hearing her mother's voice.

Elle nudges her in the ribs to encourage speaking.

"Mom, it's me," Jenna responds, snapping back to reality.

There's a moment of silence, and the buzzer goes off to let them in.

The girls stroll in quietly.

"She did not sound happy …" Jenna says to herself.

"She did not sound anything. Don't freak yourself out. How long has it been since you've seen her?" Riley asks as the three girls step into an elevator.

Jenna bites her lip nervously.

"Since you talked to her?" asks Elle, hopeful.

"Christmas."

"So you haven't seen her since the holidays? That's six months …" Elle clarifies.

"I haven't seen her since we left last year. I spoke to her at Christmas. Sort of. While we were on vacation."

Riley and Elle shoot each other a look of worry. They're about to be in the middle of a very awkward family reunion.

"I just … every time I was back here, Hana put me in a hotel. There was never any time, and she probably wouldn't approve of my lifestyle …" Jenna mutters. "Maybe we should go somewhere else. I still have my hotel room … why didn't we just go there?"

Elle puts a hand on her friend's shoulder, and the elevator stops.

They tiptoe towards apartment 1742. The door is ajar, and the three girls walk in holding hands.

The apartment is dark, save for the kitchen. They follow the fluorescent light.

Ida Ramsay is leaning against the fridge, drinking a glass of milk.

She looks up when Jenna and her friends walk in but says nothing.

"Mom … hi …" Jenna starts.

Ida looks at her blankly. She turns to Riley.

"I saw what happened on TV. Are you all right?" she asks calmly.

Riley nods, her eyes hardly puffy or sore from having cried only a few tears. She isn't particularly torn up inside, more devastated of the public airing of dirty laundry. She always half expected something like this with Hunter.

"If my daughter had kept me in the loop, I'd have something better to say to comfort you. But I'm sure that he'll get what's coming to him," Ida says, rinsing her glass in the sink and putting it on the dish rack to dry. The apartment doesn't have a dishwasher.

"Mom ..." Jenna tries to start.

"I was wondering if you'd ever care to show up. At least you're not drunk. Not like the other times you've called. You know I sleep early, yet you inconsiderately call me at odd hours ... It's late. You girls should get some rest. I'll see you in the morning."

The girls watch her as she heads down the small hallway and shuts her bedroom door. The apartment looks puny compared with all the hotel suites they've slept in.

They tiptoe into Jenna's old bedroom, kept exactly the same as she had left it, right down to the posters and unicorns.

They crawl into her double bed, squished together. Eleanor is in the middle by default because she's the smallest of the three. As she and Riley fall asleep, Jenna feels a wave of relief wash over her. Listening to their breathing, she doesn't feel alone. Memories of their sleepovers flood into her mind. Recalling their affection and comfort, of brushing each other's hair and snuggling. In the past year, she's been right beside the girls, yet totally distanced.

Jenna can't relax into sleep and walks back to the kitchen. Padding down the carpeted hallway in some old sweats, she notices a new picture on the wall and stops to investigate.

In a neat brown frame, her mother has placed the first cheque issued to Jenna, dated from before she started recording the first album. The advance cheque she sent to her mother, with the intention that it be deposited and used to pay off her mortgage, maybe buy herself a new car, even a nicer condo. But instead, the quarter of a million dollars is in a frame, mounted on a wall like a trophy from yellow-belt karate. It's right beside their last picture—from high school graduation.

She flicks on the light above the stove and rummages in the pantry. She begins to pour herself a glass of wine, not knowing how else to slow her mind down. She sniffs the rim of the glass; the dark Merlot is acidic and spoiled from having been opened so long, forgotten by Ida. It burns her nostrils a little bit, but she ignores the stench and lets the rotted vinegar slip down her throat.

"You know, you should really cut back on that stuff."

She turns to see her mother's disapproving figure in the doorway.

Ida steps into the cramped room, her goofy pyjama set on display. Flying cows are leaping over fluffy clouds. She leans against the fridge beside her daughter, dark circles under her eyes and her hair showing more white.

"I'm sorry to …" Jenna starts, sticking her hands in her sweatshirt pocket.

"What's happening to you?" her mother interrupts, clasping her hands together. She looks at her daughter steadily, not backing down.

Jenna stares at her, confused.

"You move out without a word. I never hear from you. I never see you. Your friends had to make excuses for you every time I called. Your companies are blacklisting me. Even when you're here—and I know you're here because it's on the news … you can't even be bothered …"

Ida stares at her daughter, not even in disgust, but rather pure disappointment and confusion.

"We were a team, Bean. How did it get like this? Why are you hiding?"

"I'm not hiding," Jenna says defensively.

Her mom moves to the sink to fill a glass with cold tap water, and leans against the kitchen counter across from her daughter.

"You were never that … supportive," Jenna says.

"Not like you let me. You signed a contract and then disappeared," Ida says.

The two Ramsays are facing each other tensely.

"I had to finish my work! I couldn't do it with you judging me!" Jenna exclaims, frustrated.

"I think you were afraid that I would remind you of where you came from," her mother says dryly. She sets down her glass on the counter, half empty. The beads of water on the outside of the glass slowly trickle down on the beige surface. "And I personally don't think that where you came from is such a bad place."

Jenna stares at her in shock.

"You didn't always have the fancy clothes and cars and that twit of a boyfriend, Bean. And I really hope that you haven't lost what you had inside—because then I would have been right all along," her mom says firmly.

"I have not lost who I am!"

"Then why do you keep drinking yourself into oblivion? I see the news coverage about you. I can see where it's heading, and without me or your friends there to smack some sense into you, I can't help but worry that you will crash and burn," her mother says.

Jenna stares at her angrily.

"I am your mother, Jenna. I have raised you as best I can—and I will not watch all my hard work to turn you into a good person, a decent person ... I will not watch that go down the drain. So that you can turn into some ... turn into ..."

"Turn into what?!" Jenna shouts, slamming her wine glass down on the counter beside her. The glass shatters and cuts through her hand. Not deeply, only superficial scrapes that allow small drops of blood to trickle out.

Ida Ramsay locks eyes with her daughter.

"To turn into your father," she says through gritted teeth.

Jenna stares at her mom in disbelief as her hand throbs.

"You heard me. You are turning into him, and that level of pigheaded attention-seeking stubbornness is what got him killed."

"What the hell are you talking about?" Jenna shouts.

"He died because he couldn't temper his weakness. Just like you, he became an indulgent child where everything revolved around him. He drank himself silly. And on that Friday ... he got into his car and wrapped it around a telephone pole! Because he was an alcoholic."

Jenna feels as if the wind's been knocked out of her, completely astounded.

"One Christmas, you asked me when I knew he was gone. And it was around this stage, when he stopped listening to reason, when he didn't want to get help and admit his problems—that's when I knew that, not only was our marriage over ... but that he wouldn't stop until he was dead," Ida hisses.

Jenna grabs the counter for stability as the room spins. "He wasn't in a car accident?" she whispers.

"No, Bean. He *caused* the accident because he had been at the bar all night. Like usual. I'm sorry I didn't tell you outright—I really had hoped your memory of him wouldn't be tainted. But ... seeing you like this, this is all too familiar," her mother cries, shaking nervously.

She begins to sob, and Jenna rushes forward to wrap her in a hug.

"Mom …" she whispers, careful not to put the bloody hand on the flying cows.

"I don't want to lose you, too," her mother weeps, hugging her daughter tightly.

Jenna can't formulate a response. She's staring off into space, rocked to the core.

Ida holds her daughter by the arms, looking into her tearing eyes. She sniffles, composing herself, regaining the levelheadedness she's had to have as a single mom.

"Listen to me, Bean. You are not lost. You are not like him yet. But if you keep at this … you need to find yourself, you need to think logically," her mother says, trying to warn her daughter. To scare her into sobriety.

Jenna rinses her hand in the sink, a dull stinging from the water.

She grabs her mother's glass to wash it and looks at the ring of water left by it on the counter, too tired to wipe it dry. She closes the tap.

"But who I am and who they think I am …" Jenna trails off, allowing the stress of her public identity to surface as the fibers in her body relax into tears.

The girl who commands a room and has people coveting her. With the endless supply of money to throw parties and have extravagant things. The beautiful voice is only a fragment of what she's known for, part of the character she plays.

Except, when the lights go off at night, she feels more hollowness than could ever be imagined. Unable to sit with herself, sleep vanishes in exchange for being surrounded by strangers. Commotion. Something to break the silence.

A feeling of heavy darkness, hovering. A thunderstorm never vanquished by the hint of sunshine peeking around the corner. The clouds are always there.

It is the feeling of slowness that has rooted itself so deep in her body, she isn't sure it will ever leave. The fear of starting a new day.

Maybe she can be the person she used to be and still aspire to live what she wants. Or maybe now this new person is who she is.

She starts to tell her mother about the past year.

• • •

A muted sunrise peeks through the windows of the Ramsay apartment in northern Toronto. Jenna and her mother have stayed awake all night talking, and find themselves on Ida's bed, amazed to be in each other's presence again.

"Bean ... how could you leave me?" her mother whispers, holding her daughter's hand tightly.

Jenna looks at her mom sadly, still confused by the impulse she indulged to shed her old skin and start living a new person's life—forming a fresh identity.

"Please ... don't let yourself become your dad. Don't be consumed," her mother begs, squeezing her daughter's hand. Her fingers are wrinkly, and there are freckles all over her arms.

Jenna nods, still struggling to absorb her father's truth.

"We should get some breakfast. I'll go buy some bagels for the girls." Her mom smiles, getting up and going.

Jenna remains in the bed, laying on her back and staring off into space.

She looks around at the modest bedroom, a little uneasy not to be sleeping on a king-sized Tempur-Pedic bed with Egyptian sheets. The white walls still give off a vibe of sterility and lower-middle-class reserve.

Then she remembers her schedule, her life as a star. The reality of leaving for India that evening provides a tug-of-war in her head as she realizes exactly what she's been created to be, the role she has to fill.

Am I the wannabe who lived off her friends' hand-me-downs or the powerhouse star? she wonders to herself. *I could never imagine Carter coming here to visit my mom ... but could she visit me in LA or London or Tokyo?*

The fact that she is now without her friends and going to be travelling only with Hana provides another element of resistance in her head. But it isn't something she can process right now.

Jenna rolls out of the bed and tiptoes to the kitchen to get the coffeemaker going. Drip Tim Horton's instead of imported espresso sounds pretty good right about now. Something she's missed while dining in the finest of restaurants all around the world: the simplicity of commercial coffee.

"I smell coffee," Riley croaks as she and Elle sleepily enter the kitchen. They're in her ratty kids' clothes, which still fit Elle adequately.

Jenna smiles, pouring them mugs.

"I cannot understand how you drink that!" Elle exclaims, staring at Riley's black coffee being downed easily.

"It tastes like diesel fuel," Riley admits. "But otherwise, I get diarrhea."

Jenna cringes, pouring milk in her coffee. "Maybe you're lactose intolerant or something?" she suggests.

Riley makes a weird face. "That's total BS. Whatever. It's all total crap. I'm no vegan."

Elle doesn't bother to correct her friend's inaccuracies and quietly laughs at the disdain for "alternative lifestyles."

"How'd it go with your mum?" Riley asks, leaning on the counter and exaggeratedly glancing around the apartment for Ida.

Jenna sighs heavily. "Well, I think we sorted it all out."

"That's great!" Elle smiles, putting an arm around her friend and squeezing lightly.

The door opens, and Ida presents them with a bag full of Montreal-style bagels.

"You wouldn't believe what I spotted at the checkout!" she exclaims, irritated. She pulls out a copy of the magazine with Hunter and Carter's scandal plastered on the cover.

"Well, at least they didn't get pictures of yesterday in ..." Riley laughs, trying to lighten the mood as they look over the story.

"Nope, but it made the news!" Ida shakes her head, plopping down the daily paper.

Riley stares at it with disgust. She's on the front page, overshadowing the team's big win.

"Oh ... my ... God ..." Jenna whispers as she starts flipping through the magazine exposé.

"We look like total idiots." Riley shrugs, chewing her food.

"You're not the only idiot," Elle says, her face twisting into extreme tension, as her finger follows a line of text.

Ida cuts her bagel, listening to the girls.

"Hunter White's hotshot agent produced hush money ... in excess of ten thousand dollars?" Jenna reads off the page, over Elle's shoulder.

"He knew all along," Elle says, surprised by the realization that Ben was not only aware, but an accessory to the crime.

"Oh, my lovee, what are you going to do?" Riley asks, stunned by the revelation.

"I didn't realize that we … lied to each other," Elle says, tears welling in her eyes. "How am I supposed to marry someone who lies to me?"

"Well, he didn't really lie …" Jenna offers.

"Well, he didn't openly share truth," Riley snorts.

Ida looks at each of the girls, who she's seen grow up into the women before her. The fact that they're all getting manhandled by their significant others makes her rather happy to be alone.

"How do I … I don't even … all these months …" Elle gasps softly, not sure whether she feels betrayed or angry or childish for thinking that she and Ben shared every minute detail in their relationship of perfect trust and openness. She quietly touches her engagement ring to check if it is, in fact, still there.

"I think you need to talk to him—the wedding is in, like, two weeks. Jenna's in India and Russia, and then she comes back for your wedding … so, really … you gotta confront him and get it out," Riley advises, still having the compulsion to talk in reference to schedules and plans. But she feels much more at ease this morning with her failed relationship, actually happy that it's imploded. Especially with her book hitting store shelves soon, she'll have other things to focus her attention on.

"I bet you it's some client-lawyer privilege thing," Jenna says knowingly. "I invoked that with my lawyer when I was asking him about buying weed …" She glances at her mother and stops talking.

"Point is—there's an explanation. You guys can bounce back from anything," Riley preaches convincingly.

contact burn.

[Toronto, Canada—early June 2011]

"Would you like the accents in silver or in ivory?"

Elle stares out the kitchen window of her parents' home.

The wedding planner touches Eleanor's elbow and startles her out of her daydream.

"Pardon?" Elle blushes, grabbing the table for support. "Sorry, Brigitte, I was lost in my own world …"

"Oh, honey, I know this is a lot at the last minute. But now that you are home, I need to finalize everything one hundred per cent." The kind woman's French accent is soft and soothing. She's about 40, with an olive complexion and brown hair neatly tied back with a ribbon. She is smartly dressed in a striped crewneck and ankle-length pants. Just missing a long cigarette holder and beret to complete the look.

Elle exhales, puffing her cheeks out and trying to refocus.

"Is there something wrong …?" Brigitte asks her, trying to search for the source of stress in her client's face.

Elle stares down at the seating chart created by her mother.

"Is it with Mr. Benjamin?"

Elle's eyes dart uncontrollably.

"Aha. I see now," Brigitte announces, having caught the sign.

"I need … to talk to him. I need to talk to him before I can continue all of this," Elle apologizes.

"I understand, dear. But I need to know if this is a serious matter, or only a case of nerves … before I put in orders. The tuberose is—"

"We are not having tuberose," Elle says sharply.

"Very well. I shall substitute Benjamin's request."

At that moment, her mother enters the kitchen with grocery bags, struggling to carry them.

"Madame!" Brigitte exclaims, hopping up with Elle to help.

Ben trudges in with the remaining bags, carrying double the amount of Odile.

"Ben caught me in the driveway … thank you for the hand, darling," Odile squeaks, heaving the bags on the counter.

"Perhaps we may discuss the drapings here …" Brigitte says to Odile, guiding her out of the kitchen by the elbow to allow for privacy.

Elle stares at Ben, who is still holding the bags.

"Can I get a hand?" he huffs.

She looks at him blankly, and ignores his strain, opting to start putting away her mother's grocery bags instead.

He tries to lay the bags down on the kitchen floor, unable to lift them up to the counter.

"So …" he says, breathless.

Elle focuses on putting away a box of granola bars.

"Silent treatment, huh? Is that what I deserve?"

"Oh, and what do you *think* you deserve? A hero's welcome?" Elle snaps, folding an empty grocery bag.

"Elle, come on."

"You *sort of* kept a really big secret from me. Do you know how much it hurts that you'd lie to me? And about something that happened to involve a friend of mine. A very good friend of mine. You want me to applaud you? After you run away to go protect him?"

"First off, it was a professional responsibility. I didn't actually lie to you, and it didn't directly involve your friend; it involved my client. I think you need to be reasonable and see this in a practical manner."

Elle grips a bottle of white wine vinegar tightly.

Ben blinks nervously, his eyes darting around behind his glasses. He's never seen her like this before.

Without any warning, Elle smashes the glass bottle of vinegar on the ground. The sharp smell rises up quickly, broken chips of glass scattering on her mother's marble floor.

"How could you not tell me?" she screams at him.

"It's my job!" he protests.

"Nonsense! It's Riley and Hunter! How could you not tell me?!" she repeats. "Actually, it was Riley, Hunter, Jenna *and* Carter – so that's a connect four!"

Brigitte and her mother stay right outside the kitchen, listening, and near enough to intervene if Elle attacks her fiancé.

"Elle, you have to understand that in what I do—I can't tell you everything. There are sensitive, confidential aspects of what I do. Your friend was just a casualty in this specific, isolated case. I'm really sorry. If it's any consolation, he really did care about her."

Elle's face heats up with shock. "A *casualty*? Really? So what am I? A joke? Why are we even getting married if you can't even talk to me? Maybe you can give a quote to the newspaper on that matter."

"It's not that I can't, Elle. It's that I won't. And I thought you understood this about me, about my career. This isn't going to change. I don't want to put it on you, knowing all the little bits of information that could make you a source to be pursued. It's best if you stay out of it. I've worked hard to keep you sheltered from all of this."

"So, practically speaking, when I ask my husband how his day at work was, you're going to say 'no comment'?"

Ben shakes his head at her digs.

"You know what, it's not even that you are trying to protect me, or whatever. It's that you thought you could play God and wipe up the mess for Hunter. Don't you think that there has to be accountability in life? I wonder, do you apply this to yourself," she barks.

"Elle, you know in your gut that I am absolutely, madly in love with you and would never do anything to compromise that. I don't need to play God with myself, because I am stable in my feelings for you. Nothing has ever happened, nothing will ever happen—because you are it for me."

She rolls her eyes, and he rushes up to her, placing his arms on her shoulders and forcing her to listen.

"Hunter and Riley were trying to force something that couldn't be. And because of his situation in life, I am the backup. But with you and me, there is nothing to force. That's why I want to marry you. With you, things are simple and authentic. You've seen ugliness this year, travelling with Jenna. That's the same ugliness I see in the sports industry. And that's why I love you, Eleanor Jane Bryans—because you are you, and I am me, and we are good together."

Elle looks down at the floor and lets his speech sink in.

"We're getting married in a little over a week, and I don't fully trust you," she admits, staring him straight in the eyes.

"We will regain that back. This I do not doubt. But I need you to tell me you understand my situation, that you accept me."

"I have seen Jenna stumble in after trying cocaine with Hana, and us having to tell the press she was recovering from mono. I understand that you have to have a unified front. And although I do not appreciate you handling this situation in this particular manner … at least I can tell you none of my friends will ever date your clients. Ever. That's me thinking practically."

He nods, and both of them relax.

Brigitte and Odile reenter the room cautiously.

"It's okay. We're done," Elle sighs, grabbing the dustpan to sweep up the broken vinegar bottle.

"Well, Ben, I'm assuming we will also be changing the bridal party order ... if Hunter is your best man?" Odile suggests sweetly.

"I can't pick between Riley and Jenna. Put Colette as the maid of honour. At least that way, she can brag about it to the rest of the cousins ..." Elle instructs.

"Oh, Dean will be delighted you picked her," Odile says of her brother.

"Isn't she your fat cousin?" Ben asks flatly.

"So? Hunter screwed around on my best friend." Elle shrugs, dumping the broken glass in the garbage bin.

Ben looks at Brigitte, and she averts her gaze, both of them understanding Elle's need to pair him with a less attractive alternative to Riley. Passive-aggressive vindication against the hotshot playboy.

"So, I have confirmation to change the tuberose to calla lilies ..." Brigitte starts, reviewing the list as the couple and Odile sit down at the kitchen table.

"What happened to my flowers?" Ben whines.

"I hate the smell," Elle quips.

He pouts, looking at the information put together by their wedding planner. He's picking his battles, and flowers are not worth it, especially after having won the right to continue getting married.

"The tuberose was just a casualty in this specific, isolated case." Elle grins menacingly, as the other women hold their breath in surprise at her throwing his comment back.

Ben doesn't flinch, but takes note of Elle's threshold, never wanting to see her escalate to this again. The undoing of Hunter's confidentiality agreement with the slutty random almost undid his personal life. He was not prepared for the thought that his plan could backfire. Could never know that the woman was getting paid six figures to rattle the Stanley Cup winners and overshadow their long-awaited victory with a cheap scandal.

"Shall I make coffee?" Ben asks, touching Elle's stiff shoulder.

"That would be lovely, darling." Odile smiles.

It's gonna take a lot of cups of coffee to get Elle to simmer ... but I gotta ride this out, he thinks to himself, fiddling with the brewer.

As the bold liquid steeps, he carefully observes Elle going through the arrangements before her. She has never been this disconnected from him. It's hit him in the gut, and he needs to figure out how to win her back on to his team.

sinking.

[Mumbai, India—mid-June 2011]

Jenna Ramsay is sitting at the head of a table, dressed in a sheer blue kurta with gold embroidery. She is entertaining dignitaries in the presidential suite of the Taj Mahal hotel, all the chairs and cutlery made of pure silver, giving her a heightened sense of opulence. The week in India has been spent hyping up a new single remixed by DJ Desi Ras, put together especially for her South Asian fans, and to plug the new album coming out in the fall. Hana has also been scoping out the possibility of a world tour.

"All this travel must be so tiresome," comments one of the dinner guests, a woman, the wife of a doctor, who is sitting to Jenna's right. Her husband is beside her, the cute couple is in their sixties and very much in love.

"Well, a little bit. I'm back to Canada for my best friend's wedding at the end of June, actually," she replies, tasting some masala chai. The thick cardamom taste tingles on her lips.

"Oh, how I do love weddings." The lady smiles with glee, fixing the bright green sari she's wearing and putting a palm tenderly on Jenna's hand.

"Yes, she's home with another friend, finishing all the details." Jenna grins, thankful to have avoided the monster planning involved in throwing such a big party. "My other friend has published her first book—"

"Have you seen the dress?" interrupts the woman, completely cutting the other guests in the dining room out of the conversation. They have all patiently rotated turns speaking with the famous young singer.

"No, I haven't. But I'm sure it will be great," Jenna says, smoothing her blouse. She quite likes the feel of wearing the relaxed style of Indian clothing and wonders if she could spin it into a mainstream trend back in North America.

"You are not a bridesmaid?" the woman asks suspiciously, her bangles jingling as she gestures dramatically.

"I am …"

"And you haven't been there to see the dress?" she gasps, as if she has failed performing the most sacred of duties.

"Mishtu, she is a worldwide star—how is she going to do that?" her husband interrupts, a little embarrassed for his nosy wife. "I am so sorry; she loves wedding season."

"It's all right," Jenna says, starting to retreat into her own thoughts.

This woman, Mishtu—she's right. In all the movies, women flock around wedding preparations. Trying on the dresses, having lunch and pedicures, doing bachelorette parties. But she doesn't get to partake in these rites of passage with Elle, and there's a sudden pang of jealousy towards Riley for being the more available go-to girl.

Hana Rin is sitting to Jenna's left at the table, eating her butter chicken with a knife and fork, uncomfortable by the guests' use of hand-to-mouth feeing. Jenna looks at her out of the corner of her eye and feels nostalgic for the old times, when it was her and Riley and Elle bouncing all over the world, giggling about their travels.

But as the two of them move on in their lives, Jenna isn't.

She tunes back into the conversation, and Mishtu is arguing with her husband about something.

"You'd think that by listening to us, we're the most unhappy, quarrelsome people ..." he sighs comically, making the guests at the table laugh at their verbal sparring.

Jenna smiles, thinking of what she and Carter would have been like as retirees. Trying to imagine if he would tell her secrets and hold her hand. When they are years past MTV and red carpets, when their looks would fade and leave little to hide behind.

"Well, blame it on the matchmaker, Jaanu!" exclaims Mishtu, feigning sadness to her beloved.

Her jolly, balding husband eggs her on. "I can't. She's dead—so she cannot give me a refund anyway."

Hana's cell phone rings, and she steps away from the table, having drawn a lot of glances for her flesh-exposing tank top at the conservative dinner table consisting of prominent couples like Mishtu and her surgeon husband—the life of the party.

"Is she a bridesmaid, also?" Mishtu asks, making a funny face at Hana.

Jenna shakes her head, and the guests laugh amongst themselves. She pretends to fiddle with her naan bread.

The couple begins a discussion with the others about the nature of matchmaking going online. One of the younger guests, a man in his mid-thirties, tells of meeting his wife over the Internet, of how hard it was for him as a wealthy businessman to meet someone suitable. Jenna wonders if she should attempt to anonymously take her profile online; she never meets people who take her seriously. They only want to party with her.

Hana reenters the dining room and motions for Jenna to get up and take the phone call. She has a bizarre expression on her face.

"I'm so sorry; please pardon me." Jenna smiles sweetly, relieved to be excused from having to politely decline to be matched by her new friends.

She answers the phone, and Mack is on the line, back in Toronto.

"Hey, Mack. Things are going great here. Having dinner with a few of the media owners now—"

"Jenna, I think you should sit down," he interrupts, his voice lacking the usual stern sarcasm. Instead, it has a hollow quality to it, no vibration of his personality. Almost a chilling stillness.

She slips into her bedroom and shuts the door, listening as her manager exhales heavily, starting and stopping his sentences, searching for the right thing to say.

"Jenna ... there's been a ..." he trails off.

She fidgets, standing by the window and looking out at the Gateway of India, lights illuminating the darkness—the sky above black and unwelcoming without stars.

"Jenna your mother ... had an aneurism," Mack says, trying the method of simply stating fact and cutting to the chase.

Jenna's breath stops in her throat.

"She—" he starts.

"Is she okay?" she interrupts, her voice small and timid.

Aneurism? That sounds serious, she thinks anxiously.

There is a pause on the other end. "No. She died this morning," Mack says, sighing deeply, trying to be straight with her.

Jenna's knees buckle as the sentence sinks into her brain. She drops to the ground and crawls to the wall, pressing her back into it as she curls herself up, hugging her knees tightly.

"Sh-sh-she ... *died*?"

"Yes," he says.

Jenna's eyes dance around the room wildly, as she remembers their plans to go on vacation together, to reward her mother with her first trip abroad. The image of her mom's face begins fading away without control, and she panics, unable to freeze it in her mind's eye.

"Wh-wh-what ... now?" she asks him.

"Well, we've made all the arrangements for you. She'll be cremated, and there will be a small service. So if you want to pack up and come back tonight, Hana can arrange everything. Take your time; we're handling everything," he says.

Jenna still can't speak; she can barely breathe. They stay silent on the phone.

"Jenna?" Mack's voice calls, rousing her from her thoughts.

"I ... have to go," she says, hanging up the phone abruptly.

The iPhone screen blinks off.

I didn't even ... Jenna starts to mentally list off the things that she has failed to do since their reconciliation.

She sits on the ground for what feels like hours, listening to the guests in the other room as they prepare to head home. But she can't get up and say good-bye; she is stuck to the floor.

Hana's voice rings through the suite, bidding everyone a safe journey. Once the door closes, her heels click on the marble floor as she walks in the direction of Jenna's room.

Without thinking, Jenna leaps up and runs straight into the bathroom, locking the door. No condolences will be made now. Condolences make things real, and right now—she can't process this.

"Jen?" calls Hana, knocking on the door.

"I, uh, just need to be alone," she responds, stepping into the huge bathtub and drawing the water at full force.

"Are you sure ..." Hana starts, not sure what to be asking. "Do you need anything?"

"Bath. Sleep. Sorry." Jenna replies awkwardly.

Hana retreats, leaving her to sit in the tub that is now filling with steaming water. Jenna clutches her knees to her chest. Her clothes are soaking through, but she can't feel anything. All she does is stare.

What now? she thinks, petrified. Tears don't come, she's frozen.

After almost overflowing the tub, Jenna snaps back to reality. She drains the hot water, steps out, and peels off her wet clothes, leaving them in a heap on the tiled floor. She wraps herself in a luxurious bathrobe and goes straight to the giant bed.

On the bedside table, there is a glass of water and two pills with a note from Hana.

> *Sometimes it's better to sleep and not dream. I cancelled your day tomorrow; we'll go from there.* –H

Jenna pops the sleeping pills her in her mouth and crawls between the fine sheets, hoping to vanish.

• • •

Heavy eyelids struggle to open as cracks of light come through the thick curtains of the bedroom.

"Jenna-bean, do not tell me that you got suspended!" comes her mother's stern voice. "Why would you try beat on that weak little Bryans child … I would say it serves you right for getting knocked in the face by the new girl!"

Jenna smiles to herself, almost seeing her mother's exasperation on the day that Riley socked her. The three girls were brought in the school office, and Ida Ramsay let it rip, even before the principal got to them. That was always the problem when your mother worked at your elementary school.

Jenna sighs, trying desperately to see the crease of her mom's annoyed forehead, but the more tightly she shuts her eyes, the harder she tries to focus, the more the mental picture disappears.

Her eyelids open slowly, and she's tangled up in rich, ivory-coloured sheets, sweaty and breathing heavily. She slowly looks around the master bedroom and realizes she's not in her tiny bed at home, surrounded by posters and My Little Ponies.

The bed feels like a warm incubator. She's burrowed a small sweet spot among the scentless linens. She doesn't know how long she's been there, and doesn't want to look at the bedside clock. Her throat feels dry and she sits up on her elbows to get the glass of water.

The condensation has left a neat circle on the wood night table, and Jenna stares at it gloomily, trying to recall the déjà-vu of having seen something like it before.

Then it clicks. A flashback from the last time she saw her mother, at their apartment. Her apartment. Not Jenna's anymore, not since she forcefully moved out. The night she cut her hand, but stayed up all nigh talking with her mom.

"Bean, how could you leave me …" echoes her mother's voice.

Jenna takes the big, fluffy pillow and smushes it over her head, not ready to emerge and not wanting to listen.

delicious deliverance.

[Toronto, Canada—June 21, 2011]

Eleanor Bryans stares at herself in the full-length mirror.

"Oh, my goodness ..." she whispers to herself, her breath taken away by the image reflected back at her.

The luxurious Romona Keveza wedding gown glows with the sunshine streaming through her bedroom window. The soft ivory satin makes her look as if she's sprung from a romantic period movie, and it's of such a finish that it doesn't wash her out, but rather helps her beam like Aphrodite emerging from the sea.

She's getting ready at her parents' home, friends and loved ones trickling by with warm-wishes and curiosity before the wedding ceremony.

"I love it!" she screeches, turning to face her hairstylist with tears in her eyes, touching her polished updo with excitement.

"I'm glad you like it!" he smiles back. Greg May is the hotshot hair guru who has been a staple in her family's repertoire for years. He's made a special trip to the Bryans home to help their little girl look her best.

"I ... can't believe it's happening ..." she whispers.

"Honey, I know it's a lot—trust me. But take a minute, breathe, get yourself centred, and try soak it all in." Greg advises sympathetically, as he packs up his gear.

There's a knock at her bedroom door, and Riley slips in.

"Hey, how are you doing?" she asks, checking her watch quickly as she shuts the door. They're right on schedule.

"Pretty much done ..." Elle says softly, looking back into the mirror and checking her eyeliner.

"My lovee, you look absolutely ... heavenly." Riley beams proudly, careful to find the perfect word. "Nice job, May!"

Greg takes a comical bow.

Elle's hair looks more reddish today, bringing out her green eyes like jade. Freckles dust her collarbone from the summer days.

Riley fidgets in her bridesmaid's dress, a beautiful green to complement Elle's eyes and the groomsmen's ties.

"Is Jenna here?" Elle asks, hopeful that her friend has managed to pick herself up off the bathroom floor long enough to attend the biggest day of her life.

"Yeah, she's downstairs with mimosas," Riley says, biting her lip, trying not to lick off her lipstick.

"She's wasted," Elle replies, not asking a question, but rather assuming the obvious. "Am I a bad friend for having prayed that she could not be herself today? I know that it is sad that Ida died. We were at the funeral—she wasn't. I can't believe people were hoping she'd show for autographs … I get it; it's a bad phase right now. But I hoped and wished that she could put that aside for one day … I truly wish she would realize that getting to the point of blacking out is not how to cope with a dead mother!"

"She was booked in at the salon yesterday and was sauced … Such a pity, massive change since the last time she came in. Her hair wasn't the only thing that was a mess." Greg shrugs, already familiar with the decline of the singer. He put in her first set of highlights, and every time she's been back to his salon, it's been a wildcard draw as to what version of Jenna would surface.

Riley changes the subject and stands beside her friend at the mirror, placing her hands on her shoulders. "Are you nervous?" she asks the bride.

Elle's cheeks flare a delicate blush. "No … not really. The anticipation is what's killing me. I want to see him already. You know what I mean? Get it over with!" She giggles, fluffing her gown.

"I am so happy that this fairy tale is finally happening," Riley says, brushing a stray hair behind her friend's ear. "You guys are such a great couple … it's just—if this can happen for real, then … I don't know, it's like …"

"A secret little hope?" Elle smiles.

Riley looks at her friend, surprised.

"That's what I always saw when I looked at my mom and dad. Married for so many years, but still fun-loving teenagers. Have you ever walked in on your parents having sex?!" She laughs.

Riley cringes at the thought.

"Never mind." She laughs again. "I'm sorry if it's really weird with Hunter here."

"Really? You're the one getting married, and you're worried about *me*? Please. He's the last thing that is going to get me strung out. But thank God he couldn't go to the rehearsal dinner," Riley snickers.

Elle smacks her playfully, pacing around her periwinkle-blue bedroom. "Weird that I'm not going to live here anymore. Like, really, really, live here, know what I mean?" she says, touching some of the awards on her wall.

"I know the feeling. I think I might leave my dad's place and strike out on my own …" Riley muses, adjusting her strapless bra, constricted by the gown.

Elle looks at her curiously.

"Well, now that we're no longer Top Dog's bitches … I mean, I wouldn't mind hiding and dodging all this Hunter drama. Clearing my head. Maybe work on the next brilliant piece of writing …" She laughs.

"How has this weird scandal affected the book's sales?" Greg asks.

"Actually, it spiked them, which is weird, because my book has, like, medieval mystery and random stuff." Riley laughs. "Not trendy and cool whatsoever. But I guess somehow there's a curiosity because of Jenna and Hunter? So lame."

"Well, everything will be fine, it'll happen the way it's supposed to happen. Today is *your* day, Elle. And it's going to be fabulous! Can't wait to see you in action!" Greg encourages, as he slips out.

There's a commotion downstairs, and a few seconds later, the door bursts open, and Jenna struts in. Her green dress has been modified since their fitting, now significantly shorter and more revealing.

"Mimosa?" she asks Elle, offering her a glass.

"No thanks … want to stave off as long as I can." She sighs, trying to hide her shock at her friend's state.

Jenna proceeds to drink the entire glass and set it down roughly. She pulls out a cigarette and lights up in the room.

"How's the rabbi going to like *that*?" Riley whispers through gritted teeth, as Elle stares at the ashy smoke swirling around the room.

"Elle, this is great. This is going to be great. The food … great. You look …" Jenna starts blubbering.

"Great?" Riley suggests.

"My groomsman … great …" Jenna laughs, giving a pervy thumbs-up. "I like hockey Russian players."

There's an awkward moment of silence that Jenna fails to notice as she stares around the walls.

"Shall we get going?" Riley asks, looking at the time.

"Is the limo here?" Elle asks.

"Everyone's already gone," Jenna informs her.

"They left in my limo?" Elle gasps, shocked.

"It's okay. I told them we'd take my driver," Jenna says, making a *pfft* hand gesture, sending smoke fluttering.

I hope it doesn't seep into the pores of her bedroom, Riley worries to herself, staring at Jenna's defiling of boundaries in the Bryans' nonsmoking home.

"But Ben and I were going to arrive in matching black limos ..." Elle whispers to herself.

"Now you can arrive in my Escalade. Hana's downstairs waiting."

Eleanor's eyes well up, and she looks about ready to break down. Riley steps in.

"*Ooo-kay.* So, why don't we send you ahead, Jenna, to check that everything is ready for the bride, right? Help Elle like that," Riley starts. Elle sits down on her four-poster bed, trying to stay calm.

"Yes ... check that ..." Jenna repeats, as Riley leads her down the stairs and out to the circular driveway.

After loading Jenna and Hana in the flashy SUV, she speed-dials Duncan.

"Please tell me you're stylish enough to be taking a limo to the wedding," Riley says, hiding in the living room of the house.

"Of course!" he snaps.

"What colour is it?"

"Black ..."

"Can you please, please, for the sake of making sure this wedding goes on, come to Eleanor's parents' house? Don't ask any questions; we need a ride," Riley begs.

Duncan obliges, and Riley races up to comfort her friend.

"Don't worry—matching limo on the way!" she assures, sitting down beside a speechless bride.

"Please tell me that her car was at least black to fit my décor ..." Elle sniffles, clutching a tissue.

"Bright, incandescent white—but who's counting?" Riley laughs nervously.

Elle's chest heaves as she tries to hold back tears.

"She tried," Riley points out.

"She tried," Elle concedes, but still is horrified by the thought of arriving to her conservative wedding in a monster truck.

• • •

The black stretch limousine pulls up in front of Casa Loma, the historical castle that has been transformed into a romantic backdrop for the Roberts-Bryans outdoor wedding and reception. Riley takes a quick glance around and notices there is no Jenna-mobile in sight.

For crying out loud, tell me she's here ... Riley silently pleads with the sky above.

The guests have already been ushered in and are taking their seats in the garden. The bride is led into a greenhouse to wait for her cue while the wedding party assembles behind veils of ivory satin that block the crowd's view. Green hedges act as natural walls, enclosing the wedding and making everyone feel like nymphs in a magic garden. The sun is warm overhead, getting ready to set—at least one thing is going according to plan.

Riley is paired in the procession with a college friend of Ben's. Luckily, the maid of honour is Elle's frumpy cousin, the partner to Hunter's best-man role.

She spots her brother, Brian, poking around behind the scenes of the staging area.

"*Psst!*" Riley hisses, catching his attention.

"Hey, I heard Hunter brought the Stanley Cup ..." Brian whispers, his curly hair tamed into a sleek style for the formal occasion.

His sister stares back with disdain, fantasizing about shoving her delicate bouquet down his throat.

"Well, can you ask him? I didn't see it out front, but maybe he's gonna unveil it to Ben as a present or something cool like that ..."

"Really? You're kidding. No—you go ask him if you care enough to CIA around back here looking for it!" Riley snaps, glancing at the hockey player standing around awkwardly.

"You dated him ..."

"So?"

"Sex has to equal some sort of Cup-giving power, right?"

Riley slaps him on the arm violently.

"I punched the guy in the face, man..." Brian whines, regretting defending his sister's honour at the expense of seeing the legendary trophy in person.

"So?"

"Be nice, be open to him—friendly, non-threatening ..." Brian suggests soothingly.

"I'm so fucking open and friendly, I might as well be McDonald's. Now screw off, brother dear, or I'll remove you myself ..." Riley sasses him.

Her brother snickers at her reluctance to make nice with her scandalous ex and decides to approach the athlete himself later. Potentially offer himself up as a slave in exchange to see every peewee hockey player's dream.

"You know, at least at McDonald's the smiles are free ..." Brian calls over his shoulder as his sister glares after him.

Her groomsman approaches as the event planner calls the wedding party to organize by the curtained entryway.

"Hey, Riley. Congratulations," says Sam, her escort.

"For what?" she asks—they're not at *her* wedding.

"Uh, number one best seller?" he asks in a goofy way, fiddling with his black tuxedo jacket. His handsome features look even more dapper in the snazzy attire. His dark brown eyes shine against his dark hair.

Riley's eyes pop; she's scared she may have heard him incorrectly.

I'm on a best-seller list?! she screams in her head.

He smiles at her shock. "I just saw a Tweet about it ..."

There's a sudden screech, and Jenna trips out of the greenhouse where Elle is being sequestered. She's followed by a groomsman, who hurdles over a garden gate like a track star. He briskly lands on his feet, having cleared the obstacle with the adrenaline rush. He awkwardly zips up his trousers and tries to act as if he hasn't been caught in the act.

Jenna fixes her dress in front of everyone and lines up at the front of the procession.

Elle must be exploding with rage, Riley worries. *If I were her, there'd be one less bridesmaid ...*

Sam looks back at Riley with a shrug and puts his arm out to escort her down the aisle. "I can only imagine what Elle witnessed ..." he whispers dryly, thankful to have such a sober date.

The procession begins. They march their way up to the chuppa, the Jewish wedding arc erected to honour Ben's parents. It's decorated in beautiful white flowers, the sweet scent of blossoms heavy in the summer humidity.

The crowd looks on in awe, mostly at Jenna. A few people point at Hunter, whispering. But when Elle appears with her father at the top of the aisle, a hush falls over the entire crowd as they rise from their seats.

Riley glances at Ben, and it's as if he's stopped breathing. He is mesmerized by Eleanor gliding down the carpeted runway, like a fairy in her natural element. Her father proudly walks beside her, the definition of gentlemanly class.

Elle's mother is already weeping tears of joy, her outfit accented with the same green as the rest of the bridal party, a prim hat on her head.

Eleanor and Ben's eyes lock on each other, and it's as if there is no one else sitting there, no one watching, no one whispering.

Riley glances at Jenna, who is about to cry—but probably for reasons other than joy and pride.

At the reception, the crowd lingers around the wood dance floor set up on the expansive lawn. White lanterns hang around the party, candles flickering and setting a romantic mood.

Ben's mother is already a little loosey-goosey, holding her constantly half-full glass of white wine. His father is in heavy conversation with Elle's dad, asking for an impromptu consultation about aging and brain health.

The music is turned down, and the DJ announces the official entrance of Mr. and Mrs. Benjamin Roberts.

The newlyweds stride across the garden and towards the head table, changed into more comfortable clothing. Elle is in a feminine summer dress, the material flowing as she walks beside Ben. He's changed into a pair of khakis and a dress shirt.

The crowd cheers as they approach, the DJ playing a song for the father-daughter dance. Elle beams as her dad walks her out to the dance floor.

"They are adorable." Riley laughs to her dad, who is seated at a table with Kevin.

"Maybe that'll be us one day …" Rhett smiles warmly, actually quite serious.

Riley flashes a look of fear at the thought of getting married.

"Or not!" Kevin laughs, drinking his wine.

Rhett sighs and sips his Perrier, helpless.

"Has Hunter said anything to you?" Kevin asks, leaning over to gossip.

Riley shrugs. "I think he knows better than to waste his breath."

Rhett puts an arm around her and squeezes reassuringly.

Duncan approaches them, and Riley slips away as the three men begin a heated conversation about fashion and décor trends.

She spots Jenna by the DJ, unsure of what she's up to.

"And now, the first dance of hubby and wifey! Please welcome to the stage, to sing a special number, Miss Jenna Ramsay!"

The crowd shouts in excitement, curious to see what song Jenna will pull out of her repertoire of hits.

A little unsteady from the alcohol, she sits at the black baby grand piano and adjusts the mic.

"This is for my darling lovee, Elle. Because we're not all as lucky to find love like you; some people never have it. Or it goes away," she says, not aware of the awkwardness in her attempt at a compliment.

Riley can see she's quite nervous, sweat forming on her forehead.

Please don't let her screw up, Riley begs. The stars are starting to come out, and the setting is perfect for a serenade. *She has had a lot to drink, and she is very, very sad ... but please don't let her screw up.*

Jenna begins playing.

"What song is this?" Sam asks, approaching Riley and handing her a drink.

"You know, I don't think I've ever heard it ..." she admits, listening intently.

Jenna sings a beautiful number about love and forever, her voice raspy from the excessive drinking and smoking, but still a success. She's channeling some jazz vibes. Ben and Elle dance tenderly, but watch her with their mouths wide open, appreciative for her gesture.

The crowd gives her a standing ovation, and Jenna bows, almost tripping as she tries to run off the stage.

The DJ blocks her path and hands her a microphone.

"What?" Jenna asks, looking at the device, frightened.

"Give a toast!" he says to her, trying to play off the crowd's happy energy.

Riley and Elle make eye contact across the room, both a little concerned about Jenna's inebriated state.

"Um ... okay ... so, this guy told me to toast ..." she says, laughing, trying to light a cigarette. Her hands quiver nervously as she lets the white paper cylinder sit in her mouth lazily.

"Speech! Speech! Speech!" the crowd begins to chant.

"And you're telling me to speech. Because I'm a performer. And when you want, I have to perform, right? Because that is what I *dooo*," she says. "But tonight, I am not the real performer. Ben and Elle. You are the people, even though people keep looking at me."

"Uh-oh ..." Riley whispers, hustling to the stage.

"I'm used to it. People always look at me, and take my picture, and whisper. That's okay. But tonight, my friend Elle is getting married! She loves love, you know. My mom told me that love was not forever. She's dead now. So she was right—not forever ..." she trails off, disgusted.

Riley gets on to the stage and grabs the mic. The crowd whispers nervously. Jenna doesn't even feel the tears that have started slipping down her face.

"And we are thankful for all that we have learned from our families. And celebrate being here for our dear friends," Riley says quickly, handing the DJ the mic.

She helps Jenna down to the dance floor, and Elle floats up to them, shaking her head.

Elle reaches out to hug her friend, and Jenna awkwardly obliges.

"Your song was beautiful," Elle says, trying to soothe her.

"I wrote it because I was so jealous of you," Jenna replies, shifting her weight on her feet. "Can I go now?"

Elle looks at her oddly and watches her friend scoot off to the bar, where Hana is waiting for her, having watched her client hang herself and be photographed by the wedding guests like a zoo animal.

Riley shrugs and pats her friend reassuringly, and they begin the formal meal.

As Elle becomes entangled with her guests, Riley finds herself being entertained by Sam the groomsman. They're seated at the same table for dinner, and both elect to keep a low profile.

"So what are you going to do now that you're a successfully published author?" he asks, taking a bite of his seared salmon steak.

Riley chews thoughtfully, and takes a sip of water. "To be honest, I kinda wanna get away ... be somewhere else where people didn't really pay attention to the Stanley Cup playoffs," she admits, shooting a quick glance at Hunter. He's already flocked by most of the single girls at this wedding.

"I don't blame you."

"Everyone in this city happens to know about our personal lives now because he's like a decorated warrior to them. I doubt Lancelot would have gotten this sorta coverage on the sports reels."

Sam exhales heavily. "I can see why you'd want to vanish ..." He laughs, watching an elderly couple point at Riley and shake their heads sadly. "At least they're sympathetic, right?"

"Nope. Some are totally insane," Riley admits, opting not to tell him about her slashed tire or the hate mail sent to her father's house. When one is considered a lucky charm, breaking up with a hockey empire apparently renders a beheading.

"Well, if you ever want to disappear to Northern California, you are more than welcome to use my apartment."

Riley exhales nervously, a little unsure if he thinks she's going to trek across the continent for a booty call.

"I'm leaving next weekend for a year and didn't find anyone to sublet it," he explains, realizing her thoughts. "I'm leaving to join my *girlfriend* in Africa …"

"Oh, really? That's great—how come?" Riley asks, her eyes lighting up with relief.

Sam grins, happy that they're on the same page now. "We're going to work in a community clinic. We're both doctors," he explains.

"Oh, yes, that's right! You went to Stanford Med …" Riley recalls, feeling a bit dense, especially for assuming that everyone is after sexual relations.

"Yeah. Shared a place with Ben. It was great—we were always cramming, though. When I was doing my residency, he moved to LA."

"Hey, Sam, can I ask you something?" she wonders.

He nods, finishing his fish.

"Did Ben have anyone during school?"

Sam blushes a little, trying to decide whether to divulge his roomie's details, even though he's already signed, sealed, and delivered to Eleanor now.

Riley bites her lip, regretting having asked.

"He tried. But … I think he always had someone else in mind …" Sam replies, glancing out at the married couple, who are laughing and whispering to each other on the dance floor.

Riley smiles, feeling her heart swell with joy.

They move on to dessert, and Riley finds herself looking around for Jenna. Her seat is empty, has been since at least the entrée.

There is a sudden crash and shouting, with a flurry of flash cameras going off on the other side of the shrubs.

Riley jumps up and races out to investigate.

Jenna is bolting down the laneway barefoot and jumps into the backseat of her SUV, screaming for the driver to get in. Photographers chase after her, a blur of action confusing all the guests at the reception.

Riley recognizes the person left behind in the dust of the calamity. It's the same groomsman from the garden. His trousers are around his ankles, dorky boxer shorts out for everyone to see.

Riley closes her eyes and tries to breathe. After a few moments, she turns and walks back into the party. Sam looks up and gestures frantically, asking what in the world is going on.

"Don't even ask." She mouths back.

Elle is trying to ignore the commotion, and Riley gives her an apologetic glance, motioning that the situation is over before getting back to her table. Elle shakes her head and focuses back on the guests talking to her.

Riley sits down and takes a deep breath, putting her elbows on the table and dropping her chin onto her palms.

"When can I rent your place?" Riley asks Sam.

PART III: TURBULENCE

incognito.

[San Francisco, USA—July 2011]

Riley Kohl stares at the window shades, bright morning sunlight peeking through the corners. The room seems to be glowing from the filtered rays.

She rolls onto her side on the bed. The sleep mask she wore to get through the night dangles around her neck. It's her first real day in San Francisco, and the sun outside pressures her to get up and move.

She groggily stumbles into the kitchen and opens the fridge, but it is empty and clean.

Right ... this isn't my home ... She laughs to herself, looking around Sam's apartment.

There are black-and-white photos of bridges and buildings throughout the entire place. The bedroom faces a small sitting room, which leads straight into a kitchen with standing room only dining. The bathroom is cramped at best; everything in the apartment compact and tight. But the proximity of living in the city's comfortable Marina district was well worth any awkward architectural layout.

The wood floors are cool beneath her bare feet. Riley decides to change and explore her new neighbourhood, her new city. She wiggles into her favourite Chip & Pepper jeans and grabs a bulky sweater, shoving her keys and wallet into the pockets. She opts to slide into her Converse sneakers for the long discovery walk.

She hikes through the streets, passing cafés and shops, watching families out with strollers, and couples jogging. The new sights and sounds are capturing her attention, the now-grey sky overhead not interfering with the feeling of adventure.

After a half hour of aimless walking, she finds herself standing outside of massive commotion, crowds of people flocking to and fro—even at this relatively early hour. She reads a sign for the Saturday farmers' market at the pier and claps her hands in glee—San Francisco, the essence of Northern California wholesome goodness.

As she works her way through the booths, picking fruits and vegetables to stock her empty fridge, her cell phone rings.

"Hey, lovee! How was the honeymoon?" She smiles, glad to finally hear from her friend. The newly married Mr. and Mrs. Roberts have been lost in quiet Cape Cod for the past couple of weeks, basking in fresh seafood and peacefulness. They missed her slipping out of Toronto and into obscurity, the torrential coverage of Hunter White left in the dust.

"I cannot even *begin* to express how incredible the view was—and the food!" Elle squeals.

Riley glances at her watch; it must be nearing lunchtime back in Canada.

"How is your new, temporary home?" Elle asks worriedly, the concern for her friend alone in a big city echoing in her question.

"Everything is great. At the farmers' market, stocking up on—get this—organic food. Never thought I'd really be excited." Riley laughs.

"Well, it looks like I'm going to have to start watching what *I* eat ..." Elle says softly, a sad tone in her voice.

"Yeah, I mean, I gotta say, I feel like a nimrod for not bringing my own canvas bag or whatever ..." Riley whispers, scared one of those "tree hugger" types might overhear and punch her out. "But now that I'm here, I'm kinda digging this ..."

"Yes, well ... I think I might be pregnant," Elle says, not knowing how else to tiptoe around her suspicion.

Riley squeezes the tomato in her hand too tightly, and the seeds squirt all over her fingers.

"Repeat?" she asks her friend, having heard perfectly well, but wanting to hear it again in case the fresh produce distracted her.

"Actually, I'm pretty sure I'm ... pregnant," Elle squeaks.

"You guys waste no time ..." Riley points out, wiping the tomato innards off and paying for her selections.

"I know... It's actually a bit of a shock. I wasn't expecting that it would happen this ... fast," Elle whispers. She's sitting alone in her new master bathroom, the pee test actually still on the counter in front of her. "It's kinda intense. I mean, we get the new house, get married, go on our honeymoon and pick shells off the beach ... and suddenly, I'm ..."

Riley hears a faint twinge of fear in her friend's voice.

"How do you feel about that? Are you okay with ... being a baby shelter for the next nine months?" Riley asks, as she passes by a fudge stand.

Elle pauses for a moment, upset she's even hesitating. "Of course I'm happy! I mean, this is what I've always wanted. To be married and have kids and be a yummy mummy ..." she says forcefully. "I mean, I went off birth control so I could detox my body so that … eventually … um, but it's just that this happened … now."

"Hey, you don't need to convince me! I'm the one who ran away from matrimony and all that, and with public humiliation," Riley points out.

"Have you talked to Jenna?" Elle asks, suddenly changing topics.

Riley scrunches her face. She hasn't seen or heard from her friend since the meltdown at Elle's wedding.

"Maybe … she's focusing on career stuff …" Riley responds cautiously. "I think she actually might be back in Asia."

"Okay, well, if you talk to her before I do … please don't say anything. I tried to reach her earlier today, but … no answer. I would love to hear her reaction when I tell her!" she chirps excitedly, trying to get herself pumped up.

I have a feeling she's not going to be as excited as you, Riley thinks sadly.

They hang up, and Riley realizes she's been standing and staring at the waterfront like a zombie. She shakes herself back to reality and continues walking through the stalls. She stops and gets a cup of coffee at the Blue Bottle Coffee Company to toast the creation of Baby Roberts. She takes a sip and nearly faints—it tastes incredible. Riley buys an entire bag of coffee to take home, along with organic milk and a dozen peanut butter cookies from the Miette pastry case.

"Delectable …" she says to herself, sipping the aromatic hot drink and walking through the crowd.

She buys herself fresh flowers and an entire assortment of exotic marmalades, discovering all the fun and unique offerings of the region.

Instead of walking back home, she hops in a cab to her cushy neighbourhood, watching the city unfold along the way.

She struggles up her stairs to the second-floor apartment, dragging the shopping bags into the kitchen.

"Maybe I'll cook myself a nice pasta!" she announces excitedly, storing her produce and smiling proudly at the stability she feels from a stocked pantry.

Her phone rings, and she is surprised to see a call from Mack Madison.

"Riley, I'm wondering if you've spoken with Jenna," he says, straight to the point.

"No … why …?" she replies, putting her coffee beans away.

"Because she decided to fire me via text message ..." he trails off, the confusion in his voice stirring fear in Riley.

"What?"

"Yeah. Exactly. As of ... three AM today, I am no longer her manager, and I have to say, I can't quite understand what is going on."

Riley curls up on the cozy couch by the living room window, surprised by the news. "Mack, I honestly haven't seen or spoken to her since the wedding. And even then, she was ... it honestly doesn't seem rational or anything. Why would she get rid of *you*?"

"Who else would manage her?" he gasps, his nasal voice frustrated.

Riley slaps her forehead. "Mack ... it's Hana. Obviously it's Hana. Since day one, she's been manipulating everything ... because it's not like you and Jenna were in a fight or something, right?"

"Exactly. Everything was fine. She was a bit distant, but she has such a hectic schedule. Hana was just taking on more responsibilities with her ..." he trails off, realizing the error in judgment.

"I'm willing to bet you a million dollars that it's all her. Who else would stand to gain anything from this? It's that greed ... she hated Elle and me. *Hoooly* shit did she hate the two of us. I'm sure she couldn't wait for us to get cut out of the picture."

Mack groans, annoyed. "Can you talk to her?" he asks Riley.

"Mack—she hasn't returned any contact with me. Or you. Or Elle. She's marooning herself on purpose. I think she's gotta realize it on her own ..."

"Have you seen the latest? She's already in the news for nearly breaking up a marriage with some Mexican. I knew something was up when Hana wouldn't listen to me about how much tabloid exposure she was getting ... she just kept pushing the envelope."

Riley opens her laptop and finds that TMZ has written about Jenna's late-night partying with a famous television actor and a recent invitation to model in a fashion show.

"This is bad, Riley. If she keeps going at this rate ..." Mack trails off. He's frightened to see the career he's built going up in flames.

"Oh, my God, she's doing hard drugs?" Riley gasps, reading a blog post from someone who partied with Jenna in Atlanta.

"She's out of control, probably confused since her mother's death. She never talked about it—she didn't even go to the funeral I set up, or the therapy I arranged." Mack exhales heavily. "This is what happens when you don't maintain a measure of control ... I should've been ready when you and Elle finished your contracts."

"I'm sorry. I know how hard you worked for this," Riley says to the normally quick-witted and sarcastic manager. His spirits have been steamrolled.

"If you talk to her, please try knock some sense into her ..." he begs as they end their call.

She puts her cell phone down on the couch and lets out a deep breath.

"This ... is ... bad," Riley says out loud, staring at the computer screen full of gossip. "But ... I need to not read it anymore. New beginnings."

She turns off her wireless Internet and tries to refocus on writing instead of wasting time trolling blogs for news.

She wraps herself in a Hudson's Bay blanket and decides to brew up a cup of Blue Bottle for comfort. The rich smell of the coffee revives her senses temporarily.

She stares at the computer screen, and the cursor blinks rhythmically.

What now ...? she asks herself, seeking inspiration, as she listens to the hum of people outside her window.

down but not out.

[Las Vegas, USA—August 2011]

Jenna Ramsay smiles to herself. She's staring at the massive crowd below her in the nightclub, waiting to help celebrate her second album.

Her smile feels a little stiff. She's gone through her first bottle of champagne with Hana, Carter, and their group of party people.

The DJ's voice booms through the club, announcing her presence. A spotlight illuminates her, and she is handed a microphone, the white Marilyn Monroe–inspired dress she's wearing shining under the light.

"What's up, Las Vegas! Thank you *sooo* much for coming out here tonight to support me. I am *sooo* excited for this new album—lots of music to dance to! Worked with a great new team to get it out this fall, so I hope you enjoy the new creative direction. I want to thank my new manager, Hana, and I'm so excited to party with y'all!" she says, trying to get her words out slowly and calmly. Trying.

A light flashes on to illuminate Hana, who is in conversation with Carter but turns to wave like a pageant queen.

The DJ starts playing some of the tracks, but the crowd is not quite sure how to react to the very different sound of Jenna Ramsay, Part Two.

She doesn't even notice the look of shock on the faces in the crowd. The trippy sound effects and electronic gizmos of the dance music sound too alien. She was barely even present during the recording process, not having written any of the songs herself. It was Hana's idea to "expand" her sound, and Jenna obediently followed her new confidante and leader.

Jenna stumbles back to her booth, gasping in shock as she spots Parker Ma emerge from the well-dressed crowd in the trendy Las Vegas club.

"Parker!" she shouts, uncontrollably excited to see him.

He smiles faintly, a little put off at seeing her like this. After so long.

"Hey, Jenna, I heard you were in town previewing your album and wanted to come say hi," he says, hugging her a little stiffly.

She stares at him happily, in a daze, the effects of the prescription drugs she's popped causing her to feel slow but at ease.

"I heard you dropped Mack?" he asks, lowering his voice, still surprised by the recent string of rash decisions made by his former protégé. He awkwardly shoves his hands into the pockets of his straight black jeans, rocking back and forth on his feet. He's wearing a purple vest over a grey T-shirt, looking rather alt-rock. The tattoos on his arms pop brightly.

"Yeah. Hana's been on the road with me ... she knows ... well ... it would've been nice to work with you again, though ..." she murmurs, not exactly sure what she's saying.

"Right," Parker replies, a little uncomfortable by how out of it she seems.

"How are you? I'm so happy to see you!" she shouts, grabbing his arm.

Carter struts up to them, even more blitzed than Jenna. He slaps her butt and hands her the joint from his mouth.

"Hey, who's this?" he asks, puffing out his chest.

"This is Parker! We recorded the first album together." She grins, dopey, absentmindedly holding the weed in her hand.

Parker offers his hand to the movie actor. "Hey. I saw some of your movies, man," he says, trying to stop Carter from staring him down.

"If you're not gonna smoke that, give it back," Carter says to Jenna harshly.

"Parker, have a drink with us!" Jenna exclaims, trying to break the awkward tension.

"Oh, no, that's okay. I've gotta head back to my hotel—got an early flight to Nashville tomorrow," he says, relieved not to have to hang around the sketchy-looking Carter Sampson.

A photographer rushes up to take a picture of Jenna and Parker, and Carter and Hana jump into the shot.

The flash is intense and blinds Jenna, giving her an intense headache. Hana and Carter dive back into their booth, howling with laughter.

"Well, I better go," Parker sighs.

Jenna hugs him, holding on to him a little longer than normal.

"You never wrote me back," she whimpers, uncontrollably letting her sadness come out, clinging to him.

He exhales anxiously, having been certain that all of her text messages had come from a similar state of intoxication, that she was not in a condition to actually be sincere.

Carter is staring at them but simultaneously flirting with a group of porn stars that has dropped by, waiting to meet Jenna.

Man, you are such a creeper, Parker thinks to himself, astounded by the movie star and that Jenna can't seem to see through his bullshit.

"Oh, hey, I'm real sorry about your mom …" Parker says, patting her head and changing the subject.

Jenna stares at him, a wave of nausea crashing over her as the music vibrates in her ears. Her hands start shaking; her left eye twitches nervously.

"I know you loved her a lot," he says, shaking his head.

"Are you serious? That woman was a freakin' banshee!" exclaims Carter, having overheard the condolence, swooping down on them.

Parker stares at the actor, amazed by his lack of filter. He looks to Jenna, who is like a deer in headlights, disconnected from the conversation.

Not having anything more to say, Parker disappears into the crowd, leaving Jenna to freefall into her memories.

He is saddened by the shell of a girl he saw tonight.

As he walks back to his hotel room, he remembers getting to know her back in Toronto. The unbridled creativity that flamed out of her, the intensity and energy that would push her to rerecord songs until they were absolutely *perfect*. And now, she's a puppet being dangled for her looks and image—nothing else.

I thought she could be the next real talent, have longevity. How can someone degrade into that? he thinks sadly, staring at the carpet of the elevator. And this makes it easier to miss her less, to think of her less.

indigestion questions.

[Los Angeles, USA—September 2011]

Riley stares down at the floor. She's perched on a toilet in a bathroom stall, staring at the simple white tiling. Her blue peep-toe heels are tapping against the clean floor nervously.

"Riley, at some point, you are going to have to come out, you know …" Duncan says, exasperated, communicating through the metal stall door.

"I'm going to throw up," she threatens.

He lets out a frustrated sigh. She's proven to be really difficult to deal with, unapologetic for her desire to be antisocial.

"I can't believe I let you talk me into this. As if I suddenly grew a new personality and became able to speak in public," she says, wringing her sweaty hands.

"It's not that bad. The audience in the studio is … what … less than two hundred people?" he offers.

"Yes, but the millions of people watching at home—that's worse. Why am I even here? I told you outright that there was no way I could do public appearances," she moans.

"But the public wants to meet the person behind the book. We've waited long enough—there has been no coverage on you. And for the sales you've had, *I* don't even understand how you've gotten this far without promotional work."

The door to the bathroom opens, and a person from the talk show informs Duncan that they have ten minutes until air.

"I'm not going!" Riley screams, grabbing the toilet paper holder like an anchor. She is careful not to let her bum fall through the toilet seat, not wanting to spoil the black jeans she's carefully paired with a white tuxedo shirt.

Duncan waves off the timid producer, who is talking through his headset, and secretly starts to panic about how he's going to get through to his client.

A few seconds later, the door opens again. After some murmuring, Riley hears Duncan walk out—his big, heavy feet thumping in designer loafers.

She lets out a sigh of relief—maybe he's given up and will tell the show that she is absolutely not going on air.

Now, you can go home and be the nerd you are meant to be. She grins. She's won this round.

She sits in silence, and then plucks up the courage to stand and open the door.

Riley looks at herself in the mirror, and then shrieks when she realizes there is someone leaning by the row of sinks.

"Mother fuck! What the hell are you doing?" she gasps, backing away from the stranger.

The handsome man smiles, taking a step forward.

"I was wondering how long it would take you to come out on your own," he says with a laugh, a South African accent on his words.

She looks at him with wild-eyed panic, trying to think of something to use as a weapon.

They're going to put me in restraints and take me out! she panics to herself. *He's going to kill me!*

"You know, when I first started out … I used to want to lock myself up, too," he starts. "Cut out this part of the business."

She looks at him oddly, surprised at how calmly he is speaking to her—not yelling commands or instructions, just candidly talking. He has a soothing charisma about him.

Started out? Started out what—being a teleprompter operator? She laughs to herself. He's in his mid-twenties and rather slim. A bit of a rugged cowboy look.

"My knees used to knock so much, I couldn't feel the beat of the music …"

Riley still stares at him, not trusting the man with ripped jeans and suede shoes. He's wearing a soft brown T-shirt that happens to show nice, muscled arms. His floppy smile and light brown hair …

She abruptly turns her focus away from scanning his body and looks back to the intruder's face.

"But if you think about those people out there being your friends—people who want to hear what you have to say, who like what you do—then it's not such a tough crowd, after all."

Riley takes in the food for thought, suddenly aware that her call time to the talk show stage is ticking.

"You must have friends, right? Unless you only spend your time in bathroom stalls …"

"I'm sorry; who are you?" she asks flatly, still surprised by the invasion of privacy.

He laughs heartily. "Name's Anthony Daniels," he says, too far away to offer up a handshake—and Riley is so antsy, he's scared it might be met with a slap in the face and kick in the crotch.

She stares at him, and it clicks. "Oh, the country singer! Wow, that's funny. I listen to your music. This is really great ..." she trails off, embarrassed and aware that he's become the negotiator sent in by the SWAT team, talking her down from the edge.

"It's okay. Hey, I think you're up, and besides ... I need some time alone here."

"You want to throw up, too?" She laughs, inching her way to the door, their bodies moving opposite each other, never close enough to touch. Like enemies about to sword fight.

"Nope." He smiles, walking to the urinals against the back wall and unzipping his jeans.

"Oh, dear God!" she shouts, bolting out the door. She looks over her shoulder, and there is a caricature of a man affixed to the door. In her panicked fury, she missed the ladies' restroom by a few feet.

Riley bursts into the greenroom and stands in front of Duncan, who is seated on a soft leather couch.

He stares at her, surprised she's come out from the panic room.

"What'd he say to you?" He laughs, crossing his big legs and looking up at her with wonder.

She shrugs and follows a stagehand out to the studio.

• • •

Riley wanders back to the greenroom after her interview, and Duncan is actually ecstatic by her debut live, on-air appearance.

"You were actually ... kinda charming," he says to her teasingly.

She puts a hand on his arm and lets herself have a serious moment of emotion. "Duncan, thank you for being here." She smiles.

"Well, it was the only way I could make sure you got up there. It's about time people finally met you in some capacity."

"I know. It's so weird, though. I don't want to be a character ... like Jenna." She sighs.

"Well, I must say, you handled yourself well with the questions about Hunter and Jenna," he admits, putting on his beige deerskin jacket.

Threatening to get up and leave midway through a live program sure helps ... She grimaces.

Riley grabs her purse, and they head into the hallway.

"You have to keep yourself calm. When you start operating in such a ... tense ... manner, it's dangerous. People know they've hit a nerve. Sometimes they'll dig deeper there. That's why I do yoga, to keep myself grounded and mentally detach."

"Yoga gives me headaches," Riley whines.

Duncan rolls his eyes as they walk to the parking garage.

"Do something else, then! Something that helps keep you from spinning out of control. To keep your energy centred, get control over your mind and clear yourself."

They spot Anthony approaching, wearing a dusty brown leather jacket.

"Hey!" Riley calls out to him, not so much in greeting, but more an attempt to get his attention by yelling.

"Hey, great job out there. You were actually ..."

"Charming?" Duncan coughs.

He smiles and introduces himself to her agent.

"I've got to say that I'm not really into the whole country music thing. It's a bit woo-woo for me. But I quite like your style," Duncan says.

"Yeah, it's almost more ... adult contemporary." Anthony shrugs self-deprecatingly.

But, man, can you hold a guitar and look good, Riley thinks, staring at his arms.

"Um, do you want to come get food?" Riley asks him, not polished at inviting someone to join her in a social engagement.

Anthony's eyes sparkle as he looks at her, and he seems a little surprised.

"Because, I was thinking, food could be eaten."

"That's a good thought. Yeah, sure, I'd love to. Let me make sure that my guitar is heading back to the hotel. Give me a minute?"

Riley nods, and he hustles down the hallway.

"Darling, I must now bid you farewell." Duncan announces mischievously.

"What? No! We're going to get food ..." Riley gasps, panicked, having expected it to be a party of three for the evening.

"No, no. *You two* are going to get food. I'm going to go meet my crotchety friend Mr. Bassel for fine dining that he will surely treat me to. But good job asking him out—he seems like a keeper," he says, a devilish grin spreading across his face.

"Oh, my God, what am I going to do?" she gasps, grabbing his arm violently.

Duncan shakes her off easily. "You are going to try something different and ... go with the flow," he says, coolly walking towards the exit. "Hot accent, huh?"

"Shit. Fuck. Shit," she hisses to herself, glancing around like a fugitive ready to make a break for daylight.

She contemplates making a total run for it but spots Anthony walking back down the hall.

"Hey, where's Duncan?" he asks, striding up casually.

"Oh, he ... left," Riley replies, hoping that Anthony's disappointment is enough to pull apart their plans.

"Okay, cool. Well, what do you feel like eating?" He smiles.

No dice. He's definitely interested in hanging out with her.

Riley shrugs, pushing back her cuticles.

Oh, deeear, he makes me nervous, she thinks, catching herself staring at him. His laid-back air is petrifying, but in an exhilarating way.

"Well, since you're being a pansy, I'll decide this time." He grins, leading the way.

Riley scampers after him, excited to see where he's going to entertain in such a dynamic city.

• • •

"Could you pass the pizza box?" Anthony asks, sprawled out on the floor of his hotel room.

Riley is laying facedown on their makeshift picnic blanket (the comforter), having overeaten to the point of near gastric rupture.

"You're going to eat *more*?" she asks, bewildered.

"Can't let it go to waste ..." he says, a little shocked he's forcing himself to gorge on the Mediterranean pizza they've ordered in.

Riley slides the box across the bedspread, happy to get it far, far away from her.

"Do you do this with every girl? Get them bloated and ready to die?" she murmurs. She rolls over, trying to find a less excruciating position to ease her stomachache. The dark wood floor feels soothing.

"I've gotta say, this is the first time anyone's been interested in staying in and playing it low-pro." He smiles, and then quickly frowns as he realizes there are two big slices left in the box.

"Would the hotel be mad if I threw up on their floor?" she asks aloud.

He looks at her and shrugs comically.

"Seriously, every time I eat pizza … I get like crazy stomach reactions. Yet … I keep eating pizza …" she admits.

"Stomach reactions?"

"Yeah! Like crazy di-ho. And it's even if I have one slice. Or lattes. Why the fuck am I telling you this?"

Anthony winces at the thought of fiery diarrhea.

"Sorry." She blushes.

"Are you lactose intolerant?" he asks bluntly.

Riley looks at him in shock, as if he's asked her whether she votes Democrat or Republican.

"I went through a phase where I was lactose intolerant, and I had to take supplements and drink soy milk and all this stuff … and that's kinda how I ended up deciding to go vegetarian."

Riley is horrified.

"Okay, try this. For a week, put soy milk in your coffee instead, and see if that helps," he suggests.

"Soy milk? Are you insane? It tastes like paper." Riley gasps. "And besides, I got used to drinking it black."

Anthony exhales dramatically at her argumentative side.

"Okay, okay. I'll try soy milk or whatever …" Riley grumbles.

"It's not weird, you know," Anthony says. "Lots of people go veg, or even vegan. I started seeing a naturopath—it's not a quack thing. I haven't had a meat lover's pizza in two years. And that—that was almost like giving up sex!"

Riley laughs, spitting pop out of her mouth.

He looks at her for some sort of explanation.

"I gave up sex for a year!" she shouts.

"Really?" He laughs, poking the cardboard box between them.

"Uh-huh! Well, almost a year. You want to talk about iron will …"

"Why on Earth would you do something like that?" he groans.

"Because I had to. Just had to not be … with … anyone. I'm pretty tough, you know." She smiles. "I needed to focus on other stuff. Not be defined by another person."

"That's mildly stupid. Why would you rob yourself any semblance of pleasure like that? To prove a point to yourself?" He laughs.

Riley rolls her eyes.

"So, are you still on strike?" He grins.

"Eat your damn pizza." She taunts, pushing the box further away.

She watches Anthony ferociously stuff the last parts of their supper into his mouth and laughs at their unglamorous evening.

He leans down to the floor, both of them side by side on their backs, looking out the floor to ceiling windows with a view of the city.

"Don't worry, I'm not going to kiss you," he says defiantly.

Riley looks at him oddly.

"I know you wanna make out and everything. But I'm not going to. I'm just putting it out there so you don't feel, like, nervous around my masculinity." He laughs. "I don't want you to break your strike or anything."

"I don't want you to want to make out with me," Riley jokes back.

"Good. It's settled then." He smiles.

They both continue to lie on the ground, disgusted by themselves and their caloric intake.

Anthony's hand snakes out and reaches for hers.

Riley laces her fingers between his, and they smile silently, having found a friend who likes pizza just as much.

"Let's stay here for a little …" Riley suggests softly. And the two of them stare at the lights outside, smiling to themselves, off in their own daydreams.

head in the sand.

[Miami's South Beach, USA—October 2011]

Jenna stares up at the night sky, sitting on the cool sand and listening to the ocean roar in front of her. She closes her eyes and remembers the vacation last Christmas in the Caribbean. Walking on the beach with her two friends, talking and holding on to each other like when they were kids. That level of happiness and innocent intimacy feels ages away now.

"Jen, they're waiting for you," bellows Carter, leaning over the rail of a white wood deck that surrounds the exterior of the beachfront nightclub. The loud party behind him roars back into her ears like a charging train. The luxurious VIP crowd assembled inside is joining her, Hana, and Carter on a pretentious invitation-only basis while they hang out in Miami for the weekend.

Carter stumbles down the steps and flops over beside her, laughing hysterically. He sprays sand all over her colourful Ella Moss dress, and rolls around like a pig in shit. His hands search for the joint that's fallen out of his mouth.

"Fuck!" he curses, skimming around in the sand. He finds it and sticks it back in, lighting up.

"I have to go back already?" she whines, not wanting to leave the quieter space of the beach to rejoin the hectic party. To drink and dance and get high for yet another night, in a crowd that is full of ever-changing faces. People she will never see again as she moves on to the next city, the next concert, the next party.

"Well, it's *your* party. People are here to see you and me," he scoffs.

Why do I have to have so many parties ... every night? Maybe Hana is wrong about this, she thinks to herself, wanting to go back to doing interviews with magazines and newspapers instead of being a tabloid fixture known for going out to dinner and dominating the late-night club circuit.

Carter shimmies closer and sloppily tries to reach a hand up her dress.

"Yo!" she snaps, not impressed by him intruding in on her moment of solitude—let alone wanting to go at it on the beach, like, ten feet from a rager.

"What's the matter with you? You're such a fucking bore ..." he moans, already stripped down to his wifebeater from the scorching heat inside the club.

Jenna recoils, feeling defensive about justifying her desires to sleep and rest and eat healthfully. All he and Hana do is consume like gluttonous vampires—sleeping during the day and prowling by night.

"You always make me go on top. You don't want to share drugs with us anymore. It's like you're Riley or something. Some sort of ..." he starts.

Jenna tunes out his rampage, not wanting to hear him talking about her friend—the friend who she hasn't spoken with in months, who probably is beyond angry.

"Shit, man. It's like since your bitch of a mother died, you're all *'ooh, I'm hurt and sad because she was a single mother.' Please*. She wasn't there for you," Carter wails.

Jenna digs her toes into the soft surface of the sand, burying her bright pedicure.

Carter is still complaining about something as she decides to go back into the snobby club. Anything to avoid having to hear him go on about how much she sucks.

"You're right ... she wasn't there for me then ..." Jenna says, getting up and grabbing her high heels. "But someone else was."

Carter stares after her, not sure what she's talking about, and decides to lie flat on his back, staring up at the night sky.

Jenna walks up the deck, thinking about Parker, and how much she'd rather be sitting in a studio, eating takeout food with him and drumming up new ideas.

People outside of the club are smoking and watching her intensely, enviously taking in every detail of the pop goddess. She can feel their eyes zapping her energy, making her feel weaker and more vulnerable. She slips on her stilettos and darts inside to the thumping music.

"Hey, where have you been?" Hana snaps, hovering around their private booth like a vulture. She and Carter have already downed the first bottle of the night with their entourage.

"Yeah, Carter found me ..." Jenna trails off, sizing up the people staring at her. These strangers have a universal desire to see if she's as tall as she looks, as pretty as in the pictures, as charming as claimed. And mostly to speculate if she's had any plastic surgery, or how much makeup she actually uses to get her fresh-faced look.

"Well, introduce your new single and get this party going," Hana says dryly, as if commanding a circus animal to jump through a hoop. "These people aren't paying good money to be here without a celebrity, so go, go, go!"

Jenna stares at her manager crossly and heads to the DJ booth.

"Where's Carter?" Hana shouts after her.

Jenna points towards the ocean, not turning to look back.

Walk like a linebacker, she tells herself, trying to hold her head high and throw her shoulders back to fake the confidence she lacks.

Complete strangers start flocking at her and asking for pictures. Jenna simply goes through the motions, smiling and chattering empty conversation. She flirts with the idea of sneaking out of the party early. To try recuperating some of the sleep she's lost since the New Year. Actually, since she started this intense journey last year.

The DJ hands her a microphone, and she regurgitates a scripted introduction of the new single. Her voice cracks, and she feels so tired that she can barely keep the words in order.

As the new song begins playing, the white wood floor pulses with the New Age dance beats.

In a rare moment of relative sobriety, she listens to the song and can't help but feel distressed by how strange it sounds. How foreign her voice is.

People actually like this? I really let this happen? she thinks to herself, watching the wild partygoers around her dancing (probably thanks to serious drug assistance).

This is not me. I'm not this. This sounds like chaos.

"Jenna, it would be my honour to have you join me for a drink," a man whispers in her ear, having stealthily stalked up behind her.

She's stirred out of her thoughts and turns around to find a tall, dark, handsome man hovering over her.

"Reza," he introduces himself, extending his hand to her.

"Jenna," she replies, smiling shyly, having been startled by his approach.

She glances at his decorative scarf, and then at his Gucci loafers with a bamboo-stick buckle.

"Oh, do you like my shoes?" He says with a faint Persian accent, laughing, following her gaze. His black hair is messily styled; a slight beard shows on his chiseled face.

Jenna blushes, having been caught staring.

"I couldn't decide between these Gucci shoes or these other white Gucci shoes with a metal buckle—you know which ones? So I bought them both …" he says breezily, flaunting his wealth.

"Of course you did," she mutters, and then smiles when she realizes this would be a Riley comment.

He doesn't hear her, and continues to smile flirtatiously, his tight clothing showing off his gym-sculpted, steroid-filled muscles and highlighting his perma-tan.

"So, would you like to join me?" he asks again, motioning to his booth full of beautiful men and women.

"Um … I have to find my manager …" Jenna says, looking around for Hana.

"All right, well, please come by." He smiles, kissing her hand and walking back to his posse.

Jenna begins to maneuver her way through the crowd, a little claustrophobic and teetering in her platform heels. The ogling is draining her weak energy stores, depleting her patience and giving her the impulse to yell and tell everyone to mind their own business.

"Jenna!" she hears someone shout behind her. But she ignores it and keeps pushing on. She gets to the veranda and grips the wood frame for support. She has barely eaten all day, and she feels dizzy. Hollow.

The ocean is patiently lapping up on the beach, the waves flowing no matter what is happening on the shore above. The comforting rhythm of the water calms her down.

Jenna breathes in the salty air and focuses her gaze on the shoreline. She has to blink her eyes a few times to make sure the picture that is registering in her mind is, in fact, real.

Hana and Carter are tangled in each other off to the side of the beach, unaware of their spectator.

"What the …" she whispers to herself, totally confused by the passionate exchange she's witnessing.

"Dude—there's two people boning on the beach." Someone near her laughs, as a small group of people crowd the balcony to catch a glimpse and take pictures on their cell phones.

Jenna backs into the crowd, fleeing the scene. Like a zombie, she floats back through the party, the music and happiness swirling around her. Almost to spite her.

Someone steps into her path, and she slowly looks up and sees Reza's face as he holds her by the biceps.

"I'm glad you came back." He smiles, his teeth glowing eerily.

Jenna is confused, having forgotten who the stranger is in front of her. She looks around and realizes she's in front of the table full of pretty people.

"Would you like a drink?" he asks.

Jenna nods, and a glass is placed in front of her. She looks at the mixed drink disinterestedly.

"Let's get some shots," she says, grabbing a tequila bottle off Reza's table and lining up a dozen shot glasses.

His friends start cheering excitedly, jumping up on the couches and taking pictures of their celebrity bartender.

Jenna hands out the shots, and the group toasts to her. They all start dancing and grinding on the banquettes together as she discreetly refills her shot glass. Reza leans into talk to someone, and Jenna refills a third time as the people around her take in the techno music pulsing through the room.

"Hey, let's do another one." One of the girls laughs, leaning down from dancing on the table, her boobs practically falling out of her skimpy top.

Jenna refills their glasses, and they throw back the tequila—straight and with no chasers. Nothing to dull the bitter reminder that she's got a green light to bad decisions.

Another girl pulls out a tiny bag of cocaine and signals to Jenna.

"Do you want the first?" she asks in a thick accent.

"Huh? What?" she replies, not having really understood. "Oh, no—I'm good."

The girl offers it to her again.

"Oh, no, I already had," Jenna lies, not wanting to participate in another night of uncontrollable mayhem. She fumbles for a cigarette to keep herself occupied while the rest of the group starts to lose control.

The girl nods, assuming that the star has already had her fix of the evening, and discreetly leads her friends to the bathroom.

Reza sidles up beside her, happy to see his friends enjoying the famous guest he's brought them. He's the alpha male in this circle, the provider and centre of attention.

"Do you want to sit down?" he offers.

"No. I want to get out of here," she blurts out honestly, feeling the buzz of the shots hit her like a baseball bat upside the head.

Reza seems a little taken aback and smiles darkly. He then takes his trophy by the hand and leads her towards the door, signaling that he's won her for the night.

He has his car brought up by the valet, and they get into his bright blue Lamborghini convertible. The music is still ringing in Jenna's ears, and her head pounds even more as he punches it and they take off.

"Where do you want to go?" Reza asks, looking over at her from his plush leather seat. His black hair and eyes make him seem dangerous. Dark and mysterious like a rebel ready to destroy anything in his path.

She leans her head back passively, relieved to be away from the crowd. Disappearing into anonymity at the speed of light.

A car honks angrily as Reza guns his sports car into oncoming traffic and weaves through the cars.

Oh ... I'm sure he's coked up like the rest of those airheads. Jenna grimaces to herself nervously. She has a little fantasy of the car driving off a bridge and into the cool ocean water, another way to disappear. But she continues to stare away aimlessly, passive.

"Do you want to go for a tan?" He winks at her slyly, shifting the car's gearbox aggressively. His light-wash jeans fit tightly on his muscular thighs.

Jenna looks at him, confused.

"I own salons ... we can have a drink at one of my places," he says, recklessly driving through the streets well above the speed limit.

Jenna nods, happy to be anywhere besides her own life. Away from the empty hotel room. Nowhere near her ever-present entourage.

The night air gives her goose bumps as she flashes back to the discovery she's made at the beach.

It doesn't matter whether I'm happy or sad, dead or alive ... the ocean will keep moving regardless of what's going on around it. I have to keep going, regardless of what's going on around me ... she thinks, tipsy from the booze. *Even if that means Hana and Carter.*

The sports car sweeps into a curbside parking spot, and Jenna looks out at the fancy storefront of one of Reza's salons, the trendy place where everybody who's anybody is getting primped and pampered in Miami. Where she's been invited to spa for free every time she's been in town—in exchange for some publicity shots.

"I didn't know you owned these ..." she trails off.

He gets out and opens the door of the high-tech car for her, leading her to the front door. They walk inside the dark salon and spa, Reza taking her by the hand.

At the back of the oasis, past the hallways and dozens of treatment rooms, there is a big glass wall with water trickling down it like a modern waterfall. A bar is in front of it, but it's for manicuring, even though it looks right out of the SoBe nightclub. He seats her at the "bar" and disappears for a minute. He reappears with a bottle of Grey Goose.

"Sometimes the stars prefer to have their fresh, organic orange juice spiked," he admits, laughing.

Reza pours them drinks and takes a seat across from her so that he can stare at her directly. He soaks her in hungrily.

"So, you own salons ..." Jenna tries to start a conversation, looking around at the different levels of the labyrinth.

"Yes. Salons. It turns out that every American woman likes to be touched and worshipped." He howls mischievously, still surprised by the vast success of his enterprise.

Jenna awkwardly sips her very strong drink and almost gags.

"But I guess everyone wants to look good ..." he concedes, staring down at his shoes, admiring them again. He leans into her, gently putting a hand on her cheek. His cologne is overwhelming.

"How about that tan ..." he whispers, stroking her freckled face.

He gets up and takes her by the hand, leading her to a stand-up tanning booth. He starts to kiss her, pinning her outside the metal door, and Jenna takes off his shirt like an automaton. Hot physical interaction equals sex in her mind, she's mentally tuned out every time Carter has made his moves on her.

They strip down to their underwear and stumble into the booth. The bright lights flare up as they grope at each other.

Jenna's mind slips from shock and sadness to full-on excitement as the hulky playboy devours her.

"You feel good, Jenny," he murmurs in her ear, rubbing his hand down her thigh and confusing her name in their heated stupor.

Jenna slams him up against one of the walls, kissing her way down his chest, happy to be torturing someone.

You won't forget my name when I'm done with you, idiot. She laughs to herself, feeling competitive about manipulating him with oral sex. The heat of the UV lights makes things feel so much more intense and primal.

Reza moans excitedly, as her fingers creep to his white briefs.

Suddenly, the light of the tanning both blinks off, and she stops, shocked by the sudden wave of cool air circulating through.

Reza jumps out to plug in another 15 minutes, wanting to get her to keep going. He quickly rushes back in and begins kissing and grabbing her aggressively to reactivate the mood.

Their skin feels hot to touch, the little space around them full of body heat and impulsiveness.

Ugh, I guess I do *have to go down on him now,* Jenna thinks to herself, having lost her momentum. She feels him work his way down her body, taking charge. *Equality and reciprocation.*

She squirms with delight against the bright walls.

The time on their booth session expires again as Jenna feels herself about to scream.

Reza grabs her in his arms, bumping into walls and tables along the way, knocking over bottles and supplies.

They storm into one of the tranquil facial rooms, and he sets her down on an aesthetician's table, climbing on top of her, biting at her neck hungrily.

"Condom …" she whispers.

"Are you serious?" he gasps.

"Don't be a jackass," she warns, not wanting to catch a baby from the slick stranger, let alone something icky.

He trudges off to grab a sleeve and returns, deflated.

"Don't be such a pansy," Jenna says, throwing him down on the table and getting on top of him.

Reza smiles at her annoyance and the fact that now he can tell people the famous Jenna Ramsay has been at his spa.

• • •

Jenna's eyes dart open as she hears voices. The room looks quite different from a hotel. There's harp music playing and murals of an enchanted forest on the walls. She can't remember why she's here.

"The boss's car is out front …" echoes a woman's voice, a voice that's too close for comfort.

Jenna looks down at the man spooning her on the table and cringes. She's not getting a facial in the nude, and his hairy body smells like a mix of cologne and sweat. She hops off and throws on one of the spa's plush robes, her body hurting and stinging.

Her bra and lacy underwear are on the floor, and she slips them on, searching for her dress.

Jenna opens the door a crack and can hear the spa starting to fill with clients.

She spots a pile of clothes on the floor near a group of tanning beds and quickly gets into her dress. She throws Reza's clothes into the facial room, quietly shutting the door and grabbing her purse.

What do I dooo ...? She panics, anxiously glancing around the decorated oasis. She feels helpless and alone, wanting to extract herself from the pending humiliation.

She rummages for her cell phone, which she stashed in a small clutch.

"Hana? Hi. Yeah, I … need help," Jenna whispers, still secretly upset by what she saw the night before but desperate to have someone clean up her mess.

"A driver can be here in ten minutes? Perfect," she sighs, catching a glimpse of herself in the mirror and nearly screaming.

Her fair skin is so badly burned from the tanning booth, it looks like she's been lashed and tortured.

"*Shiiit ...*" she whispers, looking at the marks on her body and the redness of her skin. Thirty minutes in concentrated sunlight has wreaked havoc on her pale, freckled body—sunspots flared all over. Bite marks dot her, three hickeys sore and embarrassingly visible.

Voices start to float closer and closer, and Jenna panics. The manicure bar still has their drinks, evidence of the late-night romp.

Thank God no one knows I'm here ... she thinks, hoping to pull off a fast exit and seek refuge at the hotel.

She slips into the tanning booth and excruciatingly waits out the ten minutes, horrified that she looks like a sundried tomato.

Jenna takes a deep breath and steps out. A small group of aestheticians and their clients stare at her with jaws dropped. She steps forward and commences the weirdest walk of shame she's ever had to do.

There are whispers all around her, wondering why she's so badly burned, if she was here all night with the boss, where her gorgeous dress is from.

As she nears the front window of the spa, she spots the driver waiting curbside for her and bravely makes her exit.

As she steps out, photographers rush forward and start snapping pictures of her, heckling and shouting. She dives into the car and collapses into a heap of sobs behind the tinted glass, humiliated that they somehow knew where she was.

clear for takeoff.

[San Francisco International Airport, USA—November 2011]

Riley is flipping through magazines at the duty-free shop, waiting to board her flight to London. She's meeting Anthony for a stop on his club tour and is beyond excited to see him again.

I'm not making out with you, she thinks, remembering his voice from their first meeting, laughing softly as she leafs through the latest *National Geographic* magazine.

She glances at Anthony on the cover of *Blender* and blushes. She grabs a copy of it and adds it to her pile. As she heads to the checkout, she spots all the gossip magazines by the cash register with Jenna on the cover yet again.

Riley grabs one and flips through it casually, fixing the glasses she's wearing for the long trip. She's in comfy sweats and trying to mentally prepare herself to sit in an airplane with dry air circulation.

The magazine story is titled "I split up Jenna and Carter," and has a picture of a handsome man in a very trendy suit. The article is about a spa owner from Florida who is auctioning off a used condom allegedly shared with Jenna and claiming to have come between her and Carter Sampson after a wild night of partying.

"For crying out loud …" Riley whispers to herself as she skims through his account of their night together. "Tanning bed? Aesthetician's table?"

She flips the page and finds a humiliating picture of Jenna, burned and trying to hide out by the pool at the Shore Club.

"Miss, would you like to add that?" asks the cashier, scanning her reading materials and cashews.

Riley looks up, feeling the wind knocked out of her, and shakes her head.

"No. No, thank you," she sighs, putting the magazine back in the display and grabbing a pack of gum instead. She has been trying to boycott the temptation, not allowing her money fuelling the machine that has been destroying her friend. She pulls some scrunched-up bills from her wallet to pay for her purchase.

"That's the number one thing everyone goes for …" The cashier admits, motioning to the gossip magazines. "The guilty pleasure.

It's almost as if those Hollywood types screw up solely for our amusement."

Riley forces a smile, still astounded by the exposé on Jenna. It's not about shopping trips and secret dates anymore. The content has become fierce and predatory; she's surprised Hana allows it to happen.

What kind of person writes that ... let alone shares that? she sighs to herself, taking her purchases and reeling from the scandals Jenna finds herself in every week. Whether it's falling down drunk or ostentatious shopping trips, confessions from her drug dealer or Carter talking about his sex life, Jenna Ramsay's innermost details have become a lucrative and sensationalistic enterprise.

"Do you want the new issue? It's got a confession from the guy who Jenna Ramsay lost her virginity to!" whispers the girl behind the counter, pointing to a box of magazines that haven't been put out yet.

Riley stares at her blankly.

"Apparently, she really sucked. I totally read the article as soon as shipment came in today," she confesses to the stunned customer. "She laid there like a dead fish."

Riley shakes her head, dumbfounded.

"Give it."

The checkout girl scans the magazine.

I can't imagine someone writing about my first time having sex, Riley thinks, remembering the awkward first time Matthew stayed at her apartment.

She grabs her purchases and finds a seat in the waiting area.

"Ha! I knew it!' she shouts, staring down at a confession from a random guy named Bart.

She pulls out her cell phone and calls Elle, not even bothering to say "hello." "Who did Jenna lose her virginity to?" she polls her friend, while waiting for her boarding call.

"Damian Hartford in senior year of high school, at his cottage when she was supposed to be staying at my house," Elle replies without missing a beat.

"Ding-ding-ding-ding-ding!" Riley replies, whipping the magazine into a trash basket.

"Why ...?"

"Because some magazine wrote this story about how she lost it to some jackass named Bart, and he goes on and on and on about how she *sucked*—like, can you believe that?"

"Bart Burns? The guy from grade eleven ancient civ. class?" Elle gasps, remembering her classmate.

"Actually, yeah, I think so …" Riley thinks, pulling the magazine out of the garbage to check the name of the claimant. She shudders when she realizes she's just picked through waste and tosses it back.

"They never did *it* …" Elle says.

"No way! She wouldn't touch him with a ten-foot pole. Right?" Riley asks. "She would've told us if she did … He was such a meathead idiot."

"Right!" Elle affirms.

"I can't believe that people have an interest in profiting from this kind of stuff. It's so wrong." Riley says, wondering if there's a chance her childhood friend neglected to share a detail, but finds it doubtful.

"Well, you saw how addictive it is for people to take pictures of her. It only makes sense that as she got more high-profile, the fascination would increase. And now that she's embraced her inner bitch, people aren't going to like her as much as the original Jenna. We know the truth, that's ultimately the only thing she can count on," Elle adds before they end the call.

Riley shudders at the realization that Jenna has hit the point of no return. That she has ceased to exist as a private citizen by letting herself be super saturated with gossip. She pops open a bag of almonds and crunches angrily, thinking about Jenna's career, already well into its tailspin phase. Just as predicted by Mack. She starts to sweat anxiously and has to unzip her North Face fleece sweater, shoving it into her large tote.

"Ladies and gentlemen, we will now board Virgin Atlantic flight number twenty to London Heathrow. First-class and passengers needing assistance only at this time …" starts the airline employee over the PA.

Riley steps forward with her boarding pass and passport.

• • •

The concert hall lights dim as the last few chords are strummed on the guitar. Riley stares in amazement at the dedicated crowd clapping as Anthony finishes his encore. He's dressed so casually, his informal style helping to create a comfortable atmosphere during his gig. The mellow music gets everyone in the mood to unwind and take it easy— the simplicity of a man and his guitar, no fuss.

She claps her hands together, her breath caught in her throat with so much pride and excitement that she can't even scream.

"I didn't know British people liked country music ..." she comments to a man standing beside her.

"We didn't know a South African could play country music like *that* ..." He laughs, still clapping for Anthony's performance. His wife hugs him, lovingly swayed by the last song.

Riley heads backstage and spots Anthony surrounded by fans and supporters.

His face lights up as she approaches, weaving through the spectators in her jeans and purple T-shirt. Her leather boots drag shyly, she's hesitant to intrude.

"So, if you're interested, my friend owns the hottest nightclub right now; we can get you set up in a booth and everything ..." a guy is pitching him as she approaches.

Anthony cuts him off, thanking him for the invitation, and pulls himself away from the crowd.

"Ready?" he asks, throwing a leather jacket over a recently changed black T-shirt. His jeans are a slim fit and worn with canvas sneakers.

"You don't have anything to do here?" Riley smiles nervously.

"Nah. I did all the interviews before the show. I'm ready to eat. The lighting guy told me about this small, organic restaurant not too far ... what do you think?"

Riley nods, happy to be feeding her grumbling stomach again.

The couple gets into a chauffeured car, which snakes its way through the crowded city's night traffic. They spend the entire car ride catching up, not having seen each other since Anthony's quick visit to San Francisco a few weeks back, before embarking on this small European tour.

"And Elle's pregnancy is going well. No serious complaints, only that Ben is travelling a lot. And I saw another crazy magazine cover about Jenna ..."

"Oh, man. That poor girl is getting devoured," he sighs, still astounded by some of the drama he sees in the entertainment industry. Anything to sell a story. He runs a hand through his light brown hair.

"I've got to say, I'm so inspired by how you keep yourself clear of it." Riley admits, impressed to be sitting alone with him in a car, going to a quiet meal, and not surrounded by total strangers drunkenly fawning over him.

"Yeah. You get over it at some point or another. Any time I'd go back to Jo'burg ... none of that glamour stuff mattered to my family. So it was a good reality check." He laughs.

Riley smiles, thinking about how indifferent her father and brother are to such novelties. Only Kevin was slightly impressed by their first shopping trip at Armani. But even then, he was upset it wasn't with Marc Jacobs himself (that came later).

"You know, I'm thinking about going back to visit soon ..." he starts to tell her.

Riley stares out the window.

"And I was thinking, maybe you could come with me ..."

"To ... South Africa ...?" she clarifies awkwardly.

Anthony nods, finding her surprise adorable.

"To South Africa where your family is?"

He nods again.

The car stops in front of the busy restaurant, and music drifts out into the street. Soft lights make the small place feel warm and inviting, but the buzzing crowd inside gives away the high demand.

"Okay!" she blurts out, a little surprised by her eager agreement.

Anthony smiles at her unrestrained transparency.

"I mean ... *ooo ... kay* ..." she says, trying to tone down her impulse response.

"Good," he winks, sliding out of the car and helping her onto the sidewalk.

"Great," she affirms, leading the way into the restaurant.

They're seated at a table in the middle of the busy late-night spot. The crowd is devouring everything from lush salads to couscous.

"You know, I made spelt pizza the other night ..." Riley informs him, quite proudly. "I got the recipe from the nutritionist that told me to try almond milk instead of soy."

"And how was it?" he asks, deciding on a burrito as they scan the menu.

"Not bad, but I need to practice it a little bit. I mean, it's no Pizza Orgasmica, but ..." she starts murmuring.

She carefully reviews the restaurant's offerings, having grown into a finicky eater since embracing a healthy lifestyle and newly diagnosed food sensitivities.

Their waiter dashes off with their order, leaving Anthony to reach across the table and grab her hand.

"You know what might be fun? If one day you came to Toronto with me ..." Riley says softly, avoiding eye contact and burning a hole into the table instead.

"What on Earth is there to do there?" he jokes sarcastically. "I've been to New York."

She feigns offence.

"I would quite like to meet your dad, though. Sounds like a pretty ... tall human being." He laughs.

"Tall is right. You know, he and Kevin are actually one of the most perfect couples I've ever known. I mean ... they just ... balance each other—but they're not too opposite. Like, Dad's definitely the more serious one. But Kevin gets that, and he can be pretty over-the-top, but not in a way that's too obnoxious ... why am I talking so much about this?" Riley blushes.

"No, no—it's good. I like to know about you," he says. "You don't normally talk much, do you? About personal stuff."

"Not about this. The gay dad thing or the scary, creative writer thing. Especially not about the train wreck celebrity friend thing ..."

"Have people offered you money for a story yet?" he asks.

"Yeah ... it's so weird. I mean, maybe if you needed the cash someone might do it ... or if you hate the person ... or if you want to feel famous for a split second. Like the fake virginity-taker guy or the douchey spa guy. But ... it's so weird. I spent so long trying to protect her from that sort of stuff, and now she's the empress of smut. She's just so different ..."

"Well, I heard her new song yesterday ... I can't believe how different she *sounds*," he admits, lowering his voice.

"The new album is shit. And probably because she had no part in it. It's not her. You don't even know her, and you can tell. Imagine what her fans are thinking! She's sold out to make something easy. For shit's sake—the songs are, like, acid-trip vibe exploratory pieces of crap!" Riley gasps, frustrated.

"But you said it's that manager chick who's the problem, right? She probably set up all the producers and collaborators for what she thinks Jenna should be like."

"Hana? Well, yeah. But ... don't you think someone has agency to decide whether to keep that influence around or not? She began to mesmerize Jenna ... and Carter's always keeping one foot in the door with her."

The waiter quickly leaves their dishes, scurrying to another table to try and manage his packed section.

"And she still won't talk to you?"

"Anth, I don't even think she *knows* how much we've tried getting in touch with her. Not with the meddler …"

Anthony dribbles beans out of his mouth, laughing.

"What?" she asks, tasting her quinoa.

"That sounds like a comic book villain. The Meddler!" he says, mocking heroic power with a fist pump.

"I'm saying that … I can see how she could get enveloped in a little Jenna bubble. But doesn't she have the power to change things around her if she really wants it? Maybe she doesn't want change."

"Yes, but speaking as a member of this particular industry, I can also understand what it's like having your head in a fog, like you're wrapped up in your own little universe. Especially if she's got people around her to reinforce it, how would she know any better? It *becomes* her reality. And if she doesn't know there's light up above … she's not going to look for it. She's going to keep walking through the mist, being led by the blind. Or rather … someone who knows that if her client gets to that light, then her lifestyle of choice is toast."

"I think that's really it. Maybe she's jealous and secretly wants to be her. What if she tries to kill her?"

Anthony laughs hysterically. "That's not funny," he says, stopping himself abruptly. "But why would she kill her? She needs her to get into all the parties." He tries to calm himself down from the mental picture of a bratty party girl like Hana Rin trying to commit a crime without breaking a nail.

Riley chews carefully, thinking about something else, ignoring the silly man-child across the table. "You know, this would've been perfect with some garlic, …" she announces, taking another forkful. "Needs a little bit more zip-bang."

Anthony smiles, raising an eyebrow. "Riley … you sound like some sort of food critic!"

She looks a little offended.

"No, no! It's a good thing. Have you thought about writing about food before?" he asks, putting a hand gently on hers.

Riley thinks about his idea for a moment.

"You know about wine. And now you know about vegetarian and vegan food, and you have travelled quite a bit. Maybe you could do, like, reviews or something …"

"But who would ever want to read what I have to say about … quinoa …" She laughs, poking her plate.

"Uh … the thousands of people who bought your book?"

Riley lets the information process in her head.

"Get a napkin and start writing what you think about this place … about the meal," Anthony suggests.

"I *have* been having a really hard time thinking of what I could do for another book, something different," she admits. "It doesn't *have* to be fiction."

"So, humour me … start jotting." He pushes a napkin at her.

Riley looks at him suspiciously but slips her favourite Montblanc out of her purse. She begins to scribble down some notes as Anthony talks about the flavours of his burrito.

"It's got a smoked … overtone …" he says carefully, thinking poetically.

Riley rolls her eyes at him and takes a bite of his sandwich, and then scribbles down some thoughts about it.

"You know what, Anth … you might just be onto something …" Riley smiles, looking down at her messy notes, starting to see what she could turn them into.

back off.

[Toronto, Canada—December 2011]

Eleanor looks down the aisle at Pusateri's Fine Foods, overwhelmed. Her grocery list is huge. Her mission to cook up a flawless Christmas dinner feels next to impossible right now. But with the help of the high-end gourmet grocery shop, she's ready to take on the challenge.

"Oh my gosh … how far along are you?" coos a woman who walks straight up to Elle and puts her hands on her pregnant stomach.

Elle recoils from the personal space invasion, uncomfortable with the attention she's getting with her rounded belly. She puts her hands on it protectively, Ben's ratty Stanford sweatshirt keeping her warm.

"When I had my first, the labour was almost thirty-six hours …" the woman shares, hoping to reminisce with the expectant mother.

Elle looks at her, horrified.

"You're having a girl. I can tell by your belly. That's so exciting. What are you naming her? I have a sixth sense for this stuff."

Elle yanks her cart away, mumbling something about having to pee. She scoots off in her Ugg boots and maternity jeans, frightened.

What a nosy idiot, hello – I'm carrying twins! Boys! Thirty-six hours? What the heck have I gotten myself into? she worries, staring down at her stomach, stopping in the cookie aisle to regroup. It's only been five months, but she's already finding it tough to move around in day-to-day life. Her ankles hurt, her back aches, and her entire body is changing at warp speed.

She heads to the meat section and picks up her specially ordered turkey. She's convinced it will unite her parents and in-laws in perfect, happy holiday cheer. Bonding over future grandchildren. As she's lifting it into the cart, her cell phone rings with a cheesy ring tone.

"Hi, *loveee*!" chirps her mother.

"Hi, Mom." Elle smiles, relieved, and takes pause in front of the deli counter. "How was Florida?"

"Sunny. What are you doing?"

"Picking up some food for the family dinner, but I can't help but feel I'm forgetting something …"

Odile Bryans hums on the line, thinking.

"I've got the stuffing, cranberry sauce, potatoes …"

"Darling, would you get me some marshmallows so I can make my yams?" Odile asks, realizing she has to get them ready for the get-together the following night.

"Of course. So, what are you up to?" Elle asks, pushing the cart forward to the candy section.

"Thought maybe we could meet for lunch ... you're where?"

"Pusateri's," Elle says, grabbing a bag of marshmallows and dropping them in her cart.

"How about I come meet you, and we can do a little shopping?"

"Okay, no problem. I want to see if I can find any cute maternity stuff. I don't want to look like such a blob," Elle says, wanting to browse the trendy boutiques in the upscale Yorkville neighborhood with Starbucks in hand and her mom at her side. Indulging in the casual, leisurely pace she can now take without a celebrity in tow. No need to schedule private shopping sessions after hours or to operate on red-alert if people came too close to them. An easy, breezy, girly afternoon sounds perfect.

"Fantastic! When is Ben back?" her mom asks.

Ben has been on a record number of business trips in the month of December alone, crisscrossing North America for almost two solid weeks of hockey games, press conferences, and endorsement negotiations—leaving Elle to kick around the house alone.

"Late tonight," she sighs, missing waking up next to her husband and having him rub her sore back.

"Oh, my! Well, maybe we can even have supper, too. Your dad is doing an emergency surgery and is leaving me all alone today ... We could rent an Olsen twins movie ..." Odile suggests sweetly.

Elle smiles to herself. The odd, childish traditions she and her mother share always comfort her. Watching movies intended for preteens with facial masks and buttery popcorn was always more attractive to her than any night of binge drinking and partying.

"We can buy some new polish, maybe do our nails!" Elle squeals happily. "But ... you might have to do my toes..."

They hang up, excited to hang out together. Elle's just happy to have someone around.

• • •

"I think Ben is going to faint when he sees the bill ..." Elle smiles mischievously as she steps into her house. Her mother helps her carry in all the shopping bags.

Elle secretly feels good about racking up the credit card bill, curious if he'll try reprimanding her for acting out. Reprimand her from across the country while away on business? What's he gonna do about it?

Elle has grown comfortable in this house, now able to find light switches in the dark with ease. Her shiny new BMW station wagon, on the other hand, still smells too clean. Above all else, she is still uneasy with being alone so much. She envisioned waking up as a couple and sharing the morning paper together every day, not her having to drag the garbage out by herself while Ben's holed up in hotel rooms on business trips.

"Well, sharing financial information confidently is a make-or-break in any marriage ..." Odile advises. She puts the bags on the living room couch and starts pulling out some of their purchases for inspection. Even for a casual shopping day, she's in tailored pants and kitten-heeled boots.

"I loved that dress on you," Elle tells her mother, who is holding a deep purple cocktail dress up to her tiny frame.

"I hope I get to wear it soon ..." she sighs, folding it neatly and placing it back in the tissue paper. Her daughter steps into the kitchen to store her groceries and make them some tea.

"Well, I'm sure to some holiday party ... New Year's, even?" Elle's voice trails from the industrial, Rhett Kohl–designed kitchen.

Odile grunts jokingly.

"Dad's not a big party person, I get it ..." Elle smiles.

"When he got that award last year—you know, the surgery thing? I had to practically drag him by the ears. Black tie? My goodness ... do you know how hard it is to force a full-grown man into a tuxedo?"

Elle snickers at the thought of her petite mother trying to overpower her father as she brings out their steaming mugs of lemongrass tea.

"How do you guys balance it all out? I mean, Ben and I are pretty similar. But at times ... I kind of ... wonder. Did you ever wonder?"

"Did? It's more like *do.* Lovee, you will always wonder. That's part of the beauty of marriage. Working with one another even though you're not carbon copies. Keeps things interesting."

They sit down on the couch, Elle putting her feet up on the coffee table, desperate to ease the tension in her lower back.

Her mother offers to rub her sore muscles and continues with her wisdom. "I think that—regardless of love and connections and romance ... it will never be possible to know a person 100 per cent before marriage. Even at my age, your father and I are still learning about one another. I think you have to remember that. That way, any surprises along the way, you realize that you're still learning. Nothing is a sure thing, just the attitude that you put into it."

"But you guys have, like, never fought. And when Ben and I argue … especially lately … I kinda worry …"

Her mother looks at her carefully, sipping her tea as she keeps one hand on her daughter's lower back for comfort. "What are you fighting about that makes you worry?"

"I thought that his promise to be around more—for when we have kids—meant that he'd be here before they arrived." Elle blushes.

Her mother nods, listening.

"I know it's tough—we're in the middle of the hockey season, and he's got a lot of new clients that got drafted in. He's so good at what he does—everyone wants him to rep them. And we were *not* expecting to get pregnant right away. Let alone with twins! But I … wake up alone and don't know if I will be okay with this once they're here crying, feeding, and pooping."

"Well, do you think he felt this way when you were away and travelling with Jenna?"

Elle scrunches her face up, having tried to avoid the thought that Ben could karmically be giving her a taste of her own medicine.

"Jenna …" Elle whispers, her heart swelling with sadness.

"How is she doing?" her mom asks, blowing the steam from her mug gently.

Elle stares down at her round belly and cups it with her hands.

"Is she on the drugs?" Odile whispers, scared of the growing fetuses hearing the negativity.

"I think so … it's almost her birthday, and I realized that I can't even send her flowers or call if I wanted to. She's isolated, like she's living in a haze or something. I don't know what more I could do. Riley and I have tried, but she has shut everything out."

"Well, I can understand the frustration of being shut out by someone you care about. Who you're worried about because they're going down a dark road, even though they are so much smarter than that," her mother hints, winking at Elle and recalling her daughter's risky college years.

"How did you get through that?" Elle asks, embarrassed.

"A lot of hope and faith. And prayer."

"But you're not religious," Elle smirks.

"So? I could still wish for the best and hope that you would have a moment of clarity …" Odile sighs, holding her daughter's hand.

"I never thought of it that way … hope and intend great things."

"Well, I always assumed you would convert to Judaism for Ben," her mom reminds her, reaching for one of their new nail polish colours and twisting the bottle open.

"I mean, I was … but … when we talked through it … we were more naturally leaning towards having a blended household. Teach the kids about Passover *and* Easter. I mean, like it or not, it's just who we both are."

Odile shrugs, coating her fingers in a dark burgundy colour that doesn't really suit her. It looks too angsty for her natural cheer.

"Well, it seems that in this day and age—and in this huge city—it's almost unfathomable to be perfectly matched. In socioeconomic, cultural, religious capacities … not even in looks and sense of style, or career potential …" Her chirpy voice trills as she takes her daughter's left foot and starts to apply a raspberry-pink colour to the nails.

"Mom—you know, you're really smart." Elle grins, always impressed by what's under the unassuming housewife exterior.

"Well, child-rearing and art collecting left me a lot of time to read …" Odile admits cheekily.

Elle stares at her mother lovingly, thankful to have her around to quell any fears during the pregnancy.

"Lovee, try to relax. You and Ben are great together—you always have been. I know it's hard without him here as a reminder. You need to take it easy. The tension transfers …" she cautions, pointing to the baby bump on her daughter.

"I know, I know. He's great. He's an amazing husband, and an amazing friend, and he's going to be an amazing dad. But I still get mad at him sometimes." Elle shrugs.

"Well, he runs away to hockey games. Your dad ran away to brain surgeries. It's the nature of marriage. Everyone needs to take personal-space detours here and there. You'll need something to run away to, also. So why don't you start thinking about what that's going to be? Start planning your next step—that light at the end of the tunnel," Odile advises. "But realistically, you're going to have your hands full for a while, so don't expect you're going to be supermom and get everything done at once. Trust me—not possible.

Elle burrows into the couch cushions, trying to imagine how her life will soon look.

happy holidays from all of us.

[San Diego, USA—December 2011]

"I think the change of scenery will be good for you." Hana smiles at Jenna, having convinced her to spend the holidays away. They are booked to stay at the Del Coronado near San Diego for a spa weekend.

More hotel rooms. More room service. More pillowcases that are without a few nights' worth of drool. Unfamiliar. Sterile.

"Yeah, I can't imagine being in Toronto for Christmas …" she whispers, thinking of her dead mother and her nonexistent friends. She watches palm trees zip past the windows of their limousine as they cross a bridge linking to Coronado Island.

"Exactly. So you need to toughen up and keep moving," Hana says, furiously tapping away on her cell phone. "You are the hottest star out there right now. This is no time to get comfortable. You need to think about your next album. We need to keep the media coverage on you—give them new stories to follow every week."

Jenna's eyes pop at the thought of recording a third full album already. The intensity of formulating ideas and pushing them into existence is energy that she simply does not possess.

"Well, I thought that I might want to take a little … pause … before I start. Be sure the current record does well, live in the now," she says to her manager.

Hana looks up ferociously, her bright, rhinestone-embellished Juicy tracksuit making her radiate even more.

"Or … not …" Jenna whispers, curling her knees up like a child, the summer maxi dress she's wearing enveloping her like a blanket.

"You don't have the luxury to stop. You are not Madonna. Or even fuckin' Celine Dion. When you stop, people will forget about you. There will be no comeback. When you stop, that's it. And I have worked too hard to let this slip away like that. I'm in this, too, Jen. And, know what—I'm tired, too. I want to go home, too. I'm lonely, too. But I do it. And you're going to do it, and you're going to like it."

Hana's voice carries through the limousine's privacy screen, her harsh barking causing the driver shiver nervously.

"I have spent all this time and all this money getting you to where you are. So get yourself together! Because you know what they're going to write about you—that you're ungrateful and that you're a fake because you don't care about anyone but yourself."

Jenna stares off in a daze, shocked by the accusations.

I don't care about my fans? I'm selfish? But I don't want to do another dance album. I wanted to do something that sounded more like me, she thinks, confused by the anger coming from Hana. *Where does she live, anyway? It's not like she has a husband or something to go home. Maybe I* am *being selfish.*

The car pulls up to the hotel, and the two women are let out. They put on their sunglasses, attempting to hide the bags and red eyes from their late night in LA. A birthday party thrown for Jenna by Alchemy Records, where she successfully managed to avoid a run-in with Mack by having security keep him away from her table—treating him as the equivalent of a commoner unfit to be in her presence.

Hana kept the security guards ferociously in check, staring down Mack, and even telling off Kwame: "What I say, goes—or she leaves your label. And do you really want to lose this moneymaker by supporting Mackenzie Madison? When did you grow a moral spine, this is business."

. . .

Beautiful red brick roofs cover the tops of the hotel's white walls, like cupcakes scattered around the oceanfront property. The beach looks quiet and calm, the sand dunes shaped by the gentle breeze.

"Miss Ramsay, what a pleasure that you chose to stay with us. We have you set up in fantastic cottage-type quarters. Marilyn Monroe stayed here while filming *Some Like It Hot,* actually." The hotel manager smiles as he takes her arm and leads her towards a footpath.

Hana waddles behind them, rolling her eyes. Jenna can feel her staring at the back of her head bitterly.

"We have you both booked at the spa for the weekend for a restorative getaway. Perhaps you'd like to take lunch in your rooms?" asks the manager.

"Do you have a bar?" Hana asks dryly.

"Yes? But do you mean like a nightclub?"

Hana nods, looking around at the beach, not spotting any cute guys.

"No, unfortunately not. But Pacific Beach or the Gaslamp Quarter are always favourites …" he offers awkwardly, having assumed they wanted a laid-back weekend retreat.

He deposits the women in their accommodations and makes himself scarce. Something about Hana Rin's intensity causes him to quiver like a lamb.

Jenna smiles when she spots a bunch of gifts piled at the foot of her bed, jumping onto it like a child.

"Ooh!" she chirps softly, curious to see who they're from and what is contained in the brightly wrapped boxes. A wave of disappointment falls over her as she realizes they're not from any friends or family. While there are plenty of goodies from famous acquaintances sitting in Hana's office, they are gifts she will probably never see. Instead, reality is that Christmas has come to her from the hotel gift shop.

• • •

"Oh, my God, he is so hot!" Jenna gasps, staring at a man walking into the bar she and Hana are in. Not even bothering to explore Coronado Island, Hana pushed Jenna to be her wingman and leave the serenity of their hotel.

"He is *stunning*," Hana agrees, hoping the blonde surfer-looking guy will happen to make eye contact with her and not the gorgeous girl beside her—as usually happens. Even in a simple black Line sweater, Jenna somehow steals the show.

Hana is trying to compensate by wearing a scandalous backless top. At least it will draw eyes away from her client, even temporarily.

The man meets his friends at the bar, and orders himself a beer. He begins talking to one of the men, and his gaze drifts to the two women, overdressed for the California beer bar.

He smiles at Jenna instantly, and she grins back. Hana feels the blood in her face boil angrily and is determined to draw the stranger's attention to herself.

"I gotta go to the bathroom …" Jenna whispers, setting down her drink and slipping away.

Hana smiles at the opportune timing. As she seductively struts towards the bar, the group of men turns to stare at her.

She approaches the blonde man. "Hi, I'm Hana."

He looks at his friends, surprised by her direct trajectory.

"I'm George," announces one of his friends, sticking his hand out for introduction and bypassing the rest of his buddies. He's mesmerized by the hot, aggressive woman. "That's Devin," he says, motioning to the blonde, but stepping out to trap her in conversation.

Hana looks George up and down, evaluating his clothes.

"Would you like a drink?" he asks, hoping to impress the LA girl with his assets.

"Manhattan," Hana commands dryly.

As the drink is served up, Jenna appears. "There you are! Why'd you leave?" she asks, a little taken aback at having to march up to the group of strangers.

"This is Devin," Hana says flatly, realizing he is not interested in her in the least. "This is Jenna."

He lights up at the introduction and begins chatting with Jenna.

"So you're in the entertainment industry?" George asks the two ladies as they discuss their work lives.

"You could say so, ..." Hana says under her breath, angry to have to be talking to the less attractive of the two men. She sizes up the rest of their group and settles on George as her prey of the evening, because at least he has a Cartier watch—in rose gold.

"Wait, so you're like, an MTV-level singer? Like *American Top 40*?" Devin asks, surprised to be talking to someone that could be played on the radio. "Sorry, I don't really listen to much new music."

"Yep. Top Forty." She blushes. More like the top of the Top 40.

Devin looks a little intimidated by her, suddenly unsteady.

"What about you?" she asks, trying to stimulate conversation and appear less scary to the handsome guy.

"I'm an engineer," he replies, a little embarrassed to seem like such a dork compared with the pop-culture icon in his midst. A flush ignites across his cheeks.

"You mean, engi-nerd," snickers George.

"What do you do?" Jenna asks, turning to Devin's friend.

The two men laugh, and he admits to being a high-profile divorce lawyer.

"What about hobbies?" she asks Devin, trying to find some common ground while Hana and George go for a round of shots.

"Surfing. And rock music ..."

"I love rock music! What's your favourite band?" She smiles.

"The Foo Fighters ..."

"That's awesome!" She laughs.

"They're your favourite, too?"

"Well ... I kinda like old school ... like soul and blues. But of rock music, I'd say they're a definite favourite." She smiles, blinking her eyes flirtatiously, not sure what else to do.

Devin drinks his Sprite silently while his friends down beers like it's nobody's business. He and Jenna bob their heads to the music being played, not sure how to overcome their conversational impasse.

"So ... how come you're here? Holidays with your family?" he tries, shouting at her over the blaring music.

Jenna looks at him, hesitant to explain her reality. So she nods in agreement—afraid he'll find it weird that she has no family and that she is spending this time of year partying instead.

"How long are you here? A week?" he asks, hopeful that they might be able to hang out under better circumstances.

"The weekend. Then I'm going back to LA."

He nods, and his body language becomes reserved. He leans into conversation with his other friends, trying to break contact with her.

I don't think he's interested anymore, Jenna realizes anxiously.

She stands at the bar, uncomfortable and mute.

Hana has pounded back her drink and is successfully overlooking the fact that she's not particularly attracted to George.

Maybe I can slip out now, Jenna wonders, not fussing over the lost love interest.

"Hey ... Hana ..." she nudges.

Hana turns to look at her, eyes already glazed over.

"Would it be okay with you if I peace out ... I need to crash ... must've drank too much," Jenna lies.

Hana rolls her eyes and gives Jenna a hand gesture that basically says, "scram."

Jenna says good-bye to George, and turns to the rest of the group with a wave. "Well, I'm going to head out. It was nice meeting all of you ..." she shouts. "Merry Christmas."

"Where are you staying? Do you want a lift?" Devin asks, surprised that her friend isn't leaving with her.

"Oh, it's okay—I'll catch a cab," she says breezily.

"What hotel is it?"

"The Del ... Coro ..."

"Coronado. Wow—that's, like a hundred-dollar cab ride. I'll give you a drive—I was going to head out soon, anyway," he admits. "I'm not much of a partier."

Jenna looks at him, not sure what his intentions are. And not actually put off by the expensive transportation cost.

"Come on," he says casually, waving to his friends.

She looks over her shoulder, but Hana can't be bothered.

Jenna follows him out to the parking lot, and they get into his beat-up 4Runner. Stickers from different beaches he's surfed are slapped on the rear bumper messily.

He unlocks the door to let her in, clearing out empty bottles of water and sports drinks, throwing them in the backseat, embarrassed.

"Sorry ... I don't normally have people ... ugh ..." he mumbles.

They get in, and he navigates to the Coronado Bridge.

"So you must travel a lot," he says, trying to initiate small talk, tapping his hand on the steering wheel as Coldplay hums on the stereo.

"Yeah. It's kind of ... a lot ..." she admits, not being able to contain her anxious giggles.

He looks at her, not sure what it so funny.

"I'm ... sorry ..." she wheezes, trying to stop laughing.

"Are you okay?" he asks, glancing away from the road for a second to stare at her.

"I'm fine ... it's just ..." she says, trying to catch her breath. "It's—this is going to sound silly—but I thought you were kinda into me. Back at the bar. And then you found out I'm this pop star ..."

Devin looks uncomfortable.

"I thought we'd end up fooling around at least. Plus, I'm not nearly drunk enough for this real talk," she giggles.

He drives down the palm-treed streets near the hotel compound.

"It's not that you're not ... cute ..." he starts.

Jenna looks at him, hoping for clarification to his hot-cold behaviour.

He inhales heavily, annoyed to have to explain himself.

"You have a girlfriend," she says, putting words in his mouth.

"No ... I don't want to random bang someone who's leaving on Sunday," he says, brutally honest.

"Actually?"

He shrugs, staring at the road. "I'm not looking for that sort of thing. I'm more interested in a relationship at this point," he says calmly. "I just turned 35, I don't do that sort of stuff anymore—it's not who I am. Who I want to be."

That was not what I was expecting, she says to herself, staring down at her miniskirt, her long, tan legs taking up the passenger seat.

Devin pulls the truck into the hotel's grand driveway.

"So you don't want to come in ...?" Jenna asks, double-checking.

He looks at her blankly and shakes his head.

She shrugs and pulls the door handle, hopping out.

"Thanks for the lift," she says flatly.

"Have fun on the island," he offers, as she turns away.

Jenna hears his SUV rumble away and feels the wind knocked out of her with his honest rejection. Empty tears roll down her cheek as she heads back to her room. She didn't even like him *that* much, yet she feels rattled by his disinterest in her predictably desirable charms.

"My energy is fucked up," she says to herself, struggling to put the key in the door, getting more agitated by the second.

Inside her room, she pulls the hotel phone onto the bed and starts dialing a familiar number. She lights up a cigarette, her hands shaking.

"Yeah ..." croaks a voice.

"Olivia, it's Jenna."

"Hey ..." Olivia rasps on the other line. "What's up ...?"

"I need to talk."

"Jenna? We talked just a few days ago for your birthday. What's wrong now?" she blurts out, her annoyance going unnoticed by her frequent client.

"No!" Jenna exclaims, frustrated. "My energy is off again—I need you to read me and tell me what's going to happen in life. I don't understand what is going on. I met someone, and he totally—"

"Where's Hana?" Olivia interrupts, now more awake.

"Back at the bar. Why—is this a bad time?"

"Jenna, it's like one AM. I was *actually* asleep."

"Oh, sorry, Liv ... I automatically picked up the phone."

"Ugh ... okay, I'm up. That's what I'm here for, right? Let me get my crystal ball—it sounds like a guy problem, right? I feel you giving off a really bad hurt ... what did this guy do?" she probes.

Back in her hip LA apartment, Olivia gets up, leaving the hot model she took home from dinner passed out in her bed. She tiptoes into the living room and curls up on the couch, not using any psychic tools, but rather preparing to pull information from Jenna to give the most general, logical advice possible. For $400 an hour, Olivia will gladly wake up at odd hours of the night to listen to the lonely star whine and worry. Desperately longing for a female friend to replace Riley and Elle, Olivia fills that void. She's even travelled with her and Hana. Psychic readings in the middle of the Mayan Riviera were not what she'd imagined when she and Hana dreamed up this con job.

"Well, what do you see?" asks the singer impatiently.

"Hmm ... no ... this person was of no significance to you. I mean, he's a Pisces, it never would've worked ..."

"Really?"

"Oh, hell yeah—he could never handle you. He'd feel eclipsed by your greatness," Olivia says, picking at her nails absentmindedly as she whips out the astrological jargon she's learned from books.

She has zero psychic inclination whatsoever, just a really incredible skill for observation. If she possessed the drive, she could have considered becoming a shrink. But blowing through her trust fund threw out any such aspirations, leaving her to dwindle in the LA party scene—until her street-smart boarding school friend devised a plan to manipulate one of her clients.

"Do you see any new prospects?" Jenna begs, hoping so badly to be rewarded with a new person in her life. A fresh start. Someone who can grasp her totality. She wants answers.

"Oh, that is tough ... I need to do another cleansing on you. I don't know how, but you got all messed up again—it's not good, Jen. I gotta meditate on you and help you clear out your energy ... stuff ..."

"Oh, no—again?"

"I think you tried to jump to quickly to the next guy—like a rebound in a way, to take your mind off everything."

Jenna sighs sadly.

"You gotta stay strong, or else it'll backtrack all the work I'm doing for you ..." Olivia warns, rolling her eyes at the ruse she's become so good at hustling. Hana would be laughing if she saw the income she's made from Jenna Ramsay alone—not counting any referrals from the singer, who now outspokenly attributes her success to Olivia. She is still astounded by the number of non-knockoff handbags hanging in her closet.

"Okay, I'll wire you the money right now—could you start the meditation for me right away? I need you," Jenna says urgently. She's become superstitious over the past few months, reaching out to Olivia to try to feel in touch with herself.

"Um ..."

"I'll double your rate," Jenna gasps, desperate.

"Okay, I will. I can see this is necessary. I'm going to hang up now and start chanting in a few minutes, okay? Take a bath and calm your mind so that you can receive my power," Olivia blabbers. "I can see there's also tension between you and Hana. Call me tomorrow. I think we need another hour to go over the effects of the night."

Olivia looks around the living room, tossing the cell phone on the coffee table and trudging back to the hot body in her bed.

new year's news.

[Toronto, Canada—January 1, 2012]

Benjamin Roberts is staring at the hospital floor, lost in a daze. He takes off his glasses and rubs his temples in distress. His baggy sweats are scented with anxiety and perspiration from having rushed to the hospital hours ago, straight from the airport.

Riley rounds the corner with two disposable cups of coffee. Her long hair is up in a messy bun, her glasses on over her sunken eyes.

She hands Ben a cup, even though neither of them will even think to actually take a sip. It's the action of having the beverage that brings comfort in the time of stress, not the actual beverage itself.

The doctor breezes up to them, still in her scrubs.

"Ben, we were extremely lucky. She's gone through a lot … the babies were in a lot of distress," she begins, motioning for them to have a seat. She takes off her surgical cap, displaying wavy hair.

Ben's face is tense with fear, not sure what news their family friend—and wife's caregiver—is about to dish out. When they found out Elle was pregnant with twins, they couldn't even fathom the possibility that she would deliver prematurely. They weren't ready for one, let alone two, babies to come ahead of schedule.

"But Mom and babies are all right for now. Recovering. I've got the boys in intensive care; you have to trust me to take care of them for now so that you can focus on Elle. The delivery was tough."

"Sarah, how … what …" Ben struggles to form even one of the thousand questions racing through his head.

"Listen, I'm not going to lie. It was a really tough delivery. Both the boys are small; one had a significantly more difficult battle than the other and got wrapped in the cord. But right now, you need to get her spirits up so that you can fight through this. Only time will tell," says Dr. Sarah Schwartz. Her pager goes off, and she excuses herself, rushing back down the hallway.

Ben is about to collapse into anxious tears. Riley stares at him in fear, not sure what to do. They lower themselves into the plastic chairs of the hospital waiting room.

She starts to try to say words of comfort, but only seems to bring him closer to the brink of a meltdown.

"Ben!" booms a man's voice, causing the two of them to look up.

Hunter rushes up to them, quickly glancing at Riley, but reaching out to hug Ben, who has sprung to his feet at the sight of his friend.

"I came as soon as practice broke. What's going on?" he asks, looking at the two of them with frantic eyes.

"The ... the boys ..." Ben starts gasping, putting his hands behind his head and struggling to breathe. His eyes dart around behind his glasses.

"They're in intensive care. The doctor says we can only wait, and that we need to focus on Elle, to get her spirits up," Riley explains quickly.

Hunter starts talking to Ben, calming him down.

Must be a guy thing. Riley smiles to herself as she wanders towards Elle's room. She stands by the doorway, staring at her sedated friend. What Riley awoke to that morning was frightening.

She had been staying at the Roberts's house for only a couple of days, a voluntary backup while Ben was away on pressing business. With a particularly concerning pregnancy, Ben was adamant about his wife having someone by her side at all times.

Riley had been in the kitchen, fixing a light breakfast for her nauseous friend, when she spotted Elle up and moving to the solarium—against doctor's orders.

"You're supposed to be in bed ..." Riley jokingly warned, following after her like an obnoxious shadow. She stood by the doorway, sipping a cup of coffee, watching as Elle carefully examined her empty art easel.

"You don't have to actually follow me," She laughed, as her friend hovered. "You know, I haven't used this in months ..." she whispered sadly, touching the wood frame.

Then, she collapsed.

Riley's china mug shattered into pieces as she sprinted to her friend, as blood seeped out of Elle.

"Stop hovering ..." squeaks the small voice hoarsely. "You're either in or you're out, doorway creeper."

Riley comes out of her thoughts and rushes straight to the hospital bed.

"Are they ...?" Elle trails off, scared of the post C-section reality she is waking to.

"No! They are alive. In intensive care, but they are alive. And waiting for you to get better, my lovee!" Riley gasps.

Elle drowsily looks away, not able to grasp how her preemies are doing. They weren't supposed to be born until spring.

Riley grabs her hand, but there is no squeeze back or acknowledgement. Elle is in her own world.

Ben and Hunter enter the room, and Ben lunges towards his wife.

"Elle! Thank God you're okay," he gasps, tears streaming down his face. Any restraint and self-control has been lost by the sight of his wife lying weak in the bed, wires and IV drips attached to her.

He covers her in kisses and hugs, not knowing how else to bring comfort or erase pain.

Riley and Hunter back out of the room to give them some privacy and start wandering the unit.

"Hey, does Elle's dad still work here?" Hunter asks, as they walk down the hallways of large downtown hospital.

"Kinda." She laughs. "He's slowly retiring. Wanted to work on his backhand a bit more. Teach the babies how to golf."

Hunter nods comically, recalling the prim qualities of the Bryans clan. Riley had to break the news to them over the phone, while they were at their Florida winter home. Odile wailed helplessly, scared for her only daughter's welfare.

"Do you think they'll be okay?" Hunter asks her, thinking of the babies.

Riley bites her lip nervously, not sure how much to talk to him. It has been a while since they shared secrets—and even then, nothing was ever totally sacred.

"Her dad says the problem could be the air supply ... they were so tiny," she sighs. "Bram got caught in the cord ..." She shudders.

"How much did they weigh?"

"Bailey was better off, but Bram was, like, two pounds." Riley grimaces. They stop in front of the nursery window. Although the boys aren't there, they both observe all the babies who are new to the world. "They said he could fit in the palm of your hand."

Hunter stares through the glass, his hair freshly washed and still wet.

"Do you play today?" Riley asks, watching him out of the corner of her eye.

"Nah, practice. Coach likes to make sure we're not out partying too hard anymore. But frickin' hell, it's New Year's Day." He groans.

"Don't swear around the babies!" Riley jokingly scolds.

He rolls his eyes but steals glances at the adorable infants.

They walk back to Elle's room. Ben is in bed beside her, holding her as she sleeps deeply.

"She's so ... distant," Ben says softly, patting her sweaty hair.

"Give her time," Riley assures, trying to smile warmly, to encourage him in the face of his wife's broken spirit.

"Go on ahead. I'll see you back at the house? I want to stay with her some more," Ben offers Riley. "They said I'll have to wear, like, a friggin' hazmat suit to see the boys in their incubators ..." he trails off, devastated.

Riley nods and pats his shoulder.

"Man, these guys were just rarin' to get out and meet y'all. They're gonna, like, have superpowers after that incubator. Wait and see— they'll have an unstoppable wrist-shot. Maybe even telepathic play-making powers," Hunter jokes. Anything to lift the mood and inspire his hockey-loving friend.

Ben smiles at the thought of little babies on skates.

Hunter gives him a nod and walks out with Riley.

"Do you want a lift back?" he offers her as they walk out into the cold winter night.

"Oh, sure. Thanks. I forgot we came in the ambulance, I didn't drive." She cringes.

"Still got the Range?" he asks, leading the way through the parking lot, referring to her bright red Jenna-mobile.

"Nope. Elle and I gave them in after we stopped working. We've been driving around in Elle's nifty station wagon. Can't believe I have a friend who owns a station wagon." Riley snorts, the snow crunching beneath her running shoes.

Hunter unlocks a dark blue Audi SUV.

"Hey! I have the same car! But it's white. What happened to your bolt of sunshine?" Riley smiles, referring to his Ferrari.

"In the garage until summer," he explains, as they hop in and head uptown. "Damn snow lasts like eight months of the year here."

Riley grins as they buckle up.

"So, I hear that your book did great," he says, trying to break the silence that has hovered over a good ten blocks. "I bought a copy."

"You did? Thanks! Yeah, I think the excitement has kinda died down now. Been trying to get my new project finished up."

"I'm sure San Francisco has been a great inspiration," he says, keeping his eyes on the road.

Does he mean San Francisco as in the city ... or San Francisco as in Anth? Riley wonders, trying to spot any hint of disdain on his face.

"It's great. A bit chilly. But the coffee keeps me going." She jokes.

"I heard Jenna's back with Carter," he says, turning to look at her with an exaggerated exhale, rolling his eyes.

"I have no idea. You know it's hard to know with them. I saw something like that in a magazine, but ... she's ... been ..."

"Busy?"

Riley nods, not wanting to openly insult her. Not returning phone calls or e-mails or having any sort of communication for the past half year would normally be classed as MIA. But not when the paparazzi can chronologically capture how she chooses to spend her days—lots of free time shopping and drinking and being a hot mess.

"It's just, I remembered something he said to me a while back ..." he trails off.

Riley turns to face him, surprised at the delayed confession.

"We were out here one night ... and he said something about him and Hana," Hunter says, shifting his weight uncomfortably in the seat.

"Him and Hana?" Riley repeats.

"Yeah. Like, that they'd been kinda ... on the DL for a while. Like, while he was dating Jenna, he was screwing around with ..."

Riley feels ill from the mental picture.

"It would really suck if all along ..."

"Thanks. I'll keep it in mind. Honestly, I haven't seen or spoken to her in ages ... but ... with Hana and Carter—it wouldn't shock me. No boundaries," Riley admits.

Hunter pulls into the driveway of the Roberts's house.

Riley turns to Hunter and smiles. "Thanks for the lift," she says, grabbing her bag and opening the car door. She starts towards the house when she hears Hunter's voice call out.

"Happy New Year, Riley," he says, smiling, and pulling away with a wave.

He drives off as Riley heads into the warm house, leaving her soggy socks and shoes by the door.

She walks down the hallway and suddenly recoils in pain. A piece of her broken mug has cut her foot. She looks at the coffee mess on the ground, and then to the bloodstains on the wood floor in the next room.

Riley grabs a bucket from under the childproofed kitchen sink and fills it with water. She begins to scrub.

After a few minutes of working on the bloodstain, Riley grunts, frustrated, unable to get the remnants to disappear. Instead she's only swirled the mess around more. She whips the sponge across the room, annoyed. Riley picks up the phone and calls her dad.

"Hullo?" his deep voice echoes loudly.

"Hey, Dad. I have a quick question …"

"*Jes,* darling."

"How do I get blood out of wood floor?"

Rhett Kohl is silent on the phone, a little concerned why his daughter is asking such a question. "*Vhy* …" he whispers. "*Vhat* did you do?"

Riley laughs out loud, realizing her father's train of thought. "Dad, really? Do you think I could kill someone?" she says, gasping for air at the thought of committing murder.

"Oh. No … I guess not? But *vhy* do you ask this?" he says quickly, embarrassed by his hesitation.

"Because Elle went into labour … and she's got … leftover on the floor. I don't want Ben to come home and see it," she explains.

Rhett sighs with relief. "I'll be right there," he says, about to hang up. "*Vait,* how is she? Are the babies born?"

Riley retells the story and Rhett tsk-tsks sadly.

"*Vell,* she's got great people behind *hur. Vee* are all here," he says tenderly.

Riley puts the sponge in the bucket and stares at the empty art easel, all the bottles of paint that are drying up.

"*Keviiin,* Riley killed a man and we *haf* to help her move *zee* body!" he calls out, away from the phone.

There is frantic gasping from Kevin, who has rushed into the room.

"You're not going to tell him until you get here, are you … gonna let him think that I just lost it and went mental," Riley observes, as her dad lets his partner have a panic attack at the implications of a murderous crime.

Rhett cackles, hanging up with his daughter.

• • •

Jenna fumbles for her chiming cell phone on the bedside stand by her head.

"Shut that thing up!" groans Carter, rolling over beside her in bed, grumpily smothering a pillow over his head.

They're in a hotel room in Boston. Their same old routine in place: paparazzi-photographed dinner, stay out late partying, stumble in blackout drunk, pass out until room service delivers food the next afternoon.

She looks at the screen, and there is a message from Riley. She struggles to read it, her eyes a bit blurry.

> *Thought you'd like to know that Elle delivered twin boys yesterday. It was a very difficult birth, and the boys are in intensive care. —R*

Intensive care? For what? Is Elle okay? A wave of dread washes over her. It's been so long since she's talked to the girls. And not for lack of trying on their part. It went from calls, to text messages, to e-mails. They slowed and eventually stopped.

There must be a point when it's been too long and people forget, right? And who's to say that the effort would even be welcomed by them now? Sometimes having history with someone means that it gets so dated that it should stay in the past. Even if they're the only people that have ever been in your corner without any shadow of a doubt, no matter how much you've pissed each other off.

It's so much easier not to have to answer to anyone. That way, no one gets disappointed or hurt or dies.

Jenna curls up into a ball, still dizzy from the night before, recovering from a bad drug trip.

Why did I let them pressure me into that? It fucks with me too much, I can't function properly. Are they trying to sabotage me? she scolds herself, thinking about the singling out done by Hana and Carter at the party last night. Any time she's ever bent to their will, she regrets it the next morning.

I'm going to need to fucking lip synch or something—how am I going to perform like this? she worries, feeling the grainy texture of her vocal chords.

She's too unstable to stand up and tell them to screw off. As much as she dislikes them, they're the only people she has.

Her thoughts drift to Elle in the hospital, and then to what her sons could possibly look like. Probably have her light eyes, Ben's strong jawline; be destined not to cross five-and-a-half feet like their parents.

Then she heads down the familiar path of nostalgia, thinking of her mom, and being overcome with a dark, dark guilt.

Jenna screams inside her head, trying to make the thoughts stop. She rolls onto her side to get closer to Carter. But he's in his own world, with his back to her.

She shakily gets up and changes. She needs to walk, but has no idea where. Anything to slow down her brain.

wild child lacking grace, destroyer of the human race.

[Los Angeles, USA—February 2012]

Hana's eyes pop open and dart around, on edge. She recognizes the setting of her bedroom and lets out a breath of relief.

"Fuck … I've never boned anyone who can bend the way you do," growls the guy beside her.

She sits up, clutching bed sheets to her chest, and hesitantly turns to see what she dragged home.

"Oh, shit, Carter …" She laughs with relief, having forgotten that they'd met up at a club late the night before—bottles of vodka able to incapacitate even the most seasoned of drinkers.

He grunts, rolling onto his side so his naked back is to her.

She devilishly grins at the fact that she can't remember how she went from commanding her booth to waking up with Carter Sampson in her bed. She had been entertaining a hot new R&B singer as a prospective client … gotten him a harem of girls and enough drugs and drugs for a small town, and then Carter swung by.

How did I get home? she wonders, clearly remembering giving the valet at the club the keys to her Porsche.

She gasps in panic and walks to the window buck-naked, her blonde extensions falling in a mess.

She looks down at the parking lot of her apartment complex and sees her sports car parked diagonally across three spots—with the driver's door wide open.

"Oh, shit …" she whispers to herself, petrified, suddenly realizing she could have died. Or killed someone. *I for sure need to take a driver next time. There's no way I'm going to prison, or wrecking my car … or …*

"Nice ass," Carter howls, walking up behind her and slapping his hand hard across the flesh.

"Ugh, whatever." She rolls her eyes, walking away from the window, shaken by the reality check of her excessive habits.

She suggestively leans into the bed, feeling the fire in his eyes rev up even more.

"How can you leave me hanging like this …?" he taunts, as he follows after her and reclines against the headboard.

Hana feels a pang of annoyance at his arrogant sexual demands and decides to torture him, sidling up, but not too close.

"You know, you should really consider taking that action movie …" she purrs, biting at his neck between kisses.

"If you can get me the part, I'll fucking do the nude scene, no question," he tells her bluntly.

"That's your advantage, the competition wants it written out …" she continues, kissing her way down his chest.

"And that's why he's not booked up for the rest of the year already …" He grins to himself proudly, having seen a big impact in his schedule since Hana began networking on his behalf.

"You won't … get back with Amy … right …?" she asks, failing to mask the jealousy towards the female lead from his last movie—the married actress Carter slept with while making rounds at Sundance.

"Please. She gave me what I needed," he snorts. "Exactly like Jenna. I think I've milked those links as much as possible; now, on to the next. Aren't you proud?"

She laughs softly at having met her match in self-absorbed success mongering.

"Well, I'll call the casting agent. I introduced him to his favourite stripper at one of my parties. This should be a nice paycheque for us."

"For us." He winks, playing into her admission of affection to him. But he has no interest in being an "us," only in sucking her dry of connections and hookups in the industry.

"So, aren't you going to go a little lower?" he cheekily demands, cupping her head as she kisses his stomach.

Hana looks up at him, feeling ungrounded by his seductive aggression, and caves in.

pressure point.

[Toronto, Canada—March 2012]

Elle stares at herself in the bathroom mirror. The bags under her eyes look ashen. Her hair is oily but fraying at the ends.

The twins have fallen into an unexpected slumber, and she has barricaded herself for the moment of unfamiliar silence.

She splashes cold water on her face, trying to stop herself from crying. She's been careful not to let the boys hear her cry. During the moments when they fall asleep, she slips away to regroup for their imminent awakening.

Her skin looks almost transparent, her energy having seeped out weeks ago. Disappearing with her sleep and personality.

She hears a knock at the front door downstairs and forces her feet to move.

She trudges to the big door and opens it to find her perky mother on the other side.

"Hi, Mom …" she whispers, grateful for the surprise visit.

Her mom takes her petite child into her arms, soothingly. "I like your sign," she giggles, pointing to the <u>DO NOT RING! Knock instead!</u> note taped by the doorbell.

Elle leads her mother into the house and to the kitchen.

"Well, I learned that when it took me three hours to get them to sleep, and then Ben's Chinese delivery woke them back up …" she trails off, leaning on the fridge for support.

Odile Bryans carefully studies her daughter's face, concern sitting heavily in her heart.

"When is Ben back?" she asks.

Elle sighs, the morning's fight with her husband still fresh in her mind. With his upswing of success as an agent, she's found herself alone a lot during this hockey season. Even with two high-demand babies, she's embarrassed to admit she needs help.

"He'll be back from Pennsylvania at the end of the week. But we've been okay." She smiles weakly, unconvincing.

"I wish you'd get someone to help you …"

Elle looks at her mother, shifting her weight from foot to foot. With one of the twins potentially diagnosed with cerebral palsy, she's having a tough enough time trying to understand what the future will bring.

"That reminds me. Your dad left this for you," Odile says, gently pulling out a portfolio from her Cole Haan bag.

Elle opens it up and finds dozens of articles about cerebral palsy—in infants, in toddlers, in family dynamics. Her dad really put a primer together!

She smiles, setting the portfolio down for future study. The possibility that Bram would have a lifelong journey with CP was enough to send Elle into a frenzy of reading and preparation when Dr. Schwartz mentioned the suspicion.

"Darling, would you consider maybe … letting a grandma sit with her boys for a couple of hours?" asks her mom, hoping to get Elle distracted enough to unwind. She looks so frazzled; a little "me time" couldn't hurt.

"Mom …"

"I feel so lonely lately, with your dad away. I wanted to stare at the babies …" She blushes, not completely lying. Her husband is being honoured at a medical conference in Phoenix. He hasn't fully retired, so the promise of more time together to travel and relax hasn't fully manifested.

Elle sighs, hugging her mom and rushing upstairs to shower and change.

After scrubbing herself and triple-shampooing, she feels instantly lighter. She wiggles into a pair of classic boot-cut jeans and slips a dark green sweater over her head.

What now …? she asks herself, feeling odd not being wrapped in her crusty sweats. No fussy babies or spit-up on her shoulder. Instead, a polished lady stares back at her—albeit and exhausted one. She brushes her hair—thinning from the stress, lackluster in colour.

She remembers the grocery list piling up on the fridge downstairs and decides to take the opportunity of a trusted babysitter to emerge from her house.

"Mom, if you can stay with the boys, I'll go to get some groceries?" she asks, walking in to the living room.

Her mother is gently humming over the babies, watching them sleep. She smiles at her daughter, motioning for her to slip out and not worry, to take her time.

Elle heads to the fridge and grabs the list off a magnetic Justin Bieber notepad, slipping into her oversized parka and zipping out the door.

She crunches through the snow and straight to her station wagon. Starting the engine, she feels an intense wave of freedom that nearly brings her to tears. She drives down to the supermarket, excited to pick up some snacks to share with her mom—maybe even crack open a bottle of wine.

She makes her way to the checkout and spots all the gossip magazines. She quickly adds them to her purchase, wondering what is going on with her distant friend. From the looks of it, a lot of partying and debauchery. And a catfight with a supermodel at a fashion show.

Elle takes her bags to the car, darkness already creeping into the afternoon sky. As she neatly positions her purchases in the large trunk, she glances around at the other cars in the lot. There are tons of luxury vehicles all around, mothers and fathers dragging their kids to the store after school hours. She spots a snobby-looking woman in a fur coat dragging her kid on a leash and feels as if she's going to faint.

Please tell me that's a joke. She stares, horrified, as the woman chirps distractedly on a cell phone while her toddler waddles behind.

"Cookie! Hurry up!" screeches the mother, irritated by her slow-moving daughter.

Without missing a beat, she pulls on the leash that is harnessing her child and yanks with annoyance. Cookie's tiny body is sent flying in the air, landing in a small snowbank beside her mother. The adult leans over and picks up her kid, carrying her the rest of the way like a football under her arm.

Elle stares after them, stunned, and whispers a secret prayer, thankful that she is a humane parent.

She glances at the video store nearby and decides to browse, shoving her car keys into the pocket of her coat.

Hmmm ... maybe she'll want to watch a movie, she thinks of her mom, deciding to stop in and to grab one of their favourites.

She prowls the aisles, staring at all the movies she's failed to watch. She stops at a DVD cover that makes her want to vomit.

Elle looks around sneakily and flips the cover of *Felons* backwards so it's not visible.

She takes her selection to the counter.

"All right, and *Princess Diaries* is due ... wait a minute ..." says the teenaged boy behind the counter.

"Hmmm?" Elle hums, a little embarrassed that he's announced her movie rental so loudly.

"You're really renting this?" he asks, narrowing his eyes.

She puffs her cheeks anxiously, looking over her shoulder at the line that's forming.

"You. *You're* renting *Princess Diaries*? I can tell it's for you," he says bluntly.

"Um-hmmm ..." she responds, totally on edge, her face starting to turn bright red.

"Were we out of something that's actually decent?" He laughs, motioning to the shelves of movies around them.

"No ..." she whispers, gripping her credit card tightly, wanting to pay and run for cover.

"You've seen it already, haven't you?" he gasps, teasingly.

Elle taps her foot nervously, not keen to admit that she's seen it well over 20 times.

"I have children!" she hisses, starting to become paranoid that the people in line are judging her.

"And you're letting them watching *this*?"

Elle has an uncharacteristic impulse to reach across the counter and throttle the oily-faced film critic, who happens to have a ninja mullet for a hairdo. She looks behind her again to the customers waiting impatiently and feels her new mommy temper kick in.

"Listen, Isaac ..." Elle says, reading his name tag. "Could you please ... just ... please ... ring this in so I can go? Go fast."

He sighs, not having converted his customer to a more refined audience, and scans the DVD.

"Well, would you like to add the new special edition rerelease of *Felons*—"

"*No!*" she shouts, slamming down her credit card on the counter, trying to avoid any trace of Carter Sampson.

Isaac looks at her, a little bit frightened, and swipes her card.

gulab jamun.

[Delhi, India—April 2012]

"What do you think of this one?" Anthony asks, sliding a dish of food towards Riley.

She dips a piece of naan into the herbed sauce and chews on it carefully.

"Mmmm! This is incredible ..." she whispers, reaching in for more and grabbing her pen with her left hand.

"Yeah, and these potatoes are pretty nice," Anthony announces.

Riley stares down at the half dozen metal saucers they're eating from, overjoyed. She's dripped the different sauces over the front of her Indian blouse, but couldn't care less.

"Too bad you won't eat this mutton ..." She smiles, selfishly devouring the meat plate.

"Hey, the best place to be vegetarian is India—so I'm not complaining." Anthony laughs, stuffing another mouthful of potato in.

Riley takes a sip of her wine.

"So I give Bukhara a five out of five," Anthony announces happily in his South African accent.

"Yeah ... I think it is certainly a five out of five ..." Riley agrees, completely satisfied by the array of food she's eaten.

Their waiter approaches the table, and Riley tries to hide her notes with the napkin, not wanting to arouse any suspicion in the kitchen. She's gone native.

"And would you care for some sweets?" asks the server, clearing some of the empty plates from their chaos. The couple has gone through almost half the menu, experimenting and adventuring with their taste buds.

"Yes!" Riley shouts, hopping up from the floor cushions they're sitting on, almost pouncing on the Indian man.

Anthony feigns embarrassment but orders himself a portion of jalebi.

"So what do you want to do after Agra?" he asks, thinking about their last few days in the country. He's performed sold-out shows, and they've packed in extra days of sightseeing.

"Well ... I don't know. I mean, it's kinda nice that we don't have everything set in stone. I need to stop by the market and pick up a few things for my dad—textile stuff. But I'm happy wandering around with you and seeing what we discover." She smiles, stealthily unbuttoning her pants to accommodate her bloating stomach.

Anthony grins and is pleased about how comfortable they feel together. He rolls up the sleeves of his long-sleeve cowboy shirt.

"Hey, maybe I should take that cameo offer for the Bollywood movie …" he says, taking a sip of wine.

Riley stares at him in shock.

"Kidding! But really, it's incredible how my music has been received over here," he admits.

"Oh! You have to see the latest pictures of Bailey and Bram!" Riley gasps, suddenly remembering and grabbing her phone, searching through her e-mail.

She hands Anthony the photos of the boys.

"Does that say 'big man on campus'?" Anthony laughs, scrunching his eyes as he points to Bailey.

"Yep!"

"These guys are awesome." He smiles, handing it back.

"I know. And Elle and Ben are the most adorable couple ever. Ever. Maybe I should go back again soon …" Riley says to herself.

"Well, I've only been to Toronto once. And it was literally off a plane, to a concert hall, and back on a plane," Anthony hints.

"Are you soliciting yourself?" Riley asks, deadpan.

"Maybe."

"Nice." She winks.

"Hey … you know the whole married-kids-house thing …" Anthony starts, changing the subject.

"Uh-huh?" Riley replies, smiling at the desserts put down by the waiter in front of them.

Anthony waits for him to disappear before continuing.

"Do you want that?" he asks, straight to the point.

Riley looks at him, expressionless.

"Like, to get married and have that whole grand affair and then get yourself a jazzy gas-guzzling SUV to cart the kids around …"

"Hey! I already have a jazzy SUV," she snaps jokingly.

"Just saying …"

Riley laughs at his line of questioning. "Honestly?" she asks.

He nods, genuinely seeking the truth, and fidgeting with the red rose centerpiece on the table.

"With *you*?" she asks.

Anthony rolls his eyes, pretending to be hurt.

"In general … not really …"

Anthony exhales, pretending to be relieved.

"I mean … I like what we have going on right now. Know what I mean? Like, how we travel and eat a lot and you do music and I write about stuff … it works. At least, I personally happen to think so …" Riley confesses.

"Yes. I agree. I mean, I would like to strap on a Baby Bjorn eventually, but … just …"

"Not yet …?" Riley finishes his sentence.

Anthony nods, smiling.

"Maybe by then, men will be able to carry children!" Riley grins excitedly, hugging her knees.

Anthony cringes at the thought.

"Or we could adopt …" he suggests.

"Wait, are we getting married?" Riley asks.

"Are we?"

"Now?" she wonders.

"No …"

"Because, really, when does someone know that they're supposed to do that?" she wonders.

"Like, how do you know when it's gone from just dating and 'hey, this person is cool' to 'hey, I should be with this person in a legal way'?" Anthony stammers. "In general, not with respect to us," he tacks on at the end.

"You mean, how does someone *know*?"

"Well, cos it's not only a romantic thing, right? There are other sides to knowing, I think."

Riley thinks carefully about what he's saying. "Right, because a lot of it is how the person fits into your life, and how you fit into theirs, no? That would make sense … but then again, you also have to redefine a new life together, don't you?"

Anthony looks overwhelmed by the existential talk, and Riley instantly regrets having indulged his nervous thoughts.

"I guess when it's time to know, you know," she decides.

"Okay, so now's not that time, right? Like, I know your friend is in the marriage and baby zone and stuff …"

"Right. Not now. But maybe sometime. If we feel like it. Then we can discuss a mini-human … or whatever," she rambles.

"Right. Mini-human. Good. Okay, I'm glad. I just didn't want you to be all, 'ooh, babies and marriage.' In case," he smiles, feeling calmer.

"Thanks for the concern. But … no. I *am* 'ooh, jalebi,' though," she winks, reaching over to his plate and breaking off a piece of his dessert.

They've neared the brink of awkwardness, but survived. It may be a bit unconventional, but it makes perfect sense for them. Riley and Anthony are walking their own paths, but side by side. There's nothing to prove to anyone, they know the other is beside them regardless.

boys' night in.

[Toronto, Canada—May 2012]

Elle Roberts pushes open her front door, her keys dangling in her mouth. She waddles her way inside to deposit her son, Bailey, into his baby swing in the living room, dropping shopping bags along the way.

A jar of pasta sauce shatters on the floor, and she holds her breath instead of swearing.

"You. Don't move," she instructs the pudgy little one, laughing at her joke because the infant can't go anywhere by choice yet. He's only four months old, after all.

She hustles back to the door and scoops up Bram from his car seat.

Elle attempts to collect the last few shopping bags and lumbers back into the house, kicking the door shut.

She secures Bram beside his brother and sets about cleaning up the broken jar, bending down in her yoga outfit and wiping the red goo.

"You know, boys. We could watch a movie later or something. Maybe order in. The night is still young …" she calls through the empty, echoing house.

She can hear one of the kids gurgling as she drops the paper towels in the garbage.

"Or we could party and be crazy. Let loose. Play music really loud and break stuff. Drink Patrón in our sippy cups …"

She walks into the living room and sees one of them spit up on his clothes.

"Or, I could change your poopy diapers. Force you to watch Amanda Bynes movies with me while I paint my toes. And if we're that rowdy … do some laundry …" she sighs, sitting down on the couch.

She turns on the TV. The sports channel is televising a game that Ben is at in Calgary. His overnight bag was packed even before she woke up.

"Honey, I'm so sorry. I have to leave tonight. I just got notice," he whispered while she snoozed in the bed—their twins asleep, miraculously.

"You're leaving again …?" Elle whispered groggily, surprised that he was being called back on the road. He had been away at least once a week since the start of the new year. It was like having kids became yesterday's news when new deals came up.

"I know. I'm so sorry. But I need to go. I can't tell the agency that I'm suddenly deciding to stop doing my job …" he argued back as gently as possible, trying to keep his voice down.

"It's not quitting—but … why can't you stay here more?"

"Because this has always been my job. For the past five years I have lived, breathed, and done hockey this way. Hands on. You know this is important to me." He tried to guilt her.

"Yeah. Me, too. Because I haven't touched a paintbrush or camera in forever. And it's obvious to see who has the more important job!" she said sternly, sitting up in bed, flipping the covers off angrily.

"You can work from home!"

"It's not that, Ben. It's that you work, and I don't. I don't have anything else to do. Because, you know what, I'm alone every single day. My kids don't speak. I don't have anyone here to *talk* with!"

With her escalating volume and anger, the babies awoke and began crying.

"You know what, I think that you need to calm down …"

"Calm down?!"

"Yes. This must be hormonal …" Ben tried to backpedal.

"Get out!" Elle shouted, throwing a pillow at him.

As soon as his sports car pulled out of the driveway, she began to cry along with her kids.

"Okay. So … what's it gonna be, lovees?" Elle sighs, turning off the game at the end of the first period.

The sky has slipped from dusk into darkness as she begins to leaf through a series of delivery menus.

Elle settles on calling in for Greek and changes her toenail colour from cherry red to burgundy, to match her deteriorated mood.

As the movie plays in the background, and her toes dry, Elle notices the babies have fallen asleep, peacefully nuzzling each other.

Elle smiles at her sweet boys and turns down the volume, staring up at the ceiling and breathing deeply.

After a few minutes of silence, a wave of emotion hits her.

"You know, I really hate when you leave," she says, starting to talk aloud to her invisible husband. "I don't like that you get to pick up and go, and I don't have that. Yes, I love my kids ... but ... that doesn't mean I'm not jealous sometimes. I want to disappear and pretend I don't have stretch marks. Maybe dress up and wear some eye shadow instead of drool. I was a hot lady!"

Why don't you tell him, says a voice inside her head.

Elle looks around, startled by the loudness in her mind.

Stop being so passive and tell him what you think, it says again, gently nudging her feelings to the surface.

She tiptoes to the laptop on the kitchen table and brings it back to the couch. Opening her e-mail, she finds a message from Riley.

Hey, booger.

> *I'm in France! Marseille, specifically. I've been slacking on the postcards, I know. You would not believe how absolutely different it is to be on tour with Anthony rather than on tour with Jenna. Like, really, who goes to Barneys and has to have an entire security team?*
>
> *Everything is going well here. Duncan thinks that my "niche market" culinary guide actually has a lot of potential. I guess there are a lot more tree huggers (I mean, vegetarians) out there than I thought. Ha. I did have this* **phenooomenal** *bouillabaisse tonight (Anth almost died when I held up an octopus bit). Everything tastes so much better when it's local.*
>
> *Wanted to check in and see how you're doing. If you need anything—moral support, wisdom, or a hit man ... don't hesitate to call! Hope to see you and the mini-humans again soon. But probably not until the holidays, I think. We're going to be working our way through the U.S., and then maybe staying in San Fran for a while.*
>
> *How's the cerebral palsy thing? Shit—that's probably the last thing you want to think about: subject change.*
>
> *I've got to run. But I wanted to let you know that I was thinking about you. Tell Benny-boo-boo I say hi. And give those heartbreakers of yours a big kiss. I swear I'm not going to become one of those creepy aunts who pinches cheeks and drinks (Long Island) iced tea in the morning ...*

Love, R

Elle smiles at her friend's frantic composition.

"She's just someone that can't really be bottled ..." she tells her sleeping boys.

Elle makes herself a cup of chamomile tea and begins to type a to-do list on the computer.

"Married—check. House—check. Car—check. Baby—check and then check it again! Career ...?"

She opens up a blank e-mail to Ben and begins to lay it out.

Honey,

I hope your trip is going well and that you're accomplishing what you need. But I'm writing to let you know that I'm kind of losing it. I'm being totally honest when I say that I don't know how much longer I can hang in. You know I support you in your work; now I need the same. I feel like I had to trade a big part of who I am in order to get all the great things in my life—but I realize now that it's not a sacrifice, but something that I need to work at retaining. So I will need you to support me by being around more. Next year, we need to make serious compromises about how we're going to live our lives. This may mean Bram and Bailey hanging around Grams and Gramps's more, or Bubbe and Zaide's. Point is, I need time and space to feel like a person, not only like crusty supermommy. Needed to say this. See you later. I love you.

Elle

As the message sends, she begins to orchestrate a plan.

"I need a location. I'll fill it with what I have so far ... but also give myself space for a studio so that I can keep creating new art ..."

Bailey's eyes flutter open and gaze at his mom.

"Don't worry, Bails. Everything is on its way to being okay," she whispers, browsing business property listings online.

He coos and closes his eyes again, almost comforted by his mother's resolutions.

man hunt.

[New York City, USA—June 2012]

The chauffeured car pulls up in front of a brownstone townhouse, a fairly recent purchase for the Jenna Ramsay estate. It's an attempt to put down roots somewhere, to have a fixed address instead of a nomadic hotel room existence.

"Home sweet home," says the kind old driver who's been assigned to her today. He has an Indian accent, his hair grey and oiled back neatly.

She rests her neon yellow fingernails on the door handle but can't bring herself to pull it.

"You know I've never actually been inside …" she admits to him, laughing softly. She's scared that she won't know the code to the alarm or that the key won't fit in the lock.

The driver looks at her sadly, unable to imagine the hollow life of the young star. Not that he consumes a lot of gossip columns, but it seems that everyone has heard of Jenna Ramsay nowadays. And her cover of an Elton John hit has ended up on his favourite oldies station.

"You know what … um … could you take me somewhere else?" She hands him her cell phone with an address on the screen.

They drive through the city and to an unassuming apartment building in Queens. Jenna's long legs gracefully flow out of the car, and she hops up the steps to look at the buzzer list.

"Jackman … McNamara … Malone … Soranno. No 'Ma' …" she whispers, running her finger down the list.

"Who is Max?" the driver asks, standing beside her and trying to read the names, having misheard her. His crisp uniform is neatly tailored to his small frame.

"Not Max." She giggles. "Ma. His last name is Ma …" Jenna sighs sadly. She towers over him in designer stiletto sandals, her trendy jean cut offs paired with a bright, frilly blouse. Perfect for the sticky night, stars hidden in the muggy sky.

He shrugs shyly.

"Oh, Shrinivas, sir … I guess it's not gonna happen," she sighs, plopping down on the cement stoop in anguish. She's been sending postcards to this address ever since she first left Toronto; the current tenant must be beyond annoyed with her.

"You do not have the correct address?" he asks, helpless.

"No. Well, yes. He must've moved …" Jenna whines.

The driver struggles to sit down beside her, trying to comfort the devastated singer. His rickety knees shake as she helps him down.

"Long night?" she asks the tired old man.

He shrugs sweetly. "Does he not know you are coming?" he asks Jenna, surprised that the young man would not be eagerly awaiting the beautiful girl.

"Not exactly … we haven't really kept in touch," she admits, staring up at the sky. Trees dot the sidewalk, their small green leaves unmoving in the humid night air.

"He doesn't know you're chasing him …" Shrinivas trails off, filling in the blanks for himself.

Jenna blushes shyly, giving away her secret pining for Parker.

"Why is he not chasing you?" he asks, winking adorably.

"I think he doesn't know that I want him … things got so complicated at the end, I feel like it almost tainted everything that was so good and pure about us."

"He was your friend?"

Jenna smiles, remembering all the nights they'd spent staying up talking and bonding. The picked-at delivery cartons, the encouraging squeezes he'd give the back of her neck.

"Honestly, he could have been my best friend—if time kept going and things didn't change. I've never been able to have that kind of conversation, a connection, with any other person, ever. He got my creative side—the songwriting and vision, which is great, for a business partner thing—but he also understood me as a person."

"Do you love him?"

Jenna laughs softly, a tear quickly brushed away from the corner of her eye. "I think I started to love him."

"And he loved you??"

She grunts, sending a current of air up to flutter her wispy bangs.

"I think … that I had a glimpse of what could be. And that it was taken away before we had the chance to really explore. I'm not saying that we're meant to be or whatever, soul mates or something. That's a bit presumptuous. What I'm saying is that I think this person is worth it enough to me to try again. Because I'd hate to think that if I didn't, I lost out on something incredible."

They sit silently, staring at the porous cement under their shoes.

"If you feel the chance is important, we must find him," says her new friend matter-of-factly.

"I think he might just be worth it …" She blushes, excited by his resolve. "I never had that kind of honesty with anyone. Like I could tell him anything. It was so safe and comfortable. I mean, almost like the guy could've been my older brother, but in a wise and protective sense instead of a weird, incesty way—know what I mean?"

He looks at her awkwardly.

"Never mind. I mean that there was a deeper connection there. Not only love and dating kind of stuff."

"What about any places he likes to frequent?" he suggests abruptly, as they try to figure out how to go forward from the front steps of the building.

"I wouldn't even know …"

"There is a bar!" he exclaims, putting up his pointer finger and trying to pull her up as he stands.

"Okay?"

"There is a bar all the young people go to. We must try this!"

Jenna looks at him wearily.

"Everyone asks to go there; this is the place that they all want. I think this may be good," he suggests with a sense of surety as he leads the way back to the car.

"It's kind of a long shot … but, I mean …"

"You do not love him to go to Meatpacking District?"

Jenna laughs. "No, no. It's not that I don't … love … love is a heavy word. I don't know if he loves me … um … It's just that I was actually thinking, maybe I should go to sleep. It has been so long since I've had a good night's sleep …" she admits, as she hurries after him.

"Sleep or love?" he asks her sweetly, putting two hands out like scales balancing, a choice between one or the other.

She bites her lip, scared that this "bar" is a long shot.

"Okay … we'll be fast …" she sighs.

"We go!"

"Yes … we go." She smiles, getting into the backseat.

• • •

"Yeah, that wasn't it, either …" Jenna exclaims, throwing herself into the front passenger seat of the town car.

Shrinivas turns from listening to his music and shakes his head sadly. "Maybe one more?"

"No ... I think it's time to call it a night ..." Jenna says, watching for any photographers lurking nearby. "And you know what's funny—they'll write a story about this tomorrow and say that I'm a raging club-a-holic!"

"I took a phone book," he offers, handing her the listing, open to the first page of Mas.

Jenna looks down and feels the image of romantically knocking on Parker's door quickly vanish. There are hundreds of listings.

"You don't want to stay and have fun? I can wait here ..." he suggests, feeling bad for the young woman, left alone after her show earlier that night.

"No. And contrary to popular belief ... I don't like to drink alone," she smirks, as he starts the car to return to her townhouse.

"Where is your friend tonight?" Shrinivas asks, carefully navigating through the night traffic.

"Hana? Oh ... she's with a man-friend of hers, I think."

"Good." He smiles devilishly.

"Yeah, I know she can be a bit much at times," Jenna admits.

"You are a very nice girl to be with her. Too nice," he announces.

She smiles weakly, not wanting to admit that she feels the same. Not wanting to entertain the thought that she's stuck with the she-devil, and by her own fault.

The car pulls up to the home, and Jenna feels more at ease.

"Would you like to come in? I'm so sorry to drag you around all night. I can make you coffee ... actually, I can't because I don't have any food ..." She laughs.

"Thank you, my dear. But I will go home. My wife leaves tea and biscuits for me." He grins, glancing at the clock on the dashboard.

"Oh, of course—I'm so sorry!" Jenna blushes, realizing that other people have families and homes to return to. Just because she's alone, doesn't mean everyone else is.

"My dear ... I hope you find him soon. He must forgive you," he says, recalling their lengthy conversation of love and fate that has played on the entire evening.

"Thanks. I hope one of these days ... we get our chance," she sighs, getting out of the car.

Shrinivas waits until she gets inside before driving off.

"He's gotta get over my stupidity, right? Drunken text messages are a forgivable offence …" she mumbles to herself as she walks through the rooms of the home, turning on all the lights in an attempt to make the place feel occupied.

It's been expertly decorated, and this is the first time she's actually sleeping there. It smells so clean and vacant that it's familiar to her nose, in a way. Like a sterile hotel room.

"I think this is dumb …" She laughs to herself, grabbing a wall decoration that looks like a tinfoil mobile from a baby's crib. She tosses it to the ground. "That is going in the garbage. I would never have bought that."

She steps into the bedroom and opens the armoire to find clothes stocked for her use. She pulls out a pair of pyjamas—opting for cozy cotton instead of a lacy teddy—and settles into the king-sized bed.

"So this is where my money goes …" she observes, looking around the room of the house that Hana convinced her to buy.

Anyone who's anyone owns property in New York, she had told her very convincingly. But when Jenna has been in New York, she's stayed at her usual hotels, never touching the house.

Jenna stares up at the ceiling and tries to let her tense shoulders relax, muscle by muscle.

She feels herself melt into the fluffy pillow, her lower back releasing the tension from her heavily scheduled day.

Suddenly, she is very aware of the fact that she is totally alone. The compulsion to dull her anxiety is trumped by the sheer exhaustion of her hollow body. She hasn't eaten well in months, surviving off of sugary drinks and cigarettes under Hana's advisement.

Another inch off that waist and you'll be a shoo-in for a Beautiful People list! she remembers hearing.

She can feel her hands starting to quiver from malnutrition and weakness, her mind loopy now that she has slowed down for rest. She pledges a secret resolution to start to feel better—to sleep and eat and get back in touch with her friends. To stop dabbling in drugs and drinking like a madman, and maybe even trim away the negative energies around her. It's a scary list of things to do, but she's also aware that her sanity and career is teetering.

"Mom, I miss you …" she whispers, dreamily. "Riley, Elle, I miss you. Parker … I miss you. Mack … I miss you, too, actually."

After saying her good-nights to the people she misses and loves, Jenna drifts into thoughts of nothing and sinks into the mattress.

clear vision.

[Toronto, Canada—July 2012]

Elle gasps excitedly as she and Ben get out of the car, her long skirt swooshing as she walks.

He's recently traded in his two-seater sports car for a more accommodating SUV (to fit Bram's future walkers or wheelchairs or canes). It took Ben a while to truly understand the extent of fatherhood, but he's happy that his car is still black and sleek. And expensive.

"Honey … it's going to be perfect …" she whispers, holding his hand excitedly as they walk through the cobblestone streets of the Distillery District in downtown Toronto. The historic zone in the middle of the city remains isolated with ancient mills and cellars, a charming and trendy spot for the artistic and elite. The old, large buildings recall an era of agriculture long forgotten, wood cellar buildings with high beams and rustic windows.

"Don't get too happy. If they know you want it, they'll have a field day …" he cautions, laughing at her glee. "Put on your poker face."

Elle tries to compose herself, and they enter one of the cavernous buildings, remodelled inside to accommodate a large gallery.

Their realtor is waiting for them by the heavy metal door, the handles aesthetically rusted to look ornate.

As they take in the bare gallery space, Elle feels all breath escape her lungs. She can see herself there. See her work colouring the empty walls and making them come to life—like a pop-up book.

The couple checks out a workspace area tucked above the main showroom.

I could put a playpen for the boys over there, she maps out to herself, looking around what must've once been an office. *Maybe build a darkroom into that corner.*

She looks down the white walls and can mentally put her different works of art on them, lining them up carefully and evenly. Letting people wander in with ice cream or coffee in hand to stare, walking dogs and baby strollers on a lazy Sunday.

The energy feels great, in line with her aspirations for the future. This environment can hold her.

After placing their offer to purchase the gallery, Elle and Ben wander down to Balzac's for a cup of coffee.

"This is really nice ... mommy-daddy time." She smiles as he puts his arm around her while they stand in the crowded lineup.

Ben kisses the top of her head, happy to see his wife excited about something, instead of exhausted or worrying or angry.

They walk their cappuccinos up the old wooden stairs and find a cozy spot to sit and talk.

Elle tells him how worried she is about Jenna. He talks about the latest inter-office news, and his favourite client who was the number one draft pick. She suggests taking their kids to the boardwalk to have slushees that weekend. It feels like they're dating again, back to sharing information instead of going on angry campaigns of silence.

"Honey ... I gotta talk to you about the fall ..." Ben starts, becoming visibly uncomfortable with introducing the topic, taking off his glasses and wiping them on his polo shirt.

Elle looks at him, dreading what she assumes he's going to say.

"I'm going to need to travel at least for a couple of months at the beginning of the season," he starts, going straight to the point—right for the jugular.

She stares at her husband, silently sipping her coffee without letting any emotion cross her face. Poker face, like he said.

"I know that I promised that I would be around more, but I'm hoping it's only for the beginning of the season."

"You did promise," she repeats, still opting for few words.

"I know. I'm sorry. But ... we have a lot of new guys that got drafted in, and I need to make sure they make good with their teams," he tries to explain. "Especially Judd—get him settled in. There's a lot of pressure when you're the top pick, when everyone is expecting you to be exceptional."

"So you're going to help those boys instead of *our* boys?" she asks dryly. "Because our type of exceptional is more complicated—"

"Elle, you know it's not like that," Ben interrupts, a bit annoyed. "You know that I'll take care of them."

"When you're here. Which, seeing how their first year of infancy went ... was not much. Ben, I specifically told you that I need all hands on deck. I can't do what I did last year. And I'm not about to ask my parents to spend the entire winter here. They already parented one generation, we can't expect our families to volunteer another."

"Elle, I promise I will be more hands-on this year. I know that you want to get back into your art business," he acknowledges.

"Right. Okay. But obviously my career is so flexible that it can flex out of existence …" she snaps, putting down her white coffee mug and glancing away from him.

Ben looks at her, wounded.

"Oh, please. You knew what you were getting into when you started this conversation," she says flatly.

His brow relaxes a little, and he blinks quickly.

"Well, I'll have to sort it out. Not like you're giving me much choice. But I will say that I'm not particularly impressed by you," she huffs, picking up the ceramic cup roughly and taking a sip of her frothy drink.

"We'll get through it …" he says, trying to be optimistic.

Elle stares at him, irritated, and not buying any ounce of sympathy he is generating. The ambitions for her gallery are already subdued by the bitterness that she probably won't be able to make headway anytime soon. Especially once regular season play begins in the fall, it seems.

You know what … fine … I will fight back. If you're going to bully me like this—I'm going to do what I want and make this happen anyway. She smiles to herself, plotting her rebellion. *You made a fuss about not leaving our kids with nannies or sitters … but I've had it with you. I can't sit on the sidelines anymore, or I'm going to go nuts and smash things. So—we're gonna get nannies and babysitters if you're going to keep on like this. And I'm gonna get a hot trainer at the gym!*

attract what you like.

[Toronto, Canada—August 2012]

Riley swings open the doors of Light Post Literary in a flurry. Her wide-leg trousers swoosh as she strides into the office, flat sandals scraping the floor and fraying the hems.

"Hi, Bernie!" she trills, hurrying past him and straight to Duncan's office door.

She bursts in, finding Duncan staring out the window, watching cranes erect the condo development next door.

"Hi?" she asks, surprised to see him off in space.

He turns, startled, holding his reading glasses in hand. "Hi."

"Whatcha doin'?" She smiles, rocking on her feet, as if she's a kid caught with her hand in the cookie jar.

"Actually? Nothing. I'm being the most unproductive person right now; it's embarrassing." He shrugs, swiveling in his chair.

"Well, not to worry. I think this will warrant an afternoon off …" She smiles, pulling a thick stack of papers from her purse. She slaps the coil-bound book down on his desk happily, the few hundred pages making a loud thump.

"Already?" he gasps, his eyes lighting up in surprise.

"Yep. Europe—for the most part—is finished!" She grins wildly. "Actually worthy of a second volume … but … we'll save that for a second-edition rerelease."

Duncan excitedly skims through the typed-up pages, getting a feel for the different culinary reviews she's put together.

"You went to Finland?" he snickers.

"Yes. Anthony was in Russia, so I skipped over for a couple of days. I must say, they have pretty good cabbage rolls."

Duncan looks ready to collapse into laughter.

"You should try vegetarianism. Even a little bit. I think it would look good on you." Riley grins cheekily, motioning to his hippie-like style of baggy fine-linen trousers.

"Just because I like meditation and chakras doesn't mean … oh, forget it. Anyway. This is good stuff," he says, tapping the draft. "I'll look over it next week while I'm in Sicily."

"Oh! Be sure to eat some good, homemade cannoli!"

"Right. But I'm going to only be there a few days before the Mediterranean yachting trip… irrelevant… well … how about we skip out? Let's grab some coffee." Duncan suggests, getting up and grabbing his leather satchel.

The two walk out of the office for the day, Bernie overjoyed to also leave early.

Riley follows Duncan through the building's underground car park and straight to his reserved parking spot.

He unlocks his luxury hybrid SUV and stashes his laptop. Opulent environmentalist.

"The alternative food guide idea was a magnificent idea." He smiles mischievously as he starts the gentle engine. "The publishers think it is going to completely jive with the whole green, carbon footprint, support local food thing. Especially around the holidays."

"Well, I can't take the credit for that little idea germination." Riley shrugs, burrowing into the tan leather passenger seat.

"That, too. You keep that Anthony Daniels around. He looks good on *you*," jokes Duncan as they pull out of the car park and start heading south towards the lake.

The car glides through the already crowded downtown streets. They head down Yonge Street, the main artery of the city, passing shops and strip clubs and theatres. Traffic chugs along as they near the Distillery District, construction sites busy developing the landscape around them.

"You know, Laith Bassel was here last month!" Duncan shares, recalling the dinner with his old friend.

"Really?"

"Came for the weekend with his wife, checked out Elle's new property …"

"Oh, that's right! Isn't the gallery also in the Distillery?" Riley gasps, remembering her friend's latest e-mail.

"Ooh—maybe we should go spy …" Duncan announces.

"Absolutely! But it's not open yet, right? It's a new acquisition."

"So? I can pick a lock," he says breezily.

Riley rolls her eyes at his theatrics, not doubting his technical abilities.

"I hear that the two wee ones are taking a bit of a toll on Eleanor," he says softly, as if he's letting her in on a secret that no one else is to hear, even though there is no one else in the car with them.

"Really?" Riley asks, wringing her hands with a slight inkling of guilt. She hasn't had a chance to reply to Elle's last string of e-mails, the hectic tail end of Anthony's tour pushing them into overdrive.

"It's the word on the street ..." Duncan shrugs. "Laith was over to her place for dinner, and her husband was in ... God knows where ... Dallas? Does Dallas even play hockey?"

"Yes, Duncan, they do. Oy. Her last e-mail *sounded* great ... she sounded great," Riley says, trying to recall specific sentences in her head. Some sort of proof that she was not, also, falling apart at the seams like her other childhood friend.

"Well, you never know. I can't imagine the pressure of having to be super perfect homemaker when you have a glossy superstar as your hubby. And a huge pop tart for a friend and a travelling ... whatever you are ..." He laughs.

"Hey—Jenna's more of a travelling ... minstrel. And I'm ..."

"See—what exactly *is* your job title, anyway?"

"Writer?" Riley suggests.

"Food snob?"

She slaps him playfully as he parks the car.

"I think that a situation like Jenna ... has so much impact on people around her, more than she could ever imagine. So, maybe Elle is trying to live in contrast to that, and valiantly trying to protect her ideal. Because, darling, for as long as I've been in this game, so much negative energy hanging around is never a recipe for long-lasting success ..." he muses.

They head up a cobblestone walkway and swing open a big green door leading into the coffee shop. The aromatic scent of the roasted beans fills their nostrils, both coffee junkies ready for a shot of heaven.

"So, do you think it's possible that what Jenna is going through now ... could be ... some sort of dark karmic effects from influences around her?" Riley asks, talking softly in the crowded lineup.

He shrugs helplessly.

They step up to the cash register to order.

"I'll have a soy cappuccino, please." Riley smiles sweetly.

"I thought you hated soy milk ..." Duncan snickers, as he pays for their beverages and a date square.

"It's grown on me." She blushes.

"Oh, Anth," Duncan jokes.

"So, anyway, I was asking—do you think that somehow, maybe she's bringing the insanity upon herself?" Riley asks, intrigued by the concept of another person's energy impacting someone.

"Well, it's only a theory ... But, consider if I think positively and care about you, then my imprint on your life—on you—is ... positive. Like attracts like," he explains. "Isn't that how the scientific explain the effects of prayer?"

"So, when Elle and I were with Jenna—the going was good because we were ..."

"Radiating love. But this woman around her now, and that maniac Carter ... I would think they're leeching her energy dry."

"And money." Riley coughs for dramatization.

Duncan rolls his eyes knowingly and continues. "You get a lot of those types in the entertainment industry. It's all about turning profit on a trend, and trying to keep control of the puppet you're dangling."

They grab their drinks and head outside to walk around.

"You know, there's this woman ... Olivia. Hana brought her in as some sort of spiritual guide ..." Riley confides.

"Pfft ... spiritual, my tush," Duncan snorts.

"Well, that's what I was thinking. I mean, I'm not really down with it all, but—I honestly don't get how this chick can be legit. Everything was so general—it could be Internet research."

"Or Hana-research ..." Duncan offers.

Riley's eyes bulge. Hana could be feeding her the inside scoop.

They look around a few shops, searching for Elle's new venture.

"It's like in dating. When I was all about the rebel thing, I attracted men similar to that, who were on that wavelength. Then I decided it was time to settle down a bit. And when I truly believed it, and was ready ... I was able to attract that caliber of person into my life," Duncan admits. "It's not just wanting something in your life—it's about creating room for it to actually enter."

"So, then, what happens to Jenna?" Riley asks.

"You mean, in an existential way?" He laughs.

Riley looks at him, serious, worried.

"To be honest ... she seems like a nice girl. But becoming more and more of a shell. Hiding in the veils of partying and all that it's so clichéd. Really? Come on. She'll either become so brittle and hollow she breaks, or ... somehow come to her senses?"

"I wish she'd listen to me—to anyone." Riley exhales heavily, staring at her sandaled feet walking on the uneven stones, her chipped pedicure annoying her.

"Obviously she doesn't want to."

She looks at him for explanation.

"It's hard enough if she has any inkling that she's fucking up, Riles. And to hear it from someone else, especially someone who's so on top of their game, is probably unwelcome heckling."

"My God, this is worse than I thought," she sighs, realizing that her friend has isolated herself from the most trusted and well-meaning people she had in her corner.

"I would advise, keep trying to compliment her. But read between the lines as needed."

"Are you for real?" she exclaims, surprised.

"I mean Eleanor, wee one. Two kids—at the same time … it's kind of a big deal," he says, pointing to the door of the Bram & Bailey gallery. "I know you've got a hectic travel schedule, but you gotta try find ways to connect and shorten that distance."

Riley stares at the locked construction through a pane of glass and feels her stomach knot as she realizes that both her friends are navigating some major turbulence.

circling the drain.

[Vancouver, Canada—September 2012]

Jenna strolls out of the airport and into the rainy afternoon. She inhales the fresh air, closing her eyes.

"For fuck's sake, you can't even wait for me?"

She turns slowly to see Hana dragging her luggage through the automatic doors, stomping like a brat in her over-the-knee boots. Her outfit is so high-fashion that Jenna pales in comparison with boyfriend jeans and a sweater.

"Sorry … I needed some air …" Jenna says emptily, trying to escape from her manager's constant presence for even a few seconds.

"Jenna! Jenna!" begin some shouts, as a small group of fans rush up to her on the sidewalk.

She absentmindedly signs autographs and poses for photos, keeping her sunglasses on, going through the motions of the familiar rituals she has to perform everywhere. The vodka-water she drank on the airplane isn't sitting right, and all she wants is to hop in a cab and make a run for it. To anywhere.

"What the hell …" Hana whines, helpless against the rain hitting her perfectly blow-dried hair as they get in to their private car. The driver silently takes their bags, and the two women stick to the SUV's leather seats.

"So I was thinking we could go for dinner. This promoter I know from LA has a partner here—supposedly really cute, too. Maybe we all can eat at Morton's or one of those oyster bars … go somewhere for drinks after. I'll see what they've got going on …" Hana starts, twirling a lock of newly darkened hair around her finger.

"I think I need to lie down for a bit …" Jenna sighs, picking at her dark nail polish, her face breaking out from the constant stress level. Her general appearance has degraded recently, getting to the point of wearing the same cozy, ratty clothes because she just feels lazy and exhausted. She doesn't even have the creativity to dream up snazzy new outfits; all she does is crawl from the bed to the bathroom to any shows or interviews, and then back to her hermit cave.

"*Oh … kay …* fine. I guess I'll wait for you, then," Hana snaps, grabbing her phone and texting with someone else.

Jenna stares out the window at the highway passing by.

"So we're on for the film festival in Toronto. There'll be a ton of hot actors there, you know, Jen. It would be the perfect time to get out there—meet some fresh talent. Get back into the dating game ..." Hana says. "Carter will be there, so we need to amp it up to compete."

"I'm not crazy about meeting another actor," Jenna says dryly, mentally recalling Hana and Carter's Miami romp.

"Hey, it's not my fault he threw himself at me ... at least now we can start marketing you as the next eligible bachelorette," she sighs. "Besides, there are plenty of hot up-and-comers that we can put you near—get people wondering, generate more buzz around you ..."

Jenna stays silent, praying for the car to supersonically speed its way to their hotel. The faster it arrives, the faster she can get out, the faster she can get into her room and barricade the door. To disappear into the bed; maybe fall asleep without any medication or booze. A nice, clean sleep without heavy feelings of dread when she wakes up.

"Anyway. All we need is for you to be at the screening of *Certifiable* so that you can support the song they used from your album, and take some pictures, and you'll be a surefire staple at Cannes from now on!" The manager laughs, imagining herself hanging at the festival on a yacht.

They arrive at the hotel, and Jenna rushes in past the photographers waiting by the sidewalk.

They scream after her, but she zooms inside and is handed her key by a starstruck employee. She sees the look of awe register on her face and runs straight to the room.

She locks the door behind her, trying to breathe and calm herself down from the brink of hyperventilation. The sight of a camera has gone from thrilling to completely frightening. She doesn't want people having part of her. Capturing her. Selling her. The way the fans hungrily eat her up with their eyes makes Jenna feel like she's a sacrificial lamb.

There's a knock at the door, and she slowly opens it a crack, paranoid.

"Room service," quivers the young man, holding a tray in front of him.

Jenna opens the door and takes the drink offered to her. She smiles and gently closes him out of her view.

Already she puts shit in my hands, she muses to herself, dumping the vodka down the large bathroom sink.

Awake but Dreaming

She turns on the TV and steps into the shower, feeling the hot water loosen the tense muscles in her neck, stiff after having flown in from Hong Kong. The aromatic shampoo stings her eyes.

As her mind wanders, she longs for forgotten simplicity. To walk down a street, or not wear makeup. To be lazy with her friends, or write lyrics while on the boardwalk by the lake.

She steps out of the shower and wraps a plush towel around herself. As the water disappears, her ears perk as she hears the familiar chorus of one of her latest songs.

Jenna cautiously steps into the bedroom and sees the television playing a commercial for juice—to the tune of Track 8 from her second album.

What the ... she thinks, as she sees the ad for the first time.

She flips through the channels and soon hears another familiar melody—Track 3. This time, it is accompanying an insurance commercial.

Jenna sits down on the foot of the bed, surprised to be seeing her work being drawn on to give the "fresh, trendsetting" vibe for such random companies.

She makes a mental note to ask Hana but is content prolonging the discussion as much as possible. The last thing she wants is to be around other people.

She picks up her cell phone and text messages Olivia, hoping to squeeze her for another soul-searching session. Maybe explore past life connections that she allegedly has to the cabaret era. Her guidance about Parker keeps her hanging in suspense, reassurances that he still thinks of her but isn't quite ready for a reunion.

As she waits for a response, Jenna starts to sift through her massive suitcase, pulling out clothes she's decided to dispose of. Bright colours and fabrics zip through the room, growing into a huge pile by the closet door until she's essentially left with her regular rotation of favourites.

"I don't need fucking eighty-thousand bajillion shoes!" she snarls, throwing the latest trends into the pile.

She calls down to the front desk, and in minutes, housekeeping is at the door with garbage bags to dispose of her waste.

"Has she lost it?" one of the maids whispers to her coworker, staring at what they're collecting.

"Shut up and bag; this stuff will sell online!" whispers the other woman, as they drag away the merchandise.

Jenna is filled with a hyperactive joy, having annihilated the alien things from the turtle shell she's carried around for so long.

"I'm going to purge everything!" she marvels, opening her laptop and starting to e-mail people hyperactively. She hits Elle, Riley, Ben, Hunter, Carter, and even Mack and Kwame with her crazy ranting, feeling a false sense of clarity.

I need to say this because if I die, I'll never have said that I love you. You were almost my best friend, and then you pulled away. And now, I don't know where I am or what I'm doing. But I am clear for a minute—I see that things around me are bad, and I'm scared! I don't eat because I feel empty; I don't cry because I feel numb. I don't know how to feel good, like how I felt when we hung out, she says aloud as she types furiously to Parker. She hits Send without even thinking and goes into a fit of insane giggles.

Her body is so drained that the laughter feels bizarre to her, like she's outside of her body and watching herself without any control over her movements. Her mind feels like it's ten feet above her head, floating in the air like a ghost.

She suddenly feels a violent crash of her emotions and drops to the ground. Her knees hit the floor hard, and the room starts spinning.

horrified hanukkah.

[Toronto, Canada—December 2012]

Elle Roberts has her twin sons in rockers by the kitchen counter. They're wailing as she struggles to juggle all the pots cooking around her.

"Boys ... please ..." she calls out to them, trying to fry latkes on the stovetop.

The shredded potato keeps crumbling as she flips the pancakes over, and she ends up throwing the greasy mess into the garbage, groaning angrily.

The phone rings, and she puts it on speaker, trying to rock her kids into calm, waving a toy at them.

"Honey, I'm sorry, but I'm not coming home tonight," Ben says over the speaker, calling from his office.

Elle drops the rattle she's holding. Her comfy sweats are splattered with food remnants.

"What?" she asks, certain she's heard wrong.

"I have to fly to Washington and get an emergency press conference going. I'm so sorry I'm going to miss dinner again ..." he says, audibly typing on his computer.

"Ben. Really? Are you kidding right now?" Elle sighs, looking at the mess around her and the two kids anxiously fidgeting.

"I know. I'm sorry, but I have to do this. I'll fly back after it, you'll see what I mean once you turn on the news," he says, growing annoyed by the e-mails popping up in front of him.

"Ben! Tonight is your Hanukkah dinner! The dinner that you made me put together because you wanted your kids to have their first darn holiday. You cannot leave me like this—I am trying to cook for everyone. This is ridiculous!" she shouts, getting the boys crying again. "I don't know how to cook fucking latkes!"

Ben is silent. His wife has escalated to swearing.

"You forgot that tonight was the party," Elle announces, realizing he thinks he's skipping an average supper.

Ben is silent for a moment. "I'm sorry ..." he finally sighs.

"You know what? Fine! It's not like I'm not used to it. You leave me here alone for everything. Like I'm supposed to be superwoman, all of a sudden. Two kids—it's pretty hard, especially when you're doing it alone. But you know what, Ben, I'll just have to suck it up, right?" she shouts, hanging up on him.

Elle sits down on the kitchen floor with her back pressed up against the wall and starts to sob. After a few minutes, she realizes her kids have gone quiet. She looks at them through teary eyes and sees that they're calmly watching their mother.

She sniffles and gets herself together, wiping her face. "Sorry, boys. Mommy needed a good cry." She laughs emptily. Something on the stove is burning, and she forces herself to get up.

She disposes of the mess around her and dials for Hanukkah help.

"Hi, you've reached Riley Kohl. I'm travelling internationally with limited cellular access, so please leave a message or send an e-mail ..." rattles the voice mail prompt.

Elle hangs up and taps her fingers on the kitchen counter.

She picks up the phone and dials again.

"Hullo?"

"Hi. Rhett? This is Eleanor ..." she starts.

"*Vhy,* hullo Eleanor! My, my ... how nice to hear you!" His voice resonates deeply over the phone.

"Rhett, I'm so sorry to bother you right now. But I'm in urgent need of help ..."

"Darling. Please, tell me," he gasps. She can hear Kevin asking for information on the other end.

"I have my first Hanukkah dinner tonight. And Ben isn't coming. I'm alone—I don't know what to do. I have children crying, things burning, and my in-laws descending in a couple of hours. I am freaking the F out if you catch my drift." She wails.

"*Gif* me your address. *Vee* are coming," he says, excited to be needed.

• • •

A few hours later, Elle looks at the scene around her and smiles happily. All their party guests are putting their coats on in the foyer, gastronomically satisfied after one heck of a celebration.

"Eleanor, my darling, I am so impressed by your dinner." Ben's mother smiles, shocked that her non-Jewish daughter-in-law came through in spades—and that her son is nowhere to be found.

"Oh, thank you ..." Elle smiles weakly, exhausted from all the preparations.

"Yes, Eleanor. This was great." Rhett smiles, buttoning his wool-cashmere jacket and hugging her. He and Kevin slip outside happily—her knights in shining armour. They helped her cook up all the food and decorate the house, Kevin spending most of his time goo-goo-ga-ga-ing over the babies and leaving Elle free to run around.

Slowly, everyone trickles out of the house, leaving her in silence. The kids are fast asleep and tucked in, thanks to her father. The dishes have been loaded in the dishwasher, extra food stored in the fridge. So she sits on the living room couch and turns on the TV, taking off her cardigan and pearl earrings. She flips to the sports channel, and Ben appears on the screen announcing the arrest of one of his clients in Washington. Elle listens to her husband for a little while.

"I don't want to talk to you until you get a home office. You're irritating," she announces, shutting off the screen, feeling the familiar sense of annoyance creep in at the sound of his voice.

She walks up the stairs to the bedroom and gets ready for bed, too exhausted to think of anything else.

get by.

[Toronto, Canada—January 2013]

"Happy birthday to you ... happy birthday to you ..." sings Ben Roberts, as he sets down a chocolate cake in front of his sons.

Elle snaps a series of pictures, capturing the grins on Bailey and Bram's faces. Their light brown hair is neatly cropped, cartoon bibs ready for the consumption of chocolatey goodness.

The Bryans and Roberts parents are joining them for the first birthday milestone, a stack of colourfully wrapped presents already on the coffee table.

With the two sets of grandparents doting on the boys, watching them smear icing over their faces, Elle slips outside for some fresh air, wrapping herself in a fleece throw blanket.

She is sitting on the back deck when she hears the glass door slide open behind her. She looks over her shoulder to spot her husband, also seeking out some quiet.

"You read my mind ..." He smiles, sitting beside his wife and handing her a glass of wine.

Elle leans her head on his shoulder, and he puts an arm around her gently.

"Ben, I'm so tired ..." she sighs, nuzzling into him.

He kisses the top of her head, staring at the snow fluttering down on the yard.

"I know, but I'm going to be here for the next few months, so you're not going to be alone," he assures her. Having requested to stay in Toronto and not travel was a big decision to take. But with his track record handling pro stars like Hunter and Judd, Ben is hopeful that his career won't suffer from the increased geographic stability. It had to happen, or else he could sense his marriage would actually crumble, his wife falling apart.

"I'm so sorry I wasn't here more, that I couldn't make this shift sooner for us ..." he trails off, disappointed to have left her to take care of everything during the last year. But thankful that he prolonged the change as much as possible.

Elle's pent-up anger and resentment caused her to have a near breakdown, straining the affectionate relationship they've always had.

It was the first time Ben witnessed her hurl breakable objects aimed at his head.

"Do you want to go away? Recharge somewhere?" he asks her, rubbing her back tenderly. "Mommy-daddy time?"

She shakes her head. "No ... things are better now. It's just a knowing of what's ahead. Being prepared as Bram grows. To be sure Bailey's got the attention he deserves with his brother around," she sighs, thinking of all the cerebral palsy research she has done.

Ben nods, stroking her hair.

"I'm not so scared anymore. I think I know what's coming ..." she says, having devoured every article on the Internet and troubleshooting worst-case scenarios in her head. Realizing that her children will need her on-point has forced Elle to gather herself back together.

"We're going to be okay soon," Ben says firmly, voicing his optimistic commitment to improve their daily lives.

She looks up at him, and he leans into kiss her.

With their relationship now ready to get back on track, she knows that they will be okay. That's all she needed.

i see the sea.

[Maui, USA—January 2013]

"This is ridiculous." Jenna laughs excitedly, staring out at the ocean-view drive down Piilani Highway on the way to the hotel.

"I know! This will be the perfect place to forget about all the Carter drama!" Hana exclaims.

"So you're not going to keep him as a client, then?" Jenna asks, sceptical.

"I meant for you …" Hana smiles sweetly, secretly wishing she could make the movie actor disappear from Earth for not calling her after their last secret romp.

"He's the last thing I'm thinking about," Jenna says dryly. "But thanks for asking," she adds insincerely, knowing by now that any reference to Carter Sampson is made with Hana's own interest in mind.

They cruise into the Four Seasons at Wailea, mesmerized by the colourful flowers and breathtaking scenery.

"A ton of A-listers love Maui … I can see why," Hana comments, watching a group of male hotel employees walk by in crisp white uniforms.

Jenna rolls her eyes at her pervy manager, then follows a bellboy to her room.

She stares out at the beach from her balcony and can't help but recall the vacation with her friends two years ago. It feels too long ago.

Jenna changes into a bright blue strapless bikini and gets ready to hit the sand.

Hana pounds on her door as she's packing her beach bag with a copy of Riley's latest book.

"*Jen!*" she shouts, rattling the doorframe—either with her fist or her bellowing voice.

She opens the door, expecting a five-alarm blaze to be the reason why she is so loud.

"Do you have any tanning oil?" Hana whines, already changed into a hot pink string bikini and opting not to cover up for the walk out to the beach.

"Yes," Jenna sighs, slipping on a jersey dress. She grabs her bag and lets the door close behind her as she follows Hana.

"Great, because there are only a couple of hours of sun left before we go for dinner, and I want to make sure I get a good tan in," Hana announces, drawing attention from other hotel guests as they walk through the lobby.

"Did you forget your sarong?" Jenna asks, a little self-conscious that people are staring at them.

"No."

"Okay, then …" Jenna laughs to herself, feeling like she's in a comedy movie with such a larger-than-life character.

They cozy up on their towels, Jenna pushing to lie out on the public area of the beach rather than sit by the hotel's exclusive Serenity pool.

Hana dozes in the sun, hungover, while Jenna stares out at the water crashing in waves in front of her.

She attempts to crack open her tattered paperback book, but her gaze is drawn to a group of surfers out on the water.

The waves aren't particularly large or rich, but they are being devoured by the three guys, effortlessly soaring on their boards.

After a few sets, they head in and park their boards near the girls.

Jenna tries not to stare.

"I know I have a hot body," jokes one of the guys, calling out to her after having noticed her watching them from the shore.

Hana's eyes pop open, and she whips off her large sunglasses to see what is going on.

"Mornin', sunshine," another guy says to her.

"Hi." She smiles back flirtatiously, admiring his hard abdominal area.

"How are you ladies?" The third smiles, eyeing them up and down in their bikinis.

"Why don't you come over?" Hana invites, motioning to the empty sand around them.

The three adventurous twentysomethings amble over to them and sit down on the hot sand, immune to the sting.

"Steve," the first guy, a very sun-exposed blonde, introduces himself. "On vacation?"

"Yes …" Hana purrs, having found her next target.

"What's your name?" asks another white guy, significantly less attractive and a lot greasier, with messy hair and tattoos.

"Hana," she says, never backing down her eye contact on him.

"Hana ... nice. Blaine," he introduces himself.

"Carver," says the third surfer, a light-skinned black guy with stunning greenish eyes and short curly hair.

"Carter?" Hana chokes.

"No ... Carver. With a 'v,'" he says nonchalantly.

"Of course," Hana says dryly, staring down at his trunks.

"Who is your mime friend?" Carver asks, pointing to Jenna, who has remained uneasily silent during their impromptu beach party.

"Oh, this is my friend Jen ..." Hana announces, elbowing the blonde to be more responsive.

Jenna forces a smile, not thrilled to have to meet new people yet again. People who will drop out of her existence in a few days, anyway. Hopefully not Google her name until after she's gone.

"She looks bored," Blaine announces.

"You should really entertain your friend better, I mean, we could always help," Steve says, flirting.

"Well ... what would be good to do?" Hana smiles, hoping to have found their gatekeepers to the island's fun and nightlife.

"Well, we're having a bonfire tonight ... you guys should come if you want to party with us," offers Blaine.

"Bonfire? Sounds fun ..." Hana says, stretching slowly and drawing the attention of the three men to her body.

Jenna rolls her eyes at the predictability of her tactic.

"We'll be right down the beach." Blaine motions.

"Better get back to work ..." Carver suggests, as the three get up.

"Where do you work?" Hana asks, curious.

He points to a beach shack near the hotel that advertises beginner surfing lessons.

The three grab their boards and head to meet their next clients, leaving Hana chuckling at the simplicity of their lives.

"I could see why someone would never want to grow up here ..." she says dryly, watching the three men-children frolic in the water with their female clients.

Jenna shrugs emptily, rolling onto her stomach, sand sticking to her butt cheeks.

Hana licks her lips, excited to get to know the laid-back boys.

• • •

That evening, under brilliant moonlight, Jenna digs a beer bottle out of the cold, wet sand. The ocean water laps up to her ankles with gentle froth. She's desperate to slip away from the rowdy group at the bonfire, Hana is already at the centre of it and prepared to pick from the selection of cabana boys she's quickly trained to worship her.

"Blaine ... would you get me another beer?" she asks in a singsong voice, battling her eyelashes. She's wearing a tight pink bikini top and snug short shorts. The guys are all in board shorts, some in logo T-shirts, some shirtless and not shy of their sculpted abs.

Blaine, shirtless and showing off his tattoos, gets up and putters off to join Jenna by the water, to dig up the beers that are buried and cooling naturally in the sand.

Carver follows him and stops Jenna before she trudges back to the group.

"I can tell you're miserable." He smiles, putting a hand on her shoulder and staring at her intensely. His hair is unkempt and lightened by the constant sun exposure.

Jenna is taken aback by his confidence. Most men have unsteady eye contact or run away when talking to an international superstar nowadays.

"Do you want to hang out, away from them?" he offers, motioning to the group laughing and shouting on the beach, the orange flames of the fire licking up into the dark sky.

The two walk down the beach by the water's edge, staring out at the ocean rumbling steadily.

"It must be nice ... surfing every day ..." Jenna smiles, watching the white cusps of the waves breaking. She gently holds her long dress from getting drenched at the hem.

"It's awesome. Get on the water any time I can. Even though right here, it's not that great. But I have a buddy in the north of the island who lets me crash with him if I get a day or two off ... and we just ..." he trails off, making a hand gesture that looks like a plane taking off.

Jenna nods, thinking that it is the equivalent feeling to when she steps out on a stage with a mic in her hand. What she used to feel with more potency.

"You know ... I could take you out tomorrow, ..." he offers, putting an arm around her neck, standing a few inches shorter than her. His dark skin is calloused and discoloured with salt residue.

"Out? Surfing? No way." She laughs.

"Why not ... you've got a good ass on you ... I'm sure you'd balance." He smiles, smacking her butt sharply.

She blinks in surprise. The beers in her belly are making his directness, the accelerated affection, a lot easier to take in. "Because the last thing I want is a picture of me—"

"Wiping out? Please—who cares? Hana's not going to do voodoo on it or anything." He laughs.

Carver is quite familiar with the fast turnaround of vacationing tourists inspired by the nightly luaus and poolside piña coladas. He's eager to see how far he can push the envelope with the attractive blonde. Something about her is more appealing than the Polish heiress that he had sex with that afternoon ... in her hotel room, while her husband was out golfing. He knows he has to close tonight, or else move on to fresh pastures.

Carver stops, roughly grabbing her arms and pulling her towards him. Before she knows it, he's wrapped her into a steamy kiss, under the full moon looking down on them.

He pulls back, still firmly holding her face in his hands.

Jenna hasn't felt such raw energy since her early days with Carter. And she longs for the excitement of meeting someone new, the racing heart of unknown territory and doing stupid things.

It could never work ... surfer ... singer ... stationed in paradise ... travelling the world, she thinks to herself of their polarities. *Holy shit, Jenna—live in the moment. He's not looking for forever, you idiot!*

She turns to him, face-to-face, and wraps her slender arms around his neck. They lean in again, and their lips touch lightly at first, and then come together fiercely.

The two fall to the sand, aggressively grabbing at each other, feeling their bodies heat up feverishly.

Carver rolls Jenna onto her back and leans into devour her neck, kissing and licking his way down it.

She paws at him but notices their bonfire group, who are not actually that far away.

"Let's go somewhere else," she whispers, stopping Carver from going any further on the public sand.

He grabs her by the hand and pulls her to their surf shack. He forces open the rickety door, and they stumble over the boards and supplies crammed in there. Jenna pushes Carver up against a long-board, the other surfboards clanging down around them. She whips down his bright board shorts in one fluid motion.

He grins excitedly as she gets down on her knees, excited to be back in control of a man, let her pent up anger out and feel a sense of manipulation by unleashing her inner bitch.

Carver closes his eyes, feeling dizzy with her attention.

"Ooh ..." he grunts, grabbing the board for support.

"Huh?" Jenna asks, stopping her manhandling and coming up for air.

Except his grunts were signals of happiness, not to actually stop and talk. As she glances up, expecting instruction, Carver lets go of his tension and ejaculates.

• • •

Hana turns her head quickly, hearing screaming coming from the surf shack down the sand.

The group quiets down as they hear frantic commotion inside, things toppling over and crashing to the ground.

"What the ..." Steve asks, struggling to get up and walking over to investigate the interruption.

As he nears the door of the hut, Jenna flies out and onto the beach like a bat out of hell. Her frantic shrieks prompt Hana to hop up and jog over.

"What's wrong?" she asks, as Jenna holds the left side of her face and wails.

She can't put words together and is panicking and gasping.

"I'll be back," she assures Steve, grabbing the blubbering singer and dragging her away by the arm.

"What the hell is the matter with you?" Hana hisses, pulling her towards the hotel with the intent of locking her up in her room so that she can resume her flirting down below.

"He ... he ..." Jenna wheezes between tears.

"He what? He kissed you? He fucked you? He didn't want to fuck you and hurt your feelings?" Hana says cruelly, dragging Jenna into the hotel and towards the elevator.

"He ... he ..." Jenna sobs.

"What the fuck did he do?" Hana shouts in the middle of the open-air lobby, stopping and forcing Jenna to answer the question.

The hotel staff look away but keep their ears tuned into the drama at centre court.

"He ... came ... in my eye!" Jenna sobs, collapsing into Hana's arms, trying to embrace her.

Hana stands awkwardly, holding Jenna up, not keen on hugging it out with her.

"Ew," Hana barks, as she drags her into the elevator. She stares at the spot on her arm where Jenna's eye was just touching and makes a mental note to disinfect her skin before returning to the bonfire.

• • •

Jenna wakes up the next morning to the phone ringing at her bedside.

She groggily thanks the hotel's front desk for the wake-up call, hanging up. She's still in the summery dress from the night before.

Except something doesn't feel right. Her eyes are droopy, and she feels uneasy; she can't see clearly.

There is a frantic pounding at her door, Hana shouting at her to get ready for their early flight. She hasn't even packed yet, and their pickup is in 15 minutes.

Jenna groans, throwing back the covers and dragging herself into the plush bathroom. She puts a dollop of toothpaste on her electric brush and lets the froth collect in her mouth.

"I need a serious facial …" she whines aloud, washing her face in the sink, hoping to get rid of the eye crusties that have formed on her lashes while she was sleeping.

She wipes her face with the fluffy hotel towel and catches a glimpse of herself in the mirror.

"Mother fuck," she gasps, deadpan, staring at the mess looking back at her.

Her left eye is so pink and swollen that puss could practically be collected from her and sold at the county fair.

She leans into the vanity mirror to examine herself, horrified.

"Car … ver …" she curses under her breath, realizing that she never flushed her eye out after the frantic episode last night. She had only popped some sleeping pills out of anxiety, eager to forget the entire mess of her surf-shack rendezvous.

Hana is back at her door, pounding again and probably waking up the rest of the floor.

Jenna runs out and throws open the door.

"Gross. What the hell happened to you?" Hana cringes, staring at Jenna's eye, her fist still midair. Her tight jeans and blouse are hugging her curves; platform heels make her seem superhuman.

Jenna pulls Hana into the room, speaking in hushed tones.

"Carver ... came ... in ... my eye ..." she reminds her manager.

Hana cringes. "You really should work on that," she quips. "Whatever, put on sunglasses, use some eye drops ... we leave *now*."

Hana turns and lets the door slam after her.

Jenna stands, frozen in horror.

Get yourself together ... you need to be in Denver ... there's an autograph signing to do before the radio show, she instructs, moving her legs one step forward at a time.

She forces herself to shower and change and opts to put huge, flashy sunglasses over her eyes for a temporary disguise. Hopefully, the irritation will disappear before landing in Colorado.

She grabs one of the only pretty things she kept after her purge-fest, and slips into an alice+olivia dress and espadrilles to accentuate her diva identity. Hopefully to also make the sunglasses less ... out of place. She rolls her lightly filled suitcase to the lobby.

In the limo, she stares at Hana and grinds her teeth, feeling fed up with her lack of empathy and constant selfishness. Even Carter has shown more sensitivity, and he's constantly blitzed.

The car takes a detour through the heights of Kula, and Jenna starts to daydream, staring at the green land around her. The dirt road is quiet—no one up this early in the morning except a few joggers enjoying the cool temperature. She hears a ringing in her ears and feels disoriented.

As they pass through the green mountains, she spots something and commands the driver to stop.

"What the hell?" Hana groans, her head pounding from her beach party drinking and smoking. "We're going to be late."

"I need five minutes!" Jenna screams manically, frightening Hana into silence. The singer jumps out of the limo and starts sprinting in her designer shoes.

"Where are you going?!"

"Ghost church! Ghost church!" Jenna shouts, racing to a small, wooden church, sounding possessed by her bizarre actions.

She drops down to her knees at the gate of the Holy Ghost Church and starts to sob.

"Please God, or Jesus or whoever—I don't even know who to pray to. Please, someone help me. I don't know what to do. Please, someone help me," she stammers. "I know I'm not ... I don't know what religion I am, whatever it is I haven't been a good one. I don't know what I'm doing. But please, help me. I need guidance. Intervene! I need you!"

A wave of calm washes over her trembling body, and she feels as if someone has put a hand on her shoulder.

"Is that you? Mom? I know I haven't been a good person. I know I've done drugs and drink like a fucker ... but I can't handle feeling this anymore ... please ... help me ... I try to make it stop but I don't know who I am," she continues, whispering to the sky.

She lies down on the dirt, trying to feel more connected to the feeling of calmness. The grainy soil and dewy grass make her feel like she's attached to something bigger. Not just floating around aimlessly like a phantom circus performer that sings on command.

She's grounded.

"I'm so sorry ... I don't want this anymore. Not like this. I want my mom, and Riley and Elle and Parker and Mack ... I don't want this like this. It's not right. Can you please fix it? Am I going to die? I want to not be here like this!"

She takes in a deep breath and shivers.

You have to keep going. Only you can create the changes. You are the fixer, her mind whispers.

Jenna scrunches her face, upset that a heavenly power has not manifested and waved a magic wand. Like how Olivia promises she can.

She gets back onto her feet and starts walking to the idling Escalade, dissatisfied by the lack of magical problem solving. How is she supposed to escape everything that she's brought into her life? It seems like a cruel joke.

Hana is staring at her from the lowered backseat window, open-mouthed.

She watches her client, crusted with dirt and soil, trudge back with a completely different disposition. *I think she's gone fucking mental.*

Jenna slides back in, and the car continues back to Kahului Airport. Jenna slips a sleeping pill into her mouth, wanting to disconnect and try finding herself in her dreams. She and Hana remain in silence until reaching their destination.

PART IV:
CRASH LANDING

crisis management.

[Madrid, Spain—February 2013]

Riley Kohl stares in shock at the photographers lining the entrance to the Hospital La Paz. The black sedan she's being driven in turns onto a side street, pulling up beside a nondescript door.

"Señorita, here you enter," instructs the driver sent to collect her from the airport.

Riley grabs her bag and opens the door. She rushes up a set of metal steps, her legs heavy with tension, and knocks on the thick industrial door. There's a commotion as photographers realize someone is trying to enter, and they start to race around the building.

A big bald-headed man opens the door and lets her in.

"Hi, thank you," Riley says, stunned. She extends her hand and introduces herself.

He shakes her hand with a death grip and introduces himself as Pierre—the head of security from an agency dispatched by Alchemy Records.

Pierre walks her through the hospital and explains the situation he encountered when arriving earlier that day.

"I had dozens of those little shits lurking around, trying to get pictures of her," he sighs in a sharp American accent—from Louisiana, by the sounds of it.

"Well, they're not so great with boundaries," Riley sighs, recalling previous experiences with paparazzi that pursued Jenna for hours on end and even into the privacy of hotels.

"The doctor has been good with letting us shut down the hall to her room. But we've had fake nurses and doctors trying to sneak in, so I've got two guys at her door," Pierre explains.

He has bold tattoos all over his body. Riley can see bright orange flames shooting up his thick neck, arching past the black polo shirt he's wearing. He's also a good XXL in size, and a comforting force to Riley's comparatively small frame.

They approach the room, with two other big-bodies out front.

Riley stands in the doorway, watching the medical team hovering around Jenna's bed. There are wires and electrodes over her entire body—red, white, and blue, like a twisted Fourth of July display.

The half dozen nurses are frantically making adjustments and taking readings, but they look more like vultures picking at the body beneath them. Her instinct is to beat them off with a stick, to help the poor, frail girl at their mercy.

"*Ebribadi* out!" comes a shout from behind her, a strong female voice with a thick Spanish accent.

Riley turns to see an older female doctor commanding everyone out of the room, her black hair tightly pulled back and secured in a bun. She steps in with Riley, and the two of them are now alone with the limp body, the door closing behind them.

"Miss Kohl, I am Doctora Carmela Fabian," says the woman, shaking her hand firmly. "I am sorry for the circumstance we are meeting. My daughter loves your book."

Riley nods, forcing a weak smile.

"Miss Ramsay came to us in very bad condition. When we found her, she was barely alive."

"What do you mean … found her?" asks Riley, her eyebrow raising suspiciously.

The doctor bites her lip nervously. "She was … left … outside."

Riley stares at her in disbelief, rolling up the sleeves of her sweater as if she's getting ready to scrap.

"A car left her … a man and woman carried her into the ambulance bay."

Riley feels the blood in her cheeks searing. "You mean to tell me that … they just left her outside? They didn't even bring her *inside* the hospital?"

The doctor nods carefully. "The man had … stupid designs shaved in his hair. The woman—"

"Was a diva, yeah—I had a feeling," Riley sighs.

She stares at Jenna, who is as pale as the white sheets around her. Not even the fake tanning makes a difference. She looks like death.

"When we realized there was someone out there, the photographers had already …" the doctor trails off, embarrassed for the vulnerability of her patient.

Riley doesn't want to hear any more. "What is her status now, then?" she asks, trying to focus.

"It was very bad. The amount of drugs … it was horrific … but I am hopeful. I will not rule this a suicide attempt. She is responding to treatment. Slowly, but getting better. We must watch and wait."

"She's going to live?"

The doctor nods gently, still a little hesitant to comment on such a high-profile patient. "I have diagnosed her quietly, this matter needs to be handled in private. We arrested a person trying to steal her chart. My team understands the sensitive nature of this patient."

Riley exhales, thankful, and stares at the beeping machines around Jenna.

The doctor excuses herself, her shoes making soft squishes on the floor as she disappears. Riley sidles up to the bed, pulling up a chair and easing herself down onto the squeaky green vinyl.

"Jenna," she murmurs sadly, moving her friend's greasy bangs from her face.

• • •

"Oh, my gosh," Elle gasps, staring at the crowd of photographers around the ER entrance. As soon as she landed in Spain, she ran straight to the car service and sped to the hospital with her carry-on bag in hand.

Now seeing the reality of how much scrutiny her friend has recently been facing each day, Elle is quite thankful to have escaped Jenna's life when she did.

"Riles, I think I'm going to need help getting in," Elle whispers into her cell phone, feeling claustrophobic from watching the people hovering near the hospital.

"Head to the side of the hospital; the security guard will let you in there, he'll be waiting," her friend instructs, sending Pierre down to meet Eleanor.

The car loops the block a few more times, Elle reaching into her bag nervously. She pulls out her journal and quickly flips to the photograph taped in it. The three girls together. More decent times.

"Okay. Ready? Run," instructs the driver, pulling up to the same metal stairs used by Riley earlier that day.

Elle grabs her bag and sprints.

A few minutes later, she enters Jenna's hospital room, gasping at the state of her childhood friend.

"Is she going to be okay?" she asks Riley, frightened, reaching out to grab Jenna's hand.

Riley nods, clearing her throat. "She was really messed up, Elle. The doctor said she was practically … circling the drain. She's going to let us take her when she's stable, no criminal charges, we gotta zip the hell outta here. But the freaking paparazzi keep sneaking around," Riley sighs, aggravated.

"That's good. We should take her, take care of her. Bring her home," Elle suggests, unbuttoning her pink cardigan.

Riley nods, holding onto her sleeping friend's hand.

"Maybe we can take her to your dad's lake house—give her some space to recover. And then see about a proper treatment protocol," Elle suggests, feeling like a pseudo-medical expert, having done so much reading and research on alcoholism and drug addiction as she watched her friend deteriorate from afar.

"Hey, did you see the latest exposé?" Elle asks suddenly, pulling a magazine out of her purse, having read it on the plane.

Riley flips to the cover story, a confessional from some baked-out surfer named Carver.

"Really? He ... came in her ... eye? This is ridiculous." Riley gasps, glancing at her unconscious friend's face, feeling sick to her stomach.

"It's disgusting. Not only that—but how Hana whores her around like this ... how else would this guy get the idea to sell his story? Carver, Carter—it's all the same."

Riley tosses the colourful magazine in the garbage bin and grimaces at the thought of all the meddling.

"Carter was part of all this, too," Riley whispers, motioning to Jenna. "He's been with Hana for quite some time, if you know what I mean. It's not really a shock to see they're magnets and working together."

"That is foul. Totally messed. Whatever, this is the end of that chapter, one hundred per cent."

"When Parker gets here, we can brainstorm about how to get her out," Riley says, anxious about the logistics in planning their great escape.

• • •

Parker Ma is led through the hospital by Pierre. With their full-sleeved tattoos, they look like members of a heavy metal band or gothic cult. He sneaks glances at the bodyguard's artwork, appreciating the crisp application of the complex designs on to his skin. He forces his gaze back to his vintage running shoes and keeps walking.

They stop in front of a room, and he quietly slips in, glancing at the two burly security guards posted out front.

"Hey ..." he whispers, stirring Riley and Elle out of a nervous, meditative state by the hospital bed. He looks down at Jenna, who is out cold.

"Parker." Elle smiles warmly. "It's nice to finally meet you in person ... well, not *nice* ..."

He nods, hugging the short girl, her face buried in his blue fleece pullover.

"Hi, Riley," he says, also reaching out to hug her.

"So, you're what all the fuss was about ..." She grins, motioning to the third chair they've brought into the room and inviting him to sit with them. "I'm glad Mack was able to track you down ..."

"Yeah. I've actually kinda been trying to keep a low profile. Ever since her album took off ..." he starts, his thoughts muddled by the sickly body in front of him.

Elle touches his arm gently, comforting him.

"How is she doing?" he asks, reaching for the singer's hand. She is clammy to touch. Her bright red nails are chipped and peeling, like the rest of her has been for so long—in total chaos.

"She sorta woke up for a bit. Still pretty weak. We've made arrangements to fly out and get her to Muskoka in Ontario lake-country, once she's strong enough. We'll get the rehab specialist up there for an intervention. But after this, I doubt it'll be much of an argument ..." Riley sighs. "We need to get professional input and help to put her back together again."

Parker shakes his head, distraught. "I can't believe it got to this point. When I saw her in Vegas ... I knew it was bad news. But I thought it was partying. I had been getting all these random postcards from her, until I moved back in with my mom—but there was never anything behind them. Totally ... random." He digs around in his bag and pulls out an orange leather journal. "Then she sent her diary to my agent, and it freaked me the fuck out. I got it last week, and called Mack and Kwame. They were both trying to get to her before she completely lost it ... but clearly, no one could get through."

Riley and Elle look at each other, wondering what her friend could have written to disturb him.

Parker looks astonished. "She's beyond depressed. But every time I tried to call or e-mail ... numbers were either disconnected or her manager blocked my path. Mack couldn't even talk to her. You know they threw him out of a party Jenna was at? That damn Hana broad had her so isolated …"

"They left her outside. Abandoned her unconscious in the ambulance bay without actually bothering to bring her in," Riley shares, feeling humiliated for her friend. Especially after watching the security tape.

Elle looks ready to vomit.

"I guess Bonnie and Clyde do work well as a team. They both clearly don't give a shit about her. Never did. She wants to monopolize and exploit her. He … well, he's a creeper, to say the very least," Riley sighs.

Elle nods thoughtfully.

"So when can we get her out of here?" Parker asks, having seen the hundreds of photographers lurking around the hospital's exits. "And more important—*how* are we gonna pull this off without causing a stampede?"

"When she wakes up and walks across the room, Dr. Fabian says we can move her. What should we do? A decoy or something?" Elle asks.

"Well, normally they do a decoy while the real person runs out the side …" Parker suggests.

"But they'll be expecting that. So what about if we do the flip, and send the real Jenna out the front and a fake Jenna out the side door?" Riley suggests, feeling rather clever. "We shall call it the Ramsay Deke!"

"Deke?" Parker asks.

"It's a hockey term." Elle rolls her eyes.

Parker looks uneasy.

"Where do we get a fake Jenna?" Elle redirects, looking at her friend's brown hair, and Parker—who is obviously a man.

"I don't think we can hire a look-a-like. Well, your hair is the lightest of us, but you're shorter than her. Or we can send Pierre to go out and buy a wig … and I could try to fake it," Riley brainstorms aloud.

"Or you could put a hoodie on Elle and let a little hair peek out. They probably won't figure out the height if we keep her in a wheelchair. Then we can lift her into the car …" Parker adds, running with the idea.

"That's perfect. That way, they don't have a chance of seeing Pierre buying a wig or anything like that, either," Elle agrees, quite aware of how quick-thinking and resourceful the paparazzi are.

"So then, I'll wheel out fake Jenna … and you wheel out real Jenna?" Riley ponders.

"Maybe I should take fake Jenna because we'll get swarmed harder than you guys as the decoy … worst-case scenario, I can grab Elle and we actually run for it," Parker says.

"Right. Yes. Safety is … crucial," Elle laughs nervously, realizing she'll be face-to-face with the wolf pack out front.

"Are you guys busting me out?"

The three of them look down at the froggy voice coming from the bed. Jenna is awake, but still a bit out of it.

Parker rushes up to her face.

"Hi …" she whispers to him.

"Jenna …" he sighs, overcome by emotion, putting a hand on her forehead as his eyes water.

"We'll talk later …?" she pleads, not wanting to expense her limited energy on what will be an intense conversation.

He nods supportively, brushing some hair out of her face.

"We have a plan," Elle informs her friend, as Riley slips out to fetch the doctor.

After the walking test is passed, the Elle and Jenna are loaded into wheelchairs and prepped for the plan. Jenna puts on Elle's Stanford sweatshirt, conveniently swiped from her husband's dresser drawer. Elle zips up one of Parker's hoodies over her cardigan.

Pierre enters the room to confirm the deployment of the two cars. "I'll go with Jenna, send the other two guys with Eleanor," he instructs, concerned about their plan backfiring.

Riley grips the back of Jenna's wheelchair tightly and, when the elevator doors pop open on the ground floor, gets her game face ready.

"She's coming, she's coming!" voices shout outside. Pierre walks beside them, as the camera shutters begin to whirr.

"Steady …" he coaches Riley, who is trying to keep the wheelchair in a straight line as Jenna cowers under the red sweatshirt hood.

"It's a decoy! She's coming out the side!" shouts one of the photographers, having spotted Jenna #2 being brought out.

The entire group of photographers rushes the side of the building, leaving Riley and Pierre free to get Jenna into the car quickly.

"Thank you for everything." Riley smiles, shaking hands with the head of security.

"Get better soon," he smiles warmly to the singer, patting Riley on the back gently, impressed by how valiant a protector she is to her friends.

"Sweet Lord ... *shiiit,*" Elle whispers, seeing the crowd of photographers stampeding towards them. The two security guards get out in front of them to deflect the rush of human bodies and cameras.

"*Paaarker,*" she hisses nervously, swatting at his hand and shrinking into the wheelchair.

He keeps wheeling forward and reaches the car door amidst the wild screaming and flashes of light.

The photographers are barking out questions to him about her condition, but he keeps quiet and still the entire time.

He calmly places Elle into the car like buckling up a child in a car seat, and they are slowly driven out through the dense crowd.

"Did I actually hear you swear?" He laughs, as she removes the hood from her head, safely behind the tinted glass.

She blushes and snickers devilishly.

after burn.

[Muskoka, Canada—March 2013]

Jenna Ramsay's eyelids struggle to open. The afternoon sun is blocked out by heavy winter clouds. The ground outside the bedroom she's in is covered with white snow, and for a split second, she thinks of sliding open the glass door and vanishing. To be free among the trees, make snow angels.

She looks around the room and hears soft chatter from outside the door. She slowly lifts herself out of bed and pads through the hallway of the wood cabin. The place looks vaguely familiar. The photographs on the wall are of wildlife and nature, the cottage heated cozily and furnished impeccably. She looks down at the cozy flannel pyjamas she's been dressed in, the wooly socks her feet are sweating in.

"I cannot believe you just did that!" she hears Riley laugh, as she enters the doorway of the living room.

Her friends are sitting on the floor around a coffee table, playing a CSI board game, the wood-burning fireplace going beside them.

Elle and Riley glance up and smile, relieved to see their friend up and about.

Parker strolls into the room with a teapot and slows to a stop.

"Hi …" Jenna trails off, looking disheveled.

He sets down the big pot on the rustic coffee table and rushes to scoop her into a hug.

She hangs on to him, feeling relieved to have his presence around.

"Come, have a sit," Riley says, motioning to the floor space around them.

Jenna slowly parks herself on top of a big cushion, with Parker at her side.

This is Rhett's place, Jenna recalls, the maple wood coffee table jogging her memory. The three girls had carved their initials in the table during a long weekend in grade five—much to the heartbreak of Rhett. Ruining a perfectly beautiful, solid piece of wood.

"How are you feeling?" Elle asks, tapping the box of their game nervously.

"Like I just about died …" Jenna mumbles.

"That's not funny," Riley says sternly.

"Sorry ..." Jenna whispers.

"We don't have to talk about it now, but we will at some point. Try to relax a little bit for now," Parker says, holding her hand tightly. Her fingers are now clean and natural, no more lacquer and acrylic.

"Do you want some tea?" Elle offers, fetching another mug. She serves them, and they abandon their game to stare at the frosty lake.

"I'm really happy to be home," Jenna says softly.

"Ben is coming up tonight," Elle says with a smile, "with a couple of boys for you to meet."

Jenna looks at her friend and knows that the boys are not romantically related. Relief. No pressure to meet and dazzle strangers. Only try to impress some babies.

Riley looks lost in her thoughts; a big sweater is wrapped around her, black tights stuffed into her wool socks.

"Thank you for coming to me," Jenna says to her friend, touching her arm and getting her attention. "I know you were there first—had to deal with a lot ... just ... thank you for being our protector."

Riley nods silently and puts a hand on her friend's shoulder.

"And Elle, I know it was a lot for you to leave your family ..."

"Oh, please! I always run away from Ben—it keeps our relationship fresh and mysterious." She giggles wildly, not quiet as funny as she thinks she is. She's wearing a sweatshirt that is way too big on her and a pair of ratty cotton shorts that say "Nice Bass" on the back with a picture of the fish.

She looks at Parker and can't bring herself to talk; there are so many thoughts and feelings rushing through her.

He seems to understand and kisses her forehead, squeezing the back of her neck gently.

"I want you all to know ... that I can never have that life again. I am a hundred per cent committed to changing everything around me. And if it takes me years to go through rehab or therapy, whatever ... I am going to do it," Jenna says, tears forming in her eyes. "I was praying so hard to start over. I—I needed to feel alive again."

"Well, I'm glad that you will make it happen," Riley says, speaking positively, not condescendingly sarcastic as is normal.

"In the meanwhile, we should consider what to do for dinner ..." Elle says, staring at the grey afternoon sky and thinking like a mommy—how to feed the troops.

"Well, how about I go into town and pick up some steaks to grill, grab some stuff for salad …" Parker offers, getting up and more than happy to give the girls some quality time. He's wearing one of Brian's strange hippie sweaters.

Elle tosses him a set of car keys, and he slips out the door with a wave.

They hear the car pull out of the driveway, and the girls decide to sit in front of the sliding glass door, side by side in a line. The curtains are drawn back, and they stare at the water.

"How long have we been here?" Jenna asks, still amazed to have woken up safely and in one piece.

"A few days," Elle hums thoughtfully.

"Are you serious?" Jenna gasps. It feels like she's woken up from a nap.

"Lovee, you were in bad shape when we got to you," Riley explains calmly. "You needed to tap out as long as your body said."

"I … can't believe … everything got so bad," she says, burying her head between her knees. The flannel pyjama bottoms catch her fat tears.

"It *was* bad. But now it *will* get better. This is the only thing that we can do—move forward," Elle says softly, gently nuzzling her head into Jenna's shoulder.

"I can't believe I screwed up my life." Jenna sniffles.

"It's not a lost cause, Jenna. You gotta reshape it. Cut out the bad influences. Not be swayed again," Riley shrugs.

"You know, there were some nights when all I wanted was to go back to the hotel and sleep. But it was like I had to go out and party, had to go out and be the crazy one … I just didn't know how else to be anymore, felt so disconnected. And after my mom … I didn't want to be here. On Earth. Anymore."

"Well, we all tried to contact you, you know. To get in touch and talk … but I never heard back," Elle says, staring at the floor.

"Me, neither. And Parker didn't," Riley says. "You even fired Mack."

"I …" Jenna trails off, feeling hurt and embarrassed.

"I had a feeling Hana didn't tell you even when I e-mailed last week," Riley says dryly. "I saw a bad story in the newspaper …"

"But still … I should've clued in earlier," Jenna says. "I felt so isolated—she was working more with her other clients, sort of leaving me to dangle … I guess I wasn't the shiny new toy anymore. I didn't have anywhere else to go."

"Of course you did. Or rather, of course you do," Elle says gently, sipping from her tea.

Jenna begins to cry, and the three young women collapse together into a heap.

"When you hit a brick wall, you can either back up and run straight into it again. Or ... back up, and bulldoze through," Riley says to her friend. "That should be the premise of my new book."

Jenna smiles through her sobs. "That sounds great! I read the first one, you know," she whimpers.

"Oh, yes, but the second one is so much better," Elle replies excitedly, clapping her hands with glee.

"So, then I take it that publishing is going well?" Jenna sniffles, composing herself, relieved for a change in topic.

"Yes. And now I live San Francisco with ... someone, sort of," Riley blushes, trying to throw in the personal information smoothly—and failing.

"With another human being? A ... significant other ... human being?" Jenna jokes, her raspy voice jumping octaves comically.

Riley rolls her eyes. The three of them are back to their old selves. It feels as if no time or drama has passed by.

"He's a singer!" Elle interrupts.

"Who? Who?!" Jenna demands, grabbing Riley's arm, intrigued by her friend's softening at the mention of a love. It's as if Riley's icy exterior has been attacked by a hairdryer.

"Anthony Daniels ..." Riley whispers shyly.

"Oh, my God, Riles—he's hot!"

Riley laughs, hiding in her sweater, blushing.

"He is. And nice! He's so good to her." Elle chimes in.

"I've been on his tour for the past ... gosh, how many months ...?" Riley wonders aloud.

"I have babies!" Elle interrupts, turning the conversation on to herself after feeling left out.

"Oh, yes. I had meant to contact you about that ..." Jenna whispers, ashamed.

"Yeah, I got your gifts from this fancy-shmancy store and figured you hadn't picked them out yourself," Elle scolds comically.

"Hana," Jenna admits.

"Yeah. They were pink. I had boys," Elle says.

"Oh, wow, what a bitch!" Riley gasps.

"Yeah, she never did quite like you guys ..." Jenna confirms.

"I knew it!" Riley says, getting up to get some cookies.

"And what happened with the pregnancy ... or the birth?" Jenna asks, vaguely recalling complications.

Elle quiets down and bites her lip. "It ... was ... pretty tough. Long story short is that I delivered prematurely, Bram has cerebral palsy, and two kids are a handful," she explains.

Jenna looks horrified, but mostly because she doesn't know what it all means.

"It's going to be a bit more on our plate. It won't get worse, so it's more like learning how to manage CP—getting early treatments and therapies, surgeries and stuff. But we've got a great team behind us now. My dad really helped in getting us prepared. For a while there, early on, when Ben was still away a lot for work, I nearly lost it. I think I freaked him out at bit. But ..."

"You're okay now?" Jenna asks worriedly.

Elle nods confidently. "Bailey ... absolutely adores his brother ... it's so sweet," she coos. "It's like he's ready to protect him already. And Ben and I are stronger than ever. For whatever comes our way. No more impulse to murder him anymore. Not even to injure him ..."

Riley reemerges, a blanket thrown around her shoulders.

"Are you getting married?" Jenna asks her bluntly.

"Hell no. No offence, Elle."

"None taken." Elle smiles, sipping her tea.

"But you're happy?" Jenna probes.

"Would you believe me if I said yes?" Riley asks, raising an eyebrow.

"Let's meet this guy and see ..." Jenna laughs. "He needs the stamp of approval."

"He got me to totally change my health habits," Riley adds. "And he's even a vegetarian. And a creative. Don't judge him for that. Or me."

"The fact that Riley is the one leading that lifestyle more than me, who introduced you all to yoga and nutrition ..." Elle trails off.

"Hell has officially frozen over," Jenna snorts.

• • •

A couple of hours later, Parker emerges through the door laughing.

"Hey, look what I found ..." he announces, having met Ben and his kids in the driveway. They each carry in a twin.

"Oh, my lovees!" Elle gasps, so happy to see them after even a few days of being apart. She scoops up Bailey, smothers Bram in kisses, and is wrapped up by Ben into a hug. He looks relaxed in jeans and a sweatshirt with a down vest, his boots covered in snow.

"Yeah, I found something else, too." Parker laughs, as Anthony struggles to carry in all the grocery bags in one shot.

Riley hops up and heads over to her boyfriend, taking some of the parcels off his load.

"I'm not mad at you, but I'm mad at you." He smiles, hugging her. "How could you leave while I was sleeping?"

"I'm sorry. I needed to see this through," Riley whispers, having regretted slipping out of their Paris hotel room. As soon as she got on the plane for the rescue mission, she felt awful.

"I could've helped you. Or … at least been woken up," he says, pretending that his feelings are deeply hurt, but actually proud of his girlfriend's fight.

Riley nods apologetically.

"How is she?" he asks, glancing quickly at Jenna.

Riley takes his hand and walks him over to her friend. Jenna hops up from the floor, ready to step into the crowd of people in the cottage.

"Anthony, this is my dear friend, Jenna. Jenna, this is *my* lovee, Anthony Daniels." She laughs, watching Elle still making goo-goo noises at her kids.

Jenna beams, surprised by the country singer her friend has become so smitten with. He's wearing frayed jeans and a long-sleeve T-shirt. Straight out of a rugged Gap ad.

"I brought steaks," Parker announces to the crowd.

Anthony looks a little uneasy.

"And … soy burgers …" Parker adds, motioning to Riley for the modifications to the grocery list.

"You're also a vegetarian?" Jenna gasps, looking at Riley.

"At times. I even tried to go vegan, but I totally don't have the balls," Riley snorts.

"Riley!" Elle scolds, pointing to the kids, unhappy with her crass use of language.

"Oh, yeah, kids. Whatever." She laughs. "You know, I happen to think that living in San Francisco has made me a lot more easy going. Really made a difference in reducing my stress levels."

Anthony rolls his eyes. "Riley" and "anxiety" are two words that will never be separated.

Awake but Dreaming 461

After dinner, and putting the twins to sleep, the three couples find themselves sitting around the fireplace and mulling over the past few years.

"It's incredible how fast things have gone," Jenna whispers, curling her feet under her bum and sitting on the floor in front of the couch where Parker is seated. He's rubbing her neck gently.

"Not so much gone, because it isn't over. More like, how fast they've come," Riley muses existentially, gesturing freely.

Everyone bursts out laughing. Her hand movements make it seem as if she's talking about male "coming."

"What? Guys, *not* what I meant!" she groans, annoyed.

"It's amazing how quickly things happen in life." Elle smiles, being the happy medium to rephrase their thoughts.

"Yes. That's very poetic," Riley says through gritted teeth.

"And on that note, I'm going to make sleep happen," Anthony says, pulling her up with him. "Flying last-minute from France … not fun."

"But it's great that you did." Jenna beams.

He nods, happy to finally meet these players in Riley's life.

Riley bends down and kisses her friends' foreheads.

"Love you," she says, waving.

They disappear into the cottage.

"I think we, as well, shall go," Elle says, gently yawning, burying her head into her husband's shoulder.

They stand up, and Elle kisses her friend's forehead, too.

"Love you," she whispers, thankful to be able to say that to Jenna. And to have her hear it.

Ben and Elle walk off, hand in hand, smiling at each other.

Jenna and Parker are left, sitting and watching the flames dance around in the fireplace.

"Thank you … for … going to me," she says softly, not sure how to express the feeling of seeing him again. Her eyes dart around nervously; part of her feels like she's daydreaming this.

His face relaxes into a certain level of gloom. "How did this happen …" he trails off, shaking his head.

"You know what? I don't even want to investigate that with you. Because, right now, all I know is that I got a second chance to be able to do this right. What *happened* can be discussed in therapy. What I *want* to happen … that's between you and me," she says, holding his hand in hers. She's trying to be brave and confident, to show him that she's serious. This is not another tantrum or attention-seeking crisis.

He puts his arm around her, squeezing tight.

"Okay," he whispers, stroking her hair softly.

They stay out in the living room all night, watching the fire die down. Just the two of them. In silence. No one else around.

sun storm.

[Toronto, Canada—December 2013]

Jenna Ramsay opens her eyes slowly, taking in the feeling carefully. She's sitting on a stool in the middle of a stage, the big concert lights illuminating her warmly.

The crowd inside Massey Hall in downtown Toronto applauds wildly, curiously watching the reincarnated performer. Free of the tabloid scandal, of the drinking and drugs, and of the crazy people, she's like a phoenix having risen from the ashes of madness. Jenna has just released a new album, under a completely different circumstance, and is back on track with the right people in her life.

"Thank you, everyone, for joining me tonight. As I'm sure you've all read, it's been an incredibly bumpy road these past couple of years. But I am extremely happy to be here today, better than ever, and sharing this with you."

The claps are thundering in her ears, and she can't help but giggle softly into the microphone.

"I wanted to have this intimate get-together not only to preview my new material for you ... but also to thank you for all your support. I worked really hard, really honestly, on this and am the proudest I've *ever* been of a record. Out of the chaos came some good. So I hope it serves as inspiration to anyone who is struggling with the storm clouds overhead, because eventually, sunshine does follow."

She looks down into the crowd and lights up when she spots some familiar faces.

"I would also like to thank you for purchasing a ticket to see me tonight. A full one hundred per cent of the proceeds are being donated to the Roberts Foundation in support of cerebral palsy research at Holland Bloorview Kids Rehabilitation Hospital right here in Toronto," she announces.

The crowd cheers as a photo slideshow plays on a screen behind her. Bram and Bailey are the stars of the montage, alongside other kids they've met during their experience at the children's hospital.

She turns to the small classical orchestra behind her and nods to the conductor, ready to start.

"Let's do this ..." She announces.

acknowledgements.

There are so people, places, and things I am thankful to have encountered along my journey so far. These are just a few of the many related to this cheeky, cheeky book…

My family: It took a while, but I finally opened my eyes, and am *skipping* down my path. I am eternally grateful for your support and encouragement. To my parents for holding their breath while I took the plunge (and buoying me when needed), my aunt for her inspiration, and my India crew for just knowing. To my grandparents for teaching me life's basic truths of goodness and integrity. I dedicate my first book to my sister – the best winger anyone could ask for (especially when it comes to style).

Jane Margaret: This project would not have happened without you. Period. You were magically, magically sent to me, and I am stoked for everything we will accomplish! Thanks for always having my back in every respect, and pushing me to hustle.

My amazingly eclectic friends: I finally shut up and did it. Now it's your turn to man up–I can't wait to see y'all shine! Thanks for lending me any stories and drama for further inspiration, and for always listening and laughing with/at me. Words can't express my gratitude for the authentic love and support.

The Contributors: Thank you all for giving me your time, talents, and input to help create. The Shaka Creative girls, my stealthy digital ninjas (JD, Tiff, Caldaroni), Al D, blackjet inc, Soranno Red… Keep building and see what manifests – take chances and Send Love.

My mentors, teachers, and guides: It might've seemed small at the time, but you've made big impacts on my life and I thank you for the bits and pieces I've gathered. Special thanks to R. Boyagoda for showing me what I want to become. To M. Magen-Ramberg for being my technicolour bodyguard all these years, and telling it like it is. The fabulous B. Bouganim for your unwavering confidence and loving light ("Yo! Are you normal?").

San Francisco: Here is where I started putting down this long-held story from page one, and I fondly remember all the adventures (especially with Blue Bottle keeping me wired, and J. Crew keeping the Fantastic

Four clothed – I adore this immensely). Special thanks to the amazing Stanford professors who inspired me to create my own reality with business acumen, yet to never lose my individuality. It took a few years, but it all finally clicked because you set the wheels in motion. And thank you to the men's water polo team at the Avery pool for giving me a reason to read outside.

Hockey: The only way I could ever last through a cardio workout at the gym. To the agents and players I've learned about and observed, thanks for showing me your world (especially to the STL Blues). Appreciation to P. Lecavalier and J. Moldaver for taking the time to coach a rookie writer. The comic relief inspired by accidentally finding myself in the Lightning locker room – golden.

Other great sources of inspiration: The authors I love to read including Joan Didion, Jane Austen, and Sara Teasdale (lovingly referenced in "responsibilities."). The worlds of fashion, celebrity, and international mayhem. The perfect drive in a wonderful car with a delicious exhaust. The vulnerability of love and heartbreak. Awakening. All the great things that bring us delight .

Holland Bloorview Kids Rehabilitation Hospital: To the magnificent children, families, and staff that I have met over the years – thank you for sharing your stories with me. Piper says thank you for the snuggles, too.